THE ATONEMENT

ALSO BYLAWRENCE CHERRRY

Commencement

School of Hard Knocks-The Re-Education of Jim Reid

ACKNOWLEDGMENTS

I would like to thank God for helping me write this book. If not for Him, I would have never finished this story. With His help maybe I'll be able to take my craft to the next level.

THE ATONEMENT

A NOVEL BY LAWRENCE CHERRY

THAT PAGE WITH THE LEGAL STUFF ON IT

"The Atonement" **ISBN-10: 0692462163**
ISBN-13: 978-0692462164

Printed In the United States of America

Dedicated to our Lord and Savior Jesus Christ.

for without Him this book never would have been possible

ONE

The sky grew dim as twilight approached, and Allen quickened his pace as he neared the entrance of St. Luke's Hospital. He knew he was running late and he hoped that he had enough time to make visiting hours and then jet over to his contracts class at Columbia, which was going to start at 7:00 p.m. Allen checked his watch. It was 6:30. "Kinda cutting it close," he thought to himself. "Next time, I'll pick something up from Manna's instead of waiting for mom to fix something."

Allen hustled through the doors and quickly signed in at the desk where the clerk handed him a visitor's pass. Then he started to one of the elevator banks in the lobby. Fortunately, the doors of one of the banks opened just as he approached and he got on with several other people that had been waiting. Someone had already pressed the button for the seventh floor, which was where he was headed to see his best friend.

During the ride, the aroma of the soup he was carrying seemed to fill the elevator. Allen checked his bag to make sure the container wasn't leaking. As he

did so, his stomach seemed to tighten and he didn't know why. Jim had gotten past the worst part of his recovery, and they had managed to reconcile their friendship. Yet Allen could not help but feel a little uneasy when he was in Jim's presence. As much as Allen cared for Jim, he felt as if there were an invisible wall between them. "It's going to take time," he told himself. Just then the doors opened on the seventh floor and he walked out and down the hall. "It's going to take time, but soon everything will be back to normal."

As Allen got closer to the room, he could hear that all too familiar high-pitched, clipped voice, mixing with what sounded like Jim's laughter. Hearing Jim laugh made him feel a bit more relaxed, but Allen was hoping they could be alone. Maybe then Jim would feel like he could talk to him. Then again, Allen was afraid of what Jim might reveal.

"I see you got some company," said Allen after he poked his head into Jim's hospital room. Jim was sitting up and in good spirits, while Tamiko was sitting in a chair next to his bed. The television was on, but it had been muted.

"That's the trend lately," said Jim.

Jim had been in the hospital for nearly two weeks. For the first couple of days he laid in a coma in the Intensive Care Unit before finally regaining consciousness. It would be several more days after that before he left the ICU altogether. Since then, he began a slow and sometimes uneven recovery. There were times when Allen came to visit and Jim would look great, but the next day he'd look like death. Lately, Jim seemed to be making consistent progress. With each passing day Allen could see that Jim looked better and stronger.

"Do you mind if I join the party?" asked Allen.

"Not at all, pull up a seat," said Jim.

"Hey, Allen" said Tamiko.

"Hey, yourself," he said giving her a peck on the cheek and sitting beside her. "Gossiping much?"

"I don't gossip. Gossip is negative. I've only been telling Jim about all the good things that have been happening while he was away."

"Mmmm-hmm, sure. Is that right, Jim?"

"Well, I didn't hear nearly as much drama as I'd hoped to, so I guess she's right."

"See."

"Anyway, I didn't think you'd still be here. I thought you were going to the movies tonight," said Allen.

"I am. In fact, now that you're here, I think this is the perfect time for me to make my exit. Take care, Jim. I'll see you tomorrow – oh, and I'll bring the pictures I promised," she said before she planted a kiss on his forehead.

"Can't wait," said Jim.

"Later, Al."

"See you, Miko," said Allen as she walked out.

"How you doin' today, man?"

"I'm still livin'. Can't get no better than that."

"You look a lot better than you did yesterday. You still having any pain?" Allen added out of concern. He knew that Jim had been struggling with the after effects of the surgery for the gunshot wounds.

"Not anymore. Whatever they puttin' in that IV drip is killin' it."

"Don't let them give you too much of that junk. You don't want to end up addicted to it," said Allen instantly regretting his choice of words. "I mean too much of that stuff could end up making you worse off."

"I hear you. What you got there?" asked Jim as he noticed the bag Allen had brought with him.

"Mamma's homemade chicken noodle soup. It's still hot. You think you can handle it?"

"You know I can handle that."

Allen moved the portable tray over to Jim's bed and set the soup out for him. He didn't know how his friend would manage with his right arm in a sling and his left leg in traction. Jim took the spoon clumsily in his left hand and managed several sloppy spoonfuls.

"You look like you could use some help."

"Nah, I got it."

After a few moments, Jim was able to orient himself to the task at hand, however, Allen could see how hard Jim had to work to do it. Jim had finished most of the soup before he gave himself a rest. Allen was glad to see that his friend's appetite was coming back.

"That was even better than I remember. I'm tellin' you Allen, your mom doesn't miss a thing. Good to know some things haven't changed."

"Sometimes change can be a good thing."

"Yeah. I guess. But it's hard when you gotta start over from scratch," said Jim as he stirred his spoon in the remnants of the soup at the bottom of the bowl.

"Hard, but not impossible. Especially if you got some help, hint-hint."

"I know. But I can't expect everyone to stop living their lives so they can help me."

"C'mon, man. You're an important part of all our lives. We missed you."

"I missed you guys, too. Didn't realize how lucky I was to have such good friends."

There was an uncomfortable silence between them for a moment before Jim spoke again.

"I'm sorry, Al."

"Jim, you don't have to go there again."

"No, I do. I really messed up."

Allen himself felt guilty about what happened to Jim. When he learned that Jim was found near death in an abandoned warehouse, Allen thought he would have a heart attack. Then when Detective Ballard questioned him about what he knew of Jim's whereabouts and dealings, Allen had to admit that he hadn't seen or spoken to Jim in nearly two years. The realization of the span of time stunned him. "How could I let nearly two years go by without talking to my best friend – the man I grew up with and was raised with?" Allen thought to himself at the time. Although he had been praying daily for Jim, Allen couldn't help but wonder if there were something else that he could have done to prevent their relationship from becoming estranged, and hence, what happened to Jim. But then he realized he had done all that he could do. Thankfully, his prayers had been answered, and now, they had the chance to start over.

"We've all made mistakes. I know I've made quite a few."

"Have you ever felt that you've gone, too far?"

"The only time you've gone too far is when you can't feel sorry and you've expressed that already."

"I don't know, man."

"Look, Jim, whatever happened is done and over with. I'm not holding anything against you and neither is anyone else. Let's just put the past behind us and move forward."

Allen looked at the muted TV screen that was playing before them as silence took over again. He didn't like the awkwardness that had started to develop between them. Allen knew what was causing it. It was the questions that loomed around them and all the things that had been left unspoken.

At times Allen couldn't help but wonder how Jim ended up here. Pastor Bynum suggested that no one question Jim or bring up the circumstances surrounding Jim's hospitalization until he was stronger. Even then, everyone agreed that it would be best if they let Jim bring up the subject first, which would indicate that he was finally ready to discuss his ordeal. Allen thought this was a prudent thing to do because he didn't want to stress Jim out and cause him to have a set back with regard to his physical health. They also agreed that it wouldn't be worth it to risk alienating Jim during such a vulnerable period in his life. In the meantime, there were a lot of questions that went unanswered. What was Jim doing at that warehouse? How did he end up in such a situation? Detective Ballard said there was another man in the warehouse that had been shot dead. Had Jim killed him? If so, why? Was it self-defense? The doctors discovered drugs in Jim's system: opiates, and barbiturates. Did Jim get caught up in a drug buy gone wrong? These were the questions that sauntered around Allen's mind. Back at home, everyone was speculating about what could've happened, but only Jim held the answers and he still hadn't said anything – to most of them at least.

Not long after Jim had regained consciousness, the police came to the hospital to question him. Allen didn't know what was said because only Detective Ballard, another officer, Vernon, and the lawyer he had gotten for Jim, were present. Vernon hadn't told anyone what had transpired, with the exception of Lena, and neither of them had told Allen anything. The only thing Jim ever said to Allen was that he was sorry. Allen could remember the first time Jim spoke. He just kept saying, 'I'm sorry' over and over again. It made Allen think that maybe he didn't want to know everything, and that perhaps everyone would be better off if Jim never said anything about what happened. The investigation seemed to be over and it wasn't like Jim had been implicated in anything. It would be best to let the past stay where it was. Allen only hoped that, whatever happened, the experience left Jim with a wiser perspective of things than he'd had before.

"I see you got the Word Network on," said Allen, trying to get some conversation going between them again.

"Yeah. I been thinkin' if anybody need the Word, it's me."

"You really mean that?"

"Yeah. I do."

"If anybody can help you, He can."

"I know. He already has."

Jim smiled at Allen, who smiled right back.

"Does this mean we'll see you back at church in the near future?" asked Allen.

"I guess you could say that."

"Good. I'll dust off your old spot in the pew."

"You sure there's still room? I mean with Tim, the handyman, and the hundred other people you and Miko done dragged up in there by now."

"There aren't that many new faces – and he's not the handyman. His name is Davis."

"Yes, of course. How could I forget? Especially with the way Miko goes on about him. But since they're an item now, that's probably to be expected."

"Wait a minute, hold up – Miko told you she was dating Davis?"

"She didn't come out and say it, but with the way she was talking, I just assumed she was. Isn't she going out with him tonight? She's dressed up like it."

"Here we go," said Allen rubbing his palm across his face. "It's not a date. She's not seeing him."

"So what is she doing with him?"

"Making a fool of herself."

"Don't tell me she's chasing him."

"It's so embarrassing, I'm not sure if I even want to talk about it. It's like she's lost her mind."

"This is certainly a first. He must be putting down some kind of vibe to have Miko wound up like that. You sure he's not an undercover player in disguise."

"Trust me – Davis is definitely not a player from what I can see, and I don't think he's done anything to lead her on. In fact, I think he's been very patient through everything she's been putting him through, but lately I can tell that Miko is starting to get on his nerves. As a matter of fact, her obsession with Davis is starting to get on my nerves. If I'm alone with the brother for five minutes, in the next five she'll be all up in my face asking me if he said anything about her."

"Hmm. I wonder how Tim is taking all this. After all, the last time I was around, he was after Miko like a spider after a fly in a web. Isn't that what his sudden conversion is all about?"

"I know what you're getting at – but that whole thing was squashed. Tim's really done a lot of growing up in the past couple of years. The only thing he's trying to do now is get right with God."

"And you're absolutely certain of this because..."

"You've spoken to him, haven't you? I know he's been by here a couple of times. Can't you tell the difference?"

"His talk is deep, but I suspect his walk is weak."

"Why would you think that? You know Tim – when he makes up his mind about something..."

"Is he aware that fornication is a no-no?"

"Yes."

"So you mean to tell me a dude who's used to having a different woman every month has just quit the game cold turkey?"

"Well – uh – yes."

"What's with the hesitation?"

"Okay, nobody's perfect and even Christians make mistakes now and again..."

Jim laughed out loud before he winced and grabbed his side.

"You okay, man?"

"Yeah, I'm okay, but I gotta be careful that I don't pop any of my stitches. But back to what we were discussing, I just knew it was too good to be true."

"No, really! I'm telling you, Tim's not the same guy. Just wait 'til you get out of here. You'll see."

"Now I've heard everything – or almost everything. Are you going to tell me about what's going on with you?"

"I already told you about law school. I'm starting my first year and with work and all, it's been a stretch, but..."

"That's not what I'm talking about. I want to hear about this new relationship thing you got goin' on."

Allen paused for a moment and toyed with the empty bag as he tried to think of a way to get off of the current topic.

"It's not that big a deal..."

"Don't try to front. Miko already gave me the hint and she didn't seem very happy about it. She said I should let you explain it."

"I'm not surprised she put it like that. There are a lot of people who aren't happy with my relationship."

"Why?"

Allen took a deep breath and braced himself for what he was certain would be Jim's reaction.

"My lady is...a single-mom."

"Wait a minute, did I just hear you right? Did you just say, 'single-mom'?"

"Yes, I did. Now before you go off the deep end, you have to consider the realities of the present time. There aren't many women our age out there that don't have kids."

"Allen, really?! 'Cause I could name quite a few."

"Still, it's not an issue for me."

"Well it should be! Look, man, I know how much you like to help people, but..."

"Save your breath. I've already heard the speech about a dozen times..."

"And you're gonna hear it one more time. Do you understand just how complicated a relationship like that is? How big a commitment you're going to have to make? Do you know how much there is at stake in a situation like the one you're in? You're only 24 years old – that's way too young to be a father and then to have to deal with some chick's baggage from a previous relationship! And let's not forget all the drama the 'baby daddy' is probably gonna have for you! How do you plan to manage all that, your job, and law school at the same time without going insane?"

"Believe me, Jim, I've counted the costs and so far I've been handling my business. Anyway, it's not like I just met this woman. I've known her for most of my life. I've loved her for most of my life."

"Oh, really? Who is she?"

"It's Callie."

"Callie?"

Allen noticed Jim's confused expression and immediately understood.

"Yeah. You know how I feel about her. I've been in love with her since high school."

"Did she tell you how she managed to end up pregnant?"

"I think we both know the answer to that."

"C'mon, Allen. You know what I mean."

"She said when she stopped hanging with us, she got caught up with some guy in a type of friends with benefits situation. Then she got pregnant and when she went to tell the guy, she found out he'd died of a drug overdose. So the dad's not in the picture and never will be."

"Sounds very convenient."

"You think she's lying?"

"I don't know what to think."

Allen noticed how quiet and pensive Jim had become all of a sudden. From the look on Jim's face it seemed he was a million miles away and it worried Allen.

"Are you okay?"

"I'm just blown away by what I'm hearing."

"I know. It's a lot."

"All the time Callie's been up here, she hasn't said a thing."

"We all agreed we wouldn't lay anything heavy on you until you were stronger. Callie and I wanted to be together when we told, you, but since the subject has come up, I thought it'd be best to just lay everything out there."

"I can't believe that Callie's a mom."

"Yeah. She had a boy. His name is Darius. He looks just like Callie. I'll show you."

Allen pulled out his smart-phone and showed Jim the screensaver picture of Darius, Callie and himself. Jim seemed to be examining it carefully.

"How old is he?"

"He's thirteen months."

Jim turned away from the screen of the phone abruptly and directed his attention to the voiceless pastor on the muted television. The last thing Allen wanted to do was to upset Jim, but it seemed all the new information was too much for him to bear.

"Are you sure you're okay?"

"It just seems like everyone has changed so much. I feel like I don't even know who you guys are anymore."

"But it doesn't mean we can't go back to the way things used to be."

"With everything that's changed, I don't see how we can."

"But that's the way life works. Yes, people change, but true friends stay together in spite of all that. For the past two years, I've been praying to God to put us all back together. Little by little, I believe He's been working things out on our behalf. Let's not waste the blessings He's given us."

Allen hoped that what he'd said had calmed his friend's fears about the future. They were both wiser than they'd been before. Their time and experience had helped each of them to mature and develop a more balanced outlook toward their friendship. This time Allen was sure there was no way anything could come between them – not even the invisible wall.

TWO

Callie paced up and down her apartment cradling her little Darius who had been fussy for the past two hours. His wails would wane at intervals, and just when Callie thought she could put him down, his cries would suddenly become more intense and she was back pacing the floor again. It was almost as if her son was playing a game with her.

"C'mon Darius, give me a break. You're not messy, you can't be hungry because I just fed you, and I checked your temperature so you're not really sick. Why can't you just settle down?" Callie said to herself. She would've had more patience for her son if she weren't so apprehensive. Allen said he'd gone to visit Jim at the hospital today, and would call her after he got home from school. It was the hospital visit that had her worried. She knew Jim was getting stronger, was able to stay awake longer, and was talking more. It was Jim's ability to talk that had her on edge.

She had made a number of attempts to visit Jim herself today, but the emergency room had been really busy. She tried again during her lunch break, but when she saw that Pastor Bynum was already there, she decided to try again later. When she went back, Mr. Sharpe was there. By the time Jim was free, it was time for her to leave and pick up Darius from daycare. She had hoped she could talk to Jim before Allen got to him again. "Allen said he wouldn't bring it up, so there should be nothing to worry about," pondered Callie who was still trying to reassure herself. Even if she was sure of what Allen would say, there was no telling what Jim would.

Callie was so distracted she could hardly keep her mind on her little boy. She took him over to the couch and put him over her knees and rubbed his back. She remembered Allen doing this to Darius on a couple of occasions. He'd said his mom had told him it had worked on him when he was little. Not long after, Darius let out a burp and passed gas several times before he began to quiet down.

"Finally," thought Callie with some relief as she turned him over and looked at him. Despite what Allen thought, Callie was convinced Darius didn't look like anyone on her side of the family. Instead, Darius tended to favor his father's side and his people weren't very good-looking at all, in her opinion. In fact, she often wished Allen could've been his father so he could have gotten some better looks. To make matters worse, Callie felt Darius had also inherited his father's cranky and whiny nature, which caused him to be given to fits of crying for what seemed to be no reason at all. Darius's constant crying was a major source of irritation and frustration for Callie, making it hard to cope with her son. Allen was a lot better at dealing with him at such times. Allen had helped her to get through a lot in the past couple of years. Callie just wished she had been able to talk to Jim and set him straight before Allen's visit. She couldn't help but wonder what they were talking about, and how Allen would feel afterward. Callie was becoming tense and she didn't want the vibe to make Darius fussy again, so she took him to his room and put him down in his crib to get some sleep. As she watched her son fall asleep, Callie reflected on the life she had built with Allen and Darius. It was a far cry from how she thought it would be.

When Callie found out she was pregnant, she felt as if her world were ending. Allen had just walked out on her, she had just thrown Jim out of her life, and had written off the rest of their clique. Looking for family support was not an option: her sister lived out of state and her mother couldn't be bothered to care much for Callie even when she was little. Callie was completely alone. At first, she believed an abortion would be the only sensible thing she could do, given her circumstances at the time. As a single woman trying to work her way to head nurse, the last thing she needed was a child, especially since she didn't know if she had the time or the emotional and financial resources necessary to care for him or her. After deliberating on the matter for a while, she began to reconsider her options. Her child was the only tangible person in her life at that moment. Aborting the child meant losing yet another person in her life, which was becoming lonelier by the minute. "If I don't have anyone else, at least I'll have this child," she thought to herself at the time. So it was settled. She was keeping her child.

It took some time to get used to the idea of being a mother. In the beginning, Callie was overwhelmed by all the responsibilities she had to assume as the sole provider and caregiver for her unborn child. She had to find a new apartment because the studio she lived in at the time was barely enough room for her.

Callie also had to think about all the different supplies she would need, child proofing the living space, and finding reliable yet affordable daycare. There were a lot of challenges involved and Callie tried to remain positive about her situation. After all, if her mother had raised two kids by herself, she should be able to handle one. "Scores of African-American women have been raising children by themselves for generations," she told herself. Her situation was nothing new, however, this fact only helped to calm some of her fears. Just because Callie could go it alone without a man didn't mean she wanted to. Being a single mother was doable, but that didn't mean it was going to be easy for her or her child; her own childhood had taught her that. Callie had always envisioned having children with a loving husband who would be there for her and their child. Callie had given up hope for her fantasy, and giving her child the life she never had, until a chance encounter changed everything.

She had gone shopping at a local supermarket when she ran into Allen unexpectedly while he was on an errand for his mom. At the time, Callie was six months along and her condition was painfully obvious to anyone who saw her. She could tell that Allen was shocked by the way he couldn't take his eyes off her midsection, much to her embarrassment. They greeted each other briefly before running off in their separate directions and Callie didn't think much more of their meeting. "With his Christian beliefs, he's probably thinking the worst about me," thought Callie afterward. She was sure Allen would never want to see or hear from her again, however, that night she received an unexpected phone call.

Though he said that he was calling to properly congratulate her, Allen had a lot of questions, and

Callie answered them as honestly as she could. He was reaching out to her and she didn't want to risk scaring him away. Since Jim had abandoned the clique, there was no sense in mentioning the affair she'd had with him. It wouldn't serve any purpose except to hurt Allen and that was the last thing Callie wanted to do. To Callie's surprise, it wasn't long before Allen was offering his assistance. He escorted her to doctor appointments and childbirth classes. He helped her to find a new apartment, move in, and decorate a nursery. Allen even got Tamiko to help him plan a baby shower for her and, when the time came, he even stood by her in the delivery room. They had been through a lot together and in the process of time their relationship had blossomed beyond mere friendship just as she had hoped.

Callie admired Allen. He was a good man and a good father to Darius. Sure there were times when he was a little over zealous with regard to matters of religion, but as long as Allen wasn't trying to force her into the church, she could over look this. Allen was everything she imagined her ideal partner to be: generous, smart, caring, and handsome. Now that he was going to law school, she also knew that it was just a matter of time before he would become a great provider as well. Callie now had the picture perfect family she had always wanted. For the first time in her life she felt she had achieved happiness. Everything was going well until the night they rushed Jim to the emergency room at St. Luke's.

Initial reports of Jim's condition were bleak. All the doctors predicted that he wouldn't last more than a few hours. Callie couldn't help but feel relieved. She felt bad about wishing death for someone who had been such a close friend. Jim had been good to her, but in her mind there were justifications for her feelings. "If Jim is still the same way he was at our last meeting, he might as well die. He'd be no good to himself or anyone else," she thought. Then that detective from the police department came. It seemed he knew the Sharpes and as soon as he identified who the patient was, he contacted them. It wasn't long before the Sharpes, the Bynums, and their friends had converged at the hospital. Allen got everyone together in the church chapel to pray for Jim. They were there every evening praying that Jim would make it, while Callie was in the emergency room, hoping that he wouldn't. To Callie's dismay, her friend's prayers prevailed. Jim survived and Callie had to think fast about what she was going to do to neutralize the threat to her happiness that had materialized.

Callie knew Allen would be determined to reconcile with Jim. At first, she tried using Jim's condition to her advantage. Jim was in the intensive care unit for more than a couple of days. This, in and of itself, limited Allen's time with him due to the fact that patients in ICU couldn't have visitors for very long. During this time Callie tried to get Allen to reconsider his relationship to Jim. She remembered their past conversation as vividly as if it were moments ago.

"Jim is my boy. We've been through hell and high water together. There's no way I'm not going to be there for him now."

"How do you know if he even wants you to be there? You said yourself, the last time you two spoke, he made it clear he didn't want to be bothered."

"He was only going through some changes. He just needed some space so he could figure things out..."

"And from the looks of things, I'd say he's done a pretty lousy job of it."

"All the more reason why I should be there for him."

"You couldn't help him before, so what makes you think you can help him now? I mean think about how he ended up at the hospital. Based on what that detective said, the circumstances sound kind of shady, don't you think? It's obvious he wasn't mugged or was just some unfortunate bystander!"

"We don't know what happened to Jim and I, for that matter, don't care. That's not even the issue. The point is he needs our support right now. Maybe I can't help Jim with everything, but I'm willing to let God use me however He sees fit. After everything we've been through together, I owe Jim that."

"Allen, I know how much you care about Jim and I'm not saying that you shouldn't. But at the same time, it just seems that this brother is determined to go down and I don't want him to take you with him."

"That's not going to happen."

"But how do you know..."

"I won't abandon him, Callie. That's all there is to it."

Trying to convince Allen to drop his friendship with Jim went nowhere and Callie knew if she continued to press him, she would risk losing his affection. So Callie resorted to another tactic: she decided to control the amount of information that passed between the two. Callie was grateful to Pastor Bynum for suggesting that Jim not be overwhelmed by a lot of questions and gossip until he was stronger. It gave her the perfect cover for not revealing the details of her relationship with Allen to Jim, and since Allen tended to have a high regard for his Pastor's advice it was easy to get him to agree. If Allen didn't bring up the subject of the relationship, it was less likely that Jim would bring up what happened between him and Callie so long ago. Shortly after Jim had awakened from his coma, he could barely put two coherent words together. His doctor had even told them that some parts of his memory might be affected for a while as well. This, coupled with the fact that Jim spent most of the time doped up on painkillers and other medications which made him drowsy and unable to maintain consciousness for more than an hour at a time, gave Callie a sense of relief for a while. Now, things were starting to change and she knew her secret wouldn't be safe for long.

The stronger Jim got, the more lucid he became, which in turn, made him more talkative. From her conversations with Tim and Allen, she realized that Jim was bringing up more and more of the recent past. Although she was certain Jim had not brought up the subject of their 'fling', Callie knew it wouldn't be long before he did. She would have to make sure she was able to get to him before that happened – that is, if it hadn't happened already.

The buzz of her intercom interrupted her reverie and nearly made Callie jump out of her skin. She hastened over to answer it.

"Who is it?"

"Handyman," she heard a familiar voice say.

Allen was obviously trying to be funny which gave Callie a sense of relief. If he was in a joking mood, then she knew that her secret was still safe. She walked over to the door, unlocked it and waited for Allen to arrive.

"Hey, beautiful," he said after he got off the elevator and headed in her direction. She noticed he was also carrying a large shopping bag.

"I thought you had class tonight."

"I did, but I was running late, so I decided to skip it. Besides, I felt like I haven't seen you two in so long, I just had to drop by. I hope I haven't spoiled your plans."

"Not at all. In fact, I'd say this is much better than the phone call I was expecting."

"Really? Then let me make it even more pleasant," he said before he took her into his arms to kiss her.

"You're right; that made my day. How was yours?" said Callie as she led him into the apartment.

"Just okay, until now. How's Darius?"

"He's asleep. He was a little gassy earlier, but thankfully I remembered that trick you showed me."

"He hasn't gotten feverish lately, has he?"

"Not for a whole week now. His immune system must be building up. What's that you've got there?"

"I stopped by the book store after I left the hospital and decided to pick up some bedtime stories for Darius. When I saw them I just had to get them. I remember my dad used to read these to me when I was a kid," he said as he took them out of the bag to show her before placing them on the coffee table.

"And you were worried that I would spoil him? Allen, you just bought him a whole bunch of clothes last week, not to mention that big birthday party you threw and all the toys you bought."

"I just want him to have everything he needs. Miko says reading to him even at this age is going to prepare him for school."

"You say that like..."

"I'm his dad? As far as I'm concerned, I am. If that's okay with you?"

"No complaints here. So, how was Jim?"

"Physically, he's a lot better, but he's still kinda down on himself. Ya know?"

"What do you mean?"

"He's feeling guilty about cutting us off and all the mistakes he's made."

"I think that's a good thing. If you don't feel guilty all you do is keep on repeating the same mistakes."

"I guess. Then there are all the changes he's heard we've all been going through. I know you wanted to be there so we could tell him together, but I told him about us."

"You what?!"

"I'm sorry, but Tamiko gave him a hint and he asked me point blank. I didn't want to have to lie."

"Of course, that little..." began Callie under her breath, gritting her teeth in an attempt to stifle her anger. "It's just that I wish you would have waited like we planned."

"I know, but at least things didn't go as badly as we thought."

"Are you saying he's happy for us?"

"I wouldn't quite put it that way."

"So how would you put it?"

"He's just concerned about the amount of responsibility I'm taking on."

"In other words, he doesn't like the idea of us being together, either," said Callie throwing up her hands.

"At least he didn't seem angry about it like my parents were. Anyway at the end of the day, it doesn't matter what Jim or anyone else likes or doesn't like. As far as I'm concerned, it's not going to change anything."

"My thoughts exactly."

"Anyway, I think he's more concerned about his own situation - like where he's going to fit in when he gets home."

"That's his problem. Jim's a grown man and he's going to have to find his own way."

"I think he will. He's going to be staying with my parents and I when he gets out. He's even been talking about coming back to church."

Callie's heart sank. Allen and Jim living together for who knows how long was making this just that much more complicated, not to mention Jim's sudden development of religious convictions.

"Is that so?"

"Yeah. I think it's exactly what he needs. It's what I've been praying about for a long time and I thank God He heard my prayer. Now if I could get one more person to come to down to church..."

"Allen..."

"No pressure. Just thought I'd suggest."

"Maybe one day. Do you want something to eat? It's going to be late by the time you get back to your mom's."

"I don't know. I have some reading that I have to finish when I get home."

"So I'll make something quick. How about eggs and rice with sausage?"

"O.K. Sounds good."

"Just give me ten minutes."

Just then, Darius started to cry.

"Oh, no!"

"Don't worry, I'll check on him," said Allen before he started off to Darius's room.

"Thanks."

Callie rushed around the kitchen gathering the items she needed for the dinner. As she was preparing the sausages she could see Allen coming back into the living room with little Darius who had since quieted down. Allen was rocking him back and forth gently and talking to him.

"Is he okay?"

"He's fine. Our conversation probably woke him up. He was probably wondering, 'who's making all that noise when I'm trying to sleep?' Right, Darius? Well don't worry little man, next time I'll keep it down. Hey, would you like to hear a story? Maybe this will help you get back to sleep. I got a good one, too. It's called, The Snowy Day."

Allen grabbed one of the books from the coffee table and took Darius with him to the recliner and began to read him the story. For the first time tonight, Darius seemed calm and content. Callie's heart melted as she watched them together. All of a sudden her protective instincts kicked in. There was no way that she could allow anyone to destroy the domestic bliss she had worked so hard to build. Callie knew what she had to do. She was determined to see Jim as soon as possible - tomorrow morning to be exact.

THREE

"So what would you recommend?" asked Tamiko as she and Davis looked over their menus. They had just been to see a Christian film called, "The Last Apostle" and Tamiko had practically begged him to have dinner with her at La Rosita, a little Latin restaurant that was next door to the theatre.

"I was going to have the pork chops, with beans and rice, but that might not be to your taste. I know you like to eat healthy and everything."

"But it's not like I'm a fitness fanatic or something. I've eaten pork before. Besides, it sounds good. I'm willing to give it a try."

"You sure?"

"Yes. I trust your judgment," she beamed.

Davis smiled back, but he couldn't help but feel uncomfortable. Every time they went out, she would always ask him what he wanted and then end up ordering the same thing. At first, he thought it was because they had the same tastes, but after a while he'd observed that she was doing this just to copy him, which was becoming annoying. It just seemed like game, like he thought this whole night was turning out to be.

When Tamiko invited him on this outing, she told him that Tim and Allen would be coming with them, however, both of them were conspicuously absent when he showed up to meet her at the theatre. In all fairness, he knew Allen wouldn't show. Allen had told him earlier in the day at work that he'd have to stop by the hospital to see Jim and then he had school afterward. Tim on the other hand, just bailed on them. Tamiko said she texted him to see what was up, but he hadn't answered and now Davis was starting to wonder if Tamiko had something to do with it. He knew she and Tim could be like peanut butter and jelly sometimes, and Tim would do almost anything she asked him to. Davis wasn't thrilled about having to entertain the possibility that he'd been cornered into yet another 'date', but this was the fifth time this had happened in the past month. She was even dressed up like it was a date: fancy black silk dress with white polka-dots and ruffled skirt, topped with a red sweater and belt, finished with black high heels. What was worse was he hated to entertain the idea that Tamiko, of all the women he knew, would ever resort to such tricks. "What happened to that sweet girl that I met not long ago?" he thought to himself. But he suspected he might know the answer to that question.

Davis knew that Tamiko liked him – really liked him – as in romantically speaking. From his personal experience, he knew that when a woman wanted a particular man, she could lose her personality as she got caught up in the chase. The only reason why Davis was willing to go along with the game was because, despite everything, he knew the real Tamiko. That girl was still his friend and he didn't want to hurt her feelings. Davis waved over a waitress who promptly took their order. When she left, Davis decided to inquire about what had been on his mind.

"Still no word from Tim?"

"I'll check my phone," said Tamiko as she took it out of her purse and turned it on. She perused the screen for a few seconds.

"I hope he's okay."

"Looks like he sent a text just as we were going into the theatre," said Tamiko, "He said he had stuff to work on at home, so he'd have to skip the movie."

"What else is new?"

"I know. Lately it seems like Tim is always busy. But that doesn't mean we can't have fun, right?"

"Yeah, I guess."

"You are having a good time, aren't you?" said Tamiko, as she eyed him curiously. It seemed as if she were trying to read his thoughts.

"I'm okay. Just a little tired, that's all."

"Worked hard today?"

"Yeah. It's a big hotel. People are always in and out and you know they gotta break something before they leave. Today it seemed like everyone was killin' the showers. I think I re-installed about a hundred shower heads."

"That does sound like a lot of work. But maybe a good hot meal with a friend will make you feel better."

"Yeah." said Davis as he slumped forward and leaned his head against his fist.

There was a moment of silence between them as Davis tried to think of something to say. He would rather not say anything because he didn't know how Tamiko would interpret, or, rather misinterpret it. He thought he had been clear months ago when he said he thought they should just be friends, but it seemed every time they were together like this, he couldn't help but feel pressured.

"So how's things going on your job?" asked Davis. He thought talking about work would be a safe topic.

"It's insane as usual. There's a new evaluation system that's about to be rolled out, and principal Stone is like a raving lunatic now, but I'm handling things."

"Do they still come in your classroom to spy on you?"

"Technically, it's not spying. They're supposed to be evaluating me. I still get observed. They come more often now, but at least it's not for a whole 45 minutes like before. Stone still hates my guts for whatever reason, but this new system is even more work for her. I'm sure she'd love to pick me apart, but she just doesn't have the time."

"Well that's something to thank God about. Now you can teach the kids the way you know how and not worry about it."

"Oh, I wish. The curriculum has been totally teacher proofed. Everything has to be according to the Department of Education guidelines. Then there's all of the paper work that eats up so much of my time - like the six page lesson plans I write every day."

"But I know you've got some extra time, now that you've finished your masters and everything. At least you don't have to worry about papers and classes anymore."

"True. And I'm thankful for that. But now I have to work on getting professional development credits, there's a new curriculum, and...I don't know. I feel like I'm working all the time. I had to plan this outing two weeks in advance, and only because tomorrow is a professional development day for our school and the kids won't be there so I don't have to write lessons. It's just a struggle to find the time to do the things that really matter to me – like spending time with the people I care about," she said taking his hand. Davis looked away, abruptly withdrawing his hand from hers, and started playing with the silverware on the table. He knew what she was trying to do, and he didn't want to go there with her.

"I hope they don't make us wait all night for our food. I gotta get up early for work in the morning."

"We could have them make it to go if you're in that much of a hurry."

All of a sudden he noticed her usual cheerful expression began to fade into a somber one. She looked down and toyed with the charm bracelet she was wearing.

"Look, I wasn't tryin' to be...never mind."

There was another tense silence between them for a few seconds. Davis didn't want to be rude, but he wanted to make it clear to Tamiko that this was not a date. The situation required that he be tactful, which was not something he was good at. He was trying to think of a way to express himself, but it was difficult because he had never been good with words. Davis was trying to think of what to say when Tamiko interrupted his train of thought.

"So how are things going in the program? This is your last year, right?"

"Yeah. Everything's been going aiight. I'm still doing good and I've already started the process for applying for my licenses."

"That's wonderful!" she said her face brightening again. "What do you think you're going to do when you're done? Like do you think you're going to start your own business?"

"I don't know if I'm ready for that yet."

"Aw, c'mon. As good as you are, you'll have a lot of jobs in no time."

"It's just that I've been praying about it and I know I need to wait for the Lord to give me the green light. Know what I mean?"

"Of course. I can understand that."

"But I figure, in the meantime, I'll just keep my job at the hotel and do a few freelance jobs here and there on the side. You know, start to build my rep."

"If you want, I could ask around the church and see if there's anyone who needs some work done. Who knows, maybe there's something my dad may need you to do around the house."

"Thanks, but don't feel like you have to put yourself out."

"It's no problem at all where you're concerned. Oh, and before I forget -" she said as she began to dig down into her purse.

"Not again," thought Davis to himself.

"Ta-da!" said Tamiko handing him a little black box that was tied with a red ribbon.

"Miko, I really appreciate the gesture, but I can't – I mean you just got me those towels last week."

"I know, but when I saw this I knew I had to get it for you. Go on, open it."

Davis took a deep breath as he untied the red ribbon and opened the box. Inside were three neatly folded cloths in different solid colors. Davis had never seen anything like them.

"Do you like them?"

"What are they? Like fancy napkins or something?"

"Nooo, silly!" laughed Tamiko "They're handkerchiefs. You put them in the top pocket of your suit jacket – you can use them when you need something to wipe the sweat out of your eyes or if you want to make your suit look fancy."

"Oh."

"I tried to get colors that matched some of the ties I've seen you wear."

"Thanks for the gift, but…I don't want you to feel like you gotta waste your money on me like this."

"Oh, don't say that. I could never feel that way. I like doing things for you. We're friends. Remember?"

"I know, but - how 'bout you hold onto these until it's like a holiday or whatnot," said Davis as he put the handkerchiefs back in the box and handed it back to her. "It would help me to feel better about taking it."

"Okay – if that's what you want," said Tamiko who looked a bit disappointed and puzzled at the same time.

Suddenly, the waitress appeared with their food, which gave Davis a convenient escape from heading into a conversation that he was dreading. He dove into his meal to try to satiate his anxiety rather than his hunger. He felt guilty about not being able to reciprocate Tamiko's feelings. At the beginning of their friendship, there were times when he thought he could. Tamiko was friendly, intelligent, beautiful, caring, selfless, and best of all, shared his faith. In fact, he had been looking for a girl like her to share his life with since he'd come to faith, but he just couldn't bring himself to commit to her. He didn't know if he was ready to handle a romantic relationship yet.

Davis had never been good at relationships and had ruined the few stable ones he did have. So when she approached him about the possibility of being a couple, he felt compelled to keep things on the level with her. Unfortunately, his honesty and frankness had done little to change her feelings. To make matters worse, instead of giving him the space and time he needed to talk to God and think about things, she started to crowd him out. It seemed everywhere he went (with the exception of his job), she was trying to be there. Then there was what seemed like the constant gift giving and errand running. The last thing Davis wanted to do was to hurt Tamiko, especially after all of the support and affection she'd showered him with. He didn't want to lose her as a friend, but given the way things were going, he couldn't see things turning out well. He looked up at her and, he noticed how she was only picking at her meal.

"Not quite your taste, right?"

"The rice is good, it's just the seasoning on the pork chops needs a little getting used to."

"I could get you something else if you don't like it."

"I'm fine, really. Actually, I was thinking about something."

"Like what?"

"I was wondering if you wouldn't mind helping me with something I'm working on at the church."

"What is it?"

"My mom is going to have this mixer for the Christian singles in a few weeks."

"What?"

"I know. It sounds lame. It *is* lame. Think of it as her way of helping people who want to get married, find a partner in a safe or sinless way. Anyway, she wants me to host it and I don't want to do it by myself. I wouldn't do it at all, only it's supposed to be a fundraiser for the grocery mobile program that's going to get groceries and supplies to the shut in elderly folks who don't have relatives to help them."

"I don't get it. Why can't you do it by yourself?"

"Because I don't want people to think I'm...looking for someone."

"So I'd be there to block for you? Make the guys think you're with me?"

"I guess you could say that, but it's not like, I'd be really 'with you' or anything like that."

"I don't know, Miko."

"It wouldn't be a real date."

"It might not be a real date, but it would feel like it. Sorry, Miko, but I don't think I can be down."

"So you're so afraid of relationships, you can't even be in the company of a woman for an evening?"

"I'm not scared of nothin'. I just don't think it would be a good idea."

"Davis, it's just a few goofy ice breaker activities and dinner – just like we're having right now."

"Look, if I had known it'd be just the two of us tonight, I...never mind."

"You mean you never would've come?" she said as her countenance dimmed again.

"Don't get me wrong, it's not that - I just – we've talked about this before and I don't wanna send you any mixed signals. I need for us to be clear about where we stand."

"Believe me, we're clear. Just forget I asked about it."

"I don't mean to upset you or nothing.'"

"I'm not upset. A little confused, maybe."

"I told you before, this doesn't have nothin' to do with you. I have to get my life straight before I can share it with someone else."

"That's what I don't understand. From what I can see, you have a stable job, your making progress in your career goals, you go to church and you have lots of friends. How much straighter can it get?"

"It's not that simple. I got a lot of personal things I need to work out."

"Was your last relationship that bad?"

"If you don't mind, I'd rather not get into it."

"Even with me?"

"Don't take it personal, Miko. You're a nice person, but I can only lean on you for so much. Some things gotta be between a man and God. I know there's probly things that you think you can't talk to me about."

"Not really."

"Not even your female stuff?"

"What do you mean, female stuff?

"You know. Things that women talk about with other women."

"I don't get it."

"In a way, I guess you wouldn't. I kinda noticed you don't have a lot of female friends. Right or wrong?"

"Wrong! Very wrong! I have a number of female friends. There are the other teachers at my job..."

"I've never seen you hanging out with them and you don't bring any of them around. None of them are your besties."

"Allen has a cousin who is a female and we're really close friends."

"How come I've never seen her?"

"Because she lives in North Carolina..."

"North Carolina! Miko, that's not a best friend, that's a pen pal. You need to get you some girls in the city to hang out with. Some ladies you can chill with and talk about things with."

"Wait a minute, why would you suggest I start hanging with a bunch of women? Unless this is your way of saying you don't even want me hanging out with you and the guys anymore."

Tamiko's defensive reaction made Davis regret his words. She made it seem as if he was patronizing her, which was not his intent.

"Nah! Nah! All I'm trying to say is - that just like you spend time with the guys, you could spend time with your girls, too."

"Or just spend less time around you, right? If you don't want to be friends anymore just say so."

"Miko, believe me, I really like having you as a friend and I want to continue to have you as a friend, but I think us being up under each other all the time is gonna mess that up...especially since I can't give you what you really want from me right now."

"I see."

"I'm not tryin' to hurt your feelings and I'm not tryin' to de-friend you. I'm just trying to be honest. I think we should try to give each other some space for a little while."

"Fine. I appreciate your honesty and I hear you – space granted. Anyway, it's getting late and I know you're tired. How about we wrap things up for tonight?"

"Aiight. I'll get the bill and we'll head out."

"Sure."

"No hard feelings?"

"Not at all."

Despite Tamiko's attempt to appear nonchalant, Davis could see the hurt on her face, and it made him hate himself. Unfortunately, he had no choice. It wasn't that he didn't trust her as much as he couldn't trust himself. There was no way that he could give himself to her or anyone else given his past. The pain he was inflicting on her now was way less than the pain he was trying to shield her from.

FOUR

"How was the movie?" asked her father when she came in. He had been waiting up for her, as she had expected.

"It was good," said Tamiko. She hastily hung up her coat, and rushed toward the staircase to keep her father from continuing his interrogation. As always, her dad could always sense when something was amiss, however, Tamiko did not feel like having one of their father-daughter conversations. She just wanted to be alone.

"You sure, baby girl?"

"Of course. I'd stay and talk, but I'm feeling wiped. I just want to go to bed," said Tamiko as she hurried up the stairs.

Once she was in her room and the door was closed, Tamiko kicked off her heels and collapsed onto her bed, face up and stared dejectedly at the ceiling.

"Now Davis can't stand me and it's all my fault," Tamiko thought to herself. "I should've never told him how I felt about him"

THE ATONEMENT

Since the day she met Davis there was not one moment when she doubted that they would make the perfect couple. For the first time in her life, she had met someone who was good-looking and Christian at the same time – a real Christian. Davis's walk seemed to match his talk. In the beginning, they grew close very quickly. They spent a lot of time together and it seemed that Davis enjoyed her company. Tamiko was certain that he was falling for her as fast as she had been falling for him. So when she gathered enough courage to suggest they become a couple she was certain beyond any doubt that he would be interested. Instead, she got the 'let's just be friends' speech – sort of.

Davis had told her that, while he liked her, he didn't know if he was ready for a romantic relationship. He needed time to sort some things out. It wasn't an out right rejection and he did say that he liked her, so she remained hopeful. At the time, Tamiko felt that she would just wait until he was ready. Time would be her ally instead of her enemy. In the meantime, she'd be there for him when he needed her. She'd show him just how loyal and faithful she could be – like any potential wife should be. If he were stuck at home feeling sick, she'd make sure to stop by and drop off some homemade soup. Several Sundays she tried cooking some of his favorites for dinner: red rice and beans with chicken, pernil, pasteles, pigeon peas and rice. Then there were the little romantic rendezvous she would set up, so they could get to know each other better: projects at church they worked on together, walks through the park, and the occasional movie or museum trip. Tamiko thought these things would show him how much she cared about him and would make her endeared to him. She never thought it would annoy him. His exact words were 'they were up under each other all the time.' It made her think of the things her mother used to say when she got annoyed and didn't want her around. "Tamiko, I can't get my work done with you up under me like this! I'm taking you to Momma Lena's!" Then he had to go and suggest that she make new female friends. It seemed to Tamiko that she'd been dumped again, and this time, she hadn't even gotten the chance to date the guy.

Tamiko had never fared that well in relationships herself, having received as many romantic pink slips as she had doled out. She'd never had a boyfriend longer than a half a year before it was over. Most of the time she'd blame the guy. Since she'd dated a few non-Christians, several of them broke up with her because she wouldn't sleep with them. Others were Christian beaus who broke up with her for basically the same reason, or because they didn't find she was submissive enough. They were obvious write-offs. But now, it seemed she'd turned Davis off. Davis wasn't some non-believer or a jerk. He was actually Tamiko's ideal guy: genuine, honest, caring, of good character, he shared her faith and her values, and he was incredibly handsome. She thought they would be the perfect couple, but the fact that Davis didn't seem to think so, made her doubt herself.

"Maybe there's something wrong with me. Maybe I'm too self-involved? What if he thinks I'm a complainer? I was going on a bit about work. I didn't mean to be negative. Maybe I was too overbearing. Why else would he ask for space?"

After a few minutes, she got up from where she lay and began to change into her nightgown. Tamiko didn't want to get into the habit of feeling sorry for herself. She tried to put her troubles with Davis into perspective. "Maybe I should give Davis some space," she considered. "With all of the time we're spending together he's probably been taking our relationship for granted." She just knew Davis's feelings would change once he had been missing her for a while. Then again, she could think of one person in their set that she hadn't connected with in a while who didn't seem to miss her at all, and though she did not like to admit it, it bothered her – a lot. "Don't even go there," Tamiko chided herself, "Davis is the better choice – or at least the saner choice." When it came to relationships Tamiko was determined to weigh her options carefully and make the right decision. Besides, she had other things to worry about, like everything that was going on with Jim.

Everyone was distraught when they heard the news that Jim had been shot. Not much was revealed about the circumstances surrounding what happened. Everything that Tamiko knew was third hand from Allen, who didn't know much himself. One thing that was obvious to everyone was that there were drugs involved. The idea that Jim could have been taking or selling drugs was more than disturbing for Tamiko. She knew Jim had be going through something really intense for him to start making such poor decisions in his life. She only wished there was something that could have been done to spare him all this, but going over the would'ves, could'ves, and should'ves wasn't going to help things. The most important thing was that everyone worked together to help Jim get better. The last time she went to visit him in the hospital, Jim definitely looked better and was in better spirits. Of all her friends, Jim was the biggest gossip monger and he was eager to hear everything that had been going on with their crew while he had been away. He seemed like the old Jim, but Tamiko could tell that he'd been through a lot. "I need to have my mind on helping Jim, rather than sulking about my problems with Davis," she scolded herself.

The loud chiming of her cell phone interrupted Tamiko's thoughts. She grabbed the phone from her purse to see who it was, even though she had intended to ignore the call. She didn't feel like talking to anyone, until she saw a familiar photo flash on the screen.

"Riley! Girl, how you doin?!"

"I think the better question is how y'all doin' up there? Daddy told me that Uncle Vern told him that Jim got shot. Is that true? Is he all right?"

"Now he is. He's going to be coming home from the hospital in a few days."

"Well I'm thankful to God for that. How'd he get shot?"

"I don't know all of the details. Jim had decided to go out on his own and no one had heard anything from him for ages. I had stopped by his apartment a couple of times, but he was never around. We almost thought he'd moved away until detective Ballard called."

"Why would Jim just cut everybody off like that?"

"Your guess is as good as mine. He and Allen had gotten into it a couple of times and the next thing we knew, Jim wasn't speaking to any of us anymore - Even Pop Vernon and Momma Lena."

"Is he still upset with everyone?"

"I don't think so. He doesn't seem upset when I talk to him."

"How's Allen taking all this? I know he's probably a mess, and blaming himself to boot."

"In the beginning he was, but now he's okay. There are other things that I'm worried about when it comes to Allen."

"You mean like his new girlfriend?"

"How'd you know?"

"I've seen the pictures on his facebook. Trust me girl, you're not the only one that's worried. That baby don't look nothing like him."

"Relax, Riley. Allen knows he's not the biological father."

"Now that just makes it even worse. And that reminds me, has Mr. Fix-it tuned up your heart yet?"

"Let's put it this way – remember when I told you I thought he was 'the one'?"

"Uh-hunh."

"Well, now I'm not so sure. We're not even dating and I got the "I need space" speech."

"Uh-oh. Now this confirms it. I've been away for too long. Y'all done turned into a heap of hot mess. I'm going to have to come up North for one of my visits and help y'all get things straight."

"For real! When are you thinking of coming? This summer?"

"Try Saturday. I started makin' plans when I heard about what happened to Jimmy a couple of weeks ago. Since Uncle Vern's is going to be a little crowded, your dad said I could stay with you."

"Really? I can't wait! Girl, we gon' have a good time – hey, wait a minute. They let you take off on your job like that?"

"No, but when you don't have a job, you can go when you please."

"Aww, Riley. What happened?"

"The salon where I was workin' closed up. The owner had mortgage troubles and that's that."

"I'm so sorry. When did this happen?"

"A month ago. But you don't have to worry about me. I still catch a few dollars here and there from the kids and the old ladies I work on in the 'hood. Besides, now I have time to do what I want to do, like visit my favorite cousins in the Big Apple."

"Well, I'm certain I can speak for everyone when I say we can't wait to see you. You know we're going to have a celebration for Jim when he gets out. It's going to be Saturday afternoon. You think you'll be here in time?"

"Miko, you know I hate parties."

"It's not a party. It's a celebration - just a few friends that sit around and have dinner together, that's all. Besides, we just want to cheer Jim up and show him that he has our support."

"Call it what you want, but I don't want to have to sit around and try to make small talk with a bunch of people I don't really know. If it's just you, Allen, and Jim that's one thing, but I can do without all those other characters you and Allen have been tellin' me about."

"Are you saying you're not even the least little bit curious about Davis?"

"Not if he's like the last dude you were seeing. What was his name again? Calvin?"

"It was Kevin, and Davis is nothing like him. He's a genuine Christian."

"So why are you talking like you're done with him?"

"I still like Davis. The problem is, I don't think he feels the same way."

"Miko, life's too short to waste your time with some loser who doesn't know how he feels. If he's not into you there's nothing you can do to change his mind. I learned that the hard way with Marcus. I gave that dude 10 months too many and I don't want you to end up wasting your time like I did."

"Davis hasn't put any pressure on me like what Marcus was doing to you."

"Really? You sure he's not..."

"Riley!"

"Just wait 'til I get up there and I'll let you know if this Davis character is worthy or not. Until then, send the others my love and tell Allen to keep his line open. I been able to catch everybody 'cept him."

"You're not the only one that has encountered that problem. He turns it off when he's at work, or he's at school, or he's at Callie's place, so it's off for pretty much all day. You know what? I'll drop by his place and tell him to call you."

"Okay. But don't tell him I'm coming. I want to let him know myself."

"No problem."

"I'll text you when I'm on my way, okay. See you in a few days."

"See you, girl."

"Yes!" said Tamiko after she had ended her call. She was certain this was the result of divine intervention: sending her favorite cousin just in time to help lift everyone's spirits. Riley Sharpe was actually Allen's cousin. Her dad, Henry-Lee was Vernon's older brother. Old Henry-Lee started sending Riley to spend summers with Allen and his parents when she was eight to keep her from getting into trouble with the rough boys she used to run with in her neighborhood. After a while, Tamiko and Allen would repay visits to her at times during winter and spring recess. They spent summers and breaks together every year until they graduated from high school. Over the years, Tamiko and Riley became the best of friends and pen pals. In fact, Riley was the only female best friend Tamiko had ever had. Thinking back on what Davis had said earlier, it really was going to be nice to have another woman around to talk to about things, and she knew that Riley could probably talk some sense into Jim and Allen. Finally, Riley and Tamiko always had a good time when they were together. Tamiko couldn't wait until Riley came. She would be just what everyone needed.

FIVE

"Finally finished," Tim sighed out loud as he made one final entry on the spreadsheet he was working on. Then he hit the save icon on his laptop and emailed the file to himself at the office. Now that he was one of the associates in business consulting at Hearns and Marshall, he had much more responsibility than his old position in business services required. Even so, things had worked out rather well. Tim was handling several accounts for some well-known businesses that were expanding their operations. In the past year, the accounts that he oversaw posted better than expected results, giving him the favor of his clients and the upper management alike. However, it was not without some sacrifice. More often than not there was work that followed him home, but lately he didn't mind it as it afforded him some distraction from the temptations in his personal life.

Tim stretched himself and took off his glasses to rub his eyes before glancing over at the clock on the table. It was only 10:00pm, which meant he'd actually finished his work early for a change and now had some extra time to himself before he went to bed.

But regardless of whether he had extra time or not, he would do what he always did before going to bed: he would spend some time with the Lord.

He walked back to his bedroom and got his Bible from the nightstand and took it to his desk. Tim never read in bed, because he knew he'd wind up reading only a page before he fell asleep. As he sat down, he couldn't help but catch sight of the digital picture frame on his desk. There were photos from his stay at John's Hopkins in Baltimore, when his friends had come to see him after the surgery. Slowly the screen cascaded from one frame to the next. The images always stirred his emotions. There was happiness, gratitude, and humility towards the Lord's goodness and mercy. Who else could have changed the nature of the tumor making it operable? Who else could have guided the doctors to remove all of it leaving him cancer free for almost two years and counting? There was no doubt about it. When Tim thought about these things he knew he had made the right decision when he gave his life to the Lord. He always kept this particular album out because it always helped to keep him grounded in his faith. He didn't want to forget what God had done for him. But sometimes the pictures brought other things to mind that he'd rather not think of – specifically the last one.

It was a picture of him and Tamiko. She was sitting on his hospital bed with one arm around him and the other holding a T-shirt that she'd bought him around his neck like a bib that had the words 'Saved by grace' on the front. Tamiko had always been photogenic. She was as beautiful in pictures as she was in person. Her smile was warm and inviting as it always was and seeing her made him wish she could be near to him now. It made him think about all the time they had spent together after his return to New York, when he stayed with the Sharpes to recuperate.

Everyday Tamiko would stop by to check on him and keep him company. Sometimes she'd bring him things – like his favorites: triple chocolate fudge ice cream, root beer, or homemade turkey sandwiches with the gravy inside. Other times she'd bring games for them to play, like chess or dominoes. But no matter what she brought, there was nothing better than the company and conversation they shared together. During his two-month convalescence, they managed to talk about any and everything under the sun. Things he'd never talked about with anyone else – not even Allen. He had told himself before he left for Baltimore that he would keep his distance from her when he got back. "We're just good friends" he reminded himself, "Besides, she likes Davis and he's probably the better guy for her anyway." But the more time she spent with him, the more time he wanted to spend with her. The effect she was having on him was undeniable and it caused him considerable anxiety. It led him to leave the Sharpes a week earlier than he'd planned without a word of warning to Tamiko. Soon after, he was back at work, and not long after that, he decided to get more involved in the church by attending Daniel's Brotherhood Bible Study class and volunteering to play guitar on second and fourth Sundays. Lately, his new busy life left him little time to spend with any of his friends, Tamiko included.

He was supposed to have gone to the movies with them tonight, but after learning that Allen had abandoned the party, Tim decided that he wouldn't go either. He felt like he'd just be in the way. "She'd probably be glad to have Davis all to herself anyway" thought Tim sadly. But Tim knew he couldn't allow himself to dwell on his feelings. So he turned the frame away from him and began to open his Bible to read.

Whenever Tim read, it was his style to simply open the Book and read whichever scripture the pages opened to. Today he happened upon the book of Proverbs, the eighteenth chapter and read, "Whoso findeth a wife findeth a good thing, and obtaineth favor of the Lord."[1]

Tim quickly flipped past the scripture after reading it. He could feel a lump begin to form in his throat and he swallowed hard to clear it and his mind. The last thing he wanted to think about was finding a wife, when he couldn't even find a girlfriend. He still didn't know how all that was supposed to work now that he was a Christian. The last time he tried to date it turned into a church controversy and some people (actually it was only Mother Rose) wanted him to be kicked out of the church. Tim continued to flip pages as he fast-forwarded through the unpleasant memories of that episode of his life. When he stopped flipping, he was still in proverbs but now he was at the thirty-first chapter, which read, "Who can find a virtuous woman? for her price is far above rubies. The heart of her husband doth safely trust in her, so that he shall have no need of spoil."[2] Tim decided to abandon the book of proverbs and the rest of the Old Testament for the book of Matthew. He started reading at the fourth chapter and continued until he got to some verses that arrested his attention.

"Therefore if thou bring thy gift to the altar, and there rememberest that thy brother hath ought against thee: Leave there thy gift before the altar, and go thy way: first be reconciled to thy brother, and then come and offer thy gift. Agree with thine adversary quickly whiles thou art in the way with him; lest at any time the adversary deliver thee to the judge, and the judge deliver thee to the officer, and thou be cast into prison. Verily I say unto thee, Thou shalt by no means come out thence 'til thou hast paid the uttermost farthing."[3]

Even after being saved for some time, there were still things in the Bible, that Tim only understood vaguely and what he had just read was no exception. But for some reason the words seem rather prescient to him. It was almost as if he needed to read this particular scripture. He knew that it had something to do with reconciling with someone who has something against you, but he didn't know why this was so important. Most of the time, if he knew someone didn't like him, he just stayed out of his or her way. He thought about if he had offended anyone lately that he needed to apologize to. He hadn't seen much of his friends, but no one seemed to be upset with him about it. The only person he could think of was Jim, but after visiting him in the hospital it seemed things between them were straight. Then there was Mother Rose, who he knew wasn't very fond of him, but he was already bending over forwards, backwards, and sideways to try to make things good between them – and not with much success either. Tim decided to keep on reading. He'd think about it later when he had a chance to meditate on what he'd read. Before he went on, Tim took out his personal journal and noted the scripture within it. Who knows, maybe he'd take it to the good pastor to see what he thought.

Tim had gotten all the way to the 8th chapter when the bleating of the intercom interrupted him. He had no idea who would be calling on him at this time of night, besides Allen with some quirky request.

Tim actually liked Allen's impromtu visits, because they were always amusing and they reminded him of his college days and the hijinks he and Allen often got into. Like the time Allen won a birthday cake in a raffle and decided to have a birthday party even though it wasn't anyone's birthday, or when they went on a scouting mission all the way to Vermont to find old-fashioned cider donuts. Tim found himself rushing to find out what Allen was up to now.

"Roger, Bradley."

"It's Miss Russell, sir," said Bradley in a very grave tone.

All of a sudden, Tim's neck felt tight and he could feel a headache coming on.

"Send her up."

Tim walked over to the door and listened for her arrival. He didn't have to wonder what she wanted, because she only came to him for one thing. After a few minutes, he could hear her leather soled platform heels clicking against the tiled floor from all the way down the hall, warning that she was near. The slow-paced click grew steadier and louder until it was right at the door. Tim opened it and braced himself.

"Mom said you're lending me $500.00 – and I'll take large bills," said Allyson as she blithely brushed passed Tim into his apartment. She was dressed in a royal blue, sheath style mini-dress with scalloped edges covered by a three-quarter, black overcoat and a funky looking pair of flesh-colored heels. Crazy looking high heels were Allyson's trademarks. They seemed to be a cross between pumps and brogues. Tim could tell she had probably just come from the salon. Her normally curly sandy-blonde hair had been blown-out straight, touched up with golden highlights and smelled like cotton candy. Allyson held out a freshly manicured hand for her payment.

"And good evening to you, too, Allyson. How are you today?"

"Just get my money, man-whore. I haven't got all night."

"Seriously? Do you have to insult me every time you see me?"

"I don't have to, but it's just more fun this way."

Tim bit his lip and tried to control his frustration and anger. "Don't give in to her," he continued to meditate, "Remember what you just read: love those that hate you, bless those that curse you, pray for those that despitefully use you. Besides, she's still your sister."

Tim turned and walked to his bedroom to get the money from his petty cash safe. Their mother had to curtail Allyson's account privileges a while ago when she started school. During her first month at the University, she drained her personal account of a whopping $20,000.00. Since then their mother only allowed Allyson a more modest monthly allowance and access to two credit cards with set spending limits. When her allowance was spent and the cards were maxed out, Allyson would beg their mother for more money claiming some emergency and be sent to Tim, who would be reimbursed if and/or when their mother felt like it. It was the only time he'd ever see his sister with the exception of the mandatory family celebrations. Even when Tim was in the hospital, she would only come to see him when their mother dragged her there. Any time they spent together, even with their mother present to serve as a referee, usually ended up in an argument and Allyson always knew what to say or do to provoke one. Tim hated the rancor that had developed between them. What made it harder to bear was the fact that things hadn't always been this way. There was a time when they were the best of friends, but that was long ago when they were both young children.

As Tim walked back out to the living room, he saw that Allyson had helped herself to some sparkling water he kept in the refrigerator, and was looking at a CD that he'd left lying on his coffee table.

"Marvin Sapp – My Testimony," she said, as she read from the cover as Tim put the cash in an envelope. "Let me guess, a gift from the midget church girl?"

"No, it's mine. I bought it myself."

"Didn't know you liked inspirational music. Or maybe you bought it to get your midget in the mood."

"Don't start, Allyson. Insulting me is one thing, but I'm not going to listen to you trash my friends."

"You won't have to hear anything else from me once I have my cash. Is that it?" she said as she reached for the envelope Tim was holding.

"Yes, but before I hand this over," said Tim, as he held the cash out of her reach, "I want to know why you need so much money lately? Especially since I just handed you $800.00 not two weeks ago."

"None of your business."

"Sorry, I don't like the idea of handing out money without knowing where it's going."

"Technically, it's not your money. Mom's going to wire it back to you next week."

"Not the point."

"Fine. I was going to use it to run away with my boyfriend to California and get high on weed," smiled Allyson. "Sound familiar?"

Tim knew what she was referring to and he didn't find it the least bit amusing. Leave it to her to bring up a particularly painful period in his past to use as material for a sarcastic barb. She always hit below the belt. He knew Allyson would just escalate her attack until he got angry enough to throw the money at her and tell her to get out. However, Tim was determined that it wouldn't end up that way.

"How do I know you don't want this for drugs?"

"Cause I'm not like you, hypocrite."

"You can leave with this money or without it, Ally. What's it going to be?"

"Why are you being such a **** ?! Getting all up in my business! What the hell is that all about?"

"Because believe it or not, I worry about you," said Tim, "Lately it seems like you've been hemorrhaging money more than usual and the fact that you won't tell me what it's for makes me think you're in some kind of trouble."

"Your concern isn't necessary. I know how to take care of myself. I'm not the one running around with some religious cult."

"It's not a cult. If you went with me sometime you'd see that."

"If that was meant as an invitation, I'll pass."

"Think about it, Allyson. Can you honestly say you're happy with your life right now?"

"You know what, forget this! I didn't come here for a street corner sermon. If you don't want to give me the money, fine. I have other means," said Allyson as she turned to walk out.

Tim didn't like the sound of that. The last thing he wanted was for his sister to end up in some compromising situation to get money.

"Allyson, wait!" said Tim grabbing her by the arm. Allyson snatched it away from his grasp.

"Here's your money."

"Finally!"

Allyson snatched it, pushed Tim aside and bolted toward the door.

"Your welcome!" Tim called after her. She didn't even look back as she let the door slam behind her.

That's the way it always went. When it came to Tim, Allyson always did her best to be as nasty and as cruel as she could possibly be. No matter how much Tim tried to get used to her behavior, it still hurt. It made him wonder what he could have done so long ago to make her hate him so much. She'd never bothered telling him and didn't think she ever would. In the past, he'd tried to reach out to Allyson, but she always put up a wall of resistance. It made him think that maybe he should just give up on her. Then that scripture in the book of Matthew came back to his mind again – the one about being reconciled to one's brother, or in his case, a sister. "I don't know," thought Tim, "In scripture it seems so simple, but I have a feeling that trying to apply it in real life is going to be a lot harder."

SIX

As she rode down in the elevator, Allyson counted her money to make sure it was all there. Despite her bluff, she would have been in some tough straights had Tim decided not to give it to her. But she always knew what to say to get what she wanted out of him. To her pleasant surprise, there was $800.00 instead of the $500.00 she'd originally asked for. The fresh bills may have clung together causing her brother to miscount them. "Too bad bro. Your loss is my gain," she thought to herself as she put it in her purse. "Anyway, Tim has a job, not to mention that fat trust fund he cashed in when he turned 21, so it's not like he's going broke." When the elevator opened in the lobby, she hurried out of the building and headed out to the driveway entrance where her sorority sisters were waiting for her. Allyson opened the door to the front passenger seat of their car and got in.

"It's about time," said the girl in the driver seat of the expensive silver sports car. She had long, dark, wavy hair and was wearing a close fitting green silk dress with a deep v-neck. "I still don't see why we had to stop so far out of our way when there's an ATM right across the street from the bar."

“You can call the shots when you’re the one that’s paying,” said Allyson as she fastened her seat belt.

“No need to snap at Courtney. How would she know that you just have to use the ATM in the building where your sugar daddy lives?” said Trish.

Allyson knew what Trish was insinuating, but she had to let it slide. They didn’t know she had a brother and she wanted to keep it that way. She was afraid that if they ever found out, they’d be staking out the New Towers waiting for the opportunity to throw their underwear at Tim, and Trish would be breaking her neck to be the first one. Allyson hated Trish more than any of the others. She was the only one whose background could come close to her own. Trish Shaw was old money black bourgeois who could trace her heritage back to the original Sugar Hill elites in Harlem. While the Shaws were not as rich as the Russells, they had a lot of clout in the social world they were all a part of because of their political connections. Allyson knew it was why she was always challenging her. But Allyson also knew that even Trish needed to be put in her place every once in a while.

“You’re right, Trish. By the way, your dad says, hello.”

“No, I think you’re confused. My dad has better taste,” said the young artificial blonde, as she pulled her coat over her slinky black dress.

“Now he does. Too bad we can’t say the same when he got married.”

“Don’t start, you two,” said Monica. “No need to ruin a perfectly good evening before it gets started.”

“I’m not the one that’s PMS-ing,” said Trish.

"That's because you're menopausing," said Allyson.

"Ouch," said Courtney.

"I just hope we get there before it gets crowded and they start watering down the drinks," said Monica as she looked at herself in a compact mirror to fix her makeup while trying to keep her long auburn tresses out of the way.

"It's not even 11:00 and the place is 30 minutes away. Honestly, Monica, try not to wet your diaper," said Allyson.

"I bet you're wetting yours thinking about Maxwell. You think you're ready to kiss and make up?"

"I'm over Maxwell. I've got my eye on someone with much more potential."

"Like who?"

"What?"

"I said, who?"

"Hunh?"

"Who? Who?!"

"Excuse me, I don't speak owl."

Courtney let out a loud shriek before cackling wildly.

"Ha-ha, how funny" scowled Monica, "By the way would you mind keeping your eyes on the road."

"You have to admit you walked right into that, Money," replied Courtney.

This was the last place where Allyson wanted to be: in a car full of self-centered, spoiled, and privileged AKA witches. To say that she hated being an AKA was an understatement. The only reason she joined was to shut her mother up and keep her from getting into her business. To Allyson, the AKA's were the lowest of the sororities on campus. Most of their pledges came from middle class and buppie families with only a few rich girls here and there. In addition, she felt being with them isolated her from the other rich kids on campus, and limited her social stratosphere. She was convinced the rich white girls that she used to hang out with had started distancing themselves from her because she was part of a black sorority. This hampered her chance to make a connection with any of the premium guys that were not in the old money African - American circles. The only consolation to being an AKA was at the same time a burden. As one of the few rich girls, Allyson had a lot of rank with her sisters that she would not have had otherwise. However that rank came with a price. She was always the one that ended up paying the expenses for nights out and the different social functions they attended.

Tonight they were headed to a bar in the burbs above the Bronx that was frequented by the Alpha Phi Alpha guys from their school. Word was out that there was going to be a crush of them there that were honoring their new pledges. All of the high profile guys would be there, and there was one in particular that Allyson was looking out for, making this event a priority. Since it was a bar and not a frat house, there would be a cover charge and then they'd have to pay extra for drinks. Allyson spent the last of her allowance on her hair, designer heels, and dress for this occasion. So she had no choice but to get money from her brother to cover the rest. Leaving her sisters hanging was not an option: to do so would have amounted to social suicide in her world. Frat communities, especially within the black bourgeois, were very tight, and if you didn't adhere to the unspoken social rules, you were excommunicated. Once you were out, you weren't let back in, no matter how much status and money you had. As much as she resented them, Allyson needed the AKAs. Being shut out of the wider American aristocracy, the black bourgeois was the only world she had access to and it was the only world that she knew how to operate in.

It wasn't long before they had arrived at the Riverdale Boat Club, and when they went inside it was packed with Alphas who were already getting sloppy drunk. Most of them were the scrub pledges that were being plied with drinks by the senior members. There were also some other AKA's from another chapter at New York University. Allyson and her sisters slinked over to a table next to one where a group of senior Alphas were sitting. Not long after they took their seats, one of the staff came to their table with a bottle.

"Courtesy of the gentleman at table 7 over there," said the woman waiting on them.

Allyson looked over and saw Maxwell raising his glass to her. She shot him an icy look before returning her attention to the party she was with.

"Here we go," said Courtney.

"I told you. I'm done with Max."

"Well, based on this kind gesture, it doesn't seem like he's through with you," said Monica.

"I don't blame Ally" said Trish, "Why would she want to get back with him after he's let the whole campus, and possibly the world, know that he prefers Kellie's homemade pie to hers. As a matter of fact, it seems he prefers everyone's homemade pie to Allyson's."

"Correction - everyone's except yours," said Allyson.

"That's because I have too much dignity for someone like Maxwell"

"Yes, we all know your dignity is reserved for guys who tip"

"Don't look now. He's coming over," said Courtney.

This was the last thing that Allyson wanted. When she began her dalliance with Maxwell, he seemed like the whole package. He was handsome, came from an established old money fortune, was well connected, had good manners and was well bred. Finally, his complexion was fair enough to pass her mother's standard. When all was said and done, he was a narcissistic jerk but this fact had no bearing on her current grudge. Most of the guys she dated were jerks. Allyson was a pragmatist: she knew that if she wanted to marry well according to the standards of her social milieu, she'd have to put up with the various eccentricities and peccadilloes of her mate. But there were certain things she wouldn't live with and Maxwell had crossed the line.

"Good evening ladies. Nice seeing you all again," said Maxwell.

"Nice seeing you, too. Thanks for the bottle," said Monica.

"You're welcome."

"Any reason you're trying to get us wasted when we just got here?" asked Trish.

"You should know me better than that. I was just trying to get your evening off to a good start. Looks like one of you could use it."

Allyson didn't even look his way. She was too busy looking for the object of her interest, when she suddenly spotted him coming back from the restroom. He was tall and well built with wavy dark hair. Like her brother, he was a lacrosse player and he was on the school's crew team. Jason Simmons was connected to the Johnson Empire fortune, which made him a worthy catch indeed. She had met him a week ago at an Alpha party and he was definitely interested in her. Since then they'd been flirting back and forth whenever they saw each other and by text. He even sent her a private picture of himself that she found quite stimulating. They definitely had chemistry if nothing else. There was no way Allyson was going to waste time with someone like Maxwell when better options were available.

"Excuse me ladies, but I'm going to say hi to my new friend," said Allyson as she got up and began to walk away.

"Before you rush off, I was wondering if I could have a word with you," said Max walking up to her once she was far enough away from the table.

"No – and don't ever come near me again. Don't think I won't file an order of protection," she said softly so that no one else could hear her.

"Overreacting a bit, aren't we. It was only a minor - spat, and I don't see any bruises…"

"It's the bruises you don't see that take longer to heal. Sometimes they never do."

"Ally, I said I was sorry. I told you, it won't happen again."

"I know it won't... because I'm not going to give you the chance," she said before leaving him where he was in the middle of the bar.

Allyson made sure to keep her cool. She didn't want Jason to see that she could let someone get her so flustered.

Jason was at the bar when she approached ordering another round of drinks for the party at his table. He looked tantalizing in his close fitting navy-blue button down shirt, tucked out with the sleeves rolled up, brown slim-fit cords and matching nubuck wingtips. As she got closer, she became intoxicated on the spicy smell of his cologne.

"Hey, stranger."

"Allyson, hi. Didn't think you'd be here since it's only Thursday. Thought you'd be hanging out at the library."

"I've decided to make Thursday the new Friday, especially since I don't have class on Fridays anymore."

"You dropped that baroque art class? I thought you needed it for your major."

"I do, but Professor Lawson is such a bore. Not to mention he's a jerk - you know, the type that likes to fail people for fun. I figured I'll wait until the summer when 'Easy A' Emmerson's teaching it."

"Shrewd move. You know, if I'd known you were coming, I'dve asked you to ride down with me."

"Too bad, huh."

"You know, I was thinking about you the other day."

"Really? Like what about," she said moving closer to him, her face barely inches from his.

"That I'd like to know more about you. You think that might be possible?"

"Depends. What do you want to know?"

"Everything. Would you like to sit at our table for a bit?"

"I'd love to but I came with my girls. I don't want to be rude, ya know?"

"I hear ya."

"But...knowing them, I may need a ride home later. Would you be willing to save me a seat in case I needed it? I'd be really grateful."

"No problem."

"Thanks. I'd better be getting back."

"See ya later."

"Don't forget about me."

"Never."

"Mission accomplished," Allyson thought smugly to herself. She had him right where she wanted him.

*****

"Allyson. Allyson, you gotta wake up."

"Hmmm?"

Allyson could hear Jason calling her, but she was still half-asleep.

"Allyson! You gotta get up."

Allyson opened her eyes, but it was still dark. It was always dark in the mornings in the fall. It took a few moments for her to remember where she was.

Jason turned on the lamp that was on the nightstand, and the light blinded Allyson for a split second. She sat up in the bed still feeling a little dazed. All the alcohol she'd drank made her head feel like there was lead in it. Then all of a sudden, she got hit in the face with a swath of fabric. It turned out to be her blue dress.

"Sorry. Didn't mean for that to happen like that. Just trying to help you out."

"What?"

"Ally, I had a great time last night and I really like you and all and I don't want you to take this the wrong way, but you gotta go – for now at least."

"What the hell?! You screw me, then wake me up at freaking six o'clock in the morning and tell me it's time to go like I'm some five-dollar trick! How else am I supposed to take it?" said Allyson as she got up and put her dress on. She was absolutely furious.

"All right, I'll be honest with you. My ex is on her way up and I don't want any drama. I really want to see you again, Ally. But right now we gotta be discreet, ya know."

"If she's your ex, then why would you care if she knows I'm here or not?"

"Okay, so she's my soon to be ex."

"I can't believe this! Jason, you are so full of it!"

Allyson couldn't believe what she was hearing. "He must think I have the word 'fool' stamped on my forehead," she thought as she collected her bra and pantyhose and stuffed them into her purse.

"Ally, please. I know I should have finished things with this chick before we hooked up, but I couldn't help it. I didn't want to risk you losing interest in me. Just give me some time to break everything to her."

"Do you really expect me to believe that? I would have more respect for you right now if you'd been honest with me up front."

"I know you may not believe it, but it's true. This chick means nothing to me."

"Yeah, I get it. That's why you're brooming me out the door right now," said Allyson as she slid into her shoes and grabbed her coat. Then she left.

"I'll call you! I promise, Ally," said Jason calling behind her.

"Whatever. I won't hold my breath," she said not bothering to look back.

She went to the elevator and waited. In the time that elapsed, her head started to hurt so badly she thought it was going to explode. She was really starting to feel her hangover and had to lean against the wall to steady herself. When the doors of the elevator finally opened, she almost knocked over a girl coming off. She was a skinny brown skinned girl with glasses who wore her hair in dreds and dressed like she was stuck in the 1970's. Allyson watched the girl walk down the hall toward the way where she had just come from. It was her. It had to be.

"She's not even pretty," Allyson huffed to herself.

When the door opened in the lobby of the frat house, Allyson had decided, she didn't want to go home. Her sisters would want her to dish on her night with Jason and had it been a true conquest, she would not have minded indulging them. In the aftermath of another romantic humiliation, all Allyson wanted was to be alone. It was still very early, but she knew there was a cheap diner nearby campus that she could go to that was open at this time of the day. As she walked along, foot traffic picked up on the sidewalks as people began to head out to work. Allyson had to take it slow because her four-inch heels could get stuck in cracks on the sidewalk and throw her down. She usually never walked more than a block in her shoes, but she felt she desperately needed to get away. By the time she got to the diner, her feet were hurting from the four-block trek. Allyson was one of the first customers in Chuck's diner. She slumped into a booth all the way in the back, kicked off her heels and put her head down.

"Morning, miss. What can I get you today?"

Allyson shot up. She didn't expect the service to be so fast, but then again, she was the only one in the diner.

"Uh – I'll have a large coffee, black, no sugar,"

"Coming up," said the woman eyeing her strangely.

"There are lots of better guys out there. Jason's not really worth it anyway. He's an heir to a media company that deals mostly in publishing periodicals. Then add to that the fact that he's not very bright. In ten or twenty years, he'll be irrelevant and his fortune will be almost nothing," Allyson reasoned to herself to assuage her bruised ego. It didn't do much to help. No matter what she said to herself, she still felt rejected and it still hurt. Allyson took out her smart phone. She scrolled through what had to be hundreds of names in her contacts, but she couldn't find one that she thought would actually care about how she was feeling right now. The loosely connected individuals that comprised her family were a joke.

The one person in her family who she felt had ever shown her any love, and who had always been loyal to her was dead.

"You gotta be strong, Ally. You're the only one you can depend on," she said to herself. Allyson had been taking care of herself for a long time. She was a survivor and she was a fighter, but at times like this she didn't know how much fight she had left. There were times when she just wanted to be wanted by someone. But she didn't want to indulge these feelings because she didn't want to be weak. Allyson flipped away from her contacts and started browsing the web. She checked out one of her favorite e-retailers and saw that there was a sale on handbags. She bought five, each in a different color and charged them to her paypal account. By the time she had to pay, she'd have her next infusion of cash and credit from her mom. "I bet Ms. Dreds can't afford one of these designer bags even at the sale price," Allyson thought smugly to herself. Then she switched over to another high fashion website to see the previews. It wasn't long before she was putting some of the items in her virtual shopping basket. "I can't wait until next week, that silk muslin is so hot. Trish is going to be so jealous when she sees me in it. I hope they don't run out of my size."

Little by little, Allyson's spirits began to lift. If only she could coordinate her life as well as her wardrobe.

SEVEN

Jim spent most of his time in the hospital either watching the preachers on the Word Network or reading his Bible, which was what he was doing right now. He was reading from the book of Psalms.

"Have mercy upon me, O God according to thy lovingkindness: according to the multitude of thy mercies blot out my transgressions. Wash me thoroughly from mine iniquity, and cleanse me from my sin. For I acknowledge my transgressions: and my sin is ever before me. Against thee, thee only, have I sinned, and done this evil in thy sight..."[1]

When he had finished, he put the Bible on the table next to him and lay back against the pillow and stared at the ceiling. Jim felt just like David. He wished the Lord would just change him so that he wouldn't make any more wrong choices that could possibly destroy his future as well as that of his loved ones. The minute Allen told him about Darius, every tense moment from Jim's past relationship with Callie replayed itself in his mind. Jim tried to convince himself that he wasn't the father. He told himself that the affair happened so long ago that there was no way he could be Darius's father.

Unfortunately, the numbers did not add up in his favor. Darius was already 13 months old, subtract that and the nine months that Callie had to be pregnant, and it brought him back to January, which was the last time he and Callie had been together. Then when Allen showed him Darius's picture, Jim immediately recognized his mother's eyes. There was no doubt in his mind that he was Darius's father and this threw Jim into a state of deep despair.

Jim had a child now – a son. Darius was an innocent life that he had helped to bring into the world. This child was really his responsibility, not Allen's. It was Jim's responsibility to take part in raising Darius, and yet he didn't even have the means to take care of himself. Not only did Jim not have anything to offer his son, but his lack of forethought had basically doomed his child to a broken home with parents that may not be able to work together for his good. If this wasn't bad enough, there was what he had done to his best friend.

Allen had been his best friend since he was seven and Allen was five. They had been through so much together they felt more like brothers than friends. Jim also knew that Callie was the main character of Allen's romantic fantasies. Allen had always loved her from afar and Jim was the only person that Allen had ever confided in about his feelings for her. In fact, it was Jim who had arranged for Allen to become Callie's tutor in school, which gave them a chance to get to know each other. Now he had stabbed his best friend in the back – twice over.

Keeping his affair with Callie a secret would've been hard enough but Jim didn't think there was any way that he could allow Allen to raise Darius given the way things were. That would be worse than what he'd already done. He wanted to tell Allen the truth, but at the same time he knew that Allen had probably deeply bonded with Darius. He could tell by the way Allen gushed over the little boy's picture. Jim was certain the revelation of Darius's paternity could possibly devastate Allen, and that was the last thing he wanted to do to his best friend.

The only person who he didn't really care for in this whole situation was Callie. He was angry about how she had obviously lied to, used, and manipulated Allen up to this point. Even the way she acted all nonchalant when she had visited him earlier, seemed to smack of duplicity. The only thing that could possibly redeem her in Jim's eyes was that she hadn't slept with Allen and made him think Darius was his. He couldn't wait until he saw Callie again.

In any case, Jim knew that he was in a pretty big mess. Not only did he feel guilty about all of the lives he had ruined while he was in the game, now the list of casualties was getting longer. He could count two more lives that were now ruined due to his thoughtless and selfish actions. Jim was tired of hurting people. He was tired of suffering in misery and guilt. So Jim did the only thing he could do. He prayed.

"Father, I admit I've done a lot of awful things and messed up my life and so many other lives in the process. I need you to help me. I'm tired of doing the wrong thing. I'm tired of making mistakes. Please bless me with the wisdom and the courage to finally do the right thing"

As he was praying, he heard someone open the door to his room.

"Hey, Jim. How are you feeling this morning?" asked Callie.

"How would you feel if you found out your best friend had been raising your child for nearly a year?"

Jim was going to be blunt and to the point. There was no use in sidestepping.

"I know what you're thinking, Jim."

"Believe me you don't."

"Who said Darius was yours? You were gone a long time."

"Callie, Please. I'm not stupid and despite my condition I can add and subtract very well. Why didn't you tell me?!"

"When you came in, you were in bad shape. Pastor Bynum felt that everyone should wait until you were stronger..."

"No, I'm talking about before. You had a whole nine months and you knew where I was at!"

"I tried to tell you! At the time, if you remember correctly, you weren't ready to be anybody's anything, much less a father. From the looks of things right now, I'd say nothing's changed."

"You can say whatever you want about me, but that doesn't give you the right to play a game on Allen. After all he's done for both of us, he doesn't deserve that!"

"So what do you think I should do? Hunh? You want me to call him in here right now and tell him about our fling? Tell him that Darius is your son? How'd you think that would make him feel?"

"Don't come here with that. If you cared about Allen, you would've been honest with him from the beginning. And you certainly wouldn't have conned him into a relationship!"

"I didn't con him! I do care about Allen, deeply."

"Please. The only person you care about is you."

"And what about you? All you want from him is a place to stay 'til you can think of your next hustle. You think the two of you will be able to live under the same roof once he finds out? Have you thought about what the others will think when they find out?"

"That's where you're wrong. I don't see how I could live with Allen and keep him in the dark like that! And as for the others, how do you think they'd feel about being lied to after 20 years?"

"Jim, please –listen to me. Allen loves Darius and Darius loves Allen. They've bonded. Allen is the only father Darius has ever known. Allen can provide for him. Why would you want to take that away from either of them? When you chase Allen away, do you think you'll be able to care for Darius in the same way? Do you think you can make Allen feel better about losing the child that he regards as his own?"

Callie's words forced Jim to consider the notion that telling the truth could possibly do more harm than if he'd just kept his mouth shut. "Maybe Callie's right. Everyone is happy right now. All I'd do is throw water on everything...like always" thought Jim. He didn't want to ruin any more lives. He'd had enough of that already.

"I don't feel good about this," he said to Callie.

"I'm not having any fun with this either, Jim. But there are other people that we have to think about."

"Fine. I won't say anything."

"Believe me, Jim. It's better this way."

Jim doubted that. He knew that truth would eventually be known. His mother had taught him that. Jim thought back to the night in the warehouse, when he prayed to the Lord for his life. "Maybe it would have been better if I had died," he thought to himself.

EIGHT

Things had been slow at the Sheraton as of late. A few of the rooms were empty since many of the summer tourists had checked out weeks prior headed for their homesteads near and far to settle back into their routines to commence the fall season. There wouldn't be any real uptick in rentals until early November when people started to arrive for the impending holidays. Davis and Allen had completed the work orders for the occupied rooms, and now they could take their time on the ones that were vacant. They were in a suite on the 6th floor. Davis was checking the lighting fixtures and fixing them when necessary, while Allen was screwing in light bulbs and engaging in other sundry tasks. Allen was at a vanity screwing in a bulb when he was beginning to lose track of what he was doing.

"You just replaced that one already," said Davis who was looking over at him from a few feet away where he was inspecting an outlet.

"Oh, right," said Allen realizing his mistake. "Sorry, my brain's a little scrambled today. I didn't get a lot of sleep last night. I was up until 3 am studying for class tonight."

"Man, and I thought my program was stressful. I take it that even part time, law school is no joke."

"You can say that again. Sometimes I feel like I don't have time to even breathe."

This was an understatement. Most times, Allen didn't know whether he was coming or going. Law school was totally different from his days as an undergraduate. He was totally unprepared for his experience with the Socratic method and it's deep probing interrogation like style of questioning. This meant he had to be more than prepared when he showed up for class, which included generating extensive outlines on readings that totaled more than 200 pages a night. When included with his responsibilities to the church, Callie, Darius, and his family and friends, Allen felt like he was running a marathon with no end in sight.

"That's because you're stretching yourself so thin trying to take care of everybody else. Just remember you have to take care of yourself, too."

"I know, but I felt like I had to stop by and see Jim, given everything he's going through."

"I thought he was getting better."

"Physically he is getting better. In fact, he's going to be getting out of the hospital this Saturday. It's just mentally, he seems a little down."

"I feel that. I was the same way when I got out years ago. Tryin' to start over is hard."

"That's why I want to throw a little welcome back celebration when he gets out. I'm not going to have much time to plan it, but I'm willing to do what I have to. Maybe a couple of us could meet after I get out of school tonight..."

"Hold up – you've already got a lot to do as it is, and you want to add planning a celebration on top of it? You need to cut back. Let your mom and dad plan it this time."

"And it will be boring. Besides, after everything that's happened between us, I want to do this for Jim. No, I need to do this for him."

"Al, I think Jim knows you got his back. You wouldn't be burning up the carpet at the hospital if you didn't."

"But I wanted to personalize this for him – you know?"

"So you plan it and then let me, Miko and Tim and them handle the details. You could tell me what you want to do and I'll fill them in and we'll organize everything. Then all you have to do at the end is show up."

Allen took a moment to deliberate on the matter. It sounded like a good idea, but he was afraid of what might happen if he wasn't there to be the mediator amongst his friends various and sometimes conflicting personalities. Then again, he desperately needed more time to concentrate on his schoolwork, which, unbeknownst to his family and friends, had been suffering. He had only been in law school for three months and already he felt as if he was falling behind.

"Alright. We'll work out the major details at lunch and you can get the others to help you."

"While you're at it, maybe you should talk to Mr. Hardy about cutting back some of your hours. He's really cool, and I know he wouldn't mind helping you out."

"Actually, I've cut back as much as I possibly can. I get out of here at 3:00 as it is. If I work any less then, that means less money and I've got too many responsibilities right now."

"But aren't your parents helping you pay for law school?"

"True, but law school isn't my only responsibility. There's Callie and Darius that have to be factored in as well."

"Doesn't Callie have a full-time job of her own?"

"Yes, but it's hard for her to handle everything by herself. I'm her man. I've got to support her."

"And as your woman shouldn't she support you, too? I think you're dealing with a lot more than she is right now."

"I don't know if I could compare going to law school to a life changing event like having a baby."

"Still, Al. It's a lot, not to mention you said this is the path that you think God wants you to take. You already put off school for a whole year just to help her out. I don't understand how she can know how important this is for you and let you take on all the extra responsibility with Darius."

"You talk as if Callie's forcing her life on me. I'm her boyfriend. It all comes with the territory. Anyway, I don't mind doing for her or Darius. Who knows? They could be a part of God's plan for me, too."

"I don't know about that. You don't even share the same faith."

"Now we don't, but who knows what could happen down the line? No one ever thought Tim would be a Christian, but he's been going strong for two years now."

"Tim's a whole different case. Al, don't think I'm tryin' to hate or nothin' but I'm a little worried that this relationship you're in might not be so good for you at this time in your life."

"Now you sound like my mom. She thinks Callie has been sent by the devil to keep me from accomplishing God's will for my life."

"Well...it does seem like she's distracting you from what you need to be doing right now."

"Oh, no – not you, too! Isn't there anyone who wants me to be happy?"

"Al, you know we're boys and I'm definitely not tryin' to interfere with your happiness or nothin' like that. But I think sometimes you gotta ask yourself if God is pleased with the choices you're making. Because if He's not happy with it, eventually, you won't be either."

"Davis, really? Callie was alone with no one to help her. Darius needed a father. How could I call myself a Christian and abandon them? Do you think God would be pleased with that?"

"No one is saying you can't or shouldn't help them. At the same time helping them doesn't mean that you have to forget about you and be everything for them. That's what God is for."

"I know what you're thinking, but this isn't about me trying to be a hero. I love Callie. When she walked out of my life, I felt like there was an important part of me that was missing, but I prayed to God about it. I prayed that He would make a way somehow for us to reconcile our differences if only so we could be friends again. Instead, I was blessed with the opportunity to have her love me just as much as I love her. I can't just walk away from that."

"You also prayed for Him to reveal His purpose and plan for your life and you told me you were sure law school was a part of that. I don't think God would give you two answers that are interfering with each other."

"They're not. I'm handling things."

"Is that why you're so tired all the time?"

Allen let out a long exasperated sigh. He was getting tired of trying to justify his relationship to everyone.

"Al, I'm only bustin' your chops about this because you're like a brother to me and I don't want to see you mess up your life by going out of God's will for you. Feel?"

"I hear you, and I appreciate your concern, but believe me when I say I got this."

"I hope so, man."

"Oh and before I forget," said Allen ready to change the subject, "my cousin Riley is coming up this Saturday, so someone's going to have to pick her up from the airport."

"That's Miko's best friend, right?"

"She told you about her?"

"She came up in our conversation last night. How long is she going to be in town?"

"A couple of weeks maybe."

"I think Miko having her girl around is going to be good for her – you know? I was telling her last night, how she needed to have some girls that she could chill with sometime."

"Right. That way she wouldn't be up under you all the time."

"I didn't mean it like that."

"Of course you did. It's okay, Dave. It's been painfully obvious to everyone that Miko's been very, how shall I say, intense toward you lately. I must say you're a better man than me. I think I would have changed my phone number and address by now."

"It's not that I don't like her. I think she's a great girl, but she's looking for a boyfriend and I don't know if I'm ready to be anybody's anything yet."

"Have you told Miko that?"

"We talked about it last night, some. But I think she might be a little mad at me, like I'm brushing her off or something."

"Don't worry about Miko. If she is, she'll get over it. She needs to start respecting your feelings instead of trying to change them. But now I have to wonder why you're so overcautious about relationships. Did you have a bad break up or something?"

"Al, I'ma be real with you. I'm not good at the long-term relationship thing. I used to roll like Tim, you know – hit it and quit it. The few long-term relationships I had turned out to be disasters. I can't say it wasn't mostly my fault, either."

"Why? You cheated on them or something?"

"Yeah, and a lot of other things."

"It sounds like you're accepting responsibility for what you've done and you know what you need to fix. You might be more ready than you think. You won't know for sure unless you put yourself out there."

"And then what if I'm not? I would never want to do Miko the way I did them other girls. I wouldn't be able to forgive myself."

"Forget about those other girls. You've made mistakes in the past, but that doesn't have to determine your future. You just told me that it's important that I stay on the path that God has for me. What if there's a wonderful woman God has put in your path right now, whether it's Miko or someone else, that you're passing up because of stuff that happened in the past."

"That's the thing. You can't just forget about the past. You have to deal with it first, otherwise it has a way of catching up to you and burning you."

NINE

Tamiko had been waiting for nearly ten minutes in the large booth at the Bistro Grill. It was a new place they were meeting at because it was equidistant from where everyone lived – that is – everyone except Davis, who was still living in the Bronx. In her restlessness, She had started making origami fortunetellers out of the napkins from the dispenser on the table. They were all supposed to be meeting to discuss plans for a homecoming celebration for Jim, which was something she looked forward to, but at the same time she couldn't help but feel a little nervous. Tamiko was hoping that Davis wouldn't be the first of them to show. She didn't want to risk having an uncomfortable moment with him, especially so soon after their last conversation. Tamiko took another napkin out of the dispenser and a pen out of her bag and began to jot down some ideas she had about the party in order to distract herself from thinking about that night. She was really getting into her work, pausing only at moments to push back wandering strands of her shoulder length hair behind her ear when, unbeknownst to her, one of the members of their party had arrived.

"Hey, do I know you?" she heard a familiar voice say in a soft tone. Tamiko spun around in the seat. Upon seeing him, she felt as if her heart suddenly skipped a beat, and Tamiko was taken off guard by her own reaction. She felt a combination of shock, joy, and anxiety all at once.

"I don't think it's been that long," she said as she got up out of her seat and he came around to face her. Tamiko couldn't believe how well he looked in his dark suit, blue shirt and burgundy tie. The color combinations made his hazel eyes sparkle like polished citrine. His thick, curly, brown hair had grown out a bit, but it had been styled rather than gelled back. In addition, he'd finally gained all his weight back, reminding Tamiko of the lacrosse jock he was when they first met. Tim flashed a brilliant smile at her and she couldn't help but smile back.

"It's been long enough. Don't I get a hug?"

"Of course."

Their embrace lasted a little longer than it should have and as they pulled out of it their eyes met. His gaze was tender yet intense, full of a warmth and affection that stirred her heart. She could feel the blood rising to her face as her cheeks burned and she didn't know if it was due to excitement or fear.

"So..." she said trying to regain her composure. Tamiko tried to say more but the words wouldn't come out. "Oh, come on Tamiko," she scolded herself. "It's only Tim."

"So what have you been up to in all this time?" Tim asked, trying to be casual.

"I think I should be asking you that question. I'm not the one who's always been missing from our get togethers lately," she said as she finally managed to rein in her emotions.

"Trust me, the only thing I've been doing is working. And yes, I realize that I've been a little out of touch, but, as you can see, I'm making an effort to have some balance in my life," he said as he followed her to take a seat in the booth.

"I guess being a business consultant is pretty intense, hunh?"

"Intense, but gratifying. I mean, I feel like I'm finally doing what I was meant to, and I'm learning a ton of new skills. I actually look forward to going to work nowadays. And what about you? I know the new school year has started already. How's that going?"

"In some ways better and some ways not. I mean now that this is my third year, I know a lot more than I did before, so my classroom is running smoothly. So far, so good, the kids are doing fine, I mean there are always a few that aren't doing as well as the others, but even they're moving along. My biggest worry is with the changes in the system overall. There's going to be a new curriculum called 'Common Core' and a new teacher evaluation system and my school is in the pilot program. This means new methods of teaching, new books, new criteria for evaluating the kids and the teachers. It's like just as I was getting the hang of things, they change everything. In some ways I feel like a first year teacher all over again."

"I know it probably seems overwhelming right now, but try to look at the bright side. You get to be in the pilot study. You're getting a front row seat to the preview, while teachers at others schools have no idea of what's coming. Second, because it's a test run, your evaluation most likely won't impact you as much, plus you get to give feedback that can influence how this thing rolls out eventually. Trust me Miko, you're in a good place."

"You're probably right," she said as she began to fidget with the charm bracelet she was wearing. "Any new social developments I should know about?"

"What do you mean?"

"Like have you made any new friends at work or at church lately? I know you haven't been around us much recently, but I'm not silly enough to think you don't have anyone else to keep company with. Who knows? Maybe you've even met someone special?"

"Miko is this your roundabout way of asking me if I'm seeing someone?"

"Are you?"

"No, and I'm not really looking for anyone at the moment," he said before taking a menu and flipping through it.

Tamiko swallowed hard before she continued.

"I don't necessarily think it would be a bad thing if you were. You know, Tim, I was thinking you shouldn't let what happened with Mya keep you from being open to other people."

"I've been over that for a while now. It doesn't have any bearing on my decision to fly solo at the moment."

"Just so you know, I'm hosting a Singles mixer as a fundraiser for the church next month. I'm sure there'll be a lot of nice young ladies that would love to get to know you – that is – if you change your mind."

"I don't think I will, but I must say, I find your sudden fascination with my love life interesting. Any reason why you want to see me coupled up with someone?"

"It's not that at all. I just don't want you to feel like you have to punish yourself for one mistake and I don't want you to feel like I'm going to judge you if and when you decide to start dating again. You're entitled to try to find the love of your life and be happy, and as your friend I want to you to know that you have my support."

"Thanks, Miko, but I'm pretty happy by myself, right now. Anyway, where is everyone? I thought I was running late when I got here."

"You know Richard. The others are probably just running late. Maybe there was some last minute emergency at the hotel. Davis would never just not show up without calling first."

"Speaking of Davis, how are things going between you two? I heard you've been spending a lot more time together lately."

"We're still just friends, Tim."

"Sounds like you're disappointed about that."

"I'm fine."

"That face doesn't say 'fine.' And you were worried about me?"

"Really, Tim, I'm okay."

Before, Tim could probe deeper, the subject of their discussion arrived. He was still in his work uniform that was stained from his hard day. His face was flushed and he seemed a little out of breath. Tim and Tamiko rose to greet him.

"Hey, Tim! Good to see you, man. We missed you at the movies the other day."

"Nice to see you, too, Dave. I really wanted to go, but you know how it is."

"Yeah. Hey, Miko."

"Hi, Davis."

"Sorry I'm late. But we had a flood in one of the rooms. You have to excuse my appearance, I didn't have time to change."

"No worries, dude. Have a seat," said Tim moving out of the way so that Davis could enter the booth. Davis sat down and slid over to make room for the others.

"After you," said Tim to Tamiko thinking she would want the seat next to Davis.

"No, you go ahead. I'd rather sit on the outside."

Davis merely rolled his eyes.

"Oooo-kay," said Tim eyeing both of them strangely before taking a seat next to Davis with Tamiko sitting next to him.

"Since we know Richard is going to be late, I say we should just get this started. We can always give him the run down later. Hopefully it shouldn't take that long."

"What about Allen?" asked Tim.

"He had to go to class, so he wrote out some things that he wanted me to run by you guys, if that's alright," said Davis taking some notepapers out of his jacket pocket.

"Right. I forgot about that."

"The Chairman of the party committee has now arrived!" a voice bellowed.

They knew who it was. Richard had just walked in wearing a long-sleeve black t-shirt with a Miami Heat jersey over it and baggy black jeans. He decided to top it off with a paper party hat from the dollar store. He also had a noisemaker hanging from his mouth like a cigar. He blew it a few times to make them all laugh.

“Rich, you’re too much,” said Tim.

“And it’s not a party, it’s a celebration,” said Tamiko.

“Call it whatever you want, as long as everybody gets to have a good time,” said Richard as he took a seat at the end of the booth near Davis. Shortly after, they all ordered their food and Davis began to start the meeting.

“By now you guys know Jim’s coming out on Saturday, so we don’t have that much time. Let’s try to get the most important stuff planned tonight,” said Davis.

“Yo, after everything that Jim’s been through, we gotta big this up,” said Richard. “We could rent some space at the community center, my cousin Malik could DJ and then we could get one of those wicker chairs – you know, like the ones that they use at the baby showers and tape dollar bills to it and...” began Richard.

“I don’t know, Rich. Based on what I’ve seen of Jim, I don’t think he’s going to be in the mood for a big spectacle with lots of people,” said Tim.

“But he was like Fitty, yo! He took 20 bullets and survived! Who wouldn’t want to live it up after that?!” said Richard.

"Exaggerating a bit, aren't we? It was more like 2," said Tim.

"C'mon man, I'm tryin' to build the urban legend – get the brother some street cred" Richard replied.

"I'ma have to agree with Tim on this one. Speaking from personal experience, when you get out of the hospital after something like that, the last thing you want is to be around a lot of excitement. If anything he's probably just going to want to sleep," said Davis.

"But if Jim's feeling down, maybe we should make it kind of festive – if just to cheer him up," said Tamiko.

"Even Al was thinkin' we should keep things on a small scale. We came up with the idea of having a backyard barbecue. He wants to do it at his folks place, so we gotta keep the guest list short," Davis responded.

There was a pause in the conversation as a waiter came to deliver their food to the table. Everyone took their plates as they continued to develop their plans.

"A barbecue in October?" said Tim.

"I know, but Al said Jim's favorite food is barbecue, and so far it hasn't gotten that cold yet. We're praying God will give us some good weather. If not, we'll just eat inside," said Davis.

"You think we could invite my man Mike and them from the Bronx," said Richard before he took a bite of the burger he'd ordered.

"Are you kidding me?!" said Tim.

"No – absolutely not!" said Tamiko.

"Who's Mike from the Bronx?" asked Davis.

"Trust me, Davis, you don't want to know," answered Tim.

"But Mike don't even smoke weed no more and Dollar sold most of his guns in the buy back program Bloomberg had out there," said Richard.

"Yeah, well, let us know when he's sold all of them," said Tim, "cause he's not welcome until he does."

"Then it's only gon' be like five people and most of them are already sitting here!" said Richard.

"Callie's not here. Then there's our other friends from church," said Tim.

"And don't forget our special surprise guest: our cousin Riley!" squealed Tamiko.

"Is this the cousin that Al said used to torture him and Jim?" asked Tim.

"Riley was just horsing around with them. She wasn't really being mean," said Tamiko.

"How she got a name like Riley? That sounds like a boy's name," said Richard.

"Uncle Henry said when she was born, she looked a lot like his mom, Florene, and he wanted to name her that, but his brother, Allen's other uncle William, had already named his daughter Florene, and he didn't think it would be a good idea to have three Florenes in one family, so he gave her his mother's maiden name, which was Riley," explained Tamiko.

"I think she lucked out. If I were a girl, I'd rather be a Riley than a Florene," said Tim.

"She cute?" asked Richard.

"Richard!" said Tamiko.

"Just askin', I'm not sayin' I'm gon try' to get wit' her or nothin'. Red is the one you gon' need to watch," said Richard.

"Wrong! I have no intention of hitting on Allen's cousin," said Tim.

"Tim, please. Let's be real. You know you can't kill that playa - don't even try," said Richard, taunting him.

"People can change you know. That's not who I am anymore," said Tim.

"So what happened to that Beyonce lookin' sister you was skipping around town with? I heard after the fun, you was done," said Richard.

Tim didn't respond. He just looked down at the table and stirred in his plate.

"Okay - Now you're crossing the line and you're just being rude," said Tamiko "So just drop it and leave him alone!"

Everyone was stunned silent by Tamiko's response. Even she seemed to be a little shocked when she realized how forceful her words were.

"Sor- ry," said Richard, looking at her strangely, "I was just playin.'"

"Not everything's a joke, Rich," said Tamiko, now lowering her voice.

"Guys! Let's stick to business, aiight," said Davis to get everyone back to the purpose of their meeting. "Al also gave us assignments for what we're supposed to be working on. Richard, you and I are going to be doin' food and drinks, while Tim and Tamiko will be doing decorations and entertainment. Is everybody cool with that?"

"Hold up. If we're over the food, does that mean we cookin'?" asked Richard.

"No. We're just buyin' it and bringing it to the house. Al's Dad is going to grill it before the celebration starts and his mom is going to do the rest. I got the list of stuff we need to get right here," he said handing the paper to Richard.

"That makes me feel better. Now I won't have to put 911 on autodial," said Tim.

"Hey, make no mistake about it, if I needed to, I could turn it out. I got skill with the grill," said Richard.

"If you don't mind, I'd rather take your word for it. Anyway, I want to know what Al means by entertainment," said Tim.

"Like think of something fun we can do while we're waiting for the food to heat," said Davis.

"This is right up my alley. You know, before you all showed up, I was sort of brainstorming different activities we could do. Tim, if you want, you could work on the decorations while I plan the entertainment," said Tamiko.

"Sorry. That's not gonna work for me," said Tim.

"So I bet you'd rather I do decorations? Right?" said Tamiko.

"Wouldn't that make more sense?" said Tim.

"Why? Because I'm a woman and I'm supposed to like to make things pretty?" said Tamiko.

"I'm not being sexist. I mean you're a teacher, for crying out loud. Aren't decorations supposed to be your forte?" said Tim.

"That doesn't mean it's all I'm capable of," said Tamiko.

"Alright, I'll give you the benefit of the doubt. Let's hear your ideas," said Tim.

"I was thinking charades would be good..."

"Fail! First of all, it's the lamest game in the world. Secondly, Jim is coming home with his good arm in a sling and a broken leg. Chances are he wouldn't be able to participate, not that he'd want to."

"What about pictionary?"

"Once again, I'll have to call 'fail', for reasons I've explained previously."

"Oh, this is a good one. We could play guess your picture!"

"Epic-fail!"

"Could you knock it off with the 'fail' stuff? You're not even giving my ideas a chance!"

"What's 'guess my picture' about?" asked Davis.

"It's a really cool game. Everyone wears headbands..."

"Okay, you lost me at 'headbands'..." said Tim.

"Just let me finish. Like I said, everyone wears a headband and the mc puts these different pictures in the headbands and you can't see them, but everyone around you can. Then you have to ask questions about your picture to the others in the room to help you guess what or who it is. The catch is, you can only ask a question that has yes or no as the answer. Sometimes I play this game with my students during choice time and it's a riot" explained Tamiko.

"Are you serious?! A game for six year-olds?! I can't imagine what else you have in mind. Musical chairs? Freeze dance? A Piñata?"

"I was planning on changing it to make it more entertaining for adults! Anyway, what's wrong with some good old-fashioned fun!"

"We get all that, shorty but you gotta remember you plannin' a big boy party. Turn that teacher stuff off for a hot minute. You gotta think of something more, uh, uh..."

"The word you're probably searching for is 'mature', " said Tim.

"Word," said Richard.

"And what would you suggest, Tim? Hmm? Since you're so critical, I can't wait to hear what you have in mind," said Tamiko.

"It's simple: We have a dominoes tournament and a movie."

"I could go for that," said Richard, "and Jim does like to play dominoes."

"And you thought my ideas were lame? Dominoes sounds so...so... elderly," said Tamiko as she folded her arms across her chest and slumped back in her seat. "And a movie! That's something he can do anytime. I wanted to do something special. Like I thought we could even do a little 'this is your life' slide show with old photos and everything."

"Miko, with everything that's happened in Jim's life, I don't think he's going to want to rewind back to the past."

"It's not like I'd be including pictures from his mother's funeral. Despite all of the hard times he's had, there were good times, too. We had lots of fun together as kids."

"Yeah, nothing makes a guy feel better than to have everyone laughing at his awkward kid pics. Sorry, but I'm going to have to give it my veto...fail!"

"Why are you being so difficult? It's like you feel it's your duty to oppose everything I suggest."

"That's because it is. I'm the sanity on this team. Everyone knows you'll turn it into a grade school prom complete with bubble wands, unless there's someone around to check you. It's probably the reason why Al paired me with you in the first place."

"You are unbelievable!"

"I know," he said winking at her.

"Alright you two, chill. You'll just have to figure out all that drama between yourselves later. Sub-teams can meet before the end of the week to iron things out. Then we'll meet back at Al's Saturday morning to get everything together."

Richard called over a hostess and each of them paid their portion of the bill, along with the customary gratuity.

"I know Jim's going to be glad to be out of the hospital. After two weeks in Baltimore I was starting to go stir crazy," said Tim.

"I'm still wondering how our boy landed there in the first place. He still ain't sayin' nothing? Not even to Al?" asked Richard.

"Nothin," said Davis.

"Maybe he's trying to put everything behind him. I know I would," said Tim, "Is it true the police interviewed him?"

“Yeah, but I don’t think they were looking at Jim as a suspect or anything like that. I suppose they would’ve charged him by now if they were,” said Tamiko.

“Not necessarily,” said Davis, “Sometimes they back off and watch you - give you enough rope to hang yourself. That’s what happened to my brother. I just hope that whatever Jim got into, he doesn’t have any plans to go back to it.”

“Hopefully his recent experience will cause him to think twice about that,” said Tim.

“They ain’t never caught the dude that shot him?” asked Richard.

“Not that

I know of. I hope this doesn’t mean Jim could be in any danger,” said Tamiko.

“He may be more of a danger to himself if he’s been…self medicating,” said Tim.

“Let’s not get caught up in a lot of guessing. Basically it’s none our business, and if Jim wants us to know, he’ll tell us,” said Davis.

“I get you. Besides, it’s over and done with. Better to look ahead,” said Tim.

“It’s getting late, and tomorrow’s another workday,” said Tamiko.

“Yeah, we all better be heading out,” said Davis.

They all bid each other good night and went their separate ways, each blanketing their reservations about the past with their optimism for the future. They were determined to view Jim’s return as an auspicious development. Jim was alive, and he was back with his family where he belonged. This celebration would be the beginning of happier times for their friend and for everyone.

TEN

Allyson gazed raptly at her tablet computer while she waited for her mother inside a restaurant. It was a little French eatery just outside down the block from her mother's office. She had been summoned here by her mother's text just the day before, which read "emergency: important family issue that needs to be discussed". Allyson wasn't alarmed at all when she read the text. Her mother usually started every text she wrote with the word 'emergency'. There was no point in trying to guess what she wanted because to Eleanor Russell a family emergency could mean anything from asking Allyson to attend a fashion show with her to announcing the death of a relative. While she was waiting, Allyson decided to take the time to work on a school project instead - adding revisions to an English literature paper she had uploaded on her tablet computer. It was hard enough trying to juggle, schoolwork, activities and social obligations without having to be interrupted by Eleanor's self-made crises.

She was halfway through her paper, when she got another instant message from Jason. He had called her two days after that disastrous morning but let it go to voicemail. He left a message telling her that he had indeed broken up with the retro 70's girl. But Allyson wasn't so sure she should trust him. In response, she sent him a brief two-word text: prove it. Then for the next couple of days he was burning up her instant messaging account with penitent pleas. "Maybe he's learned his lesson by now," thought Allyson, as she was deciding whether or not to delete the message or send a reply. In the midst of her deliberation, her mother arrived, talking on her smart phone as usual. She was dressed in her typical business gear: dark suit with a form fitting skirt, accessorized with pearls and high heels; her hair pulled back into an elegant French roll. Eleanor waved to Allyson and gave her an air kiss as she continued her conversation.

"Yes, that will be splendid. Will the Bretons be coming? Marvelous, I can't wait to get a hold of Gabe's ear. I know he's going to love my idea for his firm"

It would be another five minutes or so before Eleanor actually ended her call. In the meantime, after hastily transcribing her message and sending it, Allyson put away her tablet and took out a menu to look at. She had decided on having a salad and orange seltzer, before her mother finally addressed her.

"Allyson, your mother is about to get one of her biggest clients yet!"

"Is that what this meeting is about?"

"Oh, I wish. But before we get to that, let's put in our order."

Eleanor flagged down a waiter who took their order. When he was out of sight, Eleanor put her head in her hands as if she was in distress. Allyson was familiar with her 'oh woe's me' pose.

"Allyson, our family is in serious trouble and you're the only one that I can think of that can do something about it."

"Why? What's wrong now?"

"Allyson, how can you ask me that? Were you not there in Baltimore when we went to the hospital?!"

"So this is about Tim – again."

Allyson felt she shouldn't have been surprised. Seventy-Five percent of all of Eleanor's 'family crises' involved Tim in some way. To Allyson, it seemed that Eleanor was practically obsessed with making her son adhere to her rigid social standards. He couldn't fart without Eleanor checking to see if the smell met the family standard. It would have been enough to make Allyson jealous of her brother if not for the fact that she knew her mother didn't really care for either of them. With Eleanor everything was about control and Tim had always been the child that was more defiant, which was why he always got so much attention. Tim never directly disobeyed his mother's requests or advice. He'd simply ignore her or conveniently forget what she'd said. This was not to say that Allyson was easier to manage. Oftentimes, Allyson would ostensibly comply with her mother's wishes in order to avoid maternal interference in her life. As long as Allyson appeared to be a 'good girl' in her mother's eyes she was able to escape Eleanor's scrutiny and for the most part, live however she wanted.

"I know you're probably just as frustrated as I am right now. It's like he is determined to ruin his life and his grandfather's good name in the process. It was bad enough that he was hanging out with those ghetto people, now he's gotten himself entangled in some kind of religious cult they have."

"Well, that's Tim for you. He will do whatever he wants, no matter what anyone else says."

"The problem is he's been headstrong since he was a baby. You know the very first word he ever said to me was 'no'. I'll never forget it. He was only eight months old and I was trying to get him to wear a sunhat. Every time I put it on his head, he'd take it off, throw it to the floor and say 'no!' The only way I could get him to stop was to spank his little hand."

"Maybe you should try that now."

"Allyson, be serious! I wish you had been there when he got his second opinion before the operation. He was just screaming about how he had been healed. I told him from the beginning that those doctors at Presbyterian had misdiagnosed him, but he just wouldn't listen to reason. I mean he was making a spectacle of himself in front of all the staff: crying, falling down, and talking something that sounded like babble, to me – although one of the orderlies said it was Urdu – whatever that is. I couldn't have been more embarrassed. I was afraid that I would have to have him transferred to the psychiatric hold. And you saw how his so called friends acted when I cut off communication with them – the way they stormed the hospital and refused to leave until they saw him. I'm certain they would have tried to kidnap him if you and Terrence hadn't been there with me."

"Yes, I saw," said Allyson feeling bored. Eleanor had gone over this episode hundreds of times since they'd all come back from Baltimore and Allyson was sick of hearing it. In her eyes, her brother was just as bad as her mother if not more so: just as self-centered, callous, manipulative, and pretentious. Just like the guys she dated and everyone else in the cold, shallow world she felt trapped in. As far as Allyson was concerned, if Tim decided to run away with the cult and was never heard from again, she wouldn't be sorry in the least.

"Oh, and don't get me started on that impudent young woman. I've heard them talking and I think her father is the head guru, as they're known. I think Allen introduced Tim to them, and then those two hatched a plan to trap him. They probably see Tim as a cash cow for their organization and she's acting as the milkmaid. You know how weak Tim is when it comes to a pretty face."

"Don't remind me. So he's in a cult. What do you think I can do about it?"

"Well you know he's still upset with me after the whole fiasco in Baltimore. He doesn't trust me. But I know you might still have some influence on him."

"What would give you that idea? I mean you are aware that we don't really get along that well."

"Don't think I don't know what's going on, Allyson. Tim's not the one that starts the conflicts."

"So you're blaming me for the bad blood between us? Of course, it could never be Saint Tim!"

"Settle down. I'm not blaming you for anything. I'm simply asking you to put aside your personal feelings so that you can help save your family's reputation."

"Since when did Tim become our whole family?"

"Since he is the last male that carries the Russell name. He's the only one that can carry our family's legacy. Poppa made me promise on his deathbed to watch over him and I intend to keep that promise. It is our duty, Allyson."

It wasn't a convincing case to her at all. In fact, it was such an archaic concept, that Allyson just had to roll her eyes.

"I wouldn't be so quick to dismiss the importance of your brother's influence. Don't think that you won't be affected should your brother end up a penniless, insane, vagrant whose been caught up in some kind of cult scandal. You certainly don't think a man of great means would be interested in making a connection with someone from a family of shall we say…colorful individuals. Your aunt Helen has done enough to disgrace us as it is."

"You would think you've done more to disgrace us than anyone else," Allyson thought inside herself. She couldn't help but remember all the times she tried to explain her non-existent dad to her rich prep school friends. Everyone knew she was an out of wedlock love child to a really rich white guy that had a lot invested in keeping her a secret. The only thing that kept her classmates from tormenting her about it was the fear that she could possibly be one of their relatives.

"What if he wanted to use his money and influence to cover over my brothers indiscretions?"

"Not likely, my dear. Trust me. Most real men will avoid a mess rather than waste time cleaning one."

"My dad certainly didn't mind."

"And where is he now?"

"Haven't you read the papers recently. He got off."

"Not without having to pay a heavy cost. He'll never be the man he once was, believe me. Ally, as smart as you may be, you still have a lot to learn. You will help me rescue your brother and that's all there is to it."

"C'mon, Mom! I have schoolwork, my duties at The Spectator, not to mention my AKA responsibilities. I don't have time to run around after Tim like a private detective!" said Allyson. "Can't you just have the church investigated and shut down or something? Or why don't you just hire a real detective and get information?"

"Because I wouldn't know where to start! Besides, we have to be very careful on how we proceed. If Tim suspected that I was having him investigated, it would just cause him to run further from us. We have to get Tim to want to leave them."

"He will eventually, if we just leave him alone! Tim treats his causes and his whores the same way. Once the novelty wears away, and he's no longer the center of attention he's onto the next thing."

"I used to think the same way as you do, but there's something about Allen and those other people that has Tim fixated on them. I have to find out how they have managed to exert such influence over him."

Allyson slumped back in her chair and pouted.

"I can't believe you're acting as if I asked you to go to Canada for a pack of mints. All you'd have to do is call him more often, visit him every once in a while, maybe even go down to that church, and get acquainted with his friends, even. Is it too much for you to actually be a real sister for once?"

"Did you ever stop to wonder why this would be hard for me?"

"No, because it doesn't really matter. Keeping our family in tact is what matters. Unless this is your way of saying you don't want to be a Russell?"

"Of course not."

"Because if you weren't a Russell, you wouldn't be wearing those designer clothes you're wearing, or attending such an expensive as well as prestigious university. You wouldn't be an AKA, and you certainly wouldn't be receiving any support from me. Understand?"

"I understand."

"Good."

The waiter finally came to serve them their food, but Allyson had lost her appetite. Little did her mother know that sometimes she wished she weren't a Russell. Sometimes she wished she'd never been born.

ELEVEN

Allen was finishing up the dishes from dinner while Callie went to check on a fussy Darius in the nursery. Allen had dropped by after class to spend time with them. He knew he should have been at home reading through a case study on torts, but he felt guilty about missing time with Callie and Darius. Due to his law school commitments and time at work, they didn't have as much time to spend together as they did in the past. Dating became almost impossible. Most of the time they wound up at Callie's apartment because finding a good babysitter on short notice so they could go on a date was often difficult. But Allen didn't really care where they spent time, so long as they were all together.

With each passing day, Allen felt that he, Callie, and Darius were becoming more like a neat little nuclear family unit. It had gotten to the point where he didn't want to think about what life would be like without them. However, it was not without a lot of patience, effort, and love that they had reached this point. Sometimes when Allen thought back to where they had started out, he couldn't help but thinking that his relationship had to be the work of God's merciful intervention.

Allen had finished the dishes and was wiping down the counters when Callie reappeared.

"Darius is finally asleep."

"So he's okay?"

"Yep. He was just a little gassy. It probably had to do with all the vegetables he had for dinner."

"I noticed he's a good eater. Definitely a kid after my own heart."

"It's funny, now that you've mentioned it, but he is starting to pick up a lot of your quirks and habits."

"Really?"

"Yeah, like the way he always tries to smell something before he eats it, or the way he puts his hand to his mouth when he's thinking. His laugh is like yours, too."

"Wow. It's hard to believe he's picking all that up already."

"And you know what else? I showed him a picture of you the other day and you know what he said?"

"No, what?"

"Da-da."

"Really?"

"Yes. So I guess that means you're a good dad. Did I ever tell you that?"

"Maybe. Once."

"And you're an even better boyfriend," she said before planting a kiss on his mouth. Allen kissed her back fervently, nearly getting lost in the passion of the moment before he pulled back.

"What's wrong?"

"I hate the fact that I'm going to have to say goodbye soon. Lately, we haven't had much quality time together where it's just us or even the three of us."

"Al, you don't have to leave if you don't want to. And Darius usually sleeps through the night now."

"Callie..."

"I could understand waiting at the beginning of our relationship, when we were sorting everything out, but now we both know how we feel about each other. You know I love you and I know you love me, so what's wrong with us expressing that to each other?"

Allen didn't understand it very well himself, but he knew that he wasn't going to do something that dishonored God. It made him think back about what happened to Tim.

"I just can't – and you know why."

"Okay. I won't try to convince you to do something that goes against your beliefs. But you can still stay here for the night. You can sleep on the couch."

"And how am I going to explain that to my parents?"

"You're a grown man. You don't have to explain anything to them."

"I still have to respect them and their house since I live with them."

"Well then, I guess we have to settle for what we have if there's no other solution."

Allen hated this situation. He wanted to spend more time with Callie and Darius and he felt he owed them a deeper commitment than what he was able to give them at present.

"You and Darius deserve better than this. Maybe I should've waited until Darius was older to start law school."

"Allen, no way! You're doing the right thing. If you don't work on your future, there's no way that you'll be able to give Darius one."

"You do realize that I have seen you both for a total of about two hours this whole week, and the other day I had to cut class to do it."

"It's okay, Al. I know you're doing the best you can."

"I have to find a way to do better. In fact, let's start next weekend. This Saturday is Jim's homecoming, but next Saturday is going to be all about us."

"That sounds wonderful. What do you have planned?"

"It's a surprise."

"Great. I love surprises."

"But I will tell you that it's going to be the three of us during the day and then I have something special planned for just the two of us in the evening - and you don't have to worry about finding a babysitter, because I'm going to take care of that."

"Even better."

"And now, we still have an hour or so before I have to head back. You want to watch some TV with me on the couch."

"I could think of something better."

Callie pulled him close and kissed him as the two made their way to the couch. Allen tried to keep his head together, but Callie was making it difficult as she sent her hands to roam around his body. Part of him thought that he should just leave, but part of him thought otherwise. "I can stop things before they go too far," his other half suggested. They had been in this situation before and each time it was harder and harder to pull himself back from the brink. Allen didn't want to have to keep doing this. He wanted to be able to give in to their love, and to spend more time with his family. There was one possible solution, but Allen pondered if he was truly ready for it.

TWELVE

Large dark clouds huddled together overhead looking like someone had spread a large gray blanket across the sky. There had been heavy rain earlier in the day. The large drops of water had managed to knock leaves off the trees and litter the streets with them. After the rain, the winds picked up a bit, often taking the leaves into a little whirlwind. Tim walked carefully through the Bynum's drive so as not to slip on them. Once he was at the door, he gingerly rang the doorbell, and prayed.

"Who is it?" said a shrill voice.

"It's me, Mother Bynum – ma'am," said Tim shifting the bag he was carrying from one hand to the other. He was a little disappointed that his prayer had not been answered.

"Whom does 'me' refer to?"

Tim struggled to keep a straight face. He knew she was probably looking at him through the peephole.

"Tim Russell, ma'am. Tamiko's friend."

"Oh. What do you want?" she asked through the closed door.

"Tamiko and I were supposed to meet to discuss the details of the celebration we're planning for Jim. Is she available?"

"One moment, please."

Tim could hear her walking away from the door. Mother Bynum was worse than some of the bouncers at the nightclubs he used to frequent. Given how she felt about him, he knew he might be waiting outside for a while. Luckily for Tim, it wasn't that cold, even though it was late October.

After several minutes, he could hear the sounds of the two women arguing behind the door, before Tamiko opened it.

"Tim, I'm so sorry. Come in. I hope you weren't waiting long."

"Not at all."

"Let me hang up your raincoat," said Tamiko, as she took his coat. "Would you like me to put your bag away as well or is that for our meeting?"

"Actually, it's for you. I got you a desk caddy."

This was no ordinary caddy. It was printed with pink and lavender flowers, which he knew were Tamiko's favorite colors, covered in lace and scented with potpourri. There were many different sized slots and a little drawer at the bottom that contained matching post-it notes, and notepaper.

"Oh, thank you," she said looking a little bewildered. "It's lovely."

"And this is for you, Mother Bynum" said Tim extending a box to her.

"Well this is quite unexpected – what is it?" she said taking the box gingerly and looking at it warily as if he'd just handed her a bomb.

"It's a spice rack, ma'am. Several weeks ago at dinner you said your old one broke."

"I don't recall saying that."

"I do," said Tamiko. "You talked about it all evening."

"I didn't say I never said that. I only said I didn't remember saying it," she said holding the package awkwardly. The she looked down at his shoes. "How very nice of you. I hope you wiped your feet. I just mopped and vacuumed."

"Sorry, ma'am."

Tim went back outside and made sure to thoroughly wipe his feet on the mat at the door.

"Tamiko, please be a dear and put these things out of the way."

Tamiko silently obeyed her mother's request, while Tim came back inside. Mother Bynum was standing in the middle of the room, her arms folded across her chest. She looked very forbidding in her dark dress and matching expression. She was staring at him as if he were a pile of garbage someone had dumped in the middle of her living room, his gift having imparted no effect on her mood. Tim decided the best way to save himself from her passive-aggression would be to be ingratiatingly polite.

"So how are you today, Mother Bynum?"

"Blessed as always, Ted. Thank you."

"It's Tim, ma'am."

"Isn't that what I said?"

"You called me – never mind."

"Tamiko, do you really think it's wise to be entertaining guests on a school night when you have work to do?" said Mother Bynum to her daughter who had just come back from her errand.

"We're just trying to organize Jim's homecoming celebration. It shouldn't take that long."

"She's right. It'll only be a half-hour tops."

"I should hope so. Your father will be here soon and after a long day at the church he's going to want to eat his dinner in peace"

"Have a seat, Tim. Would you like anything? Something to drink?" said Tamiko.

"No. I'm fine, thanks."

"Oh! I forgot to get my notepad. Excuse me, Tim, I'll only be a second."

"No problem."

Tired of standing, Tim cautiously moved toward the sofa, all the while Mother Bynum's eyes followed him like targeted missiles. Tim took off his suit jacket and laid it on the arm of the sofa before sitting down. Mother Bynum remained at her post standing guard.

"Young man, I will remind you that guests are entertained on the first floor of this house only and I do not expect to meet with you on any of the floors above, especially in the presence of my daughter. Is that understood?"

"Yes, ma'am," said Tim as respectfully as he could and struggling to conceal his exasperation.

"And I will also make you aware that, under no circumstances, is my daughter allowed to have male company at this house when either myself or the Pastor is not present."

"Mom, he knows," said Tamiko who had reappeared with a legal pad and a pen. "You say it every time he comes over."

"Tamiko, I will be finishing dinner, if you should need me," said Mother Bynum before she reluctantly returned to the kitchen.

"Thanks, mom, but I don't think I will," she said before plopping down on the loveseat across from Tim with a pen and pad. "Okay – I thought we'd start by discussing decorations, since that's the least controversial of our duties" She was looking at her pad and not at him, which she often did when she was in a bad mood. Tim decided to try to lighten things up a bit.

"What?"

"I said, I thought we should start by talking about the decorations."

"I'm sorry, it's kinda hard to hear you when you're sitting so far away."

Tamiko let out a huff and came to sit next to him on the sofa.

"Better?"

"Much. Now I don't need a megaphone to talk to you. By the way, are you upset with me?"

"Annoyed is more like it."

"Why? Because of what I said the other night?"

"You called all my ideas lame!"

"Miko, I was just jerking your chain. You know? - Like old times. I thought it would bring you out of your mood. You looked kind of sad when I came in."

"I wasn't in a mood. I was just concentrating."

"You sure?"

"Yes" she answered a little testily. Whatever the problem was (though after their conversation last night, he assumed it had something to do with Davis) it was still bothering her. He could tell she wasn't ready to talk about it so he decided to let it go – for now.

"Okay - if you say so. Would it make you feel better if I said I'm sorry?"

"Is that what your gift is all about?" she said as she ran a hand through her hair.

"No, I wasn't trying to buy my way into your good graces if that's what you're thinking. It's just that I was getting your mom the spice rack and I didn't want you to feel left out."

"That's another thing - why did you buy my mom a spice rack?"

"Because she needed it. Plus, I'm trying to do like the scriptures say and do good to those that hate you."

"My mom does not hate you," said Tamiko beginning to brighten.

Tim sent her a look that conveyed his skepticism.

"She's just being a worry-wart. That's all."

"What would she have to be worried about?"

All of a sudden Tamiko looked a little nervous.

"She thinks that you...I mean - she thinks that I..."

"What?" said Tim softly. Her hesitation made Tim curious.

"You know what? Never mind about what she thinks. It's ridiculous and we've wasted enough time. So, anyway, like I was saying, I was thinking of decorating things according to a theme. I had two ideas in mind. The first is a New Year's theme, since Jim is starting his life over, and the other possibility would be a football theme. Sort of like to let Jim know that we're all there for him, the same way we'd cheer on our favorite football team. I was thinking we could all wear jerseys in Jim's favorite colors: green and gray, and we could all have different numbers. What do you think so far?"

Tim had gotten lost in thought studying her. He couldn't help but admire how beautiful she was – her medium length dark brown hair, parted to one side, that grazed her shoulders, her glowing chestnut complexion, and her deep liquid dark brown eyes. Her dress was a loose, jersey material that draped delicately over her petite but shapely figure as she lounged on her end of the sofa with her legs tucked in against her. Tim had never really noticed how radiant she was until recently. He had always thought she was merely cute before, but now he found her completely captivating. What made her stand out from all of the other women he dated was that she had a natural beauty. She didn't need make up, or those creepy eyelashes that looked like spiders, or the hair extensions. Everything about her was real and genuine which he found comforting.

"Tim?"

"Oh, sorry," he said snapping out of his daydream. "New Year's sounds kind of formal and I doubt anyone's going to want to dress up so they can sit around at home and eat barbecue. I'd go with the football thing. But do you really think we'll be able to get the jerseys on such short notice?" He had to remind himself that he couldn't afford such indulgences of mind.

"Don't worry, I'll take care of the jerseys. I know a place that can get it done pretty quickly. It's the same place where I got my students jerseys for our school's field day. Besides, we're not getting that many. There's only about eleven of us altogether and I know everyone's size. I'll call them tonight and they should be ready by the afternoon of the celebration."

"Okay, if you say so."

"I was also thinking we should have tumblers, napkins, and all of the party favors to match the color of our jerseys, too."

"Wait a minute – what kind of party favors are we talking about?"

"You can relax. There aren't going to be any bubble wands; just regular party hats for those who want to wear them, balloons, streamers, noisemakers, horns, and those felt banners like you see on college campuses. We could even get novelty banners with like those funny sayings on them - things like that. And maybe we should even have everyone dress in green and gray just to keep with the theme."

"Sounds a little cheesy but I think Jim could use some cheese in his life right about now. It'll make for a good laugh if nothing else. But about the dress code: What if our guests don't have anything to wear in those colors?"

"No one has to wear both colors. They can wear all green or all grey in the shade of their choice. Anyway, they're basic colors. It's not like we're asking people to wear mauve or taupe."

"Fine. I'll agree."

"Now, we have to finalize the entertainment portion..."

"Which I still think should be a dominoes tournament and a movie."

"C'mon, Tim. Why can't we have a little slide show about Jim? After all, the party is in his honor."

"I told you, no guy wants people gawking at his awkward kid pics."

"But I have some really sweet ones that I know would cheer Jim up."

"Maybe and then maybe not. Jim's past is loaded. When you're as depressed as he might be, even good memories have a way of turning on you and making you feel bad. Nothing would sink our celebration faster."

"How?"

"For example, let's say you put up some graduation photos, and he starts to associate those with his past aspirations to be a lawyer. Next thing you know, he's all bitter about how he didn't get that legal assistant job, he goes into a race rant, and it snowballs from there."

"What if I just use the ones from when we were kids?"

"And what if those pictures remind him of when his mom was alive, and he starts to miss her."

"I guess you're right."

"If I were him, I'd rather sit through that headband thing."

"Really?!"

"I was speaking relatively, Miko."

"What if we have just one round?"

"Miko..."

"Please."

"You really want to play this game that badly? Why? Do the kids at school play for money or something?"

"Tim!" she laughed, nudging him in the shoulder.

He knew he was going to look like a punk in front of Allen when he found out what was on the events list, but he couldn't resist Tamiko, not when she looked at him the way she did. At least she was looking at him now. Tamiko seemed to be in a better mood and he liked seeing her in such good spirits. Besides, Tim didn't think it would hurt the festivities any.

"One round during the appetizers and that's it."

"I promise, you won't regret it."

"I hope not."

"Now are you going to bring the dominoes or should I try to find some."

"I have a set, but we're probably going to need at least five or six if there's going to be a tournament."

"So, we'll have to get more. Oh, and about the movie..."

"Don't worry about that. I already streamed it on my laptop. It's that film 'Courageous.'"

"Oh! I've always wanted to see that."

"And now you'll get your chance."

"So that's it. I guess we're done then – and in less than 20 minutes."

"I know your mom will be happy about that. Anyway, I'll report back to Allen tonight, and I'll pick you up early tomorrow. We'll do some shopping and then we'll head over to Al's and set up.

"Great. Do you think you can get here by 8:30? I know this amazing dollar store in mid-town where we can get everything we need and they open at nine."

"You got it. See you tomorrow."

"See, you."

Tim put on his suit jacket, and Tamiko went to retrieve his raincoat from the foyer closet before she escorted him to the door. He had not walked more than a few feet from the entrance when he heard her call him back.

"Tim!"

"Yes," he said turning suddenly.

"Thanks again for the organizer. It's really beautiful."

"Your welcome, Miko."

Tim could feel his temperature rise as he walked down the drive toward his car. When he got in he noticed, that she was still standing in the doorway looking out. "Don't get your hopes up," he warned himself as he started the ignition and backed out onto the road. Whatever was going on between her and Davis, he wasn't going to take advantage. Still, he couldn't help but look forward to being able to spend some time with his best friend.

THIRTEEN

Allen was keeping watch at gate 13 of LaGuardia Airport and had just finished off a coffee he got from one of the overpriced chains that were in the terminal. Considering it tasted like dishwater, he couldn't believe what he paid for it. He wouldn't have bought it at all if it weren't for the fact that he needed the energy. He had been up late at a study group last night after work in preparation for moot court on Monday. His friends had done a great job planning the celebration for Jim, and he was surprised they were able to work together in his absence without incident. He wanted to be able to sleep in, but he felt guilty about not doing any of the major work for the party so he insisted on picking up Riley from the airport. He had to fight for the job with Miko, who was more than thrilled that her best friend was in town. Allen himself was also looking forward to seeing one of his favorite cousins whom he hadn't seen in person in years.

Allen checked the board again, and then looked at his watch. She was supposed to be on flight 419, which was supposed to have arrived twenty minutes ago. He hoped he hadn't missed her somehow. He scanned the crowd of people heading toward the gate, but he couldn't find her. He was worried that he wouldn't recognize her when he saw her since it had been so long. "What if she's changed her looks?" he wondered. He went to throw away his empty coffee cup before returning to his post. Then he saw a huge afro among the crowd. Allen knew that afro anywhere.

"Riley?!" he called out.

The afro picked up its pace and it wasn't long before he could see her clearly. Her afro was pushed back by a dark green bandana. She was wearing a cute little ladies hunting jacket over a grey camouflage t-shirt, and green army pants and desert colored army boots. She also had her signature gold hoop earrings. Despite the fact that her clothes were decidedly not feminine, the fit was. The camouflage did nothing to hide her svelte, hourglass figure. Her caramel complexion was glowing with the brightness of health.

"Little Al!" she screamed as she threw her five foot ten inch frame on him for a bear hug. Allen picked her up off her feet.

"Little? I haven't been little since I was thirteen. Are you forgetting that I'm a whole five inches taller and sixty pounds heavier than you now?"

"But you're still two years younger, so there!"

"Girl, you look good! Old NC has been good to you," said Allen pulling out of the embrace and taking her luggage from her as they began to walk to his car.

"Thank you, sir. You don't look too bad yourself. Where's Miko? I thought she was coming with you."

"She wanted to, but I asked her to stay at the fort and help get everything ready for Jim's celebration."

"Oh, that's right – the party. Look, Al, you and Miko better be glad I love Jimmy like I do, otherwise I'd have you take me straight to the Pastor's and I'd stay there 'till it's over. I'm not sure if I'm ready for those other folks y'all carry on wit.'"

"Aww c'mon, Rye. You gotta be more social."

"I can be social, but from what you and Miko have told me, I'm not sure these folks are gonna be my cup of tea. I mean, you got your baby-momma, hustle-man, a bougie player, and some passive – aggressive dude with commitment issues."

"Where on earth did you get all that? I hope I never said anything to give you that kind of impression."

"You didn't because you see the best in everybody. I fill in the blanks you leave out, then get Miko's take and make my own judgment."

"Trust me, they're all good people."

"Just tell me they're the type of people who know when to go home. I don't think I can take one of those parties like my brother Wilson throws where people don't even think about leaving until 3 am."

"Trust me, nobody will be around past 10:00, and that's if Jim can handle it."

"Wait a minute – what do you mean, if Jim can handle it? Is he in a wheelchair or something? I thought Miko said he was gonna be okay."

"He is, but you have to remember he's still recovering from surgery, not to mention he's got a broken arm and a broken leg."

"Man. And y'all still don't know what happened?"

"Negative. And that's another thing, Riley – I know you like to play detective sometimes, but..."

"Don't worry, Miko already let me know what's goin' on when I texted her last night. I'm not gonna ask Jimmy any nosy questions. I promise."

"Good to know," said Allen. They stopped at the car, where Allen loaded her luggage in the trunk, then opened the car door for her to take a seat.

"But don't think that because I'm not saying anything, I'm not taking notes."

"Riley – remember your promise. Jim needs our support, not our meddling."

"Who said anything about meddling? I know Jimmy's a grown man and he has his own life to live. I only meant I would be observing my surroundings, that's all."

"Uh-hunh. I have no problem with your observations. Trouble is, you can't see something without saying something."

"I only say something when there's mess somebody's trying to hide. If everybody's clean, won't be nothin' for me to talk about."

That was the thing about Riley – if anyone had anything to hide, she'd definitely be the one to find it. Allen knew Jim might have some skeletons, but he was content to let sleeping dogs lie. The last thing he wanted was for Riley to start waking them up, because if she did, he knew someone would definitely get bitten.

****

Allen put the car in park and got out to open the door for Riley and then proceeded to the trunk to get her suitcase when he heard the sound of the front door opening followed by a high pitched squeal.

"Riley?!!!"

"Miko?!!!"

What followed was an incoherent mix of screams of excitement and rapid chatter. As he headed back with her suitcase, he saw Riley and Tamiko embracing with the former lifting the latter off of the ground and spinning her around. It reminded Allen of how they were when they were little girls.

"Girl, I can't believe how long it's been. You look so good!"

"So do you. I see you still tiny!"

"And you still love your army pants, hunh."

"You know that. Comfort over cuteness has always been my rule. But I got my colors right, as you can see."

"I see. So how's everybody at home?"

"We're fine, you know Wilson...."

"I know you two are really happy to see each other, but I think there may be some other people that would like to meet Riley, too," said Allen pointing to their friends who were standing in the doorway watching. Riley let out a huff, rolled her eyes, and turned her back to the audience to face Allen.

"I feel like I'm getting a headache."

"Don't start" said Allen lowering his voice so the others couldn't hear. "Just give them a chance, Rye."

"Allen's right. You're going to love them once you get to know them," said Tamiko grabbing her arm and leading her toward the house.

"I bet."

As they neared the entrance of the house, the crowd parted to let them in and Tamiko served to herald the entrance of her old friend.

"Everyone I want you to meet our cousin Riley Sharpe, who has come all the way from down South to be with us," said Tamiko.

Riley put on a half-hearted smile and waved to everyone. All of the young men stood staring unable to utter a word. Riley stood there in front of them self-consciously pulling on the curls at the nape of her neck. Then Daniel looked around curiously at the others before stepping forward.

"Hey, Riley. Welcome back," he said giving her a man-hug.

"Thanks, Dan. Glad to be back."

"Girl, you don't know how I wish it was summer. I still got my old super soaker and I'm ready to settle the score."

"The last I remember, the score was 55 to nada – and trust me, you don't want to go there. I'd still have you runnin' back to you mamma soaking wet and crying like always."

"I'm a big boy now, Rye, if you haven't noticed."

"Bigger, but obviously not badder, at least not with that dorky lookin' bow-tie you sportin'.'"

"Excuse me, D. But you have to allow me to introduce myself to this young lady. Name's Richard."

"Hello, Richard."

"Ump – ump – ump," said Richard, as his eyes roamed her figure. "Girl, you must be a thief."

"Come again."

"Cause you done stole my heart."

Richard took her hand and tried to kiss it, but Riley snatched it back. Several of the others began to chuckle to themselves.

"Is this guy serious?" said Riley as she looked back at Allen.

"Don't mean no harm, sweet thang. Just tryin' to show my appreciation for your overwhelming beauty."

"And I would've appreciated it if you'd done so in a more respectful way."

"It's okay, Riley. He's just playin,'" said Allen.

"Well, I don't play like that," said Riley.

"Oh, all right. It's like that?" said Richard backing away.

"I don't know what type of women you're used to dealing with, but I'm a lady and you don't step to me like that. Learn how to come correct."

"You know what...forget this. I'm going to check on the chicken."

"Yeah, you need to go somewhere," said Riley under her breath.

"Anyway, Riley we have some other friends we'd like you to meet. This is Tim Russell. My old roommate from college," said Allen.

"Nice to finally meet you, Riley," he said smiling at her. "I've heard a lot about you."

“Heard a lot about you, too” said Riley, who shot a knowing glance toward Tamiko before returning her critical gaze to Tim and folding her arms across her chest.

“Good things, I hope.”

“Interesting things would be a better way of putting it.”

“I'll take that. It's better than being boring. Is there something wrong? Why are you looking at me like that?” said Tim after noticing the odd way she was looking at him.

“You look different than in the pictures I've seen.”

“How so? Better or worse?”

“Just...whiter, that's all.”

“Now that's something I've never heard before.”

“Hmph – I doubt that.”

Tim's jaw dropped.

“Don't get offended. It's not like I've never met a swirl before. As a matter of fact, there's plenty of y'all down south. It's just that the one's I've known are at least a *little* tan. Tell me something, is your momma all black or is she a swirl, too?”

“Oooo-kaay,” he said as he started to back away. “Well, I'd love to stay and chat, but Jim's going to be here any minute and I have to finish putting up the streamers in the backyard. Excuse me.”

“What's his problem? I just asked a simple question.”

“Riley, did you have to go there with the color thing?” whispered Tamiko.

"Where I come from people talk about stuff like that all the time. I mean, you are who you are. What's the big deal?"

"We'll talk later," whispered Tamiko.

"And where is your honey pie, Allen? What's 'er name – uh, Cassie?"

"Callie is running a little late because she had to drop Darius off with the babysitter, but she'll be here."

"You mean I don't get to meet Darius?"

"I told her she could bring him, but she didn't feel it was appropriate."

"Aww, man. He was the only one I was looking to meet. Anyway, my head is throbbing. If you all will excuse me, I'm going up stairs to lie down for a spell. Let me know when Jimmy gets here."

"But you haven't met Davis yet" said Tamiko. She had grabbed a reluctant Davis by the arm and was guiding him over from where he had been standing.

"Oh," she said before turning around. "Hi, Davis."

"Hey."

"There - we've met. Now can I go lie down before my head explodes?"

"But we have another friend who's coming..." began Tamiko.

"Really? I'm definitely going to need to lie down," said Riley interrupting her as she headed upstairs.

"I'll get you some aspirin," said Tamiko following behind.

"Are you sure she's related to you?" asked Davis.

"I know. Riley can be a little hard to take sometimes. She doesn't have a lot of people skills," said Allen.

"She's nice, once you get to know her though," added Daniel.

"No offense, but I'm not sure if I want to. From what I've seen so far, she seems to think she's all that," said Davis.

"Truthfully, she can be a little bossy. She tends to think she's everyone's life coach, but she promised me she's not going to try to get up in anyone's business. That's the last thing that we need," said Allen.

"Amen," laughed Daniel.

FOURTEEN

As difficult as it was to get dressed, Jim was glad to be able to wear his own clothes again. As always, Momma Lena knew just what he needed: his favorite baggy, short-sleeved ribbed knit t-shirt, his green fleece jacket, and track pants with the Velcro side closures on the leg that would accommodate his cast. Pop Vernon had helped him get himself together while Momma Lena went to the nurse's station to wait for the paperwork. After spending three weeks in the hospital, Jim was glad to leave, but he wished he could've returned to his own apartment instead of moving in with the Sharpes. He would have felt better about being with his family if he didn't have such an explosive secret that lay pulsing in his heart like a live landmine. The worst part was Jim knew it would be revealed, but he didn't know when it would come out or how the people he loved would react. Thinking about it filled Jim with dread. Jim faced a long road ahead of him and he had trouble feeling good about any of it, which left him in a state of depression that was worsened by the cocaine withdrawal. Part of him wished he had some coke right now, but the other half knew just where that would lead.

"You feelin' alright?" asked Vernon, noticing Jim's somber expression.

"Yes, sir. I'm okay."

"You don't look it. Somethin' botherin' you?"

"Pop, I don't want to be a burden to you and Momma Lena any more than I already have. I can stay at the co-op and get a health aide to help me, that is, if I still have it."

"Don't worry yourself about none of that. Your momma and me don't mind havin' you round, and the co-op will be there when you get back on your feet. You need to take them two weeks to relax and think about what you wanna do."

"I been thinkin' for a while now. Startin' to feel that going back to church might not be such a bad idea."

"Glad to hear that. Pastor's got counselin' services on Wednesdays and Fridays."

"I don't know about no counseling."

"Jimmy, are you forgetting I was there when them cops took your statement?"

"I'm not planning on picking up those old habits again, Pop."

"I know you not 'cause counselin's gonna help you with that. If you gon' stay under my roof that's the way it's gonna have to be. You hear me?"

"Yes, sir."

Jim did not like the idea of going to counseling even though he knew he needed it. He didn't want to reveal the extent of his problems with drugs to his friends. Jim knew that everyone was aware he'd been smoking, but he didn't want to have to explain about the coke and the other drugs. He was afraid of what they might think.

"Look, son. Don't think I haven't been where you are now. I remember when I came to this city from Charleston thirty years ago. I didn't have nothin' in my pockets but my hands, and yet the Lord worked. He still works. Don't worry too much about what's gonna happen down the line. You do what you can and believe God will work out the rest."

"Thanks, Pop. I appreciate you."

"I'm always here for you, Jimmy."

Vernon gave him a hug, just as Lena was entering the room accompanied by the nurse.

"Is everybody ready?" asked Lena.

"I guess so," answered Jim.

"Oh, Jim! Just look at you! You look so much better. I think he might have even gained a few pounds. Wouldn't you say so Vern?"

"He should have with all that food you kept sending down here."

"You know that hospital food don't do nothin' for nobody" opined Lena "No offense," she added hastily when she remembered the nurse's presence.

"None taken," said the nurse, "If you could just sign these Mr. Reid, you'll be good to go."

Jim took the pen and scribbled his signature as best he could with his left hand. When he was done the nurse collected them.

"Good luck, Mr. Reid, everyone," said the nurse before she left.

"Thank you."

"We better get going. We don't want to be late."

"Late for what?" asked Jim.

"Oh, me and my big mouth. Never mind what I said."

"Al and the others done cooked up a little surprise for you."

"Vern!"

"What? I ain't spoiled nothin'. All I said was it's a surprise. I never said what the surprise was."

"Let's get him home before we ruin it any more than we already have. C'mon, Jim."

It couldn't get any worse. Jim knew Allen and the others probably went out of their way to throw a celebration for him. They had done so much for him, and what had he ever done for any of them? What had he ever done for anyone? Jim believed he didn't deserve a party. While the others believed his return was a reason for celebration, Jim did not. Once his secrets were revealed, he knew it wouldn't be long before they felt the same way.

FIFTEEN

"WELCOME HOME!!!"

Their salutation was followed by an acoustic assault made by plastic flutes, horns and noisemakers. There was a large banner that read "Welcome Back" and green and gray balloons floating around along with the aroma of barbecued chicken." Everyone who was there was wearing green football jerseys over their clothes, and some had on those ridiculous looking, dollar store party hats. The fact that he already knew about this surprise did nothing to prepare him for the experience of it.

"Is all this racket necessary?" grumbled Vernon. "The boy just came out of the hospital and y'all gonna send 'im back with a ruptured ear drum."

"It was Tamiko's idea," said Allen pointing at her.

"Allen!" said Tamiko as she jabbed Allen playfully in the stomach.

"It's okay, Pop," said Jim.

"Time for the group hug!" said Allen.

"Be careful with him, now. He's only got one good leg and arm as it is and you don't want to break them, too" warned Lena.

After the hug was over, they all carefully backed away to give Jim some space. Jim was totally overwhelmed by their outpouring of love and affection. He turned away from them for a moment to wipe tears from his eyes.

"Welcome back, man," said Allen putting his hand on Jim's shoulder.

"Al, you and the others didn't have to go through all this."

"I know we didn't have to. We wanted to."

"Now it's time for our surprise guest. Jim, you'll never guess who's here to see you!" said Tamiko bubbling over with excitement.

"Okay, now you got me worried. Who's this 'special guest'?" said Jim feeling a little diffident.

"She's talking about me."

The voice was unmistakable. He turned to see her easing her way between Tim and Richard to come to the front of the group. Jim couldn't believe his eyes.

"Riley?"

"The one and only."

"But how – when – what are you doing here?"

"I heard you needed some TLC so I decided to come up North for a spell. Are you glad to see me or what?"

"You know I am, girl, come over here!" he said motioning to her to come over for a hug.

Jim couldn't believe it. Riley had come all the way from North Carolina just to see him. Under other circumstances, he would have been ecstatic about her visit. Through the years they had become as close as siblings, as they played together, went on little 'adventures' and shared secrets. Riley was one of the few people that really knew him, and sometimes he even felt as if she could see through him. As such, he didn't know whether to feel comforted or terrified.

"Hey, little mama!" said Vernon, "Don't forget about me."

"You know I could never Uncle Vern," she said stopping to greet her uncle with a hug.

"Oh, Riley it's just so good to see you. How you doin' chile?" said Lena who had given her a peck on the cheek with her hug "You look like you done grew about four more inches since the last time I saw you."

"I'm fine, Auntie Lena. Don't worry, I'm still 5'10" and I hope I don't get any taller than that."

"Don't count on it if you're a Sharpe. Folks on my side run tall."

"Don't I know that," said Allen.

"Alright. We've done our part. I got to go meet Smitty for the game and I know your momma got to get to the church. Don't make no mess while we're gone and if you do, make sure you clean it up."

"Dad, we got it."

"And y'all can drink anything you want in there, but don't drink my Royal Crown cola."

"It's okay dad. We have our own drinks."

"And don't forget to leave some of them eats for me and your momma. We didn't fix all that food just to get a work out."

"Don't worry, Pop Vernon, I'll definitely make sure of that" said Tamiko.

"See you later, baby," said Lena who kissed Allen on the cheek before leaving. "Have a good time everyone!"

"But not too good!"

Allen and the others said their goodbyes to Allen's parents before they gathered to give Jim personal greetings.

"Hey, Jim. We missed you so much," said Tamiko taking her chance to get another hug.

"Missed y'all, too."

"Yeah. Who else is gonna help us keep it real, dude?" said Tim.

"Thanks, Tim."

"Hey, Jim," said Callie stiffly. She paused before giving him an awkward hug.

"Hey," replied Jim, who didn't bother to hug her back.

"Lemme pay my respect to the six-billion dollar man here!" said Richard.

"I don't know about all that," Jim smiled.

"Nah, man. You pulled a Lazarus on us. We gon' celebrate that."

"But before we do, there are some more people who want to shout at you. You remember Davis Martinez, right?" said Allen.

"Yeah. Nice to see you again, man."

"Same here," said Davis.

"And you know Daniel."

"Lil' Rev, how you doin'?" asked Jim, pulling him in for a man hug.

"Good. How about you?"

"I'm makin' it."

"Good to hear."

"And last, but not least, this our new friend Chris."

Jim stood frozen. He hoped he was the only one who could hear how hard and fast his heart was beating in his chest. It became hard to breathe. There was no doubt about it. It was him - the guy he used to call 'Way-lo.' He had his hair had grown out a little and shaped into a curly Caesar cut. He was wearing a gray, long-sleeved tee underneath his football jersey, and gray jeans with green and white suede sneakers. Chris looked a lot younger now that he had gained even more weight and developed some tone to his physique, which made him blend right into their set. He could tell that Chris was just as shocked as he was. So now Jim knew the church crowd Chris had been running with – Jim's own crew. "Just keep cool," Jim cautioned himself.

"Nice to meet you," said Chris with a bit of diffidence as he extended his fist for the pound.

"Yeah. Nice to meet you, too," said Jim, greeting him back. It was taking a tremendous amount to affect the nonchalance of a blind, initial encounter.

"Chris just joined our church a couple of months ago," said Allen.

Another specter from his past had emerged and settled itself right in the midst of his own home. So far, it seemed Chris wasn't going to call him out on their past relationship, and he wondered why. 'Was this part of a revenge plot?' he wondered anxiously. Then he thought about their last encounter before he got shot. At that time it seemed that Chris bore him no ill will, but could he have changed his mind? Jim began to wonder about what Chris had told them already. Had Chris spoken of the things Jim had said and done to him? If he had, how long would it be before everyone figured out Jim was the man Chris had talked about? How would they react when they found out Jim was a drug dealer? Now Jim was tense. This was supposed to be a relaxing day with his friends but it was turning into a huge ordeal. Now Jim would have to spend the next several hours pretending to be happy and carefree when he was anything but, and hope that Riley wouldn't notice. Though the celebration was just getting started, for Jim it couldn't be over fast enough. "Jesus, please get me through this," he prayed within himself. Meanwhile, Allen began to direct the festivities.

"Now that everyone's gotten acquainted, I want to welcome you to the Jim Reid homecoming day celebration! Whoo-hoo!"

Everyone clapped and cheered along with Allen in response and some blew their horns and noisemakers. When the noise died down, Allen continued.

"I am going to be your MC for the afternoon and evening, and as such, I want to let you know what's going on. First we're going to mingle a little bit because it's kind of early and the food's still heating. During our mix and mingle period we're going to have a few appetizers and a quick game of 'guess my picture.'"

"Say what?" asked Chris.

"It's corny, but it's fun. At least that's what the entertainment committee told me," said Allen sending a wary glance over to Tim and Tamiko. "At any rate, it'll be quick. Then, after the mix and mingle, we're going to start the dominoes tournament, followed by dinner and a movie. Sound good everyone?"

Tim blew his horn, which made the other's laugh. Daniel and Tim helped Jim over to the couch to sit and the others went to attend to matters related to the party. Allen and Davis went into the kitchen and a few minutes later Davis emerged with the appetizers: spinach rolls, fried zucchini, and a dip platter. Then Tamiko and Tim went around handing out construction paper hats to all of their guests. Soon after picking up appetizers, everyone began to get into groups and have conversations. Jim was trying to keep track of Chris when Riley approached.

"I'm sticking to you Jimmy. I'm not tryin' to parlay with these other folks."

"Still anti-social, I see."

"'Til God changes me. I got you some eats," she said handing him a plate with a spinach roll and some zucchini. "Oh, and here's your game hat."

"Thanks. You didn't want anything for yourself?" asked Jim before taking a bite of his spinach roll.

"I hate spinach, and I tasted that fried squash thing and it wasn't for me. I'm saving my appetite for the barbecue. Anyway, how you feelin' now? Tired?"

"Not as tired as I was of being cooped up in the hospital."

"When do your casts come off?"

"In two weeks. After that I'm gonna have to do rehab. They had to put pins in my knee and leg to reconstruct it and I gotta learn how to walk on it."

"Sounds like you're gonna need some help. How'd you like it, if I was your unofficial home health aid?"

"Rehab's going to take a while. How long do you plan on staying?"

"Til just before Thanksgiving. Just in time to see you up and about I hope."

"That's a lot of time out here. You're not worried about your job."

"I'm more worried about you."

"You don't have to be. Look, Rye, I don't want you to feel like you have to sit around and take care of me. As much as I appreciate you being here right now, I don't want you neglecting your situation for mine."

"Gee, I just got here and it sounds like you're trying to get rid of me."

"I'm not. I just don't want to be poor Jim."

"Jim, I'm not here because I feel sorry for you. I love you, man. I just want to see you back to the way you used to be – you know – happy."

"I am – and I'd be even happier if I knew my friends were taking care of themselves."

"That means you don't have to worry about me and mine. We're fine. Daddy and Mamma Shirley just celebrated their 20th Anniversary. Wilson just started working for this new computer software developer, and yes he's still trading toys with his annoying geek friends. Bennett talks to us now and can do more for himself, plus he doesn't do as much hand flapping as the doctor calls it, and Junior nailed the SAT, and is thinking about going to Al's old Alma Mater. Me, I'm still doing hair, and before you hear it from Miko, yes, me and Marcus broke up."

"Glad to hear you all are doing well. Except for that last part."

"Breaking up with Marcus is good news in my book. He's not even worth talking about."

"There's more where he came from."

"I hope not. Marcus was bad enough. If there's any more like him I hope they go extinct."

"You know what I mean. There are plenty of other guys out there to choose from."

"I know. Right now, I don't mind being by myself for a while. It'll give me time to figure out why I keep picking losers. Speaking of losers, what's your take on Al's new girlfriend? I know already you don't like her," said Riley lowering her voice.

"What would make you say that? Callie's been friends with us for years."

"You didn't look like you were glad to see her."

"I'm just not thrilled about Allen taking on so much responsibility, that's all."

"I don't think anyone is. Miko says Allen knows he's not the daddy. Any of you know who the daddy actually is?"

"Riley, let's not be all up in Allen's business. Callie's his choice and if that's what he wants, then just be happy for him and leave it alone."

"Okay-okay, I wasn't planning on starting anything," said Riley, who was so taken aback by

Jim's abrasive response she was speechless for a few minutes. Jim, realizing how he had overreacted, tried to ameliorate the tension. He didn't mean to put her on the defensive. That would arouse her suspicion, which was the last thing he wanted.

"I didn't mean for it to come out like that. I'm sorry I..."

Before Riley could respond, Tamiko and Tim came over to chat.

"So, Jim, are you excited to have Riley back with us?" asked Tamiko.

"Not as excited, as I know you are. I bet you got your sleeping bag hidden around here somewhere, ready to stay the night," said Jim.

"Actually, Riley is staying at my place," said Tamiko.

"For Real?" said Jim brightening a bit. He considered it a fortunate turn of events. If Riley were preoccupied at Tamiko's maybe she wouldn't have time to get in his business.

"Yeah, after all, it's going to be a bit crowded around here," said Riley.

"You sure you gonna be able to make it a whole month with Mother Bynum?" chuckled Jim. Riley narrowed her eyes at him.

"What's so funny?" asked Tim.

"My mom doesn't always think Riley's such a good influence," said Tamiko.

"I can handle Mother Bynum," said Riley.

"You might want to change out of those pants before you go over there," said Jim snickering.

"Shut up," said Riley.

"But they're not going to even have a chance to butt heads because I have so much planned for us to do. The city has changed so much since the last time you've been here and there's lots of things I thought we could do together. I was just talking to Tim and he's going to get tickets for us to go see that new Christian play, 'The Choice' that they're showing off Broadway," said Tamiko.

"Well, well, well, how nice of you, Tim. Will you be accompanying the girls on this little adventure?" asked Jim.

"No. Since Miko doesn't get too see Riley so often, I thought it would be a nice way for the two of them to spend time together by themselves," he replied.

"You'd pay for my ticket and you don't even know me like that?" asked Riley.

"Al and Miko are like family to me, so that means you are, too," said Tim.

"You really mean that?" said Riley.

"Of course," said Tim.

"Then can you do me a solid? I could use $20.00," said Riley.

Everyone laughed.

"What y'all laughing about? I'm serious. I could really use $20.00. I was going to ask Miko, but since you put yourself out there..."

"Riley!" said Tamiko.

"It's not a problem, Miko," said Tim taking out his wallet.

"Tim, man, no - you don't have to go there. Riley you need to stop," said Jim.

"No! People need to watch what they say," said Riley.

"Here you are. Sorry, I don't have anything smaller," said Tim as he handed her a fifty-dollar bill.

"Thanks, man. 'preciate you."

"Riley, you are going to pay him back every last cent before you go home," said Tamiko.

"It's not a big deal, Miko," said Tim.

"See, we cool. Like the man said – this is a family thang," said Riley.

"Oookaaay. Soooo – Who are you and what have you done with Tim?" asked Jim.

"What are you talking about?" said Tim.

"I mean first you got saved, now your engaging in selfless acts. What's going on with you bro?" said Jim.

"Just growing up I guess. I've learned there are more important things in life than getting ahead and stockpiling cash," said Tim.

"And what brought this on?" asked Jim.

"I've been through a lot while you were away. You remember that really bad health scare I told you about?" said Tim.

"Yeah?" said Jim.

"I didn't tell you this before because I didn't want to freak you out, but I even had to have surgery."

"For real?" said Jim, looking at Tamiko for confirmation.

"Yes, we were all worried for a minute, but then we had faith that God would intervene," said Tamiko.

"I know I wouldn't be sitting here right now if it weren't for Him. Nothing like nearly losing your life to make you think about what's really important," said Tim.

"Losing your life? What was wrong with you?" asked Jim.

"It was a brain tumor," said Tim after a nervous pause. Jim could tell that it was difficult for him to talk about even after all this time.

"You mean, cancer?" said Jim. He couldn't believe what he was hearing.

"Yeah."

"Wow," said Riley.

"But he's fine now," said Tamiko "He's had several physicals since the surgery, and the doctors haven't been able to find anything."

"I guess you know you're blessed," said Jim.

"So are you, dude. You were pretty bad off, but I thank God for answered prayers."

"Amen," said Tamiko.

Jim knew his friends were right, but at the present moment his second chance didn't feel much like a blessing, but a huge burden.

*****

After a few more minutes, Allen came back to the living room with some 2X3 inch pictures. It seemed that the game was about to get started.

"Everyone, if I could have your attention. It's time for the guess the picture game to start. I'm going to need everyone to find a seat," he said.

Everyone sat in the living room in a circle. Allen explained the rules of the game to the guests before taping a picture to each person's hat. Instead of using pictures of common objects, Tamiko had decided to take pictures of the guests and others that they knew and use these pictures for the game. The players would have to guess who was in the picture on their hat. The game wasn't very difficult and everyone was able to guess the person in his or her picture within the customary three guesses afforded them. The incorrect guesses elicited a lot of laughter and light-hearted banter from the group. The overall levity the game created helped Jim to relax a bit. He also noticed that Chris wasn't talking a lot, which also gave him a sense of relief. When the game was over Tamiko collected the hats, while Allen collected the pictures. When they were done, Allen started the dominoes tournament.

"Okay, now we're going to get started with our dominoes tournament. Now I know everyone here knows how to play dominoes, but some of us are more advanced than others so I created brackets. We'll play as partners then winners in each partnership will move up until we have a winner"

Allen brought out a chart with the playing pairs on it. Tamiko was paired with Chris, Richard was to play Callie, Davis faced off against Riley, Jim played Daniel and Tim went head to head with Allen. After the first round, Callie, Chris, Davis, Jim, and Tim were left. The others milled around and watched the remaining pairs, cheering on their favorites. Allen headed back to the kitchen to check on the food that was heating. After the second round, only Callie and

Jim were left, but the final round would be postponed when Allen came in from the kitchen to announce that dinner was ready.

It was still daylight and the afternoon autumn air was crisp enough to lightly ruffle the fringes of the umbrella over the table. Everyone filed into the yard and took a seat at the picnic bench as Allen and Davis helped to serve. Jim, Riley, Tamiko, Richard, and Daniel took up one side of the bench while. Callie, Allen, Tim, Chris, and Davis occupied the other side. It was a little tight with so many people, but this didn't dampen the spirit of the guests at all. The table was filled with all of Jim's favorites: barbecue chicken and pork ribs, macaroni and cheese, red rice, corn on the cob, and salad. There was a cooler of sodas off to the side where the guests could choose from cola, iced-tea, and seltzer. This was the most tense time of the evening for Jim because, it was around the dinner table that people did the most talking and he was afraid of what would come out of Chris's mouth and what Riley would think of it.

"It's kind of cloudy out here. I hope it doesn't rain," said Callie.

"I did hear that it was supposed to rain this afternoon, but it looks like God's holding it back for us," said Allen.

"So, Jim, how does it feel to be back?" asked Tim.

"Good. But I have to admit I feel a little out of the loop. So much has happened since the last time I've been around."

"But you've been caught up on all of it," said Allen, "there aren't any more surprises left that I can think of."

"Yo, Al, can we tell him 'bout what happened at the hospital when we went to see Tim?" asked Richard.

"I don't know, man..."

"It's okay, Al. Jim knows about my surgery."

"And Rich is itching to tell it, so..."

"Jim, check this out. Tim's mom had the hospital on lockdown. There was a special visitor list and you had to have two types of ID. She even had a private security guard in front of his room. It was crazy! We had to try like three different times. It was like trying to get close to the president!"

"So how did you guys get in?" said Jim.

"You know I know how to parlay with the best of them and I knew how to read the situation. Now, the last time we went, we were finally able to get passes and get upstairs but then when we got up there, they had this big security guy in front of the door and he told us we couldn't see Tim. So Al tried to reason with the brother, 'bout how we had come a long way and everything, but he wasn't tryin' to hear nothin'. Then Miko started getting a little hysterical and she was crying real hard and I seen the guy staring at her like she was crazy, so I took him aside and I told him a little story, slid him some cheese – just like I do at the club. Next thing you know we was in."

"You were crying?" asked Tim.

"We hadn't heard from you since you left and I was worried. We all were – right, Allen?"

"We were worried, but you were the one with the drama," said Allen.

"Tim, how come you didn't tell them what was going on?" asked Jim.

"I couldn't. The doctors felt that it would be best if I had the surgery right away. I entrusted my mom with my phone and told her to contact everyone to let them know what was going on, but instead, she wiped all your numbers from the cache," explained Tim.

"Cold snap!" said Jim.

"Cold is right. Anyway, Rich, you ever gonna let us know what you told that security guy?" asked Allen.

"I just told him that Miko was Tim's fiancée and his mom didn't approve of the marriage because they was from two rich families that was at war with each other, kinda like Romeo and Juliet."

"What?!" laughed Tim.

"Richard! How could you?!" said Tamiko.

" 'Cause I knew he would fall for it. He looked like a sucka for drama. Dude was readin' a chick-lit book when we rolled up on him. Anyway, it was for a good cause. We got in."

"But it wasn't over. Tell Jim what happened next," said Allen.

"Oh, yeah – then Tim's mom showed up with his sister and some thick brother (and you know they don't like us no way) and they started yelling at us. Makin' a scene all up in front of Tim, getting' him upset and everything. I was like how you gon' set it off like this when yo' boy tryin' to get better?"

"For real?" asked Jim.

"For real! Then the doctor and the nurse came and they was ready to bounce everybody, and his moms was trying to make it seem like we was startin' the trouble and the sister she was real nasty. You know she had the nerve to call Miko a 'ho'" continued Richard.

"No, she didn't!" said Riley.

"She did. But we checked that."

"So did you guys end up leaving?" asked Jim.

"No, cause they asked Tim who he wanted to stay and he chose us. So the double-stuffed-Stedman-Graham-lookin' brother and the ferocious females had to go."

"Wow. And I thought my family had issues," said Davis.

"I now believe you, Tim. Your mom really does have control issues. How did you manage dealing with her all those years without becoming a basket case?" said Allen.

"Easy. It's called boarding school," said Tim.

"And what's your sister's problem? Why is she so...so...so...mean?" asked Tamiko.

"You too nice, Miko. I was thinkin' of a whole other word," said Richard.

"I know you haven't seen the best side of her, but she isn't all bad. At least she wasn't when we were younger. It might be hard to believe, but she used to be a sweet, bubbly little girl. I remember I used to call her cupcake because when she was little she would always beg me for cupcakes," said Tim.

"Really? What happened to her?" asked Davis.

"Life, I guess. She and I have been through a lot, and maybe she was affected more deeply. I just pray for her, now."

"Maybe we should all pray for her. She needs it," said Allen.

"She's not the only one," said Richard sending a glance in Riley's direction.

"Speaking of prayer, Allen, tells me you're thinking about coming back to church," said Daniel to Jim.

"Uh...yeah," said Jim.

"When you do, you might want to join the Brotherhood Bible study we have going on. It's just a bunch of us getting together to discuss what being a man means according to the Scriptures. We meet after church on Sundays from 2 to 4"

"I don't know man," said Jim.

"Everybody here is in it - Allen, Tim, Davis, Chris, and some of the other young brothers from our church. It's a real support group where we exhort each other and strengthen each other with the Word," said Daniel.

"Yeah, and with everything the enemy is throwin' at us nowadays, it's a real help. Fa real," said Davis.

"I'll think about it," said Jim.

"It's helped me a lot," added Chris reticently, "I don't know if I would have been able to stay clean the past 10 weeks without it," Chris was looking straight at Jim when he spoke.

"Congratulations, Chris! I can't believe it's been that long already," said Tim.

"Word, we're really proud of you, man. Look how far He's brought you. If only those dealers could see you now," said Allen.

"That's right, and he's been going wit me and Davis to the gym, too. He's gettin' all swolled up and everything," said Richard, "I know they wouldn't want to try to mess wit' you now"

Jim winced at his words as if he were hit in the stomach.

"I don't worry about them anymore," said Chris.

"Jim, are you okay?" asked Callie.

Jim looked around at everyone. They were all eyeing him strangely, especially Riley.

"I'm fine. I'm just getting a little tired."

"If you need, we can cut the celebration short," said Allen.

Jim felt he should take advantage of his friend's offer. The day had been pure agony and a nerve had been touched. He'd had enough.

"After all the work you guys put into this, I don't want to ruin it," said Jim.

"This is about you and you can cut it off whenever you want to. We all understand that you still need time to recuperate," said Allen.

"Yeah. I think I'm gonna do that. You guys can stay out here if you want, but I think I'm going to call it quits," said Jim.

"Aww. But you haven't even opened your presents yet," said Tamiko.

"You heard him, Miko. The celebration is over. Let's clean up," said Allen.

*****

Jim was in Allen's room standing by the door. He was actually propping himself up on a crutch and the doorknob, waiting. When he saw Chris come upstairs to use the bathroom, Jim knew he had to take what could be his one and only chance to talk to Chris alone. Jim had to find out what Chris had told the others about his past.

When he heard the toilet flush and the water running, Jim peaked out. There were a few tense second before the door opened and Jim made his move.

"Chris," he called out to him softly.

Chris heard his name, but couldn't see who was calling him. He looked around for a moment, and Jim opened the bedroom door wider so he could be seen.

"Chris!" called Jim a little louder this time.

This time Chris saw him. He stood motionless with a suspicious look as if he didn't know if he should trust Jim.

"Come here for a second. I just want to talk to you."

Chris came to the door and Jim motioned to him with his head to come all the way in. Jim was tired of propping himself up and sat in the armchair by the door.

"I didn't know these was your people, Jay – I mean, Jim."

"Look, man you don't have to be worried about me. I'm not going to try to hurt you. I couldn't even if I wanted to."

"What you want?"

"I just want to know how much you told them about everything."

"They know I had a habit, and I told them about some of the things that had happened to me, but I ain't name no names or nothing.'"

Jim breathed out a sigh of relief.

"Jim, I'm not lookin' to put the past on blast. I know you tryin' to start over just like I am."

"I appreciate you, man."

"Just so you know, Smoke and Bricks dead. Smoke killed Bricks then Trace killed Smoke. Now Trace got all the spots, and that's all he wanted in the first place. So you don't have to worry 'bout them."

"Thanks for the information."

Chris turned to leave.

"Just make sure no one sees you go out."

He nodded, looked out and left.

Jim struggled as he used his crutch and his one good arm to get out of the chair and limp his way back to the bed. As he lay down, his burden shifted a bit, making it a bit easier to carry. His drug-dealing past was securely under wraps – for now. He closed his eyes and tried to go to sleep, but he couldn't. There was this pulsing heat in his chest. At first he thought it was indigestion, but then he realized it was something else. It was the landmine hiding inside his heart.

SIXTEEN

Callie knew something was up when she saw how Jim and Chris reacted to meeting each other. It seemed to her as if they'd met before and were both surprised to meet each other at this party. She even noticed how Jim kept eyeing Chris throughout the celebration, which made her even more suspicious. Then her gut confirmed it when she saw how Jim went grey when Chris started talking about his past. The only question that remained to be answered was how Jim and Chris knew each other. Callie knew that Chris had been a heroin addict and Jim had been smoking weed for a while before she broke up with him. There was the possibility that they had done drugs together. "Perhaps Jim had ended up doing heroin as well" she thought to herself. Whatever it was she had to find out.

After Jim had retired to Allen's room, Callie was determined to corner Chris to find out just what the connection was, however, her attempts were thwarted due to all the cleaning up that was going on. Allen had asked her to help him clear the table while Chris was taking down decorations in the living room. When the clean up was nearly done, Chris excused himself to use the bathroom, which Callie didn't think much of. She would wait until he came back and then offer him a ride home. After a while, Callie got anxious and went upstairs to check on Chris. They hadn't known Chris very long and unlike Allen, she couldn't trust such a new acquaintance to have the full run of the house, especially one that had been a heroine addict.

As she went up the stairs, she heard someone call Chris's name. She stopped so that who ever was beckoning couldn't see her on her way up. After a moment, she continued on and she saw Chris enter Allen's room closing the door after him. This was her chance to find out what was going on between them.

Callie crept over to the door and tried to eavesdrop on their conversation. It was difficult because the men were talking in low voices. However, she did hear Chris say that he wasn't going to "put the past on blast", and how he mentioned that Jim didn't have to worry anymore because some guys named Smoke and Bricks were dead. Callie listened until she heard the tread of feet toward the door. Then she went into the bathroom and waited until she heard Chris go down the stairs. When she felt the hallway was clear, she came out of the bathroom and went downstairs behind him.

Now everyone was bidding each other goodnight and getting ready to go home. Callie had to act quickly if she wanted to get to Chris.

"Chris, would you like a ride?" asked Callie.

"Actually, he's riding with me," said Davis before Chris could respond.

"Crap!" thought Callie. Now the interview would have to wait.

"Besides wouldn't that take you out of your way? I know you have to pick up Darius from the sitter," reminded Allen.

"That's right," said Callie remembering her son. In her haste to get information about Jim she nearly forgot about Darius.

Callie wished the others goodnight and gave Allen a peck on the mouth before leaving for her car. She was still pondering her next move on the way. She had to find out who Smoke and Bricks were and Jim's connection to them.

On sudden reflection, Callie realized that talking to Chris might not be such a great idea. He had just made a pact with Jim to keep quiet about the past. He probably wouldn't answer her questions and may even go back to Jim and tell him that she had been inquiring about it. Callie thought she would take another route. She decided to use her street smarts to figure it out. She knew some shady people who might know, like the woman who used to be her former neighbor from the projects. She and Callie used to go clubbing together back then, but she got caught up in drugs and ended up a prostitute. They didn't hang together any more, but whenever Callie went by that way to visit her mother, she'd holler at her old friend. If Smoke and Bricks were dealers or addicts from the area, she might know something about them. In any event, Callie had to know what Jim was hiding and she had to figure it out before the others did. She needed that tactical advantage just in case Jim's conscience got the better of him.

SEVENTEEN

Riley was sitting in front of the vanity wrapping a scarf around the front of her afro before getting ready for bed. Meanwhile, Tamiko, dressed in her pajamas and bed robe, was outfitting the air mattress on the floor with sheets and pillows. They'd had a long day with the barbecue and then coming back home to watch the 'Courageous' movie with Tim. Now it was time to turn in. Tamiko herself was in no hurry to get any sleep. Now that Riley had gotten a chance to meet all of her friends in person for the first time, she was anxious to know what she thought, especially with regard to one person in particular.

"So, what do you think?" asked Tamiko, ready for the start of a long session of sister-talk.

"Hunh?" said Riley who seemed to be lost in thought.

"I mean what do you think about our new friends?"

"I think *your* friends aren't the kind of people I want to hang with."

"I should've known you would say that. May I ask why? I mean as far as I can tell they've gone out of their way to be nice to you."

"Nice? You call that nice? Richard made a pass at me, Tim was trying pull a snow job on me, and Davis was giving me attitude the entire time. Not to mention that Chris fella is just plain weird."

"Richard *was* trying to be nice. That's just his way. And I told you Tim got saved so he's not the same guy I wrote you about five years ago. Chris can be a little spacey sometimes, but I can't believe you thought Davis was rude. He has to be the nicest guy I've ever met. Sometimes he can be quiet, but that's only because I think he's a little shy. He's really very sweet and sensitive."

Riley's revelation took Tamiko by surprise. She had always valued her cousin's judgment when it came to people, because she was rarely off the mark. She had expected Riley's distaste for the others, but she believed Davis to be of such impeccable character that not even the ultra-critical Riley Sharpe could find fault with him.

"Miko, that's your infatuation talking. Trust me, this guy is no good. He was practically glaring at me when you introduced him, and when we were playing dominoes, he barely spoke two words to me and was huffing and sighing the whole time."

"You brushed him off when I tried to introduce him..."

"I brushed him off because he was acting like he didn't want to be introduced."

"Who would, after the way you chewed up Richard and Tim?"

"Richard needed to be put in his place, and Tim's just too sensitive about race stuff."

"Everyone thinks Davis is a great guy."

"I bet his ex-girlfriends don't."

"Of course his exes wouldn't, especially if he's the one that instigated the break up – which would have to be the case because who would want to break up with a guy who's sweet *and* drop-dead gorgeous."

"Miko, are you listening to yourself? You do realize he used to be a banger, right?"

"That was a long time ago before he got saved – almost a decade ago."

"Still, saved or not, bangers tend to be emotionally unstable people with a lot of issues. I used to date one, if you remember."

"Riley, I'm not that naïve. I'm well aware of what his life was like before coming to faith. He's shared parts of that with me. But Davis is nothing like Tyrell. Davis has left that life, and Tyrell was still out there when you were dating him."

"So Davis has left the life. How do you know the life has left him?"

"Because I've seen how his faith in God has changed him. God can change anyone no matter what their past."

"God can change you, but the devil can tempt you, too. Believe me, Miko. I know what I'm talking about. If this guy is asking you for space, give it to him."

"I have been giving him space, since that's what he wants, but I don't want us to be through."

"It's not always about what we want, but what's best."

"I know, but then I'm right back to where I started – alone, without the possibility of finding anyone and as old as I'm getting..."

"You're only 23 years old!"

"And I'll be 24 in less than two months. Add to that the time it takes to find the right person, and then who knows how long for the relationship to grow, I may not be married until I'm 40."

"Wait a minute, am I hearing right? Is Tamiko Bynum worried about getting a man?"

"Not 'a man,' the 'right man.'"

"What happened to working on your teaching career and your work in the children's church? What happened to fulfilling God's will and worrying about the guys later."

"Who says it isn't God's will for me to have a husband?"

"If you think it's God's will, then why are you worrying about it? If it is, it'll happen. Just be patient and let Him lead you to the right one. If you try to make it happen according to your time, the only thing you're gonna get is a mess. Trust me, I learned that the hard way."

"But you don't understand – every other time I would meet a nice guy who wasn't a Christian, or a Christian guy who wasn't so nice, but Davis is a nice guy and a Christian. In fact, I never thought I would ever meet a guy as good as Davis. If he isn't the one for me, then who is?"

"When Samuel came to Jesse's place he thought Eliab was the perfect guy to be king, and so did

Jesse. He was the oldest and strongest son of the bunch, but God said, no. Then they looked at the other brothers, thinking it would be one of them, but God still said no. He saw what they couldn't. Now you might think Davis is perfect for you, but that doesn't mean he is. Remember God can see what you can't."[1]

"But when we met, I felt...I felt...different."

"Mamma Shirley would call it hot and bothered."

"No!"

"C'mon, Miko. You're human. Everyone has felt lust..."

"It was not lust!"

"Okay, strong attraction, if it makes you feel better. But you can't let your flesh get the best of you, especially when we know what the Word of God says."

As much as Tamiko hated to admit, Riley had a point. In the past year Davis had become a near obsession, occupying more and more of her thoughts, and pushing God to the sidelines. Maybe Davis wasn't the only one who needed space.

"Okay, you're right. I need to stop obsessing about who I'm going to end up with and just live my life."

"That's right. When the right one comes along, God will let you know."

"I thought I already knew."

"I know," said Riley putting a reassuring arm around her. "I was talkin' to Mama Shirley about this kinda stuff a while back, right after I had broke up with Marcus and she told me when God let's you know – you'll know. Most of the times we get mad and want to reason and resist, but we know in our hearts that's what God wants. He may have someone for you right up under your nose, someone you haven't considered at all. I bet when David came in and stood before Samuel, he was probably thinkin' 'Now I know you don't mean this!'"[2]

They both burst out laughing. Tamiko was feeling a lot better – definitely a lot less anxious than she had been feeling days before.

"Who knows where your future husband is. But I will tell you one thing, he wasn't at that party we had today. With the exception of Jim and Allen, everything else there was the clearance pile."

"It was a celebration! Besides, the only guy there that I like is Davis."

"You may not like them all, but I think there's one that may like you."

"If you're talking about Daniel, I'm already aware."

"Girl, please. Daniel's interest is nothin' but politics. I'm talking about someone who's romantically interested."

"And who would that be?"

"Mr. Snow Job."

"Tim?"

Tamiko's heart jumped unexpectedly.

"Uh- yeah. Did you not notice that he was following you around the whole time."

"He did not!"

"OK, maybe not the entire time, but for a good piece. Then there was the way I caught him studying you while we were watching the movie. You better watch out, girl."

"You're starting to sound like my mom."

"You know I tend to go out of my way to disagree with her on everything, but I have to give her props this time."

"I know you're good at reading people, but believe me your radar's off on this one. Tim's never really liked me that way."

"What? You mean the player, never ever even tried to run any game on you?"

"Nope. I'm not really his type at all. All the girls I've ever seen him date have looked like pop-star divas or supermodels."

"If he's a real player it has nothing to do with looks, so much as the challenge. He might just be trying to see if he can bag you 'cause you seem hard to get."

"Tim's saved now. He's put that life behind him."

"You sure. Those kind of habits are hard to break."

Tamiko couldn't help but think back about what happened between Tim and Mya for a moment. She would never forget the day that Tim just suddenly introduced her to their group. He told her they had met one afternoon after he had been dismissed from the Brotherhood Bible study. Mya had been attending a doctrinal class and was waiting for her brother to pick her up. She was definitely Tim's type: a tall, voluptuous, long-weave-wearing, barely-dressed, honey-colored sister. Tim had assured everyone that they were taking things slowly and that he wanted a real relationship. Despite his assurances, everyone had their reservations – everyone except Tamiko.

Even though everyone else doubted Tim's resolve, Tamiko did not. She even talked to him privately about the situation and the temptations present. Tim seemed so earnest and sincere. Yet not even three weeks later, their relationship ended followed by a melee between Tim and Mya's brother outside the church and a scandal that had not been heard of since Deacon Jenkins was caught stealing money from the tithes collection. Tamiko had never been more disappointed in her life. In fact, heartbroken would have been a better word to describe what she felt. She even found herself crying about it for a couple of days, although she didn't know why. Afterward, Tim did repent and seemed sincerely penitent about his actions. To Tamiko, he seemed like a helpless addict, driven by impulses that were beyond him. Only God and prayer could help him overcome them. While she believed Tim loved the Lord, she didn't know if Tim truly knew how to submit so the Lord could change him. Thinking about this in light of her cousin's suspicions, Tamiko knew she had to keep a certain amount of emotional distance between herself and Tim – whether she liked it or not.

"You're right. But God is the one that does the breaking. We have to have faith that He will. I can only pray for Tim. Who knows, one day Tim just might make a great husband, but I don't think I could wait that long."

"Yeah, infinity would be a long wait. I only wish Allen were as cautious as you. He's the one I'm really worried about. I'm not feeling him with that Callie girl. I remember her from when I visited in the summer of '03. I'll never forget when she called me 'country'. Haven't liked her since then."

"Don't waste your time with Al," said Tamiko as she settled down in the airbed. "He won't listen. Everybody's talked to him about Callie. Even Granny Eloise!"

"You mean to tell me Auntie Lena's mom called all the way from Jamaica!"

"Yep. So you know this is serious."

"It is, especially after what I noticed today," said Riley as she retired to the full sized bed.

"What did you notice?"

"I'll tell you once I have it all sorted out. But believe me that Callie is sittin' on top of a whole lotta mess."

EIGHTEEN

Davis sat on his couch, staring at the cell phone he'd laid on his living room table. He was wondering if he had enough nerve to go through with what he knew he had to do. "God please give me the strength to do this," he prayed. He had gotten Evie's new number from an old acquaintance they'd had in common, and his sister had told him where the others lived. There were a million reasons why he shouldn't do it. "What if she hung up on him?" he thought. He couldn't blame her if she did. "What if she decided to make a situation out of it?" he mulled anxiously. The last thing Davis wanted was trouble. Even if he did get through to her, it wouldn't erase what happened in the past. "What difference would any of this make?" he asked himself. The questions would only lead to excuses, and after reading the scriptures, he realized there was no excuse that could hold water against what the Word of God said.

"You need to do this, man," he told himself. "You been sitting around here too long, lettin' this hold you back. If you really want to get better, you got to deal with this. That's what you learned in counseling the other day. The Word says it, now you gotta live it." He had been thinking about how things went down between him and Tamiko and what Allen had told him at work several days ago. It was time to move forward, but not before he dealt with the reckoning.

Davis picked up the phone and dialed Evie's number. As he waited for her to pick up, he tried to think about what he was going to say. Davis felt his mouth get really dry, so that it seemed like his tongue was stuck to the roof of his mouth. After five rings he was ready to hang up, but before he could, he heard the click of someone picking up the line.

"Hello," said a gentle female voice.

"Evie? It's Davis," he said, his voice a little raspy. There was a pause on the other end of the line leaving Davis to wonder if she had hung up.

"You still there?"

"How the hell did you get my number? Why are you even calling me?" she said in a more stern voice.

"Look, I know we're over and everything. I'm not lookin' to hook up with you or nothin' like that. I just wanted to know if we could talk."

"You wanna talk, then talk."

"I think it would be better if we did this face to face."

"Don't even think I'm falling for that again. You got anything to say to me, it's now or never."

"I – I understand if you don't trust me. I want to apologize for everything that went down between us. I was wrong. I shouldn't have treated you the way that I did when we was together. I'm sorry."

"Yeah, I've heard that too many times from you, Davis. It's beyond old."

Evie was jaded and Davis couldn't blame her. He had apologized to her over and over again throughout their relationship, promising her that things would be different, that he was going to change and every time he broke his promise.

"I know, but I mean it this time – with everything I got."

"You always mean it. What's supposed to make this time different from all the other times?" said Evie flatly.

"I've given God control of my life. I done left the streets. I'm not drinkin' or doin' the drugs no more..."

"Yeah, well, good for you. Excuse me if I don't give a *d**n" she said cutting him off. He could tell by the bitterness in her voice that he wasn't convincing her. In fact, Davis was having a hard time convincing himself. He'd had the same issues with women since coming to faith, which was why he'd stopped dating entirely.

"You're upset and I can understand that..."

"No, you don't understand, Davis. You have no idea what you took me through – how much I've suffered because of the things you did to me. I lost my friends, my job, my home, and even some of my own family won't speak to me because of you. At one point, you had me so twisted I thought I'd even lose my mind – and you wanna step to me with this 'sorry' nonsense again?"

There was a brief silence between them. He could not refute her words. Davis felt she was right. His apology would never be enough.

"If I could take everything back..."

"You can't – so don't think I'ma fall for your little act, and we gonna be chill like nothing happened. You tried to break me, but you failed. I have a life now. It's not the best life, but it's my life and I'm not going to let you tear down what I've worked so hard to build," she said her voice quivering.

Her words were as sharp and precise as a doctor's scalpel. Davis could not shield himself from the deep truth of her pain, her voice resonant with her suffering. His choices, his actions had consequences for others that could not always be rectified with expressions of penitence. The fact that she had moved on, did nothing to exonerate him from what he'd done, for he knew that he had left scars on her life that served as witness to what he had allowed himself to become.

"Believe me," said Davis as he tried to keep his voice from cracking "I don't want to hurt you any more than I already have. I'm just asking you...if you can forgive me."

"Forgive and forget, right? Would that make you feel better? Clear your conscience so you can move onto your next victim?"

"Evie, please..."

"Go to hell, Davis. And don't call me no more."

Davis lost his grip on the phone and covered his face with his hands as the tears leaked from behind his tightly closed eyelids. He took deep breaths to try to calm himself. Davis had known going in that this task would not be easy, and he knew there was always the possibility of rejection, but none of that prepared him for the emotions that were welling up in him at the present moment. Shame, grief, guilt, self-deprecation, fear and anger swirling inside his breast like gases on the verge of combustion. Images of his past self confronted him, mocking him in his present.

"She's right. You don't deserve forgiveness. 'Cause deep down, you know you're still the same n**ga you used to be runnin' the same bull. That's who you are and who you always gonna be, kid" Then he remembered what happened between him and Allen at the Christmas celebration not that long ago.

Davis got up from the couch and grabbed the porcelain lamp that was sitting on top of the end table and hurled it across the room. It hit the wall on the opposite side and broke into shards. Then he kicked over the coffee table nearly sending it into his TV stand opposite it. Davis stood shaking and he covered his face with his hands again taking long deep breaths to calm down. He started to repeat a psalm he'd memorized:

"Hear my cry, O God; attend unto my prayer. From the end of the earth will I cry unto thee, when my heart is overwhelmed: lead me to the rock that is higher than I..."[1]

By the time he had finished the recitation, the funnel cloud inside him had dissipated. He took his hands away and opened his eyes. He immediately set the coffee table aright and replaced the magazines and other things that had been sitting on it. Then he walked over across the room to clean up the mess he had made with the lamp. When he saw it, he stopped in his tracks. It was the lamp Tamiko had given him as one of her friendly gifts. It had been steel blue and shaped like a beehive with Japanese writing on the side. He'd always taken meticulous care of it, hoping to make it into his own personal keepsake. Now it laid spread out across the floor in different sized jagged pieces, wires hanging out of the base like the entrails of a gutted fish. Davis felt deeply ashamed and angry with himself. He just wanted to be different: to get rid of all of the filth and scum, but there was a darkness inside him that just wouldn't let go. As he knelt down to pick up one of the shards of broken lamp, terror suddenly took hold of him. "God, please," he prayed, "please help me. I need you...I need you."

NINETEEN

"Greater Apostolic Church of Christ, Julius Bynum Pastor," read the sign in front of the building. "This has to be the one," thought Allyson. She knew the words Greater Apostolic were in the title and she had heard her brother mention the name Bynum before. She put her car in park and got out and looked around. It was a modest looking, pastoral church: a red and white brick structure no bigger than a two-story walk-up. The service had probably been underway for some time because she could hear the music all the way across the street, however, she could see that there were still a good number of people who were entering, so she didn't have to feel self-conscious about interrupting anything. Even so, Allyson couldn't help feeling somewhat on edge, as she didn't know what to expect.

She smoothed down the front of her designer pink and gray, tweed suit, adjusted the strap on her leather purse and tipped her matching felt hat with tweed bows and proceeded to cross the street to the entrance of the church. When she got there, she wasn't about to take her four-inch, flesh colored, patent leather, platform pumps to the stairs, but walked up the wheelchair access ramp. Upon opening the door, she was jolted by the loud music and the stage lights that were being used to light the sanctuary. It would have been enough to send her back out had she not seen a familiar face that confirmed this was indeed the place she was looking for.

"Praise the..."

Allyson could tell he was shocked to see her and it made her feel at ease and more in control. She liked shocking people.

"Hi, Allen," she said giving him a sly smile and taking the program he held in his hand. "Would you know where my brother is?"

"He's over by the altar, performing in the band. He always plays guitar for us on first and third Sundays," said Allen pointing to the area where Tim was.

Allyson followed the motion of his hand with her sea green eyes that finally happened upon her brother in the midst of the worshippers. She couldn't help but feel embarrassed when she saw him totally absorbed in his task.

"Yes, I see," she said after swallowing hard. "So where do you all sit?" she said trying hard not to show how uncomfortable she was.

"We usually sit up front when we're not on duty. I'll show you."

Allyson grabbed his arm and Allen led her down the aisle. As they walked along, it seemed like a lot of the other members were losing their minds. They had passed some woman vehemently banging her tambourine while doing some type of crazy dance.

Then there was a man who was doing what looked to be the same kind of babbling that her mother told her Tim had done at the hospital. He had his head back and he was crying with his arms stretched out in the air, palms upward. There were a few rational looking people who were sitting or standing and just clapping their hands but the majority of these religious devotees looked to her as if they were high on something. There were even people in the choir that had lost it. The atmosphere in the church was unnerving, indeed. "What the hell has Tim gotten himself into? What have I gotten myself into?" she thought while holding tightly onto Allen's arm.

Allen stopped when they had reached a pew that was the third from the front row.

"Here we are."

Allyson was astonished. This had to be the worst row yet. Every single person there was going crazy, especially, the older woman on the end who had even taken her shoes off.

"Are they...okay?"

"Yeah," said Allen giving her a funny look. "They're just praising the Lord."

Allen left her there to take her seat, but Allyson was still hesitant. None of them seemed to have noticed when she approached, and she was actually glad about that. She took a seat at the end of the pew farthest away from them, leaving several spaces between them. Allyson couldn't help staring at them as they engaged in what she considered to be such wild behavior. The older woman was starting to run back and forth near the aisle. There was also an older man who was bent over and looked like he was running in place. There were even some younger people in her row that looked like they could be Tim's age. They were probably his friends. One young man was swaying back and forth on a crutch, crying while another was dancing next to him. Finally, just over from them, were two young women who were almost as bad as the older woman on the end. The first was a taller woman in a pants suit with a huge afro, with what looked like a tea cozy attached to it with a hairpin. The other was much shorter and prissy looking in her three quarter sleeve foulard print secretary dress with a pleated skirt and decorated with a bow tie at the neck.

"Hallelujah! Glory to Your name! Praise you Jesus!" the shorter woman called out in a loud voice.

Allyson felt like she recognized this woman's voice. She could barely see who it was because the woman was wearing a cloche hat and had her hair swept forward which obscured her features. Allyson moved forward just a bit to get a better look at her. Now she was able to recognize who she was. "Not the crazy midget girl!" she thought. Allyson moved back to the end of the pew and tilted her hat to the side so the midget girl wouldn't be able to recognize her. Then she sat back and perused the program Allen had given her. It seemed the service went from 11:00am until 2:00pm. Allyson checked her watch: it was only 12:00pm – there were still two more hours to go. "Good gravy!" thought Allyson "I only hope it doesn't get worse. If they start some kind of cult ritual stuff, I'm outta here!"

After a while the music stopped and the service settled down. Some guy came up to the Altar to announce a meditation period and Allyson was thankful for that. The loud music and shouting parishioners were starting to give her a headache. During the meditation period someone sang a solo and the rest of the church was quiet, with the exception of a few members who called out ever so often- or praised the Lord, as Allen described it. After the meditation period was over a really tacky looking older woman came to the altar to welcome people. Just like the rest of the people in this church she was all drama. She had an enormous purple satin hat with huge white taffeta flowers reminiscent of something from the Victorian era. That combined with her purple silk floral print beaded dress made her look ridiculous from Allyson's point of view. "Now I know why Tim likes it here. He probably feels right at home amongst his own kind," she mused. After the tacky woman left, some guy came up and announced different events that were sponsored by the church.

Now it was starting to resemble a normal church service. "The sermon will probably be next – boring!" She could already feel her eyelids growing heavy with fatigue. She knew the next time she came on a scouting mission to Tim's church she would have to forgo drinks with Jason, with whom she was on more than friendly terms again, now that he had gotten rid of the boho chick he was with. Allyson sat back and leaned her head to the side into the corner of the pew. After a while she, began to zone out in her own thoughts. "I should be safe so long as I keep a low profile," she thought to herself as she yawned deeply. "When the service is over, I'll just grab Tim and get out of here before anyone notices. With any luck I'll never have to come back."

*****

"Allyson. Allyson!"

She heard someone calling her. It was probably Courtney.

"Just go ahead of me, I'll shower when you're done," said Allyson still half asleep. She had forgotten where she was.

"Allyson!!!" said Tim, shaking her.

"Oh!"

Allyson awoke with a start to see her brother and his friends surrounding her. She noticed her hat had fallen from her lap as well as her purse and scrambled to pick them up with several of the gentlemen assisting. Then she stood up, adjusted her hat, and smoothed out the creases in her suit.

"It was a very long service, I must say."

"Allyson, what are you doing here?" asked Tim looking bewildered.

"You invited me, duh."

"And you said you would never set foot in here."

"I've a right to change my mind. Aren't you going to introduce me to your friends or are we just going to stand around and stare at each other?"

"These are my friends, Davis Martinez, Jim Reid, Chris Lodon and you already know Allen and Tamiko. And this is Allen's cousin Riley Sharpe. Everyone this is my sister, Allyson."

They all greeted each other stiffly and they were all looking at her as if she just dropped out of the sky, her brother in particular. She knew Tim was probably trying to figure out why she was here and she was trying to think of a good explanation that wouldn't arouse his suspicion before he asked.

"It's nice to see the faces to match the names to. Tim has spoken very highly of all of you and this...institution. It's made me curious enough to want to come and see things for myself."

"That's nice to hear. Did you enjoy the service? I mean, the part you were awake for at least," said Allen.

"Sorry, but propaganda tends to have that effect on me. Oh – look at the time. It is rather late and I have more important things to do. Tim would you care to escort me to my car?"

"Of course. If you'll excuse me for a moment."

"Nice meeting you all."

Allyson grabbed his arm and Tim escorted her up the aisle to the door. Neither one of them said anything until they were outside the church doors.

"I am sooo glad that's over. I was afraid, I'd never make it out of there in one piece."

"Okay, so now do you want to tell me what this little visit is really about?"

"I already did. I really was curious to see what you do here."

"Allyson, please. I've known you and my mother long enough to know better."

Allyson had to give her brother some credit. Though he was a jerk, that didn't mean he was stupid. He was well aware that she despised him and would never spend any time with him unless his mother forced her or unless there was an agenda. There was no way Tim wouldn't have known what they were up to. She'd have to come at this with a totally radical approach – one that would give her a significant advantage, no less.

“Alright, I was sent to spy on you. Mother’s worried about the integrity of the Russell brand.”

“Not this again. Why can’t she just let me live my life?”

“Because being the only male with the Russell name, you’re the savior of our family,” she mocked. “Like you’re not enjoying this.”

“Believe me, I’m not. You don’t know how many times I wished you’d been born a boy just so she’d cut me a break.”

“Who knows? She just might anyway– depends on what I report back to her.”

“What do you mean?”

“Timothy, we can both make this work to our advantage. Our mother is determined to get information, which I am in a unique position to provide. Now I can relay information that portrays your activities in a favorable light or I can present information in a way that will increase her anxieties and subsequently her interference, hence, making your life miserable.”

“And what would I have to do to gain your so called assistance?”

“Just a small donation to the Allyson Russell fund every once in a while.”

“Not happening, sis.”

“Have it your way. Then I tell her exactly what’s going on and how you and these crazy people carry on like a bunch of chickens with the heads cut off. Maybe I’ll even say that your chief guru drugs people to make them act like that.”

"Say whatever you want. The way I see it, you need this escapade to carry on far longer than I do. Once your job has ended so will the stream of money that I know my mother is paying you. And don't try to kid me. I know you'd have nothing to do with this foolishness if it wasn't so."

"Would you rather she employ me or a real detective? Because if our deal doesn't work out she'll just hire someone far more insidious who can do way more damage at the expense of your precious little friends."

"Let me ask you a question, Allyson: would you rather be paid something or nothing?"

Tim had her in a corner and she hated it. Even when they were younger, he always knew how to pull the rug out from under her feet. She did need the bonuses her mother was giving her for this little escapade. At the same time, she didn't like the idea of helping Tim without getting something out of it in return.

"I don't like doing favors if its not worthwhile."

"I know. So I'll make this more palatable for you."

Tim took a pen out of his jacket pocket and a piece of paper. He started scribbling something on it.

"I have to get back to church because I have a Bible study to attend. In the meantime, I'm going to give you this," he said handing her the piece of paper when he'd finished writing.

"What's this?"

"It's the address to Allen's house. I want you to come to dinner there tonight. It starts at 5:30. Don't be late," said Tim as he began to walk back to the church.

"How do I know I'm not being set up to be an offering for some kind of crazy, ritual sacrifice?!"

"Don't be ridiculous!"

"I'm not coming!"

"You have to! It's part of your assignment!"

"I just wasted 3 precious hours of my time in that silly church and now he wants me to come to some stupid dinner," thought Allyson petulantly. Tim was right, though, it was part of her mission. Her curiosity also was beginning to get to her as well, as she began to wonder what she would learn or find when she went.

TWENTY

The Brotherhood Bible Study was well underway as Daniel was concluding a series of lessons called "Holding Your Vessel" or particular instructions on how men should walk in the Lord. The past couple of Sundays, he talked about the things they could do for their mental, and spiritual well-being and today they were to begin to talk about the physical side. Tim was trying to stay focused on the lesson at hand, but a part of him was trying to figure out what Allyson and his mother were up to. Most likely another plot to separate him from his God, his friends and the church since their first attempt while he was in the hospital in Baltimore failed. Thinking back on that incident, Tim really didn't want to have anything to do with either of them anymore. Now he understood that scripture that he'd heard Miko sometimes quote: the one about Christ being sent with a sword and how the father would be against the son and the son against his own father.[1] Maybe he needed to accept the fact that his family did not want to be saved and just let them go. But then he remembered that scripture that he'd read several days ago:

> 'Therefore if thou bring thy gift to the altar, and there rememberest that thy brother hath ought against thee: Leave there thy gift before the altar, and go thy way: first be reconciled to thy brother, and then come and offer thy gift'.[2]

At the time that he had read it, he pondered the possibility of reconciling with Allyson, but it just didn't seem possible. It wasn't that Tim was against reconciling with her. He'd tried in the past, but it seemed that nothing could get Allyson to put aside her anger toward him. He understood that a lot of the bitterness and anger that she directed toward him was due primarily to the circumstances they were born into: a family created out of an adulterous affair, with self-absorbed parents who were struggling with their own identity issues and couldn't invest much in their children. As such, Tim really didn't have much against her. However, he knew that there was something else. Allyson had something against him personally and it went deep. Whatever it was, it was most likely the motivation for her involvement in his mother's latest shenanigans. But then he had another thought. "What if this is no coincidence?" It made him think back to how things worked out for him at work a couple of years earlier. Maybe this was a sign God had been working on their behalf, and that he should reach out to her. He'd have to pray to God to show him how. "In any case, we'll see what happens at dinner tonight," he mused before Daniel intruded on his thoughts.

"Tim?"

"What?"

"We were talking about the different ways a man can sin against or defile his body making it impure. Do you have any suggestions? Allen mentioned tattoos, piercings, and carvings, and Davis mentioned drugs and alcohol. I was wondering what you think we should add?"

"I'd say a poor diet. In the book of proverbs it speaks against gluttony and in Leviticus Moses spent a lot of time distinguishing between things that were clean and unclean to eat and there had to be a reason why God ordained that. I'm assuming that was for people's physical as well as spiritual health."[3]

"Good. We'll add that," said Daniel as he turned to write it on the whiteboard. "Now can anyone think of anything else?"

"All the men looked around at each other, but no one said anything."

"Now all the others seem self-explanatory, but I will add one more to our list."

Daniel wrote on the whiteboard in big block letters: FORNICATION.

"This is the biggest obstacle for some us brothers in our Christian walk," Daniel continued.

Tim slumped down in his seat and pulled at his tie. All of a sudden he felt hot and the air seemed a little thin. He felt like he knew whom Daniel was directing this part of the conversation toward, and wished he could disappear. Fornication was certainly a big issue for Tim who was used to having women for his amusement on a regular basis. Since coming to faith, he knew that what he was doing was wrong and had stopped cold turkey. The first six months weren't that hard since he was recovering from surgery and after that acclimating to his new job kept him busy, but then he started to get restless. It wasn't that he wanted sex – in fact, the longer he abstained, the less he wanted it – but he did miss having female companionship. After seeing Allen and Callie together and Tamiko pursuing Davis, he started to feel that maybe it was time to find a special someone for him. So Tim decided to date only girls from their church reasoning since the Pastor and most of his friends who frequented the church were true to their faith, everyone else would be as well. If that were the case, then the women at this church wouldn't be as much of a temptation as the average woman he'd meet in the city. At least that's what he thought.

One of those women he'd been interested in was Mya. She was beautiful, a good conversationalist, and she seemed to be just the kind of woman he needed to help him take his mind off a certain unattainable one who had managed to steal a good portion of his heart. They went on a couple of dates and things were pretty innocent – that is until they had dinner at his apartment one night. After dinner, she asked if she could use the bathroom, and Tim thought nothing of it. However, he was totally astonished when she came out without her clothes! It was weird because this hadn't ever happened to him before. He had no idea how to respond, except the way he used to.

Tim hated thinking about what happened that night. He felt so guilty about what happened afterward, that he felt he had no choice but to end the relationship with her. Little did he know how much drama would ensue from that one decision. Tim felt as if that was God's punishment for his sin. He knew it was wrong, but the problem was that he wasn't exactly clear as to why it was wrong. In any case, he just hoped Daniel would lecture and not call on him for his take on anything. He was the last person that could say anything on this topic.

"Just to be clear, do we all understand just what fornication is?"

"It's basically premarital sex," said Allen.

"Exactly. If you are not married and the woman you're with is not married, it's still wrong and you're defiling your body. Let's look at today's scripture reading."

Everyone read the scripture passage together. It basically, said that sex outside of marriage was corrupting the body. This was like saying that sex was evil. "But how could sex be evil if that was how people showed affection?" thought Tim. It was necessary to populate the earth, and he'd always been told it was a natural appetite just like hunger or thirst. So how could it be wrong? He wanted to ask Daniel, but he didn't feel confident about raising the issue.[4]

"So what do you guys think about what you just read?"

"I think its saying that as a Christian we have to even treat our physical bodies as a holy vessel because Christ lives in us and He's holy. Like the scripture says 'Be ye holy for I am holy.'[5] It's the Christ that's in us that we have to be aware of and respect. I think that's why he tells us in Romans, 'that ye present your bodies a living sacrifice, holy, acceptable unto God, which is your reasonable service.'[6] That's the life we are supposed to live and that's why Christ sacrificed Himself. But when we treat our bodies casually, and you're out there getting' yo' freak on, it's like treating Christ and his sacrifice like it's nothing," answered Davis.

"That's a good reading of it Davis and I like the way you referred to other scriptures to back up your points. I'd say I agree with you. Does anyone else have any revelations they would like to share?"

"I think it's defiling your body in that it's a sin, and we know all sin is going out of the will of God. In this scripture he tells us what his will is when he says, 'Now the body is not for fornication, but for the Lord; and the Lord for the body.'[7] I think he's saying our primary purpose is spiritual for God and not physical for ourselves. So when we go out of the Lord's will and get caught up in the physical part, we are going to suffer. If you think about all the consequences of premarital sex, there is a lot of suffering like all of the children born out of wedlock, the STDs that are passed around and just all of the jealousy and violence that can come from it. I think God wants to keep us from that. That's how He shows that He loves us and we honor that and glorify Him by honoring our bodies and submitting to His will. I think that's why it says in Corinthians 6:20, '...glorify God in your body and in your spirit which are God's" said Chris.[8]

"Word," said Brother Darryl, the oldest member of the group, "cause we belong to Him. That's why we submit, because once you are a Christian and Christ puts his Spirit in you, you are not under your own will any more, but you want to do what He wants you to do."

"Amen, brother" said Daniel.

Now Tim was starting to feel like he was getting lost, but he was afraid to ask any questions because he thought they would misinterpret his intentions.

"But hold on – I get what you guys are saying about how as Christians we need to live holy lives and honor God and all, but what does sex have to do with it? It just seems like you're saying sex is a bad thing," said Allen. "And if fornication is a sin, how come there's no commandment against it, like there is for adultery?"

As always, Allen was the man. Tim was grateful to him for asking the question that was on his mind and probably some of the others as well.

"Don't get me wrong brother. No one is saying that sex is wrong or bad, or that it should not be enjoyed. It's sex *outside* of marriage that we have to worry about. Even though there's no commandment against fornication, it is clear from our last reading in Deuteronomy, that fornication is not allowed.[9] In fact it tells us that the penalty for fornication was that you had to marry that woman and you couldn't ever divorce her.[10] If we really think about it, we understand that there's no commandment because it wasn't really necessary. It was well understood by the majority of people at that time how destructive fornication could be as brother Chris just told us."

"Even if the two people love each other and are consenting and are responsible about it?"

Tim thought he knew why Allen was taking that angle and he was interested in hearing what Daniel was going to say.

"I see where you're going with this Al, and I'm going to level with you. First, a lot of guys want to think 'well if I'm into her and I love her and she loves me, what's the problem?' I say, and I think God would agree, If you really love her, you offer her your life, not 15 minutes in the sack, or a couple of months as a bed buddy. So if you don't want to marry her, you probably don't love her. You might like her, but you don't love her."

"Wooah," said Allen, "I never thought of it like that."

Tim hadn't thought of it that way either.

"Secondly," continued Daniel, "there is no such thing as responsible sex if it is outside of marriage. None of man's methods of interfering with God's processes are foolproof. We all know condoms can break even when used properly and your girl's birth control can't protect against STDs. So as I said earlier, if you want to make a responsible choice, you get married and stay faithful to your spouse."

"But how are you going to know if you're in love unless you have sex?" asked young Brother Jerry who was the youngest guy in the group. He couldn't have been more than 19 or 20.

"Sex is not love, it is merely one way to express love. Love develops by spending time with a woman, talking to her, getting to know her, opening yourself to her emotionally, not physically. That's how a lot of guys get messed up: they get caught up in superficial stuff, like they think because the sex is hot, they must be in love."

"I been there," said Chris.

Everyone laughed. Tim had to admit to himself that he had been there a couple of times when he was younger.

"That's because a lot of us men don't really understand what the proper context for sex is. It's not a sport or a recreational activity as it's portrayed in the media and it has nothing to do with expressing manhood as we discussed previously in lessons on Godly manhood. Sex is the consummation of marriage or the physical manifestation of the commitment that marriage is. It is a part of the commitment in and of itself. When you have sex outside of marriage, it's like you're cheating on your future wife."

"I don't get it. How can you cheat on someone you're not married to yet?" Tim couldn't help blurting out.

"Look at it this way – Sex is supposed to be exclusive to marriage, so any kind of sex outside of that is breaking the pact. If you can't respect the sexual part of the commitment before you're married, you're going to have trouble respecting it afterward."

"So like if you take it out of context, you're abusing it and it loses its value?" asked Allen through a yawn.

"Exactly. It's like what some people do with drugs. Drugs can be great when they are used in the right way. But when you abuse drugs and you are taking them out of their proper use, not only do they lose their value, they can become harmful. With sex it's the same thing. When you engage in promiscuous behaviors you are dulling yourself physically and emotionally. Then when you finally do decide to settle down, you'll find you have a hard time achieving real intimacy, connecting to women or even experiencing physical satisfaction. That's what truly sabotages so many marriages."

"And I guess it would follow that the promiscuous lifestyle is not only harmful to ourselves, but to others, too," said Tim quietly.

"True. 'Cause we have to admit, when you're out there trying to game women to get in their pants you're doing it out of pure selfish desire and ego. Many of us try to play it off by saying that if the girl is down there's nothing wrong with it. But we should know that if a girl is willing to put herself out there like that then all we're doing is taking advantage of someone who obviously doesn't feel good about themselves and leaving them worse off than when they started. It's like seeing a man who's been beaten half to death and you come up and take a turn at hitting him just because you can. A real man, especially a man of God doesn't do that."

Tim couldn't argue with what Daniel was saying. Thinking about his past from this new perspective made him feel like the man-whore his sister often called him. It even made him hurt inside to think of what he had done to himself, and the other women he had been with. No wonder Allyson had very little respect for him. He definitely agonized about how his past might affect his relationship with that special woman he wanted to be with. Now he felt so unworthy of her, especially since he knew she was saving herself for her husband. Tim used to think he had so much to offer any woman, now he doubted if he had anything to offer at all. He knew that the woman he had feelings for expected a lot more than financial security and a hot night in the sack. But above all that, he was living for God and he knew that the old Tim wasn't the man He wanted Tim to be. Tim didn't want to be that guy anymore either. It made him think of his mistake with Mya again. He didn't want that to happen again. He wanted his life to honor God, every part of it.

"So let's say you've been living that lifestyle and you want to come out of that. You try to stop, but you find yourself doing things you don't want to do."

"That's our flesh, and as long as we are in these bodies, the Devil will try to use that to interfere with our walk with Christ, but we can't surrender to it. Instead, you have to surrender to God. In the

Romans it tells us, 'Know ye not, that to whom ye yield yourselves servants to obey, his servants ye are to whom ye obey; whether of sin unto death, or of obedience unto righteousness'[11]. You have to be obedient and you have to surrender everything to His will. Like brother Darryl said, you can't live by what you want anymore. It has to be what He wants."

"But how do you surrender?"

"You believe what God says and you do what he says from your heart because you love Him. You allow his Spirit to guide you instead of relying on your own will and desires. You don't question Him because you know that you can trust that He always has your best interests at heart."

"But what if you get into a situation with a woman that – from circumstances beyond your control – goes a little too far?"

"There are circumstances that are within our control that God will warn us about so that we don't have to get into the temptation or so that we can escape it. One thing that I don't do, as a man of God, is allow myself to get in compromising positions with the opposite sex. That means no dinner at my place alone, no romantic weekend get aways with just the two of us, no intimate touching, none of that stuff. I also will not date girls who dress too provocatively."

"For real, bro?" asked Brother Jerry.

"For real. When I court a woman, I take her out to a public place, we have a good time then I take her home and then I head back to my crib."

"Doesn't that take all of the spice out of the relationship?" said Brother Jerry.

"Not at all. But it does take out the superficial stuff that gets in the way of getting to know the lady you are courting. Like I said, a relationship is more than the way she kisses, or the moves she puts on you, or how she looks in her little black dress. It's about getting to know her as a person and finding out whether or not she would make a compatible spouse."

"I must say, brother Dan, you've given me a lot to think about," said Tim.

"That was the plan, brother. Looks like we're out of time for today. We're actually going to continue on this topic, next week. I want each of you to find some scriptures that show how Godly men respond to temptation in this area. Then I write down things you think you can do to prevent falling prey to this particular sin."

Tim and the others thanked Daniel for his time before they began to leave the little recreation room the class was housed in. Chris left with Daniel who was giving him a ride home. Davis, and Tim were getting ready to leave when they noticed that Allen was still sitting at one of the desks. He was fast asleep.

"Looks like we got another sleeper," said Tim.

"Hey, Al! Wake up!" said Davis.

"Hunh – what?" said Allen jerking out of his sleep.

"Bible study is over. Time to go home for dinner," said Davis.

"Oh, man. Give me a second, alright," said Allen stretching himself.

"Take your time, buddy," said Tim.

Tim took another look at his friend. His eyes were bloodshot and he looked as if he had aged ten years overnight.

"Al, are you ok?" asked Tim. It was weird seeing Allen like this. He was used to the strong vibrant Allen whose energy infected everyone else. It was jarring to see him so lifeless and worn.

"I'm good. Just a little tired."

"Law school that rough?"

"I'm managing."

"How much sleep did you get last night? Twenty minutes?" asked Davis.

"I got a couple of hours."

"What's a couple hours?" asked Tim.

"I crashed at 5:30, 6:00, something like that."

"And you had to get up for church at 8:00! That's like 2 hours!" said Tim.

"Like you've never done it," said Allen.

"Once, twice a month maybe, not on a consistent basis," said Tim.

"You need to cut back on something before you make yourself sick, Al," said Davis.

"I agree with Davis. You can't keep going like this," said Tim.

"C'mon, you don't have to be overly concerned. Once I get a hot meal in my stomach I'll be good to go," said Allen.

"Where? To the morgue?" said Tim.

“Oh, stop it. I think I remember a time not so long ago when a certain somebody was working real hard...”

“And not only did I take a vacation, but I also went to the doctor, just as you recommended. Remember?”

“I remember you took your own sweet time about it, too. Anyway, I don’t think my situation is as urgent.”

“Yet.”

“It won’t be. Now that Jim’s home I’ll have more time because I won’t have to go by the hospital anymore, so that’s going to give me an extra couple of hours right there.”

“I hope so.”

“Besides if I were you, I’d be more worried about what your sister was doing here today.”

“I know exactly what my sister was doing here – spying.”

“She’s spying right now, but you better hope it doesn’t lead to anything else. Your mom is scary, man – almost like a soap villain. You better hope this isn’t part of some elaborate plan they have to kidnap you and keep you locked in a secret room where they try to brainwash you into believing you’re someone else.”

“Please. My mom’s bark is much worse than her bite.”

“Oh, after what I experienced in Baltimore, I think her bark is bad enough on its own.”

"That reminds me, I think I should tell you that I invited Allyson to Sunday dinner. I hope you and your parents won't mind?"

"Are you for real? My parents won't mind, but I do. I can't imagine why you would want to do this to us?"

"Relax, I'll handle her. I'll have her sit next to me, and do damage control."

"You better, bro. My mom, Davis and Pastor are saints, and Miko, Jim, and I know how to hold our tongues, but your sister's mouth in the same room with my dad, Callie, Riley and Mother Rose? That's like a throwing a lit match in a dry forest."

"Sorry, Al, but I won't be there. I promised my mom that I would come down and have dinner with her. Then I got some other stuff I gotta take care of," said Davis.

"Sad to hear that man. We could have used the extra leveled head in the room. But I can't ask you to take time away from your mom," said Allen.

"Don't sweat it, Al. I been around girls like her. She probably won't start nothin' 'cause she won't be in her own territory. Know what I mean?" reasoned Davis.

"Exactly what I was thinking. She knows she's outnumbered, so she might behave herself, and if not, I'll apologize to everyone for her and take her home," said Tim.

"Alright, then. Let's go," said Allen.

"Sorry to put you out like this," said Tim.

"It's okay, man. It's like the Word says, 'All things work together..." said Allen.[12]

Tim was sure it would.

TWENTY-ONE

The dining room table was crowded with people and even though it was late October, it was stuffy and hot, so much so that Allyson shed her suit jacket and placed it on the back of her chair. The fare was very pedestrian: pot roast with roasted red potatoes and gravy, collard greens and banana pudding for dessert. None of it looked appetizing, as the meal seemed very calorie heavy, however it did smell good. Even so, Allyson found herself pushing the food around on her plate. There was no way she was going to eat collard greens – ever. The crazy older lady, who turned out to be Allen's mother, seemed to be a pretty decent hostess though. She was nice and she didn't mind catering to Allyson's special diet needs, like going to the store to get her the seltzer water and wheat crackers she wanted. In addition, the people weren't as loud as they seemed to be in church, which made Allyson feel less apprehensive. Everyone was talking and laughing, enjoying themselves and each other. Nothing like the dinners she'd experienced with her own family - the formal, rigid affairs, full of affectation yet lacking genuine affection. “Keep your guard up,” she reminded herself, “That’s how these cults get you. They make you feel like you’re family.” Allyson noted there were a lot of strange members in this family.

All of Allen’s family was here, including a cousin who looked like a throwback from the ‘70’s with her huge afro and some chick that Allen had for a girlfriend. There was the disabled broke guy whose name she forgot, the midget girl, her tacky, uptight mother and her guru dad. Allyson couldn’t believe the guru would condescend to have dinner with them. Most religious leaders that she’d ever read or heard about kept themselves aloof from their flock. Then again, maybe Allen’s parents had some type of high rank in their church’s hierarchy or something like that. Allyson was content to listen attentively to their conversations to see what she could glean about what went on amongst them. She learned that the disabled guy had just come home from the hospital, and was living with Allen and his parents so they could take care of him. Allyson however, found Allen to be the most distracting. She had always thought he was hot. She was tempted to make a move on him despite the fact that he was poor. Allyson could have cared less that he had a girlfriend. “It’s not like I wouldn’t give him back when I was done with him,” she thought. But she didn’t want to jeopardize losing Jason who was her ace right now. In any event, Allyson could see that Tim still had some kind of attraction to midget because every time she opened her mouth Tim looked her way. It made her wonder if they had ever slept together. Allyson went along making mental observations and notes in this fashion during their conversation at the table.

“Where’s Davis?” asked Tamiko.

"He said he was having dinner with his mother and then he had some things to do" said Allen.

"Oh."

"Don't worry, Miko. He'll probably be back with us next week."

"I'm not worried about it."

"As well you shouldn't. People should eat with their own families," said Mother Rose, "I would worry about someone who never ate dinner with his own family"

"Jim, I saw you in the congregation. Are you visiting or back for good?" asked Pastor Bynum.

"For good, Pastor," answered Jim.

"Sure am glad to hear that. Makes my heart feel good to see all these young people coming to the Lord."

"Amen, Pastor. I noticed the congregation's getting bigger. Mother Hardy said when she came late she and hers couldn't barely find three seats together," said Lena.

"Yes. Deacon Ford said we have about 50 new members, but they're mostly young people as the pastor said. Twenty-something," said Mother Rose.

"You say that like you sound disappointed Mother Rose," said Pastor Bynum.

"Oh, I know that we should be glad for any lost soul that finds the Lord, but I find the younger converts are not as dependable. They're a member one day and then gone the next. Especially after the doctrinal classes when they realize that membership within the body of Greater Apostolic Church of Christ means you must have a walk that's worthy of our calling. The Lord is not going to bless mess and neither will we," she responded.

"I wouldn't worry myself none about the ones that don't wanna do right, Rose. Like you said, they don't last. But we should pray for them just the same," said Vernon.

"Some of them leave. Then there are others that sit up in the church and cause confusion with their gospel rap, and all the dating around nonsense, which is nothing more than fornication. They don't even want to adhere to proper standards of dress. It's always these younger women coming to church in sundresses, skimpy skirts, and don't get me started on the ones wearing pants. It is written: the woman shall not wear that which pertaineth unto a man" said Mother Bynum looking right in Riley's direction.[1]

"Pastor, can I ask you a question?" said Riley.

"Of course," answered the Pastor.

"When the Bible says that a woman should not wear a garment pertaining to a man, do you agree that means women should not wear clothes that are made specifically for men?"

"Yes, that's what the language means."

"So if I'm wearing something that's made specifically for a woman, it's okay? Right?"

"Well, I would be inclined to say yes. A woman should wear what's made for a woman and a man should wear what's made for a man."

"Now if I buy an article of clothing to wear to church, or anywhere else for that matter, then that means I should buy from the women's department since those clothes are made for women. On the other hand, it would be wrong of me to buy clothes from the men's department because those are made for men. Right?"

"Can't argue with you so far."

"Therefore I think it can be safe to say that a woman should not wear men's pants to church. Would you agree Pastor?"

"Yes, I would have to agree, Rye" chuckled the Pastor.

"Pastor Bynum, I promise you, I will never wear men's pants to church or anywhere else, if I can help it."

Allyson, had to chuckle to herself at Riley's rebuttal to Mother Rose's invectives. Despite her awful fashion sense, Allen's cousin had wit and moxy. She could respect that.

"Looks like we might have another lawyer in the family," said Vernon.

"Pastor! Please do not encourage her. You and I both know very well that pants were originally designed for men only," said Mother Rose.

"So were hats, belts, shirts, and underwear," said Riley.

"Okay, let's talk about something else. We don't want to be like the Pharisees, now. Remember it's not what's on the outside that counts," said the Pastor.

"Still, the outside is a reflection of what is within," insisted Mother Rose.

"Mother, we will discuss this later," said Pastor Bynum.

"Allen, what's that you're drinking?" asked mother Lena as she studied the can next to Allen's plate. "That's a mighty small can for a soda."

"It's just an energy drink, mama,"

"You mean like those ones with all the caffeine?"

"Yeah, but this one's not as bad as some that are out there. I only drink them when I need to study"

"You better be careful, Al. Those things aren't good for you. There are other ingredients in there beside caffeine that can wreak havoc on your system," said Tim.

"I've heard they're no good for your heart, and with your history, you don't need none of that. Find strength in the Lord, and leave them so called energy drinks alone" said Lena.

"History? What's she talking about, Al?" asked Callie.

"When he was a baby, he had an irregular heartbeat," said Lena.

"How come you never told me this?" said Callie.

"Because it's a non-issue. That was a long time ago. I was a born premature. I had a lot of other things wrong with me then, but I'm fine now," said Allen.

"Never could play sports in school. Had to settle for chess club," said Vernon.

"C'mon, it can't be that bad, or they wouldn't put it out there," said Jim trying to defend Allen.

"They'll put anything out there if it makes money. From what I hear, some folks even dying from that mess," said Vernon as he dipped a chunk of potato in some gravy. "Allen, you gon' have to leave off that."

"But, those were people who had more than several cans at a time. I don't intend on doing anything like that."

"I mean it, Allen. That's yo' first and your last drink. If I see any of those things turn up in the fridge, they're goin' down the sink. You hear me boy?"

"I hear you," sighed Allen.

"Mr. Sharpe, Allen's a grown man, and you're treating him like a child," said Callie.

"Callie, it's okay. It's not a big deal," said Allen.

"Allen may be a grown man, but he's living in my house, which means what I say goes. Ain't that right Allen?"

"Yes, sir."

"I don't know what's wrong with you children today. I'm 53 years old, and I don't need no energy drink," said Vernon.

"In all fairness, Mr. Sharpe, Al's got a lot he's trying to manage, what with work, law school, church and..." said Callie.

"And a ready made family to boot," said Riley, interrupting Callie's defense. "Maybe you should drop some of your commitments, Al. I can think of one in particular," said Riley, sending a cold look Callie's way, before taking a sip of seltzer from her glass.

"Everybody, please! Just because I had an energy drink, doesn't mean my life is spiraling out of control. You're acting like I'm doing..."

Allen stopped mid-sentence and looked over at Jim. Allyson looked around. Everyone seemed to be uncomfortable. She wondered what it was all about.

"Just trust me when I say I'm handling things."

"Alright, we hear you. But remember you can't do it by yourself. Trust God to help you" said Lena.

"I will – I mean I am," said Allen.

"So Allyson, you haven't said much this evening. I hope you're having a good time with us," said Pastor Bynum to their guest taking the conversation into another direction.

"I'm not much of a talker," she said with a bit of a start. She didn't expect them to bring her into their conversation. "I like to think of myself as more of an observer of human behavior"

"I heard you got the chance to observe our service today. I'm curious to know what you thought of it"

"It's certainly was louder than any other service I've ever attended"

"Of course. The Bible says make a joyful noise unto the Lord.[2] That's what we do at our church. We praise him so that He knows how much we love Him and how grateful we are for His mercies toward us"

"It seems your god must have a hearing impairment,"

"Allyson!" said Tim, shooting an angry look her way. "I apologize Pastor Bynum"

"What?!" said Allyson.

"Father, forgive them for they know not what they do.[3] Or say," said Lena shaking her head.

"It's okay, Tim," said Pastor Bynum before returning his attention to his sister. "I guess you don't believe in God"

"No, I don't. I hope that doesn't offend you," she said.

"Young lady, we're not offended by your unbelief, but no matter what your beliefs are you need to respect ours, especially when you're in my house," said Vernon sharply. "Is that understood?"

For a minute she thought Poppa had come back to life in the form of Allen's father, their manner of reprimand being so similar.

"Absolutely – sir"

"Do you mind if I ask why you don't believe?" asked Pastor Bynum.

"If you must know, it's because I think the concept of god is an ideal just like good, love, fairness, truth, and justice. They're all concepts people made up when they started to form societies. Since man is feudal by nature, these ideals were created to moderate people's behavior so we don't live in a state of constant war. In reality there are only the strong and the weak. Weaker people invented concepts like good and evil and such to keep the stronger people from destroying them. The concept of 'evil' particularly is used as a boogey man to guilt stronger people into giving up their power for the sake of the weak. It's how the weak ensure their own survival," said Allyson with an air of smugness.

"Sounds like philosophy 101," said Tamiko. "A la Nietzsche"

"So lemme get this straight – you're saying if I decided to beat you down right now and take your wallet, it'd be okay because I bested you. Like because since I proved I'm stronger I deserve it, right?"

"I'm not sure you understand me," said Allyson. Given that Allen's cousin was taller and more muscular than herself, she felt that there needed to be some clarification.

"Oh, I think I do. You better be glad there are people who believe in those concepts you mockin', otherwise I'd have myself a cute little pink purse," said Riley.

"I was trying to explain that Right, Wrong, Good, and Evil along with all the other ideals are culturally relevant. They change from nation to nation, culture to culture, and from one generation to another. That's why there are so many different religions and that's why even the religions themselves change from one age to the next. They change along with the needs and power structures of societies," Allyson continued. It all seemed so obvious to her, and she believed there was no way they could refute her logical argument.

"Do you really think that's right, though? To change your morals based on what's expedient or on politics?" asked Allen.

"It's not about what I personally consider to be right or wrong. My feelings are irrelevant. It's what is," said Allyson defending her position. They were all staring at her as if she were to be pitied.

"Says who?" asked Pastor Bynum.

"Research has uncovered tons of anthropological evidence," said Allyson.

"Why should I trust their research? Man's been known to be wrong about things before. When my daddy was just a young boy, scientists and anthropologists had a lot of so called evidence to support the idea that African-American's were not human. Turned out they were egregiously wrong. Why should I trust them in this case? Who's to say this philosophy you've heard is a version of things that they're using to try to control people like me"

"I know what you're getting at. Your kind likes to believe in absolutes: you believe there is only one god, one standard for what should be considered right and wrong. You believe in absolute Truth. Absolute truth is a theory that's never been proven. Experience tells us that there is no such thing"

"So you don't believe in absolutes"

"Exactly. Absolutes can't be trusted because they can't be proven"

"And you are positively certain that there is no absolute truth. There could never ever be any other explanation, right? Is that what you believe?"

"Of course"

"Then you contradict yourself. You do believe in absolutes. You just believe that there is absolutely no such thing as absolute truth. I guess that means your idea can neither be proven or trusted"

Allyson sat shocked. Never had she had any religious person answer her in such a way before, but she wasn't ready to concede to the guru's argument.

"But it can't be proven. Evidence shows there's no such thing as Truth. If there was, then why do different peoples have their own versions of what Truth is supposed to be?"

"I'll tell you why: 'Because that which may be known of God is manifest in them for God hath shewed it unto them. For the invisible things of him from the creation of the world are clearly seen, being understood by the things that are made, even his eternal power and Godhead; so that they are without excuse: Because that, when they knew God they glorified him not as God, neither were they thankful; but became vain in their imaginations, and their foolish heart was darkened. Professing themselves to be wise, they became fools, and changed the glory of the uncorruptible God into an image made like unto corruptible man, and to birds, and fourfooted beasts, and creeping things. Wherefore God also gave them up to uncleanness through the lusts of their own hearts, to dishonour their own bodies between themselves: Who changed the truth of God into a lie, and worshipped and served the creature more than the Creator, who is blessed for ever. Amen'"[4]

"Amen, Pastor!" said Mother Rose.

"And what does that mean?" asked Allyson.

"It means that one thing all people have in common is that they have an awareness of and a desire to worship God. No matter where you go in the world, there isn't a culture that doesn't worship something. God created us with that desire and it is only when we worship the true and living God that we feel complete, whole, and satisfied. Unfortunately, many people have refused to worship Him as he is. Blinded by lust, power, selfishness, pride, fear or greed, they turn from worshiping God to various religions. Religions are man made and oftentimes man centered. They are a set of prescribed rituals and practices, nothing more. These rituals, in and of themselves, can do nothing for anyone unless they are tied to true faith in the One True and Living God and that faith is based on the sacrifice that his Son Jesus made. That is why even religions that claim to worship God can often be pagan in nature. Too many times people trust in a certain ritual or practice and not God himself. Their faith is about using the ritual to get what they want in order to fulfill their own desires and purposes, rather fulfilling God's will and purpose for their lives," explained the Pastor.

"Praise God, Pastor! Hallelujah!" said Mother Rose.

"But what about those of us who don't have a religion or believe in anything?" asked Allyson.

"Everyone believes in something, even the atheist and the nihilist. If you didn't believe something, you would have no belief to express. If you didn't believe in something, you'd have no reason to persuade me to believe anything other than what I believe. Atheists indeed have a religion and human intellect is their god. Their church is the university and their worship is debate and research," said Pastor Bynum.

"I will admit that you're a good debater, Mr. Bynum, however I'm still not quite persuaded," said Allyson, however, she could not help but to consider the words he spoke and where they came from. They were very powerful indeed, and she had to admit that she had exhausted her arguments, but Allyson could be as stubborn as her brother at times. She hated to admit that she was wrong even when it was proven to her, simply because she didn't like the fact that someone else could be right.

"I kind of figured, but I'll keep praying that one day God works through someone or something to change your mind," said the Pastor.

"I don't see why you keep browbeating her. I think we should respect her beliefs and leave her alone, rather than badger her into believing something that's more acceptable to you," said Callie.

"No one is trying to badger her. Just like for her to see things from a point of truth," said the Pastor.

"Exactly. How can he know the way of life and not share it with her? He wants to help her. That's what the preaching of the gospel is about, Callie," said Lena.

"How can you be so sure your way is the right way?" said Callie.

"Because the Bible says so!" said Mother Rose.

"Who says the Bible is right?" said Callie.

"God does! He's the One that wrote it!" replied Mother rose angrily.

"That's what you think! Where's your proof?!"

"Let me tell you something…" began Mother Rose.

"Now, Rose, just calm down. You can't get through to someone that way," said the Pastor.

"Honestly, how can you all be so hypocritical! You jumped down her throat when you felt she disrespected your beliefs, now you're disrespecting hers?!" said Callie who was becoming more and more emotional by the minute.

"You need to check your girl, Al," whispered Riley to Allen who just ignored her.

"Callie, that was not my intention," said the Pastor.

"I certainly wasn't offended," offered Allyson. She had no idea why this woman was getting so upset. It's not like they were all arguing and the dude was yelling at her.

"Exactly. Pastor Bynum wasn't disrespecting her. He was just explaining…" began Tim.

"So why did he express the fact that he wants her to change? As if she even needs to change? No one has the right to tell another person what they should or shouldn't believe," said Callie.

"Al, you better check her before Uncle Vern does it, southern style," warned Riley again, motioning to Allen's dad who was looking more irritated by the minute.

"Callie, calm down," said Allen taking hold of Callie's arm.

"No!" she said snatching away from his grasp, her eyes fixed on the Pastor. "You're supposed to be a man of God and yet you're being so mean spirited and narrow-minded!"

"Now hold on! I got to get up in this right now. There's a way to disagree without being disrespectful and you done crossed the line," said Vernon.

"I can't believe this! So expressing an opposing view is disrespectful?" said Callie.

"When you start calling people names and fixin' your mouth to tell somebody off it is. You don't ever have a right to get up in the face of your elders, especially if he's a man of God and he's in my house!" said Vernon.

"Vernon, it's all right, she's just..." began Pastor Bynum.

"I'm sorry pastor, but I don't think it is. Now, If you don't like what the pastor got to say, you can go to him on your own time and discuss it rational like you got some sense, but you sho' ain't gonna sit in my house and sass the Pastor like you his momma! And if you don't like what I'm puttin' down you can leave right now!" said Vernon.

"It would be my pleasure," said Callie before she stormed out of the dining room.

"Callie!" said Allen following her.

"Let her go, Allen! Let her go," warned Vernon. "I got a feelin' she come back in here, I'ma have to take my belt off! Some of these young folk today just don't have any manners."

"You took the words right out of my mouth, Vern. I can't believe the gall of that young woman!" said Mother Rose.

"You know what the Word say "For we wrestle not against flesh and blood, but against principalities, against powers, against the rulers of darkness of this world, and spiritual wickedness in high places," said Lena.[5]

"Amen," said Mother Rose, "And that's a devil if I've ever seen one."

"I wouldn't say that. She's just a lost and confused soul. Vernon, I was gonna try to talk to her," said the Pastor.

"Uhn-uh, some people don't want to talk, they just want to fight. I felt the zeal of Phineas welling up in me.[6] Wasn't no way I was gonna let that nonsense slide. Sometimes you just got to rebuke the devil."

"Pop Vernon's right, Daddy. That's just the way she is. I just feel sorry for her," said Tamiko.

"I am truly sorry for you, Lena. I have no idea what Allen could possibly see in her!" said Mother Rose.

"You and me both. Now I know how Isaac and Rebekah felt when Esau married those two Ishmaelite girls," said Lena.[7]

Now that the conflict had subsided, Allyson felt it was her cue to leave. She'd had enough excitement with these people for today. It was now almost 6:00 and there were things she needed to do for school.

But at least they were interesting, especially the afro-girl, and Allen's dad who seemed to be the reincarnation of her beloved Poppa.

"I hate to interrupt, but it is getting rather late and I have school work I have to finish," said Allyson.

"Oh, but you haven't had dessert yet. Do you want me to fix you a serving to take home?" asked Lena.

"That won't be necessary. I think I'm quite full."

"Are you sure? I noticed you didn't have much to eat. I hate to have people walk away from my house hungry if I can help it."

It seemed as if Mrs. Sharpe was actually trying to show some type of motherly concern for her. While her manner seemed quite inviting, Allyson was wary if she should trust it.

"No, thank you, Mrs. Sharpe. I'll be fine."

"I'll walk you to your car," said Tim.

"Okay, then. Goodnight dear and God bless you," said Lena giving her a hug – a real hug. Not the stand off-ish pats her mother gave. Allyson was startled by such an endearing gesture from someone she'd only known for a few hours.

"Goodnight, Mrs. Sharpe."

All of the others bid her farewell and Mrs. Sharpe made her promise to have dinner with them again before Allyson and Tim left.

"Your friend, Callie, has issues."

"Tell me about it. Nothing like you were expecting, was it?"

"No. They're not as big a freak show as I'd hoped. Still strange none the less."

"Will we be seeing you next Sunday?"

"If my investigation warrants it. I feel I've seen a lot already."

"Remember it's to your advantage to extend your research. I'm sure our mother can afford it."

"Like I said. We'll see."

"Allyson."

"What?" she asked peevishly.

"I'm glad you came."

Allyson closed her car door, put the car in drive and drove off. She didn't care how Tim felt one way or the other. The only thing that mattered to Allyson was her own agenda. So far, there seemed to be nothing really dubious about the people that her brother was hanging around. Honestly, they didn't seem to be a cult, either. Most cult churches were members only and did not appreciate visits from outsiders unless they had been halfway convinced before they showed up. The fact that they tolerated Allen's agnostic girlfriend, and even her own views were indications that the church was just what it was – a church. Overall, they just seemed like as bunch of folksy, superstitious, people who were really enthusiastic about worshipping their god. It all left Allyson puzzled. What would Tim want with these people? Did he also think Mr. Sharpe was like Poppa? He was a very country version of Poppa though. Maybe Tim was attracted to these people because they were like a real family. Even she had to admit that although they were a bit strange, they were not as bad as the mess of loosely connected people that she had to call family. The only way she was going to find out what Tim was doing here would be to spend more time with him and the rest of them. So far things hadn't turned out so bad. They weren't obnoxious people. Allyson didn't mind the prospect of being around them just so long as she didn't have to become one of them.

TWENTY-TWO

Callie walked quickly down 153rd and Broadway in the area known to most as the polo grounds. After working a double-shift at the emergency, Callie was able to get off work early and decided to take advantage of this opportunity to continue her investigation. After that dinner fiasco, Callie was determined to try to get Allen away from as many bad influences as possible, but she had to be patient and deal with one thing at a time. First, she had to work on breaking his connection with Jim. She'd worry about his domineering family of religious zealots later.

It had been a long time since she'd lived in the projects around here with her mother. It had been dangerous back then during the height of the crack wars, and had only become marginally less so after the Giuliani reign of terror of the late 90's. But Callie was known in these parts; she had connections and she felt this afforded her some protection in such a dicey neighborhood. She had partied with a lot of different people from these parts during her high school years, and remained on good terms with them, no matter what happened to them. Some of the cool guys ended up becoming drug dealers, and some of the 'fly girls' ended up on welfare with a couple of kids. There were some that ended up strung out, but she never allowed her own marginal success in life to cause her to look down on them. Callie knew that in America, any success a black person enjoyed was tenuous at best and a job loss or health crisis could throw her into the same kind of situation – just like the friend she was looking for right now.

It hadn't been that long since she'd seen Valerie, though nowadays most people called her 'Spade', which was shortened from "the Queen of Spades", because she used to know how to hustle at the epynonymous card game. Sometimes Callie would see Spade when she took the subway home from work instead of driving. The last time she saw her was a couple of weeks ago in the train station at 125th Street and Broadway where the 1 train ran. Spade was standing at the far end of the platform, looking dazed and confused, and holding a box full of raffle candy. She had on a dirty, short cut, brown wig, and a cheap-looking, revealing outfit that was stained. When Callie stopped to say hi, she found Spade was trying to sell the candy. She was probably trying to make some money on the side, since her pimp was probably taking most of the money she made as a prostitute. Callie bought several bars. Although it was very likely that Spade was going to use the money to get high, Callie still wanted to show her old acquaintance some support.

No matter how many times she'd seen her it was hard for Callie to believe she was looking at the same Valerie Taylor: the girl that every girl in the Essex Houses wanted to be. She was beautiful, popular, and she had a little after school job at a trendy retail chain, which helped her to be able to afford nice clothes. Finally, she had every boy on the block wanting to be her boyfriend. She went to a different high school than Callie, but they knew each other because they had been neighbors in the same building. Valerie and her mom were always having a party and Callie was always invited. When Valerie wasn't partying, she was at the club, and she usually invited Callie to go along with her. At the clubs, guys always flocked to her, but then would pretend that Callie was invisible. When Valerie saw how they were treating Callie, she would check them and let them know that guys who disrespected her friends would not be getting any attention from her. "What happened to you, Val?" Callie wondered about her friend.

It might have begun that day when she knocked on Callie's door asking to use the phone to call a cab because her mother had just put her out. It was strange because up until that point, Val and her mom had always been the best of friends. Val had told Callie she was going to stay with her father, but it wasn't a few months later that she saw her going into a park restroom with some shady looking dude.

Callie shuddered, and she couldn't tell if it was the cold wind or the memory. She buttoned the front of her jacket and tied the belt tight to keep the cold out and picked up her pace. Callie had to move quickly. She only had a short window of time before she had to pick up Darius from daycare. Callie slowed her walk when she got to the area where she knew the local drug spot was in. She stopped at the block before it and kept an eye out. She didn't know if there were cops watching, and she didn't want to be mistaken for a regular customer. Since there was a bus station nearby, Callie thought it prudent to continue her stake out from there, so as not to arouse anyone's suspicions about what she was doing. There would be three buses that came and went before she spotted the object of her interest.

As suspected, Spade was leaving the spot and heading down the street. Callie got up from her perch and followed her until she was near a run down shelter on 151st Street. Callie tried to make it seem like a chance encounter, by bumping into her from behind.

"Oh, excuse me," said Callie, as Spade turned around to see what had hit her.

"Cal?"

"Spade?"

"Hey girl! How you doin'?" said Spade giving her a peck on the cheek.

"I'm good. And you?"

"Still goin'. You still a nurse'?"

"Yeah. I got off early today, and I was rushing to pick up my son. Sorry I bumped you"

"Oh, that's alright as long as it's you. How's your baby boy? Last time I saw you, you said he was getting' big."

"Yep, and he's walking and even doin' some talking, now. Already had his first birthday."

"Really?"

"Yes."

"Ain't that somethin'. Time flies, don't it? Seem like yesterday we was hanging out at the clubs."

"I know."

Spade looked out into space for a moment, and her smile faded. She looked down at her clothes and the looked at Callie's before staring at the ground.

"Well I don't want to keep you, I know you have to go, so..." she said turning away.

"Before you go, I wanted to ask you something?"

"What?"

"Do you know a guy named Chris Lodon?"

"Chris...Lodon?" she said looking confused, "I don't know...what he look like?"

"Tall, kinda fair-skinned, kinda thin, real soft spoken..."

"Maybe. I'm not sure," she said peering at her narrowly with mistrust. Callie understood what she was doing. It was the code of the street: you don't put anybody's business out there to just anyone without gauging the person's motive. Now it seemed obvious to Callie that she knew who Chris was, and had been close enough to him to want to protect him. In order to get Spade to trust her, Callie knew she would have to be creative.

"It's just that he goes to the church my boyfriend goes to and he hangs with us sometimes. He mentioned you the other day, and I told him I see you 'round the way sometimes. He told me to say hi if I saw you again," said Callie, hoping this bluff would pay off.

"Oh! I know who you talkin' bout now! You talkin' bout Way-lo – at least that's what we used to call him 'round here. How's he doin'?"

"Good, good."

"Yeah, he told me before he left from 'round here, he got saved. He asked me if I wanted to move into his building downtown and join the church and all that, but I need to be close to my job, you know. Besides I don't have time for church folk and all that."

"I get it. I'm not into church either, that's my boyfriend's thing."

"Tell Chris I said come see me. It's been a while."

"I will," said Callie who was a little disappointed. It seemed their interview was ending and so far, the only thing she learned was that Chris was indeed a drug addict from around this area. But she needed to find out his connection to Jim.

"One more thing, Spade," said Callie, hurriedly "Was there another guy that used to hang with you all? Somebody named Jim?"

"Nah, I don't know nobody named Jim? Whenever me and Way-lo – I mean Chris, used to hang out, it would be me, him, Passion, Dray, Boots, and maybe Gizzy and Ol' School if they wasn't locked up."

"You sure? Because the guy seemed to be from round here. They were talking about some guys named Smoke and Bricks."

"Word?"

"Yeah, somethin' about how they died."

"Nah, they got put down. Bricks got shot up in that warehouse off from Riverside with this other dude named Jay. They was in the game – workin' for Smoke. Smoke got away but he didn't get far because the cops found him dead in his car over by the Manhattan Bridge."

"Who's Jay?"

"I just tol' you. He was one of the guys workin' with Smoke. He was a skinny guy - maybe your height, or a little bit taller, with a dark brown complexion and a goatee. Kinda look like Sean Wayans back in the day, but a little darker. He was crazy as hell."

Callie knew exactly who she was talking about. The description fit Jim perfectly, with the exception of the 'crazy' part. Now she was onto something.

"Really?"

"Chris used to buy from them when he was usin', but Jay would do him dirty. He'd do Chris a favor and then turn around and beat the hell out of him – for no reason. That n**ga used to beat Chris like a slave. Jay had some serious problems. But he got it back. I think he might've died, too. I didn't hear nothin' 'bout no funeral, but I don't think he had any kinda family to even have one. Shame," said Spade.

"Yeah. It is. Oh, my goodness," said Callie as she checked her watch "I have to go get my baby. I would love to keep talking but..."

"Don't worry about it, girl. I gotta be someplace myself. I'll see you around."

"See ya, Spade."

"Oh, and remember to tell Chris, to see me."

"I will."

Callie headed back up the street to her car with a confidence she hadn't known for a while. Callie had always known that there was something that wasn't right about the whole situation Jim had been involved in. Now she knew that Jim was not just a user, but he was a dealer, and a ruthless one, based on Spade's account. No wonder Chris was so quick to keep Jim's past a secret. The guy was probably scared to death. The thought sent chills down Callie's spine.

All these years she thought she knew Jim. He was the last person she would have suspected to be involved in the game at that level. How could the guy that she had always known to be so compassionate and caring engage in violent acts of brutality against another human being? Yes, she knew he was on a treacherous path, when they ended their relationship, with the drugs and the drinking but she never thought he would have sunk to such a level. It made her wonder if he had gotten to the point where he was actually involved in a murder. The very thought made her neck tighten with apprehension. Then she thought about the argument they'd had at the hospital. It made her angry to think about how Jim tried to put a moral guilt trip on her that day. "He has the nerve to talk about how I'm scheming after everything he's done," she seethed. There was no way that she could allow Jim to have any part in her son's life. She didn't even think it was a good idea for Jim to be a part of Allen's life anymore – whether Allen liked it or not. Given this new information, Callie felt something had to be done.

Callie would have to proceed carefully. "Jim may indeed be as crazy as Spade says he is," she thought. Maybe the death of his mother, and his derailed career aspirations were just too much for him to bear. The last thing she wanted to do was to set Jim off in such a way that would trigger any violent proclivity he had. She didn't want Allen or her child to be hurt because she had provoked Jim to do something self-destructive. Callie would keep her cards close to her vest and she wouldn't show them unless she absolutely had to. In the meantime, she would have to think of a solution. She would have to find a way to get rid of Jim, but she would need to enlist his cooperation in order for the plan to work.

Then as Callie sat down in her car and started the ignition, the idea popped into her head. It was brilliant. Not only would Jim go for it, she had no doubt that his whole family, even Allen would agree to her idea. She couldn't wait to pick up Darius and get home so she could call Allen to see how he felt about it. If he went along, then she would have Allen be the pitchman because she knew his family was starting to dislike her – intensely, and they would be more inclined to go along if they thought it was Allen's idea. If all went well, Jim would be out of the picture before Thanksgiving.

TWENTY-THREE

"How was class?" said a voice as Allen walked through the door. He thought everyone had gone to bed, but noticed a light in the corner by the kitchen door. It was Jim. He had been reading his Bible and was waiting up for him. However after everything that had happened to him today, Allen was not in the mood for company. He still had a lot of work ahead of him for tomorrow's class and he was exhausted. It was 10:30 and all he wanted to do was sleep, but that was not an option.

"Like always," he said followed by a long yawn.

"Mom left your dinner in the stove."

"I know."

"If you need to study, I can sleep on the couch tonight. Mama Lena already made it up for me."

"I won't put you out, man."

"You're not putting me out. I'd rather anyway cause it's hard getting around in that tiny room with my crutches and everything. So don't worry about keeping me up alright."

"Okay. If that's what you prefer."

"You alright, man. You don't seem like yourself."

"It's just been a long day. I'm gonna take my food upstairs so I can get a head start on tomorrow's lesson."

"Alright. Good night, Al."

"Night, Jim."

Allen went to the kitchen and got his tin foil wrapped dinner from the oven and put it on a serving tray that was on the counter. He then headed upstairs to his room trying to manage the book bag and the tray. When he got to his door, he had to put the tray down in order to open it. Then he took it up once again along with the bag and went inside where he put his tray on the desk and turned on his lamp. Afterward he went over to his book bag and pulled out a paper from inside the front compartment and sat on his bed as he stared at it. It was a midterm exam that had been given in his contracts class. Most law school professors didn't give midterms or papers. A student's grade was based on the end of year final and participation in class discussions. This particular professor decided to be magnanimous and give a midterm to allow the students to see how they were faring in the course. Allen couldn't get over the red 'C' that was on top of the paper. He had never in his life seen a grade this low on any exam he'd taken – ever. What made matters worse, was that at the graduate level, a grade like this was not a passing grade. A 'C+' was barely passing. Allen was filled with confusion, shame, and dread. There was no way that he could tell any of his friends or family about this. "I'm flunking law school and I just started. How in the world could this be happening?" Allen wondered.

When he went to office hours after class, the professor explained that he needed to develop a more panoramic view of judicial precedent when making application to modern contexts. After their conversation, Allen totally understood what the professor was saying. However he wished he had more time to fully digest what he was reading. Allen spent most of his study time cramming, and he felt he understood very little of anything. Attending study groups helped at lot because when he was able to exchange outlines with others he could see some finer points of the law that he had missed, but he would have to go more often than he did if it was going to really be effective for him. The problem was always time. There was never enough time.

Allen had re-tooled his daily plans so many times that they didn't make sense to him anymore. He had worked with Mr. Hardy to negotiate a new 30-hour workweek from his old 45-hour week. Then he cut out his morning and evening devotions, and reading his Bible was limited to Sundays when he read along with Pastor Bynum and when he prepared for the Brotherhood Bible study class. At first, Allen felt convicted about sacrificing his time with the Lord, but then he began to look at things differently. "After all, if law school is in his plan for me, He knows how time consuming it is and He would want me to do my best," Allen surmised. He couldn't even fathom compromising his time with Callie and Darius, even though his friends and his family were constantly telling him they were a distraction. "How can I neglect the woman I say I love or her child? I don't think God would be pleased if I did that," Allen further rationalized to himself, "I barely spend enough time with them as it is." At any rate, Allen was still giving time to the Lord. He said his prayers in the morning before he left for work and again before he went to bed. He was serving in the church, ushering on first and third Sundays and he was in the brotherhood Bible study. He was giving a lot of time to the Lord, even if it wasn't as much time as he used to. Still, Allen needed to find more time if he was going to bring up his grades. He needed time for study groups, but where was the time going to come from?

It was now 10:45. Allen couldn't waste any more precious time with his thoughts than he already had. He took out the contracts textbook and the accompanying case study book that he had for the class and set them on the desk next to his dinner with a yellow legal pad. Then he unwrapped the foil from the plate he'd brought upstairs: turkey meatloaf with rice pilaf and green beans. Allen took a bite of each entrée on the plate, before reaching into his bag again to bring out a bottle of water and an energy drink. Allen knew that his family would kill him if they found out, but he felt they were being overly dramatic. "I'm a grown man and I know what's best for me. A little energy drink never hurt anyone. It's like soda with a little extra kick. Anyway it's not like I'm doing drugs," Allen reasoned.

Allen opened his book to the page for tomorrow's reading began taking notes, alternating attention between his meal and the work in front of him. He would only stay up until 2:00 am so he could get enough sleep to get through the day. Allen had barely gotten a few notes jotted down before the sound of his phone interrupted his flow. He stopped what he was doing to check to see who it was. It was Callie. He had to take it. "She wouldn't be calling this late unless it was important," he thought as he answered his phone.

“What’s up? Is everything okay? Darius isn’t sick, is he?”

“No, everyone’s fine on this end. I know it’s late and you’re probably busy, but I just wanted to check in with you. I called earlier, but I guess you got out of school late today, hunh?”

“I had to go to my professor’s office hours. No big deal. What’s on your mind?”

“Just wondering how things are going between you and Jim. I know it’s a lot trying to work, go to school, and entertain your best friend at the same time.”

“We’re fine. It hasn’t been a problem at all, so far.”

“Is he still depressed?”

“Somewhat from what I can tell. But I think being around family has been good for him. He was even reading his Bible when I came in. It’s gonna take some time, but I’m confident the old Jim will show up eventually.”

“That’s good to hear. I was worried that his emotional funk would start to rub off on you.”

“I hope you’re not about to go into another ‘Jim’s going to bring you down’ rant”

“I’m not. I was only thinking that he might be a little worried about having to start his life over. You said he lost his job at the MTA, and now he’s temporarily disabled and has no prospects for one.”

“Right now, he’s just worried about getting his casts off. We’ll deal with that other stuff when it comes to it.”

“But I was wondering if the city is such a great place for Jim to start over.”

“What are you talking about?”

“I’m saying with the high unemployment rate, and all the temptations here, maybe Jim could use a change of scenery.”

“You mean he should move out of New York?!”

“Don’t get so excited! No one’s suggesting he just go to some no-man’s land all by himself. He could go some place where he has family and friends.”

“And where would that be?”

“How about North Carolina? After all, you said your family is Jim’s family. I’m sure Riley and your other cousin’s would look after him. Plus, I’ve been hearing there are lots of job opportunities that are opening up down there.”

“I don’t know, Cal. Jim’s been gone for a long time. I was kinda looking forward to us just chillin’ like old times.”

“You’ll still have a chance to re-connect with him. I’m not saying he should go down south right away, or that he should never come back, but you can’t argue that he shouldn’t explore his options a little more.”

“And you’re sure this has nothing to do with putting distance between me and Jim’s corrupting influence.”

“I was thinking about what would be best for both of you. You do have three more years of law school to go, and you have enough to worry about as it is.”

“Callie, it’s not like I’m trying to help Jim all by myself. My mom is here, so is my dad...”

"So you're saying that this new adjustment's been easy?"

Allen had to admit that it was going to take some time to get used to the new situation. Would it have been easier for him if Jim weren't there? Maybe. But Allen realized that when you're trying to be there for someone, it wasn't always going to be about what was comfortable for yourself. Jim was already trying to accommodate Allen's needs regarding laws school. Thinking about this made Allen feel guilty. He didn't want Jim to feel neglected by him or even worse, to feel like a burden. In addition, down south, Momma Shirley didn't work like his mother did, and Henry Junior was still in high school, so Jim would have a lot more company during the daytime instead of having to hobble around the house by himself, which he would have no choice to do once Riley left.

"O. K. Maybe you're right to consider it as an option."

"Do you think you might make the suggestion to him?"

"If things don't work out for him here, I will. But let's see what the Lord decides. Anyway, while I have you, how's Darius?"

"Good – He's even been trying to walk by himself now."

"Really? Man, I wish I was there to see him."

"Don't worry. I recorded it on my phone. I'll let you see it when you come over on Saturday."

Allen's heart sank.

"I wanted to be there when he took his first step."

"Allen, don't worry. Darius will have plenty more moments for you to be there for: like his first day of school, and his first time riding a bike. He's a got a ton of growing up left to do."

"I know."

"It's getting late and I don't want to hold you any longer. I know you have a lot of work to do."

"Yeah, you're right. I better be going."

"See you Saturday."

"See you."

When Allen ended the call, the time came up. It was now 11:30. He only had 3 hours left to study and he'd only gotten through 30 of his 250 page readings. Another thing that always worked against him was traveling back and forth between his place and Callie's place. He'd have a lot more time to spend with Darius and Callie if he lived there. If he lived there, he would be able to check in on them every day rather than once a week. He wouldn't have to worry about being interrupted by phone calls because he'd be there already. However he knew that he couldn't live with her without being married to her.

Then he considered what Daniel said during their Brotherhood Bible study meeting last Sunday: "If you really love her, you offer her your life, not 15 minutes in the sack, or a couple of months as a bed buddy." Allen knew he loved Callie, and she was definitely the woman he saw himself spending the rest of his life with, but he still had reservations. First, he wasn't sure how she felt about marriage. In the past, she'd suggested they move in together, but she never suggested marriage. The last thing Allen wanted to do was to scare her away with a proposal. Then there was the annoying little fact that she wasn't a Christian. Allen could not deny, considering after what happened at their last Sunday dinner, that she was any closer to becoming a Christian than she was when they started dating. It took him two hours to calm her down that Sunday evening and he had to be careful not to say one word about God in order to do it. It would take nothing short of a miracle to get Callie into the church.

"Lord, I need a miracle right now," Allen prayed out loud. There were so many things that weren't fitting together that he needed to fall into place. "This all has to work out somehow," Allen insisted to himself. He then opened his energy drink and took a long swig before directing his attention back to the work in front of him. "Everything will work out the way it's supposed to," Allen continued to reassure himself. He was certain that God would make everything work out the way he wanted. He just had to trust Him.

TWENTY-FOUR

The night was damp and foggy as Tamiko and Riley made their way up the escalator in the mall on 153rd Street. Looking from behind, Tamiko felt as if they were rising through a plume of smoke. However there was no heat, only a raw chill that tried to poke through her trench coat. They had come for some special art supplies that Tamiko needed for a class project the next day. When Tamiko looked over at her cousin, she couldn't help noticing the annoyed expression on her face.

"I promise, I'll only take five minutes. I know what I need and where I can find it,"

"Don't they have the same discount store in Harlem?"

"They do, but they don't have googly eyes or pipe cleaners which I really need right now."

"Alright," she huffed resignedly.

They went inside and Tamiko got a basket from the area where the carts were. Tamiko was trying to make their trip as quick as possible, since it was late and she still had some work to do for school. She quickly made her way down to Aisle 7 where the arts and craft supplies were and picked up several bags of the googly eyes and pipe cleaners.

"Are you sure that's going to be enough?"

"I'm just buying enough so I don't have to come back again."

"Please tell me they're going to reimburse you for all that."

"I'll get some of it back."

"I could definitely not be a teacher."

"Do you think there's anything you need while we're down here?"

"I don't really need anything, but I wouldn't mind stopping at that food court to get a snack afterward...that is, if you don't mind."

"Of course I don't, but I can't believe you're still hungry. We just had dinner before we left."

"You know I can't live off those skimpy portions your mama serves."

"She's just trying to be health conscious."

"Funny, I thought she was being cheap."

The store wasn't crowded so the lines weren't very long. The ladies were able to make their purchase rather quickly before heading to the food court. They were halfway there when Riley's sharp eyes spotted someone familiar sitting at one of the tables.

"Wait a minute," said Riley stopping in her tracks, "Isn't that Davis?"

Tamiko also stopped as soon as she heard his name.

"Where?" she asked as she began to look around.

"Right over there at that table in the corner where the pizza stand is"

Tamiko scanned the area carefully. Then she recognized his trademark fade and work clothes. She also noticed that he was sitting with an olive-skinned, Latina woman with long dark brown hair, wearing a dark suit. They both had coffee and it looked like they were in the midst of deep conversation.

"Stand over here so he can't see us," whispered Tamiko as she pulled Riley into an aisle full of bakery goods. Even from where she and Riley were standing they could still see them. Tamiko could hear snippets of their conversation, but they were speaking in Spanish.

"I wonder who she is?" said Tamiko.

"Me, too. You want to go over and say hi?"

"Absolutely not! He'll think I'm stalking him. I'm supposed to be giving him space, remember?"

"Doesn't look like he needs so much space now. I told you he was no good."

"We don't know what that's all about."

"It'd be a lot easier to find out if they weren't speaking Spanish."

"She could be a relative for all we know."

"Girl, please. She don't look nothin' like him."

"Not all relatives look alike. Tim doesn't look a lot like his sister."

"Still, I think you should go over there. I'm not sayin' you should make a scene, but you need to let him know that you know what he's up to."

"He may not be up to anything. Let's go," said Tamiko who was beginning to feel uncomfortable. "I don't want him to see us and think we're spying on him." She turned away from the scene, not knowing what to think of it.

"Why are *you* feeling guilty? It's not like we followed him here from his job. It's called a chance encounter. If he's not up to anything, he shouldn't mind running into us."

"Their conversation looks pretty intense."

"So he won't mind us interrupting it," said Riley grabbing her arm and pulling her out of the aisle where they were hiding.

"Riley, no!"

"C'mon girl, you know you want to. You just as nosey as I am."

"Riley, stop! This isn't funny!" said Tamiko snatching away from her.

"I'm not playing. You need to let this dude know what time it is," she said grabbing hold of her arm again.

"I don't even want him to know I saw him here."

"Too late, he's seen us. Let's go," said Riley who continued to pull her forward.

Tamiko looked over and saw Davis looking at them. As their eyes met, Davis's face went pale. The girl he was with didn't notice and was still speaking rapidly in Spanish. However she stopped when she noticed Davis looking over her shoulder.

"Hi, Davis" said Tamiko forcing a smile.

"Hey" he said. He didn't look like he was happy to see her at all. Neither did his guest. In fact the girl looked as if she had been crying.

"Didn't know I'd run into you here. Riley and I were picking up some supplies, when she noticed you from across the aisle," said Tamiko.

"She gotta name?" asked Riley.

"This is Stephanie. Stephanie this is my friend Tamiko and her cousin Riley," said Davis languidly.

"Nice to meet you Stephanie," said Tamiko.

"Nice to meet you, too" she said, shaking Tamiko's hand weakly and avoiding her eyes. Then she returned her attention to Davis. "Look, it's getting late and I have to go."

"We didn't mean to interrupt you. We were just stopping by to say hi," said Tamiko.

"No, it's okay" she said to Tamiko while trying to force a smile. "See you around Davi. Good luck and God bless you," she said to him before planting a kiss on his cheek, collecting her things and walking away. Davis just looked down at the coffee cup in front of him.

"Davis, are you alright?" asked Tamiko. He didn't look like his usual self. In fact now that she had been looking at him closely it looked as if he may have been crying as well.

"I'm fine," he said still looking away from her.

"Was that your cousin?" asked Riley.

"She's an old girl-friend of mine," said Davis quietly.

"Interesting," said Riley as she arched her eyebrows at Tamiko.

"Davis, I – we didn't mean to bother you. I mean I hope we haven't caused you any trouble," said Tamiko.

"I wasn't trying to get with her if that's what you're thinking," he said looking at Riley, who rolled her eyes at him.

"Davis, you don't owe anyone an explanation," said Tamiko.

"He doesn't?" said Riley.

"No," said Tamiko firmly to Riley before returning her attention to Davis "Goodnight, Davis."

"Goodnight, Miko."

"Let's go, Rye,"

"I didn't even get a chance to get my snack."

"Let's go!" Tamiko insisted.

They walked away, but after a few steps Tamiko looked back and Davis was still sitting at the table looking dejected. Her stomach was in knots. There was definitely something wrong, but Tamiko didn't know if she really wanted to find out what it was.

*****

Tamiko tried to keep her mind on the work in front of her. She had finished writing tomorrow's lesson plans and was working on organizing data she had collected on her students through assessments in order to preparing for her first assessment meeting of the year which was a week away. This year, more monthly assessments were added. There was a new sight word assessment, as well as a numeracy assessment on top of the reading level tracking sheets, math unit tracking sheets, and writing tracking sheets. Tamiko had just finished the three latter sheets and was now beginning to tackle the sight words assessment. She was trying to find a way to collate the information she had gathered on the student's sight word knowledge. She had given all of the students a baseline sight word exam and was trying to figure out how to level her students based on the information, but there was so much information that she was having trouble organizing it all. Every child was assessed on 100 words over a three-day period. The only thing she was certain of was that they all needed to work on learning the words. The 100 words were broken down into distinct groups of words such as gold words, silver words, bronze words and the like which made things even more complicated. Then add to that the scene from the discount store that nagged at her brain, making it hard for her to concentrate. Then, just as she was trying to format the spreadsheet she was trying to make, her computer froze.

"Awwwww, c'mon!" said Tamiko as she frantically tapped the 'esc' key.

"Computer giving you trouble?" asked Riley who was coming in with a tray that had two cups of hot tea and a plate of mini-crescents. She put the tray on the vanity before walking over to the desk where Tamiko was sitting with her computer. "Try pressing control, alt and delete at the same time. That's what Wilson tells me to do."

"But then it will re-start and I'll lose what I was working on. I guess it doesn't matter though. It's not like I had any idea what I was doing anyway. Just thinking in circles," said Tamiko getting up from her desk and sitting on the airbed.

"Maybe some of this tea will give you a brain boost. It's just like you like it with honey and lemon. I got some mini crescent rolls too, if you want," said Riley handing her a cup.

"Thanks, Rye. I'll just have the tea. I've been thinking about what I could do to make this spreadsheet, but I'm blocked."

"I hope there's nothing else on your mind that's blocking you."

"If you're referring to who we saw at the food court, when we went to the discount store then I'd have to admit that it is bothering me. I know that it shouldn't, but it does."

"Miko, we've had this conversation before. You're supposed to be living your life, not obsessing. "

"I'm not obsessing! It's just that he looked so sad and depressed."

"Mikooooo, don't go there."

"What? Even if we're not together he's still my friend. I still care about him."

"Even so, you shouldn't let yourself feel sorry for him. That wasn't sadness you saw – it was guilt. We caught him in the midst of his crooked little caper red handed."

"They were talking. It's not like we caught them kissing or something."

"Miko, he was obviously trying to get back with his ex! At least she was smart enough not to take him back."

"He said he wasn't. Davis wouldn't lie to me."

"Instant message alert: When it comes to relationships, all men lie!"

"There weren't any indications they were on a date. I mean, who takes a date to the food court of a discount store and then wears their work clothes?" said Tamiko.

"A cheap date, that's what. Yes, they're out there. Believe me girl – what you saw tonight was a huge red flag. Didn't you see the way that girl ran off when we got there? She's his ex so she probably knows more about him than you do. If she doesn't want him back, I'd think twice before I got together with him."

"I don't think she's upset with him. She kissed him on the cheek for crying out loud."

"She told him good luck, too, so she was more likely kissing him off."

"Regardless, I didn't get the vibe that he was interested in her. It seemed like they were just talking. From the way it looked it had to be about something really disturbing – like maybe a tragedy they both experienced. Whatever it was, it probably has something to do with what's making Davis afraid of relationships. I just wish he felt he could talk to me about it."

"That would be red flag number two. If he feels that he can't talk to you about what truly bothers him, do you think that you two would really make it as a couple? That's what relationships are all about Tamiko: communication is key. I think you need to deal with the fact that this dude is just not for you."

"But if he's not for me, I wish God would let me know why."

"Just let it go already. Goodness, why is it that we women insist on having our losers? All dwelling on him is going to do is ruin your life and you don't need that especially when you've got bigger things to worry about: like that thing you were working on just now."

"Yes, the endless amounts of data that has to be analyzed. The problem is I have no idea how to turn it into a spreadsheet without it becoming ridiculously tedious. I would ask Allen to help me, but he's drowning in law school stuff."

"I'd help you, but you know I don't know anything about data or computers. What about any of the others? Can't they help you? Like, what about Daniel? He's a computer geek."

"No way. He'd think I was interested in him and he'd spend the entire time trying to chat me up rather than actually helping. Not interested."

"What about Mr. Snow Job? He's got to know his way around a computer."

"Stop calling him that. Tim happens to be a very nice, genuine guy."

"Oh, you and Allen like everybody."

"And you like nobody. Anyway...Tim might be able to help, but he has a new job with a lot more responsibility so he's probably as busy as Allen. I don't want to be a burden."

"You know he won't mind."

"If it's all the same I'd rather not. Besides, any time I have male company, my mom goes off the deep end and starts accusing me of throwing myself at him."

"That's because that's the type of woman she used to be, and she's putting that on you. Now she wants to re-write her history and make herself a saint. You remember what your grandma Emma used to say about her, right?"

"Daddy says Grandma Emma didn't think any woman was good enough for him."

"I second that. But, back to what we were talking about. You better ask somebody if you don't want to end up getting fired."

"I'll pray about it. Anyway, how's being Jim's home health aide going?"

"Nowhere. All he does is sit on the couch, watch TV, read the Bible, and sulk all day."

"I guess we can't expect so much, so soon. It's only been a couple of days since he's been out of the hospital."

"But it's more than that. I really do think he's depressed about something."

"It might have something to do with what landed him in the hospital in the first place. You know, we never really found out who did that to him. Maybe Jim's afraid of that person."

"Could be that. Could be a number of things. I only wish he'd talk to me – or to anybody for that matter."

"He very well may be. Since he's back in the church, maybe he's talking to God about it. He can do more about whatever's bothering Jim than anyone else."

"True. If that's the case, I hope he's not just talking, but doing some listening, too."

"I think so. I think it's even a miracle that he even wants to have a relationship with God again. After Mama Merta died he was so angry and bitter at God, and everyone. I was really afraid for him."

"Yeah. He took it really hard.

"I didn't think Jim would ever come back to the Lord. I don't know what happened to Jim out there, but I'm glad for it if it helped to save his soul."

"Like Mama Shirley say 'Ain't nothing or nobody too hard for God."

"I don't know. I could think of one person – like our special surprise guest at dinner last Sunday."

"Who you talkin' bout? Goldilocks or Allen's barracuda."

"Goldilocks?"

"That's the nickname I'm giving her to help me remember who she is. This place is like grand central, I gotta come up with some way of keeping track of all these characters you know."

"I was referring to Allyson, but you're right. Callie doesn't seem like she's going to be joining the church anytime soon, either."

"But you never know how God will work. I can't wait to see what He's gonna do."

"Neither can I."

TWENTY-FIVE

The sounds of stirring in the room had awakened Allyson from her sleep. It was dark, but there were a few rays of daylight that peeked from between the folds of the drawn curtains of her room. She could also hear the heavy drops of rain battering the windows. After wiping the sleep from her eyes, she could see Jason walking back and forth, gathering his clothes that were scattered about. It seemed he was getting dressed to go out. Jason never really liked to stick around long after they'd been intimate, but this was the first time he seemed to actually try to sneak away from her. However, she wouldn't allow him to get away so easily.

"Going somewhere?" she asked, her voice groggy with sleep. She pulled the covers close to herself to cover her half exposed body.

"I know this looks kind of bad, after I said we'd do breakfast, but I was going to send you a text to explain everything."

"What's to explain?" asked Allyson, who couldn't wait to hear what his excuse was this time.

"I've got a lot to do. My dad's charity luncheon is today and he's going to have some important clients there that he wants me to connect with. Then I have deadlines to meet for an article I'm working on for the magazine, and a paper that I have to finish for my medieval literature class," he said as he slid into his pants.

"You didn't tell me any of this last night," said Allyson sitting up in the bed, pulling her knees to her chest under the covers.

"You didn't ask. And it certainly wasn't on my mind then."

Allyson got up from the bed and walked toward him where he was standing near the dresser, buttoning his shirt. She came up behind him and embraced him, pressing her body against his.

"I'm sure your dad wouldn't mind if you were a few minutes late," she purred into his ear. Then she began to kiss the back of his neck in an attempt to seduce him into staying. She was surprised when he pushed her away and continued to dress.

"Sorry, Ally, but this is much more important."

There was always something that was more important. That's the way the men in her social circle were. Women were no more than tools they used to satisfy their carnal desires. If you were lucky, you could get to be a trophy wife. Allyson had hoped to become Jason's trophy, but so far, there were signs that it was unlikely. Had he considered her a trophy, he would have asked her to his father's business luncheon to show her off, rather than sneak away from her to attend it. However, their relationship was in the early stages and there would be time for her to be introduced to family and acquaintances. She knew she had to be patient.

"I'm starting to feel like I'm dating a vampire," she said "The only time we're together is at night. During the daytime hours, you make yourself scarce."

"Don't start with the griping. I'm stretching myself thin as it is to make time for this relationship. If you're going to start laying guilt trips on me..."

"I was just joking, Jayce. Lighten up."

"Oh...sorry. Didn't mean to bite your head off. I'm under a lot of pressure this week."

"I can help you with your paper if you want."

"Thanks. You're better at the lit classes anyway. I'll send you the file and you can finish it," he said. By now he had his shoes on and was grabbing his keys from the dresser.

"I'll see you next week?" said Allyson who had now put on her robe and was walking over with him to the door. She was hoping that he would remember that her birthday was the Wednesday. Allyson made sure to mention it every time they were together last week.

"We'll see. I'll call you," said Jason giving her a peck on the lips before hurrying away.

That was not what Allyson wanted to hear. "Maybe he's going to surprise me," Allyson thought hopefully to herself trying to subdue the fears that loomed in her subconscious. She had no pretensions about them being in love or anything, but she thought they had a common understanding about what was expected between them. Even if he didn't love her, he was supposed to respect her and help her keep up the appearance of a happy couple. But so far he wasn't doing a very good job of it.

Allyson decided to go into the kitchen of their suite to grab a bagel and some juice. When she entered into the living space who was there but Trish and Courtney who had just come in from an evening of partying. Trish was wearing a strapless black lace cocktail dress, and Courtney was wearing a silk turquoise sleeveless shell and matching pleated mini skirt with open-toed flesh-colored boots. She could tell they were half drunk or hung over by the way they were staggering in.

"Hello, ladies," said Allyson blithely as she walked to the cupboard to grab a package of bagels.

"Hey, Ally!" said Courtney snickering. "We saw Jason sneaking out as we were coming in. Hot date last night?"

"Court, please. I am not some sixteen year old who feels the need to share every detail of her relationship with her friends," she said as she cut into her bagel.

"That's what you call a relationship?" asked Trish.

Allyson made sure their eyes met when she gave Trish a dirty look. She would have liked to slice her like the bagel she was dressing.

"I know it's all confusing to you, Trish, since you've never really been in one before. Remember, Johns don't count."

"Sorry. It's just that I thought relationships only involved two people."

"Trish!" said Courtney snickering before she nudged her with an elbow. Allyson knew something was up.

"What are you getting at Trish?"

"You should go to Fabian's. It's a little seafood restaurant in the Village."

"Trish, shut up!" said Courtney who was falling down laughing.

"Really! You have to try it. I think you'll be surprised by what you find there."

"You wanna tell me what you think is so funny, Court?"

"I'm not laughing!" she said as she rolled around on the floor hysterically.

"You know what? Both of you can go to hell" said Allyson as she took her food and stormed back into her room.

When she got inside she put the food down on her desk and put her head down. She wasn't even in the mood to eat her bagel anymore. She knew what Trish and Courtney were implying, but then again they may have been trying to play mind games with her. As far as she knew, Jason had dumped the bohemian princess. In any event, she didn't care if Jason was seeing someone else as long as she was his primary girlfriend or 'the trophy'. She just wished she'd known about it before they did – that is, if their insinuation was even true. If there were competition, she'd have to check it out to make sure she had the advantage. Now on top of snooping in Tim's business, she had to do some investigating into Jason's dealings. Her life just couldn't get any more complicated.

"zzzzzzz" went the sound of Allyson's vibrating smart phone. It was right next to where she had laid her head on the desk and when she heard it, she was startled. Then she checked to see who was calling her. Just when she thought things couldn't get any worse, they did.

"Hello, mother."

"Allyson, darling, how are you? I hope I haven't caught you too early."

"No, I was just..."

"So how are things getting on between you and Tim?"

"I went to that church or what have you. Tim's one of their musicians. He's also in some type of Bible class they have there. I guess that's some kind of indoctrination seminar or whatever."

"But what kind of message is this guru sending to those people? Is he a faith healer of some sort or one of those prosperity preachers? Or is he like that Dwyer character with all that power of the mind jazz."

"I didn't hear the sermon. I fell asleep."

"Allyson, this is important! We have to find out why Tim is attracted to these people!?"

"Alright, alright. I'll take notes next time. Anyway, then he invited me to dinner with them and..."

"You were able to have dinner with them? So soon? You didn't eat or drink anything from them, did you?"

"No, I didn't..."

"Because they often drug people you know. But what did you find? That had to be very interesting, indeed. Is he rich like that televangelist in Atlanta? Does he have connections?"

"We ate dinner at Allen's house, so I don't know what the guru's house looks like. He doesn't dress like he's rich or anything."

"How large is the congregation? Does he have one church or are there other chapters?"

"I'm guessing it's just the one church. It doesn't seem like a huge outfit, but they fill all the seats. The guru's wife said something about they added fifty members, but they were mostly young people in their twenties, like Tim."

"Preying on impressionable young people. I should've known."

"I don't know about that. The old lady said the young people don't tend to stay very long. She'd rather have older members."

"In that case, they may be looking for people who can give more money. What else did they talk about?"

"Not much after that. All they talked about was Allen's health issues and God. In fact they tried to convince me to join them but..."

"But is Tim giving them any money? And what about the girl, is he involved with her?"

"I don't know yet. I only went there once. This is going to take some time, not to mention an appropriate church wardrobe."

"I thought I gave you $4,000.00 the other day?"

"That was for my AKA luncheon and homecoming. Most of my suits and dresses are much too short to wear to church."

"Oh, fine, but I want to impress upon you the importance of your job. I'm not looking for schoolgirl gossip. I need you to use your reporting skills to get access to information that we can use to gain leverage. Find out what kind of church this is and what that guru's intentions are. See if you can find some skeletons that are hidden in their closets – something that would get Tim to see these people for the phonies that they are."

Allyson thought it was ironic that her mother, of all people, would call them phonies. So far, Allyson wasn't getting that vibe from any of them at all. She couldn't help remembering how patient the pastor was when Allen's girlfriend jumped down his throat. She recalled how warm and caring Allen's mother had been towards her and how real her hug felt. Finally, she remembered Mr. Sharpe, who reminded her so much of Poppa.

"What if they're not phonies?"

"Allyson, my dear, I've been around a long time. Trust me when I say your average Christian is nothing but a hypocrite."

Still Allyson wasn't sure that these people Tim was hanging with were your average Christians. At least something inside her hoped they weren't.

TWENTY-SIX

Jim flipped from channel to channel looking for something interesting to watch as he sat propped up on the couch where Riley had left him. He usually watched the preachers on the Word network, but at this time of day, the charlatans were on, namely some dude named E.Z. Monie who was about nothing but money blessings. Jim knew he wouldn't be interested in anything this guy had to say after he saw him doing a praise dance in a pile of money the parishioners had thrown into the isles. There was a cooking show on one channel, but they were making some fancy gourmet dish that looked pretty disgusting. Jim didn't think crayfish would taste good with peanut butter. Then there was an old black and white movie on another channel, and an old episode of his favorite kids show on another. He decided to give the remote a rest for a while, now that he had found something to distract him from the black hole that was his life.

Pop Vernon said that he should be taking this time to seek the Lord's guidance on how to move forward with his life, but so far it seemed as if God was keeping quiet. Jim had been reading the Bible and praying, but he still hadn't gotten any kind of revelation about where to begin in order to start his life over. From his perspective things seemed bleak. The only job experience he had since college was working for the MTA, and with everything that happened, there was no way he could go back there. He didn't know what else he could do with a B.A. in political science. He had no money to go to graduate school. The last time he tried to get a job, he couldn't even land a position at a fast food restaurant. Jim felt helpless, and he wondered why God was not intervening on his behalf now to give him some direction. He knew that it had to be God that kept him from being killed in that warehouse. "Why would He deliver me from death only to abandon me now?" Jim pondered. Then he briefly thought about the secrets he'd been keeping. Jim couldn't help but entertain the possibility that the multitude of sins he was hiding was standing in his way.

"This isn't working," Jim thought to himself as he changed the channel again. He didn't want his mind to go there again. There was nothing he could do about those things. Thinking about them only made him depressed and fearful. He was getting tired of these feelings. He was tired of not being able to feel good anymore. He wanted to lose himself in something. So he changed the channel and happened upon another cooking show. This time the lady was cooking soul food: oxtail stew and collard greens. Now this was more suitable. Jim just kept his focus on the oxtails the woman was braising in the pan. He envisioned himself pulling the meat off the bones with a fork and tasting them.

"Let's go out for lunch today" said Riley as she stormed into the room. Jim's attention was still on the TV and what she said barely registered with him.

He didn't even notice that she had her coat on and was holding his open to help him put it on.

"What?" he said.

"I said, let's go out. I know you've got to be tired of being cooped up in here by now," she said almost sounding as if she were demanding him. The last thing Jim wanted to do was go outside. He only had one good arm so using the crutch they gave him at the hospital was near impossible.

"I can barely get around in here and you want to go out?"

"We can use the wheelchair that Aunt Lena got you."

"I'm not using that thing. I feel worthless enough as it is."

"Using a wheelchair doesn't make you worthless. Just be glad this is only temporary and not permanent."

"I don't want to go out anyway."

"Well, I do. I don't want to waste my visit to the city sitting around here all day."

"You can always go by yourself."

"But I don't know the city that well. I was hoping you could make yourself useful and be my tour guide."

"Do I really look like I'm ready to do battle with all those tourists at Empire State Building?"

"You should know I wasn't planning on going all the way out there. I was hoping you could show me that place where we got pizza the last time I was in town. Now, they had some good pizza."

"You mean Leo's Harlem Hand-Tossed?"

"That's the one with them swirl dudes that know how to rock pizza, right?"

"Yeah. I guess I wouldn't mind going there," said Jim relenting. He was beginning to think that maybe the fresh air might do him some good and he was certain that Riley would be less inclined to ask him about his personal business in public. In any event, it had been a while since he'd had some decent pizza.

"Alright then," she said helping him into his jacket, "the chair's waiting out by the door."

"Riley!"

"Now, Jimmy, you know I can't hold you up on them crutches like Al and them can. You gotta weigh like 180 pounds!"

"I've seen you take down a brother that was 200 pounds."

"That was my adrenaline at work and I was armed with an aluminum baseball bat."

"But that thing is gonna be such a hassle."

"That pizza shop can't be more than a few blocks away from here."

"Aiight. I'll take the chair, if it makes it easier for you."

"It will. Now let's go."

*****

It seemed like ages since he'd been in Leo's. After he had ended his friendship with Allen, Jim would avoid the place because he was afraid of running into Allen here. Allen loved pizza and Leo's was his favorite. They'd been regular customers since high school. Jim liked the fact that it was one of the few black-owned businesses left in Harlem that hadn't been pushed out by the gentrification, which had occurred during the last several years. There was a marriage of Italian and African-American culture that could be seen throughout the place. Maps of Italy and Africa, as well as pictures of Leo's Italian grandfather with the likes of Adam Clayton Powell, Jr., Percy Sutton, and David Dinkins decorated the place. Leo and his brother Tony were some really good dudes, too. They always supported the community, especially the high school that Jim and the others had attended. If it weren't for Leo and Tony, there wouldn't be a Chess Club at the New Visions Magnet School. It was nice to patronize a place where he was welcomed and respected.

When he came in with Riley, Jim felt like a teenager all over again. Seeing the little tables with the red, white and blue plaid tablecloths, the black metal chairs, and the marble counter with the case of zeppolos, beef patties, and garlic knots on display brought back fond memories. In the midst of it all was Leo, his son Brian and his nephew Tony, Jr. who worked with him to service the customers. Leo was a short fair-skinned brother with a thick build, whose age could only be told by the gray that was starting to come in around the edges of his curly jet-black hair.

"Hey, Jimmy!" said Leo as he entered the restaurant "What happened to you?" The man was genuinely alarmed when he noticed Jim's condition.

"It's okay, Leo. I'm alright. Just a few broken bones. Not a big deal."

"You was in an accident or somethin'? I know I hadn't seen you in a long time, but...man."

"Don't worry about this, man. I'm good."

"I'm sure you are, cause you got this beautiful doll right here lookin' after you," said Leo smiling at Riley. "I bet you think I don't remember you. You the cousin, right? Rhonda is it?"

"It's Riley."

"I knew it started with an 'R'. How's thing's down south?"

"Everyone's fine. Thank you."

"Now what can I do for you two today?"

"We'll have two jumbo slices: one plain, one pepperoni. And two medium colas."

"Comin' right up, son."

As Leo prepared their order, Riley pushed him over to a table by the window and sat opposite him.

"Now aren't you glad you came out?"

"Sort of," said Jim.

"Still thinkin' 'bout what you gonna do with yourself?"

"I've been praying, but He's not answering."

"Just give it some time."

"I'm running out of time. My first week is almost up and I've got one week left. Thing is I need a job and I don't see any opportunities in any of the fields I'm cut out for."

"But you went to college. Ain't that 'sposed to give you some kind of advantage?"

"In theory, but when you live in a city that has very few job openings and a glut of college graduates, it kinda undercuts any advantage I may have had. You see where Allen's workin' don't you?"

"So? You gotta start somewhere. Besides, I'm sure if you ask Allen or Tamiko or one of the others, they'll help you find a job."

"Maybe, maybe not."

"You gotta be positive, Jim. You could've been dead right now, but thankfully that wasn't in His plan. He's keeping you for a reason, and I don't think it's to sit around and mope all the time."

"I'm not moping."

"Yes you are, and it's worrying me a little bit, 'cause this is not the Jim I know. I feel like something's eating you and it's more than not being able to find a job."

Jim froze. He couldn't look at her, nor did he know what to say. He was thankful when Leo interrupted them to bring their order to the table.

"Here you go: two big jumbo slices. Let me guess, you're the pepperoni?" he said to Jim as he put the trays on the table.

"As always."

"And here's your drinks. Enjoy."

They thanked him for the fast service, and Jim started in on his slice so that he wouldn't have to continue their conversation. He thought that if he just ignored what she had said she'd leave it alone. But neither of them had gotten halfway through their slices before Riley took up the topic again.

"Why'd you cut everybody off, Jim?"

"I was going through some stuff. Everybody was going gung-ho with the Lord, and at the time I couldn't see why He was so great. I couldn't get into that, but now..."

"So what did you decide to get into? The game?" she said lowering her voice so no one around them would hear.

Jim felt his stomach knot-up at the mention of it. 'How could she know?' he thought to himself. He couldn't say anything.

"Let's keep this on the level," she said. "Everybody knows you was on that stuff. You obviously didn't have a job, and you had to have some way of paying for it."

"How do you know when I lost my job? It could have been last month for all you know."

"Don't play with me, Jim. You know I know better than that. Nobody gets beaten and shot up over a $100.00 heroin debt. You don't get marked unless there's way more money involved or unless you're the one that's way more involved."

It was no use. Riley knew how to read the situation. She wasn't as sheltered as Allen or Tamiko and had been experienced with what went down on the streets. There was no way to spin this; he had to tell the truth – some of it, anyway.

"It's not what you're thinking. I wasn't planning on being in that life forever. I was on my way out when I got hit."

"Jim, what were you thinking? Did you forget about what happened to your dad?"

"Look, I was desperate, aiight. I couldn't find a job and I had a whole lot of bills. I needed a way to stay afloat until I could think of somethin' legit."

"You could have come to your family."

"I didn't realize that then...I wasn't thinking. Trust me, that part of my life is over."

"Not if there are people out there who want to finish what they started."

"I know for a fact those guys are dead."

"How would you know that? Unless you..."

"No! I didn't...The guy I worked with thought I was stealing from him. He was the one that was after me, but there was another guy he had a beef with who shot him."

"Still, how would you know this unless you were still dealing with someone on the inside? Is it that Chris guy?"

"What would make you think that?"

"Cause you know him. I saw the way he looked at you at your welcome back party, and I know his story. Was he one of your customers?"

"I guess you could say that. But that's over now. I don't ever want to go back to that life again. I wound up doing a lot of things I really regret" said Jim. He couldn't tell her about Angela or the two boys known as Rollo and Zee. It had been hard enough for him to come to terms with the fact that he had taken part in murder – even if it was technically in self-defense.

"Is it those regrets that have been bothering you?"

"Yeah."

"What's done is done Jim. God forgives you for all that. I'm not holding it against you and I'm sure the rest of the family wouldn't either."

"If you don't mind I was hoping we could keep this between ourselves."

"The Bible says there's nothing hid that won't be made known[1]. You're not going to be able to hide it forever. If I was able to put two and two together, it won't be long before the others do, too."

"They don't need to know about this. It doesn't have anything to do with them."

"If it affects you, then it's going to affect them."

"I intend to come clean about everything when the time comes. But if no one's asking, I'm not telling. I think I've put everyone through enough as it is."

"You're not still messing with that stuff are you?"

"Do I look like I'm messing with it?" said Jim who was more than a little annoyed by her question.

"That's not an answer."

"No. I'm not taking anything," he said making sure to look her straight in the eye.

"Are you gonna get some counseling or something? Maybe you should ask that Chris fella about what he's involved in at the church."

"I'm thinking about it," said Jim, although he felt he didn't need any counseling services. He'd been doing fine so far on his own.

"And there's nothing else that's bothering you?"

"What I've told you isn't enough?"

"I don't mean to give you a hard time, Jim. I care about you. If you're going to move forward you have to be able to let the past go and the only way to do that is to deal with it. Hiding, pretending and half-lying is only gonna weigh you down."

"I'm being straight with you."

"So there's nothing between you and that Callie girl that I need to know about?"

Jim felt the hairs on his neck stand up. It seemed like Riley had suspicions. He had to remember to keep cool.

"I told you Callie's a friend," he said doing his best to seem casual.

"Didn't seem like it at the barbecue. You hugged her like she had Ebola and you didn't have two words to say to her the whole afternoon. Same thing at dinner last Sunday. Big change from the last time I was here."

"I told you before, I'm not very happy about how she's using Al to help her take care of her child, that's all. It's not fair to him with all that he's trying to do."

"So why not take her aside and straighten her out instead of avoid her?"

"Al's crazy about her. I don't want to mess things up for him. He deserves to have some happiness and if that means I have to keep my mouth shut, so be it."

"Who's to say that she'll make him happy? He doesn't look it right now."

"Who's to say what can happen in the future? Didn't you just tell me to be positive? They could work out after all."

"Do you really think the father of her child is dead? It sounds just a little too convenient if you ask me."

"And nobody's asking you," he blurted defensively. Riley's eyes seemed to widen with a sudden awareness that put Jim on edge. She fixed her interrogative gaze on his face as she leaned forward towards him and folded her arms on the table.

"Looks like I've touched a nerve."

"That's because Al's my boy and I'm not going to let anybody start stirring up crap in his backyard. Not even his cousin."

"All I did was ask about this baby's biological father. If Allen knows it's not him, and the guy is supposedly dead, why would that be such a big deal?" she said narrowing her eyes at him.

"Exactly. It shouldn't matter who that kid's dad is, so why even bring it up," said Jim summoning his confidence. "Al loves that kid like he's his own. If Al's willing to step into the void and be a dad, who are we to say that he shouldn't? After all, that kid needs a dad. Why mess that up for either of them?"

"You and I both know that Al is too young to be anybody's father! He can barely take care of himself! He still lives at home and he just started school again for crying out loud."

"He's also a grown man capable of making his own decisions. Even if we don't agree with them, we still have to give him respect."

Riley was backing down. His passionate defense seemed to relieve her of her suspicions, for now.

"I respect his decision, but that doesn't mean I can't be concerned about what's he's doing. Especially about what could happen to that little boy."

"What are you talking about?"

"I'm talking about the fact that Allen seems to think he can pretend to be this child's biological father. One day somebody's going to have to sit Darius down and tell him the truth. That child is going to have to know who his real father is, dead or not. If they let him find out on his own, he's going to be one angry person with a lot of issues."

"What makes you so certain of that?"

"Because my brother Wilson had the same issues. His mother died when he was a baby. Then daddy married my mom a couple of years later thinking she could be his mom, too. But soon he was asking them those hard questions, and daddy tried to avoid them by changing the subject or telling him to shush because he didn't think Wils could handle it. Next thing you know, Wils started acting out by picking on me and Bennett, getting into trouble at school and such. So daddy just decided to tell him the truth about everything: told him about how his momma died of heart failure, gave him pictures of her and the letter she wrote to him before she died, told him stories about her, took him to visit her grave and all that. Not long after that Wils stopped acting out. He was more at peace with himself cause that part of him that was missing was filled in a little bit."

"But Wilson was already four years old when you're dad married your mom. He already knew she wasn't his mother."

"That's right. If he knew and it was having that affect on him, how do you think this little boy's going to feel after so many years when he learns that Allen is not his biological father? How do you think he would feel if he knew his parents deliberately lied to him all that time?"

"I wonder how he would feel if he had to find out his real father was nothin' but some bum who couldn't do anything for him any way."

"How would you know that?"

Riley was becoming suspicious again. Jim had to think fast.

“Allen told me he heard from Callie that the guy died from a drug overdose.”

“You know my mother was practically the whore of Babylon and a drunk to boot, but I’m glad I know who she is. Now that doesn’t mean I love Mama Shirley any less, but it’s important to know. I guess it gives you a kind of closure to know where you come from.”

“I guess I never thought about it that way.”

“Because it’s never been an issue for you, but in my patchwork family we had to make sure to keep everything and everybody straight.”

“Right. Anyway, I’m tired. How ‘bout we get this wrapped up to take home.”

“Alright. I’ll do that.”

Riley took their leftovers to the counter to be bagged and paid the bill leaving, Jim to reflect on their conversation. He had never considered how keeping his secret about Darius’s paternity could actually harm his child. The last thing he wanted to do was to cause Darius any kind of psychological trauma that could negatively impact his life. Now Jim was in a real bind. It seemed like he was cursed if he told his secret and cursed if he kept it. The landmine he had been harboring was becoming more and more volatile. He had to find a way to defuse it or it would destroy the people he cared about.

TWENTY-SEVEN

Tim was still going back and forth with himself as he approached the Bynum home for the third time this week. Though he had resolved to keep his distance from Tamiko, he had to admit that he was more than happy when he got a text from her asking for help with something she was working on at school. It was a little odd because the message was so short and brief, which was very unlike Tamiko, who wouldn't even use internet shorthand in her texts. At first thought, he was leaning towards making an excuse for why he couldn't help, but he really couldn't find one and it caused him to feel guilty. He did not want his personal feelings to keep him from being a friend and he knew the task wouldn't take more than a couple of hours. 'What could happen?' he said to reassure himself.

He gave the doorbell two short rings and waited for Mother Rose's caustic greeting, but was pleasantly surprised when the door suddenly opened.

"Hey," said Riley looking like a military service woman standing sentry by a checkpoint, her expression stoic. She always wore army pants and combat boots. She had to have them in every color under the sun. Today they were lavender, pink, and purple camouflage and matched her lavender t-shirt and violet button down. She had the front of her hair braided into an intricately ornate pattern of cornrows with her afro forming a crown behind them.

"Hi, Riley," said Tim "Is Miko around? She asked me to help her with something for work"

"She's somewhere in here," she said stepping aside so he could come in.

Tim came in but was a little unsettled by the way Riley seemed to be looking him over. The last time she did that she publicly humiliated him. He was wary about saying much of anything because he was afraid of how she'd respond and he could tell that she wasn't very fond of him, and he attributed this to what he observed was her over protectiveness toward Tamiko. He was hoping Tamiko wouldn't be long. For a few minutes they stood facing each other awkwardly.

"You can sit down for a spell if you want, while I go get her," she said before going upstairs.

"Thanks," said Tim as he took off his jacket and placed it on the arm of the chair before sitting down and taking his laptop out of his bag. He was just glad to be left alone. Then he turned it on, so that it would boot up while he was waiting. Then he took out his ac adapter and was plugging it into an outlet when he sensed someone was standing over him.

"Todd?!" said Mother Rose, her call sounding almost like a reprimand. Tim dropped his cord at her feet.

"It's Tim, ma'am" he said quietly rising to greet her. "Nice to see you again Mother Rose" Tim held out his hand for a shake, but Mother Bynum stood with her arms folded in front of her.

"May I ask what you are doing in this house?"

"Tamiko asked me to..."

"Tamiko Elizabeth Bynum!" said Mother Rose as she walked away from Tim and headed toward the staircase.

Tim sat back down and waited. But it wasn't long before he could hear the high shrill sound of Tamiko's whining, mixed with her mother's angry barks, and Riley's southern drawl. "Maybe this wasn't such a good idea after all," he thought. It just seemed odd that Tamiko would not have told her mother that he was coming over. She'd always done so in the past. Unless, she didn't because she knew her mom would give her a hard time. The last thing he wanted was for his visits to cause trouble between Tamiko and her mom. If that were the case he'd stop coming altogether and just see Tamiko when she was at Al's or when they all went out together. As Tim continued to muse over the matter, the three women came down stairs. First was Mother Rose, with the usual sour look on her face, followed by Tamiko who seemed very uncomfortable, and finally Riley who was struggling to keep a straight face, as she seemed to find the situation amusing.

"Excuse me, Todd, but there seems to have been a miscommunication."

"It's Tim, Mother Rose," said Riley.

"Yes, yes, of course," said Mother Rose waving her hand at Riley before returning her attention to Tim. "You see, our friend Riley has been playing a little joke, as it were. She has confessed to me that she took liberties with Tamiko's cell phone and sent you a message to come over. Tamiko had no idea what had happened, until now when she checked her phone."

"Really?" said Tim.

"With all due respect, Mother Rose, I wasn't playing a joke. Miko needed help and she was too proud to ask, so I asked for her. She was gonna flunk her assessment meeting and get fired, if I didn't."

"That is not for you to presume. Tamiko is a college educated young woman, who is quite capable of completing her work on her own. If she needed help, she would have asked one of the young ladies at the school."

As the two women argued, Tim couldn't help but look at Tamiko. She was standing pigeon-toed, looking down and fondling her charm bracelet, which was what he noticed she often did when she was nervous or feeling uncomfortable. He didn't know if it was the scene her mother and her cousin were making or if it was something to do with himself, since she wouldn't look his way. He wanted to know what she was thinking. Tim wished she would say something – anything.

"In any event, please accept my apologies for any inconvenience our friend may have caused you, but as you can see your services are not required. Now I know you must have a lot of work to do yourself so I wont hold you..."

"Mom, it would be even more rude to ask him to leave after he's come all this way."

"Tamiko, it is a school night and you have a lot of work to do."

"And Tim has come to help me. Right, Tim?"

"That was my intention."

"Tim, I'm so sorry for all of the confusion. I would understand if you wanted to leave, but I'd appreciate it if you didn't."

"Miko, I don't want you to feel obligated to have me here. I mean, I understand that all this isn't your fault, so If you really don't want me..."

"You see, Tamiko, he's not offended at all. Therefore if he wishes to leave..."

"I do want you – I mean your help," said Tamiko.

"In that case, I guess I'll stay."

"Then it's settled. I'll go upstairs and get my files and my computer. I won't be long." she said before heading back up the stairs.

"Well, this is still my house, and I say that on school nights, there are going to be limits on how long guests can be entertained. I expect this young man to be on his way home by 8:30 and no later. Is that understood Tamiko?"

"Yes, mother," she called from upstairs.

"Young man, I will remind you that the ground floor of this home is the only place where guest are allowed..."

"What if he has to go to the bathroom?" asked Riley.

"This is none of your concern. I am not addressing you at the moment, although I will have a few choice words for you later when the Pastor arrives."

"Sorry. Just askin."

"I'm going to finish fixing dinner. I can't wait until Pastor comes home. The foolishness I've had to deal with today."

"Let Miko know that if she needs me, I'll be right upstairs," said Riley as she eyed Tim warily.

"I'll let her know," said Tim politely.

As soon as Riley went up, Tamiko came back down. She was casually dressed in a loose fitting, three-quarter sleeved button front smock dress. It fit like a sack, but no matter what she wore, to Tim she looked beautiful. When he saw that she was struggling with what she was carrying, he met her halfway up the stairs to lighten her load.

"I'll take some of that," he said taking her laptop and a box of files she had, leaving her with the external hard-drive.

"Thanks."

"So what are we working on?"

"It's a sight-word assessment I gave to the class. It's like a list of 100 words, which are categorized by color, or level. Now I have to find a way to organize the information so that we can see how the students make progress through the levels. I tried using the levels themselves and then listing students. Then I tried listing the students and then the levels on the opposite axis, but that was a disaster. I have to make one simple table and I'm out of ideas of how to do that with all this information."

"Don't worry. I know what we could try to make it easier. Have you ever heard of a data filter?"

"What's that?"

"It's like having a spreadsheet where you can view different aspects of the data using the filters and print out different graphs and charts. The only thing is it takes a while to design your filters and put in all the data."

"You mean I couldn't just cut and paste from what I already have?"

"Not really. Sorry."

"So we'll have to re-enter the sight-word information for all of these students."

"How many students do you have?"

"Twenty-five. But we don't have any kids who knew all 100 words. Most of them capped out at 25."

"So it shouldn't take that long. I have a blank template on my hard drive that I'll transfer to yours. I'm a fast typist, so after you come up with the filters you want, I'll create the actual spreadsheet and type in the info. Then we'll trial it and print some things out to see if it's what you want. Sound like a plan?"

"Excellent. Let's get started."

*****

"Now for the moment of truth" said Tim in an imperious voice trying to be funny.

"I can't look."

"And...it works!"

"It does? Explain it to me. What am I looking at?"

"Look, here's your class, now you can click on a filter to view whatever aspect of the data you want, for example if you want to know about how many children know their gold words, you just click here and then it will show you a break down of your students that know them. You can see that 2% of your special ed kids know them, 85 % of the general education, 30% of your English language learners, and so forth. Then if you click here, you can even filter by word to see which words are the ones in each group that most of your students don't know."

"Wow, this is so cool."

"Yeah, like here you can see how all the students missed the word 'because' of the silver words, the same with the word 'where' of the copper words."

"This is incredible. It's like I can see exactly what they need to work on, and how to get started."

"And you can print reports, like I said earlier. I'm saving everything in the assessments folder of your external drive so it'll be easy for you to find."

"Tim, you are such a life saver. Words cannot express how much I am appreciating you right now."

She put her arms around him and hugged him tightly before planting a kiss on his cheek.

"I guess I'll take that as a thank you," said Tim as he turned away from her to put away his laptop, hoping she wouldn't see the color rising to his face. "You might want to also save one for Riley, since she was the one that sent out the S.O.S."

"You're right. I do owe her one."

"So why didn't you ask me yourself? After being friends for so long, you should've known I'd be willing to help you with anything."

"I know, but I didn't want to monopolize your time. You have your own work to do and I know it's not fair to expect you to drop everything for my little crises."

"Honestly, Miko. I don't mind. It's not like I've got a lot going on like Al does."

"But you'd have to admit, if I was constantly bothering you all the time, you'd get annoyed."

"Tamiko, you could never annoy me."

"I used to, a while back when we were all in college. I remember whenever Allen invited me to go with you two somewhere you'd have this look that screamed 'Aww, man not her!'"

"And if I remember correctly, you weren't too pleased to see me, either. You wouldn't even talk to me directly. You'd always tell Allen to tell me something."

"Because I thought you didn't like me and I didn't want to antagonize you. When we first met, you didn't seem very happy to meet me."

"That's because you were looking at me like I was from another planet."

"I didn't mean to. Allen was always telling me about what a cool brother you were, so I just assumed you were – but then you looked-"

"Whiter?"

"I wasn't trying to be..."

"I know you weren't. At least, that's what I realized later. It's just that I've encountered a lot of different responses to who I am, and unfortunately a lot of it's been negative. People look at you and try to figure out what you are so they can put a label on you. To some people I'm not black enough and to others I'm not white enough. I guess it's made me a little oversensitive over the years."

"Understandably."

"So I never really thought you were annoying. Weird maybe."

"What?!"

"Not in a bad way. I mean you're different from any woman I've known. Extraordinary might be a better word."

"How's that?"

"Because you're kind, loving, and honest. You see the best in people and you help them to see the best in themselves. You don't look for what you can get, but what you can give. You have courage and integrity that allow you to stand up for what you believe – and you have faith that's unfeigned. When I think of you, I think of that scripture in Proverbs that says "Who can find a virtuous woman? for her price is far above rubies (Proverbs 31:10)"[1]

"Really?" she said quietly as she looked into his eyes. She seemed as taken aback as he was by his admission. "What makes you say that?"

"Because of the way you've always been there for me – and I have to give you credit because I haven't always been the easiest person to be there for. Even when I start to get on everyone else's nerves you always stick up for me."

"Oh, Tim. I think you give me too much credit and not enough to yourself. I'm not a saint and you're not the worst guy in the world. I actually think you're pretty...wonderful."

"I'm sure there's a lot of things you'd like to change about me if you could."

"Maybe. But no one's perfect. Truth be told, I think you have way more good qualities than bad ones."

"You mean that?"

"Of course. Everything you said about me, I could say about you. I could also add that you're open-minded, and you're not afraid to open yourself to others even though you might get hurt. Like the way you keep reaching out to your sister."

"Yeah. I wish I could say things were getting better between us, but ..."

"But she came down to the church and had dinner with us. It's a good start if nothing else. Even if she's just spying, at least now you two have the chance to get a dialogue going."

"More like a monologue. I talk and she either ignores or insults me – and I still haven't gotten to the bottom of why she's angry with me."

"Do you think it may have something to do with your grandfather's death? You told me she stopped speaking to you after that."

"I have no idea. She was really upset when he died – we all were. It wasn't until some time afterward that she started treating me like dirt."

"She could have been angry about his death and was taking it out on you."

"No. We've had some really big arguments over the years since then, and she's made it pretty clear her gripe is with me. The fact that I don't know why she's angry is probably what frustrates her more than anything else."

"I don't think that's fair. She can't expect you to read her mind."

"But how could I have hurt her that badly and not know what I did? I mean she's my baby sister. If something bothers her it should be apparent to me, don't you think?"

"Allen has done things to hurt my feelings without realizing it, but I didn't hold it against him. One time when we were in high school, he ran off to Hershey Park with Daniel and his other chess club buddies and brings me back, a t-shirt that's two sizes too big. I was so mad at the time, I could have whipped him with that shirt."

"Because he got you the wrong size?"

"No!" laughed Tamiko, "I was upset because I was supposed to be his friend and he didn't even tell me he was going or invite me to go with them. Plus, he knew I wasn't doing anything that weekend."

"Ooooh! Okay, I get it now."

"That's because I explained it to you, which is my whole point. You can have a situation that can be seen by different people in different ways. You can't ever really understand why she's upset unless she tells you. Even if you manage to figure out what it is that set her off, you still won't know why that bothers her unless she explains it."

"Which will be never. That's why I've been praying for God to reveal to me what it's all about. Then hopefully, she'll want to listen to what I have to say."

"It may not even take all that. God has a way of working things out. You just keep reaching out to her."

"You're right. And after everything God has done for me, I shouldn't doubt him now."

"Amen."

"But enough about my family and their problems. How are things here? Have you and Riley had a chance to have a girls night out?"

"Not yet, because I've had to work, but I'm looking forward to Friday when we go to see the play you got us tickets for. Thanks so much again."

"Any time, Miko. Remember to tell me all about it when you get back."

"I will."

"You better. I've been telling you all my stories, now I want to hear some of yours."

"Being an only child, I don't have a lot. Most of them you've heard already, and the rest I know you've heard second hand from Allen."

"C'mon, Miko. Given how your mom is, I would think you should have hundreds."

"She's not that bad."

"Miko, you're 23 years old and she just gave you an 8:30 visitor curfew. I'd say she's moving into Eleanor Russell territory."

"My mom isn't controlling, just a little over-protective, that's all."

"I bet – like the secret service. Tell me..." he said looking around and then leaning towards her "do you think we're being recorded right now?"

"Shut up!" said Tamiko chuckling as she slapped him playfully on the arm.

"That artificial flower arrangement over there looks suspicious. I think one of the flowers may have a camera hidden inside. My guess is the yellow one."

"You're insane," she said laughing.

"As a matter of fact, I'll bet that if I even approach that staircase over there, an alarm will suddenly go off, there will be lights flashing, and a net will drop down from the ceiling..."

"Stop...stop," said Tamiko gasping between fits of laughter.

"No, no. Let's see. I think it could happen," said Tim. He got up and slowly walked over to the staircase, Tamiko's eyes following him as he went. Just as he was about to put his foot on the first step, a beeping sound took them by surprise and they both shrieked in shock. Tim hurried back over to the couch where he'd been sitting. They both found the irony of the moment hilarious.

"I was right! I knew it! I've initiated the doomsday sequence!" laughed Tim. Tamiko had rolled off the couch and was on the floor doubled over with laughter, while the beeping continued.

"What's going on out here?" asked Pastor Bynum "What's that beeping? And why are y'all laughing like that?"

Tamiko tried to explain, but could hardly say anything because she couldn't get a handle on her laughter and Tim was experiencing the same thing. Then just when they had both begun to compose themselves, Mother Rose suddenly appeared out of thin air with a timer in her hand from which the beeping sound originated. When Tim and Tamiko saw her, they both fell back on the couch laughing.

"There doesn't seem to be much work going on here. And what, may I ask, is so amusing?" said Mother Rose.

"It's nothing. We just didn't know where...that sound was coming from," said Tamiko once she had recovered from her hilarity.

"Rose, why do you have that timer?" asked Pastor Bynum.

"Because it is 8:30 and that means visiting hours at this residence are over."

“Is this really necessary?” asked the Pastor as he put the palm of his hand to his face.

“Yes it is. We have rules and it is our duty as parents to enforce them. Tamiko, I trust you were able to complete your work before you and your friend decided to start playing around.”

“Yes, mom. We’re done.”

“Good. Now, as it is already late, I’m sure that this young man would like to go home...”

“But he missed dinner. Tim, are you sure you wouldn’t like something to eat before you go, son?” asked Pastor Bynum.

“Pastor, Tamiko has to get up early for work tomorrow.”

“Now, Rose, it’s the least we could do after how he helped Miko. A lot of the restaurants might be closed by the time he gets home.”

“No, thank you, Pastor Bynum. I’ll be okay. I have something I can throw in the microwave at home.”

“Are you sure?” asked Tamiko, “I could fix you a plate to take home if you’d like.”

“Thanks for the offer, but I’ll be fine. I’ll see you around.”

“Thanks again. I really appreciated your help.”

“Anytime. Let me know how your assessment meeting goes.”

“I will, and I’ll pray for you and your sister.”

“Thanks. We’re going to need it.”

TWENTY-EIGHT

So far, the day Allen had planned seemed to go from bad to worse. He had planned for Callie, Darius, and himself to attend a children's fair in Central Park, and then he and Callie would have dinner on the ferryboat later on, but an unexpected change in the weather ruined everything. Allen woke up that morning to find several inches of snow had covered the sidewalk below his window and it was still coming down fast. He managed to salvage the day by taking Darius to the Children's Museum in lower Manhattan to explore the exhibits. After that, they had lunch together at Emily Ann's before they dropped off Darius with his mom while they got ready for a romantic evening at Callie's.

Allen prepared her a homemade candlelight dinner of her favorites: Chicken parmagian, ravioli, and Caesar's salad. Even with the last minute change in plans the day was turning out to be everything Allen had hoped for. The ambiance created by the candlelight, the food, and the sound of Callie's Stylistic's CD playing in the background made everything just that more intimate and romantic. Allen looked at Callie who was sitting across from him at the table eating her meal and he couldn't help noticing how beautiful she was. He loved her smooth ebony skin, and her long, thick, natural mane that flowed over her shoulders. She had a long slender face with high cheekbones and a pouty mouth that he found irresistible, especially when she was wearing that sparkle lip-gloss like she was tonight. He even noticed the way the stretchy material of her lavender off the shoulder dress clung to her slender figure. Allen was drinking her in with his eyes because he wanted to remember her at this point in time. He wanted to remember everything, because he knew that this was going to be one of the most important nights of his life.

"Allen, I have to say, I am having the time of my life right now," said Callie, taking a sip of the white wine Allen bought to go with their dinner.

"Good. That was my intention. I was afraid this night was going to be a bust with the way the weather turned out. I originally wanted to take you for dinner on the ferry."

"I think this is even better. It's just the two of us, alone, and far away from the stress of everyone and everything else."

"I hear that."

"Al, I've been thinking and I want to apologize for making a scene at dinner last Sunday."

"Apology accepted."

"I know your family means well, but sometimes they're enough to make a person snap."

"Let's not waste time talking about them. I just want us to enjoy what we have right now."

"You're right. You can't know how much I appreciate your taking the time to plan all this."

"Callie, I'm your man and I love you. It's what I'm supposed to do. But I do have to admit, there is an ulterior motive for all this."

"Really? I didn't think you were capable of such things."

"Seriously, Callie, I wanted to talk to you about us."

"What about?"

"Do you remember when I talked about how you and Darius deserved better?"

"Yes."

"I've been thinking that you need a brother that's ready to make a full commitment, and I was thinking about whether or not I can be the type of man that could do that for you."

"Allen, I told you that I was willing to take what you could give."

"You shouldn't have to settle, Callie. That's why I've decided..."

Allen paused while he reached into the pocket of his coat. He took out a little black velvet jewelry box and put it on the table.

"...to ask you if you would do me the honor of becoming my wife," he said as he opened the box to reveal a diamond ring. The gem wasn't as large as he had wanted it to be, but he hoped that she would accept it for now.

Callie looked shocked, but Allen couldn't tell if she were happy or just simply horrified. She had put her hand over her mouth and stared at the ring in the box. As dark as her complexion was, Allen could see that she was becoming flushed. He was starting to regret his proposal as he was beginning to think maybe he hadn't thought out how much she would be affected by it. He might have been ready, but there was the possibility that Callie wasn't.

"You don't have to give me a yes or no right now, but I'd like to know what you're thinking."

"Allen, I never thought..." she said as tears began to drop from her eyes, "I never thought...I can't believe...yes!"

"Did I hear you right? Did you just say 'yes'?"

"Yes! Yes! With all my heart, yes!"

Allen felt relieved. He took the ring out of the box and put it on her ring finger. It was a little loose, but neither one of them seemed to care. They got up from their seats to embrace in a passionate kiss. For Allen it was the realization of his high school fantasies. The girl of his dreams had just agreed to be his wife. It made everything he had gone through in the past several years worthwhile.

"You have no idea how happy you've made me right now," he said.

"I was thinking the same thing about you."

"Now that you've said yes, I intend to dedicate my life to making sure you don't regret that decision. I love you, Callie."

"I love you, too, Allen," she said before kissing him again.

"So, when do you think we should have the ceremony?"

"Soon. I've never liked the idea of long engagements. How about you?"

"It's going to take time to arrange everything, not to mention I'd like to get married in nice weather. Would June be soon enough?"

"I think that would be wonderful."

"June it is then. I can't wait to tell everybody."

"I can," she said noticeably crestfallen. "If no one's crazy about the idea of us dating, you can imagine how everyone's going to feel once they find out we're engaged."

"Our announcement is going to be just that – an announcement. I'm not asking for anyone's approval. As far as I'm concerned, they're going to have two options: they can share in our happiness or they can sit out quietly."

"I know you're close to your family and the last thing I want to do is ruin your relationship with them. Maybe we should sit on this news for a while, until they've gotten used to the idea of us."

"We've been dating for nearly a year already. If they're not used to us by now, they're never going to be. I think the sooner we tell them, the better. That way they don't think we're rushing into things."

"They're going to think we're rushing regardless. I still feel that we should wait to tell them. I'm not talking months, but just a few weeks. We could make it a Thanksgiving surprise."

"Oh, I get it. That's actually a great idea. When we go around the table and talk about what we're grateful for, I can tell everyone about how grateful I am that you said yes."

"And I'll be keeping my fingers crossed under the table when you do."

"Let's not be pessimistic. I know everyone will groan and moan for a while, but I have no doubt that everyone will be on board by the time June rolls around. Now I'm going to be in a tough straight because I have to choose a best man and I got a three-way tie going on. Maybe I'll just have three best men, if that's okay with you."

"What are you talking about?"

"I'm talking about Jim, Tim, and Davis."

"Jim? I thought you were going to talk to him about moving to North Carolina."

"I said I would do that if things didn't work out for him here, which remains to be seen. At any rate, he's most definitely going to be in the wedding."

"If he even wants to be in it, given the funk that he's currently in."

"I'm confident he will."

All of a sudden, Allen noticed that the song, "Betcha By Golly Wow," was playing. He remembered that this was the same song that was playing when he and Callie danced at their senior prom. It made Allen feel as if somehow this was meant to be.

"Sounds like our song is playing. Would you like to dance?"

"Of course."

Allen and Callie allowed themselves to be swept along with the sweet and simple melodies of the song and its sentiments. For Allen, this evening marked the beginning of the best days of his life. He could see their future in his mind's eye. They'd settle down for a couple of years while he went to law school, then when he got a better job, they'd add onto their family. Allen could see all the holidays they'd spend together and all of their special moments as a family. There was no reason to doubt that he and Callie would last a lifetime.

TWENTY-NINE

"Lord, it's me again. I know you're probably tired of hearing from me, but I can't help it. You're the only one that can help me. I'm sorry about the things I've said about You in the past, and I'm sorry for not keeping my faith and trusting you when Mama died. It's just that losing her hurt so much, and I didn't understand then like I do now. Look, I know I should just be grateful that I'm alive right now. You could have cut me off and sent me to hell, but You had mercy on me. I don't have the right to ask You for anything else, but...I need you. Please, help me. My life is a mess and I know it's my fault. I made a lot of stupid mistakes and I know I've got a lot to pay for. But I don't want the people that I love to have to suffer because of what I've done. Show me what I need to do to fix things. I'll do whatever you want me to, just show me..."

Jim had managed to sit himself on one of the carpeted steps at the altar where he was praying. He had come to the church early with Pastor Bynum who was up in the office with the other clergy and ministerial staff preparing for today's service. Jim wanted some time in the church when it was empty and quiet because he was hoping he would be able to hear the voice of the Lord speak to him about his situation.

The secrets he was keeping locked away inside him were making a hole in his spirit that was causing him unbearable pain. All Jim could think about was what he had done. His guilt had become a demon that tormented him daily. Every time he tried to feel good about something, his guilt would rob him of his joy. It wasn't simply the wrong that he had done that bothered him, but the fear of what would happen when everything became known. He couldn't help but think back to what Riley had said to him at Leo's that afternoon: 'There's nothing hid that won't be made known.'[1] Riley had already figured out a lot, and there was no doubt in his mind that she had begun to entertain the idea that he had some connection to Darius. How long would it be before the others started making the same connections? What would they think if they found out? Then he thought about how the longer he kept this secret the worse the outcome would be. What would he do if an angry Darius confronted him eighteen years from now about what he'd done? What could he say? The possible answers to these questions filled him with anxiety. But this was the beginning of his problems.

To make matters worse, ever since he'd stopped taking cocaine cold turkey, Jim felt as if a cloud of depression were hanging over him. He had been praying to help him combat it, but not getting an answer made him feel even worse. Sometimes, in his desperate search for an answer to his depression, his mind would wander back to that magic powder called cocaine. There was a small part of him that felt if he could have just one little hit every once in awhile until he could feel better on his own, he'd be all right.

Jim knew how dangerous going back to his habit was and when that part of him began to stoke his urge, he would fight against it. But lately that little part of him had been growing.

Jim still had not signed up for the counseling services at the church. He had begun to entertain the idea after Riley had suggested it during their lunch at Leo's. He even called down to the church office to get information about it, but when he found out Davis was one of the counselors, he balked. He didn't want anyone from his set to know about the extent of his addiction, even if the information would be treated confidentially. "Besides, if God can't help me, counseling sure can't," he thought to himself. So he sat at the altar waiting for the Lord to move and felt more despondent with every moment that He didn't. After a few moments, he heard footsteps coming from the stairs leading to the prayer room. When he looked up he saw one of the last people he wanted to see coming down.

"Praise the Lord, brother," said Davis upon seeing him.

"Praise the Lord, man."

Part of Jim's reservation toward Davis stemmed from the fact that he didn't know him very well and his first impressions of him had been clouded by jealousy. Davis seemed like a nice guy, and under different circumstances, they might have become best friends. At present, Davis's presence made him feel a bit self-conscious and Jim hoped he was only passing through to somewhere else and would leave him alone.

"I'm not interrupting nothin', am I?"

"Nah, man. I done said my piece. Sometimes I just like to sit and listen – ya know?" said Jim hoping Davis would take the hint. Instead, Davis sat down next to him at the altar.

"You just got to trust Him."

"Now that's the hardest part."

"I'm not gonna lie, you right about that. But it's the only choice we have. It's like Job said, 'though he slay me, yet will I trust him...'"[2]

"Davis, you were in the life, right?" asked Jim. It had just occurred to him that he and Davis had something in common.

"Yeah."

"You ever done anything during that time of your life that you regret? Something you thought no one would forgive you for?"

"That would be just about everything. There's no way to come through that without getting hurt or hurting someone else. Every day is nothin' but senseless violence. Sometimes I get a little depressed thinking about all the things I did back then."

"How did you learn to move on from that?"

"First off, I know a lot of the things I did was because I didn't know any better. For a long time I thought the way I was livin' was normal – like that's how it was suppost to be. If I had known then what I know now, I probably wouldn't have done most of the stuff I did. I definitely wouldn't have gotten into a gang – period."

"But there had to be things you knew were wrong."

"Yeah. There were things that I knew was wrong, but I did it anyway. I try to do like the Lord says – ya know? I had to humble myself, cop to what I did, and ask people for forgiveness. Some people forgave me, but some haven't and I can't fault them for that. I can't bring dead people back to life and I can't heal the scars I put on people's hearts. It's real easy to mess things up, but you can't always fix things."

"That's the problem. It's all the things you can't fix. It's like a burden you have to live with the rest of your life. I mean I know God forgives our sins and everything, but when there are things that constantly remind you of how you messed up...it's like you just can't get past your past."

"True that, but the way I see it is you have to repent, deal with it, accept the consequences, and then trust God to handle the rest. That's the only way to get past the guilt. I've been going through some things because of some issues I hadn't really dealt with, and that's what's been helping me.

"I'd be afraid of what God might allow to happen."

"Sometimes you just gotta man up and go through. I'm not gonna say it's easy or it's not gonna cost you nothin' cause just recently I realized there are some things I gotta give up on. You just gotta trust that in the end God will work things out."

"Maybe you're right, man."

There was something about Davis's words that resonated with him. It almost seemed like God was speaking to him through Davis. Just like what happened with Way-lo that day at the McDonalds. Jim knew what he had to do, but he was afraid. The prospect of his family's hurt and disappointment filled him with unbearable shame. The thought of losing everyone he loved and being alone again was terrifying. "If only there were some way that they could find out without me having to actually deliver the blow personally," he thought. But that would make him look worse in their eyes. Not only would they feel betrayed, they would also think he purposefully deceived them.

After a while, the ushers and ministerial staff began to come downstairs and take their places to greet the host of congregants who were waiting outside to be let in. Davis went downstairs to the choir room to rehearse with the other members and Jim went to the pew where he and his family usually sat. While he waited for them to arrive, he decided to read his Bible. He decided to pick up where he left off in the book of Matthew:

"Watch and pray, that ye enter not into temptation: the spirit indeed is willing, but the flesh is weak. He went away again the second time, and prayed, saying, O my Father, if this cup may not pass away from me, except I drink it, thy will be done"[3]

The passage summed up how Jim felt. He didn't want to have to go through with what he knew he had to do, even though he had just told God that he would do anything. At the same time, he knew it was best to resign his fate to the will of the Father, just as Christ did. In the end Christ drank the bitter cup. He suffered unto death for sins he didn't even commit to save people like Jim. The least Jim could do was suffer for something he actually had done. Still, there was a fear that tugged at his heart. Jim wanted to do the right thing, but he needed the strength and the faith to go through with it.

THIRTY

Allyson walked through the doors of the church expecting to see Allen, but was greeted by another usher, an older gentleman, who simply flashed a warm smile her way before handing her a program. She felt more at ease this time, now that she knew what to expect, and she thought she was better dressed for the part thanks to the salary her mother was paying her for her investigative skills. Allyson was certain her black and camel colored Italian merino crew-neck sweater dress that came to the knee, and her beige cloche hat and trench coat were well in keeping with what many of the other female parishioners would be wearing and help her to blend seamlessly into the aesthetics of the church environment. Allyson stood for a moment and looked over the sanctuary thinking about where would be a good place to sit.

"I was hoping you'd show," said a voice coming from nearby.

Allyson turned around to see where it was coming from. She thought she recognized the voice. It was none other than, Tim. He looked as if he was glad to see her. Allyson hoped he wasn't getting any funny ideas. She couldn't help being related to him, but there was no way they were going to be friends again – ever.

"I have a job to do."

"Of course. Would you like me to escort you to where we're sitting?"

"That won't be necessary. I'd rather sit in the back."

"Are you sure? I thought you'd want a front row seat to record your observations."

"I saw enough of that last week, thank you very much. And frankly, you're enough of an embarrassment under normal circumstances. I certainly don't want to be anywhere near you when you're in some sort of praise mode like you were the last time I was here. Anyway, I find the saner people of this church tend to occupy the back rows."

"Are you going to be available after the service is over?"

"Why?"

"Mrs. Sharpe was wondering if you could help her serve dinners in the church hall across the street. They're kind of short of staff and they could use some help."

"Why the hell would you think I'd want to do that?"

"You're right. Forgive me for thinking that you would want to do something for someone other than yourself."

"Oh, don't try to guilt me. They're your people, not mine. Why don't you help them?"

"I would, but I have Bible Study class, and it wouldn't be fair to Daniel."

"I'm just a visitor here. Don't you have any other members available?"

"I wouldn't be asking you if there were. But if you don't want to, I can't force you," he said walking away.

Then Allyson had a second thought. The experience might be useful in helping her to find out what goes on behind the scenes, and learn what this place and these people were really all about.

"Tim, wait!"

He stopped and turned to look at her.

"I'll do it."

"Thank you. You can meet them up front after the service"

"I'm not doing this for you. Like I said, I have a job to do"

"Don't remind me"

He was about to turn away, but turned back suddenly.

"Allyson, do you think one day, we could meet up just to talk..."

"No"

Allyson turned and walked away without saying another word and took a seat in the second to last pew near the entrance. As she crossed her legs, she diverted her attention to the praise team that had gathered at the front of the church signaling the start of the service. She had no interest in hearing anything Tim had to say. A famous writer once said, that one should believe what people do and not what they say. As far as she was concerned, there was nothing that Tim could say that would change how she felt about what he had done to her. She had seen Tim's true colors a long time ago, and she was determined to treat him accordingly.

As the service got underway, Allyson went through the church bulletin to distract herself from the bitterness that was welling up inside her. There were times when the memory of his transgression would flash before her and she felt as if she were reliving it all over again. All of a sudden she was eight years old, laying in her bed, and crying herself to sleep for what had to be the thirtieth night in a row after the recent death of her beloved Poppa, one of the few people in her life that she knew actually loved her. In the midst of her sobbing, she heard a tumult coming from Tim's room down the hall. It sounded as if someone was tearing the room apart. Amidst the racket she heard the agitated voices of her mother and her new nannies, Safi and Anna, and another masculine voice. She wondered what they were doing. Allyson got out of bed and went to the door and poked her head out. They were in Tim's room and the door was open. There was a police officer standing outside writing on a tablet and her mother was in the doorway directing the two nannies who were inside.

"Search the armoire and all the dressers–thoroughly! Check for secret compartments! If there are any papers check every word!"

"Yes, ma'am," said Safi.

"Anna, check under the mattress," said Eleanor.

"Ms. Russell, can you tell us who was the last person to have contact with your son?" asked the officer.

“He was last seen at school...he was supposed to have lacrosse practice, but the coach said he never showed,” she answered.

“Do you think you could give us information on some of his friends? Maybe we’ll get a lead from one of them”

“Oh...I don’t really...” she began. She rubbed her forehead as she did when she was trying to think, “Anna, do you know anything about Tim’s friends? You know the boys that stop by sometimes?”

Allyson immediately picked up on what was going on and her heart was beating out of her chest. She ran down the hall toward her mother and the officer.

“Tim’s missing, isn’t he? Did someone kidnap him?” said Allyson.

“Allyson, sweetheart, please. Go back to bed. Your brother has not been kidnapped. We’re just trying to find out where he is right now,” said Eleanor.

“But if you called the police...”

“Just as a precaution, my dear. Trust me, Allyson, everything is going to be fine.”

“That’s what you said about Poppa, and he’s dead!”

“Allyson, this is not the time!” said her mother, who had to stop her self from reaching out and shaking her daughter. “Safi, please put Miss Russell to bed.”

“Yes, ma’am,” she said as she emerged from the room. “Come now, little miss. Let’s go back to bed,” said Safi holding out her hand to Allyson.

“No! I want to help,” said Allyson. She knew she was taking a real risk considering her mother’s temper. As long as the officer was here, she knew her mother wouldn't dare strike her, but when he left, she would pay. But she wanted to help Tim, and she was willing to endure her mother's cruelty if it meant having him back home and safe.

"Allyson, do as you're told!"

"The police will find him, miss," said Safi as she pleaded with the little girl, and looked back fearfully at the angry expression on her employer's face.

"I'm his sister. I know who his friends are and I know his girlfriend, too," said Allyson as she ignored the other adults and appealed directly to the officer. "He talks to them on his laptop all the time."

"Do you mind?" the officer asked Eleanor. She merely nodded her assent. The officer stooped down to Allyson's level and introduced himself to her and asked her what she knew. Allyson told them everything she knew about Tim's friends and where they lived. She also made sure to tell them about the girl. Allyson knew Tim was crazy about her because she had caught them making out in his room on more than one occasion. She only hoped what she was telling them would be useful in finding Tim. She didn't know if someone had done something bad to him or if he had gotten lost somewhere. She just wanted him back safe.

"Thank you for your help, sweetheart. I promise I'll do everything I can to make sure your brother gets home in one piece. Now go to bed and get some sleep, ok."

"Yes, let's go, Miss Ally," said Safi as she took Allyson's hand gently.

They both started back toward her room, but Allyson kept her ears open to hear what the adults were saying.

“If we could have the computer, it would help,” said the officer.

“It’s gone,” said Anna who was out of breath after turning half the room upside down.

“Does he usually take it with him?” the officer asked.

“Sometimes, if they having a project at school or something like that,” replied Anna.

When they got to the room, Allyson burst out into tears.

“Oh, miss, don’t cry. Mr. Tim hasn’t been missing that long. The officer will find you brother. He promise you,” said Safi, as she gently stroked Allyson’s hair.

“What if he doesn’t? What if some evil person like...killed him or something? That happened to this kid I heard about on the news,” said Allyson.

“You need to stop watching the news. You too young for that. Anyway, Mr. Tim is a big strong boy and he know how to take care of heself. He could have went someplace with he friends after school and they got lost or something.”

“But what if he’s hurt and he can’t get home, like that time he went camping with Stuart and Gary and they left him in the woods by himself while they got a ride from Gary’s sister.”

“We find him then, and we will find him now, little miss. Don’t worry you head and get some sleep now. ‘Right?”

Safi tucked Allyson in and left, but there was no way the younger girl could sleep. She had just lost Poppa and now Tim was gone, too. Tim was the only person left in her family that she could trust, the only other person who had ever been there for her in any capacity. She couldn't imagine living without him. She hoped with every fiber of her being that he would be found alive, and soon.

It would be two weeks before they had heard anything. During those two weeks, Allyson rarely slept, but crept around the house during the night to listen in on the conversations her mother had with her close friends, Aunt Morgan, the nannies, the police and Hurst when he finally decided to get involved. During the day she would have Safi drive her around to different places in the city where Tim would hang out with his friends, to check to see if he would appear, but he never did. Allyson had never been so scared in all her life. With Hurst's help, they finally found him in California and had him detained in central booking at a local precinct. Her mother and Hurst went in the latter's private jet to pick him up and bring him back, meanwhile the nannies filled her in on what was going on.

"See, I told you they'd find you brother - all the way in California, no less. It's a good thing you told them about the girl because that help a lot. Turn out she was missing, too and they get them both together."

"Did kidnappers take them there?"

"No. He and the girl come there all by theyself."

"You mean he ran away?"

"Yes, Miss."

"Why would he do that?"

"I think he was still sad about your Poppa being gone and he felt stressed, maybe a little lonely even."

"But why would he feel lonely when I'm here?"

"Mr. Tim is a big boy and you're a little girl. He need help you can't give him."

"Was he going to stay there with that girl forever?"

"I don't know nothing 'bout that, Miss. I think he woulda come back after while. Fourteen is big, but at that age you still need a mommy and a daddy."

"He didn't even say goodbye to me," said Allyson as tears spilled down her cheeks.

"Oh, little Miss Ally, come here," said Safi, who had stopped her work to take Allyson in her arms. "I'm sure Mr. Tim didn't mean to leave you. He probly just ran off without thinkin' much. Sometimes when people's heart hurt they head don't work to good. You brother always love you."

"No he doesn't. He's just a liar! Just like the rest of them! And I don't care if he ever comes back!" said Allyson as she snatched herself away from Safi and ran to her room.

"Miss Ally, that's not true!" Safi cried after her "Miss Ally!"

Allyson locked her door and threw herself on the bed letting her face sink into the pillow that muffled her sobs and absorbed her tears. "How could Tim do that to me? How could he leave me here all by myself?" she thought at the time. If he loved her he would have taken her with him like he did that girl, or at the very least he would have told her his plan. She thought he always told her everything, just like she always told him everything. After Poppa's funeral, Tim promised her that they would work together and take care of each other, but now it seemed that was just another empty promise like the ones her mother and Hurst made all the time. She would have expected a betrayal like this from her parents, but not from her big brother. Not the brother that used to read her bedtime stories in silly voices, let her sleep in his room when it was thundering outside, took her to the Carousel at Central Park on Saturdays when he had nothing to do, and played tea party with her and her teddies even though he thought it was dorky. This couldn't be the brother who taught her how to draw princess cartoons and calmed her down before recitals when she was so nervous she'd throw up. Now it seemed that brother died with Poppa and now she was truly alone. Everything and everyone she had trusted in had either left her or betrayed her.

Allyson swallowed hard, and gritted her teeth to stifle the tears that were trying to well up inside her, as she remembered where she was in the present. She had tried to convince herself that she couldn't feel that hurt anymore. Nothing could hurt her anymore. "Don't let yourself go there, Ally. Remember you're strong; you're a survivor. You don't need anybody. The only person you can trust in this world is you," she admonished herself.

She was glad when she felt her phone vibrating in her purse. When she took it out and looked at the screen, she noticed she'd gotten a message from Jason. He had invited her to dinner on Wednesday, and they were trying to settle on the time. Jason wanted to meet her at Menagerie at 5:00, but that was cutting it close because she had a class that ended at 4:00, so she sent a text suggesting they meet at 6:00. The invitation renewed her hope that he'd remembered her birthday after all, which put her in a better mood. While she was waiting for his reply, she decided to go shopping on the internet for her birthday outfit. She wanted to look really special and let Jason know just what kind of woman he had. She had just purchased a cute little aqua paisley, silk mini dress when Pastor Bynum or what she'd call Harlem's own Reverend Lovejoy approached the altar.

"Go head and praise Him for a little bit before I get started here," he said addressing the congregation. Shouts of praise resounded all over the sanctuary. Allyson felt like she was getting a headache.

"Praise the Lord, bretheren."

"Praise the Lord."

"Since today is communion Sunday, I got a short one for you all today. But just because it's short don't mean its not going to be heavy. Amen?"

"Amen."

"My subject today is: He is God. The message is coming from the book of Daniel, chapter four, verses 29 through 37. When you find it say Amen."

Allyson yawned and pushed some of her curly ash blonde locks over her shoulder, as the parishioners searched for the scripture. She was tired, but not enough to fall asleep as she did last time. She decided to stay awake and listen to the message to find out his angle so she could give the information to her mother. Suddenly, Allyson felt a tap on her arm. When she looked over she saw that an old woman was offering to share her bible with her so she could read along. Allyson did not expect such a gesture. The woman was smiling at her and seemed to be offering out of kindness – not what she expected based on the stereotypes she had of church folk who she had always thought were mean and judgmental.

She would have waved away the woman's offer, but instead she decided to accept it, glancing down at the page.

Allyson had heard of this king before in an ancient history class she'd taken in high school. She knew Nebuchadnezzar was a real king who lived during the pre-Christian era, but didn't know much else about him. She wondered how the good reverend was going to get an hour-long sermon out of this particular snippet of the Bible.

"I know that God is real. I know that He is and that he is God. There are a lot of people who don't know this fact. They think everything in this world is according to man – dictated by human flesh. And I don't understand how anyone can believe in man. Man has let us down so many times. Man relies on his research or his science to help him understand this world and how it works, but how many times has science failed us. Science told us that African-Americans weren't people. We now know that wasn't true. They told us women's wombs made them crazy, but now we know that's not true. Science told us that certain drugs were okay, but then a year later, the same drugs had to be pulled because they killed people. Every time you look around there's always something that man and his science thought was true, but in the end, it turned out it wasn't true. Some of the things they've said were so crazy, you'd have to ask yourself why would people even give that a second thought. Did you know they got doctors today that want to say that pedophilia is not a sickness? Now you know that's wrong. You can't even trust him for the weather half the time – weather man say it's going to be sunny and you go out there without your umbrella and sure enough it rains all over you. But you can't tell man that he doesn't have it going on."

"You can't tell some of these men that they might be wrong. They want to argue with you and tell you about their degrees and their experiences and the work that they've done. They think it's all about them. As we read the scripture passage we see Nebuchadnezzar was just like these men."

"Nebuchadnezzar believed that everything that he had came from his own strength, wisdom and power. He was full of himself and he refused to acknowledge God. He probably thought he was a god in his own right. But then God put His hand on Nebuchadnezzar, hallelujah! He took a man at the height of his power and intellect and brought him down to the level of a beast of the field. It reminds me of what it says in the book of Psalms, 'verily every man at his best state is altogether vanity,'[1] and when he says 'Man that is in honour, and understandeth not, is like the beasts that perish.[2] Just when you think you're something big, God will show you just how little you are. Nebuchadnezzar was scraping and drooling, his hair sticking up like birds feathers and there was nothing he could do about it. He had lost his mind. There was no kind of psychological therapy in all the world that could have helped him get his mind back because what God does, man cannot undo. Nebuchadnezzar scraped and drooled until the time that God had appointed, or until He was good and ready. How many rich and powerful men today get a disease like cancer? They go all around the world thinking they can use their money and influence to get a cure, but it doesn't work. It is not until man has an encounter with God that he realizes who God is. After his encounter, Nebuchadnezzar had no other choice but to admit that God is real and that He lives."

"Here we go," thought Allyson, smugly. "More science bashing. Granted, there were scientists that made mistakes, but scientists have also made some really important discoveries that have benefited humankind. Scientists discovered the world wasn't flat. They also came up with transplant surgeries, antibiotics, computers and other useful inventions. There had to be some kind of error in order to get to these successes. That's what progress is all about. It has nothing to do with a god." Allyson was getting restless. She felt he was more convincing at dinner than he was during this particular sermon. However she would continue to listen to see where this message was going.

"Many people see man imitating God and think that because of the few things God allows him to do like Himself, that there is no God. God allowed Pharaoh's magicians to do enchantments like some of the miracles that He worked through Moses. God allowed sorcerers like Simeon to bewitch people. God allows men today to play around and call themselves cloning, using in-vitro fertilization, making artificial hearts and the like, but there's always a limit to what man can do. There was a point when Pharaoh's magicians couldn't do what God was working through Moses to do. They couldn't use their enchantments to bring darkness across the sky and hailstones of fire. Simeon could do a lot of things, but he couldn't lay hands on anyone and have them filled with the Holy Ghost as God worked through the apostles. Even today, a man can call himself making an artificial heart – I read a story about how the fake heart was still going, but the man was dead, praise God! If God wants to call you home, there's not a man on this earth that can keep you alive. Man can manipulate these cells and the like, but he can't make something out of nothing! God formed a world from nothing – he didn't need any cells or anything else! God spoke and it appeared –how many men can claim to do that! He formed man from the earth and breathed the breath of life into him! When have you ever heard a man do that! Jesus Christ called Lazarus back to life after the latter had been dead in his grave four days. Have you ever heard of a scientist that could do that? Y'all don't hear me! I'm telling you that man has a limit, but God has no limit!"

"Hallelujah! Glory to God! Glory!" said the old woman next to Allyson. Her exclamation made Allyson start a bit. It's seemed the old woman was not the only one who agreed with the Pastor. There were many people calling out praises to God.

"Some of you still want to argue," continued the pastor, "you want to say that man is on a path to progress. The longer we live, the smarter we get, better things are going to get. I say what kind of progress have we made? Going from the telephone to the cell phone is not progress. Going from the horse and carriage to the airplane to the space shuttle isn't progress. Over the years man has been able to change ***how*** we do things, but not ***what*** we do. For all our technological progress, no one has ever been able to solve the problems that have plagued mankind since the fall of Adam and Eve. For centuries, man has been searching for a way to bring world peace, but has he ever done it? For centuries, man has been searching for ways to end poverty and crime, but has he found it? Man has made peace accord after peace accord, policy after policy, law after law, ruling after ruling, but nothing he does can legislate the human heart. Decade after decade man has been trying to prevent natural disasters, disease and sickness – has he ever been able to do it? When it comes to these things we are in the same state that we were in thousands of years ago, but we just have fancier gadgets. We keep trying to solve these problems but there is only One that will be able to solve them. There is One that will bring peace, there is only One that will end poverty and sickness. My Bible tells me that the only One who will bring perfection to the earth is Jesus Christ!"

Allyson couldn't argue with this particular portion of the Pastor's message. From the way the world looked to her, man did seem to be like a dog chasing his tail. So many scientists, politicians, businessmen, celebrities, and philosophers in the world all claiming to have the answer to the world's problems and in the end their work would be proven to be miscalculations, error and sometimes outright lies meant to deceive. But then whom could you believe? Who could you trust? Should she even believe this Bynum character?

"So you see I can't put my trust in man," continued the Pastor as he reached the conclusion of his message, "I know some of y'all say you trust me, but I can't even say I trust myself from time to time. I have to put my trust in the Lord. As it is written: 'God is not a man that he should lie, nor the son of man that he should repent'.[3] I know that I can trust God because his Word is always true. The apostle Paul wrote, 'Let God be true and every man be a liar'.[4] When He speaks it comes to pass. I know that I can trust God because He is Wisdom. He knows what I don't and his knowledge is perfect. I know that I can trust God because He is all powerful and there is nothing that He can't do. Finally, I know that I can trust God because He is love. He loved us so much that He sent his only begotten Son, Jesus, to die for our sins. That's right, like the Word says 'For when we were yet without strength, in due time Christ died for the ungodly'[5] and 'But God commendeth his love toward us in that while we were yet sinners, Christ died for us'.[6] We didn't deserve the grace that He gave us, but He did it anyhow. How many of you know many people who would do something good for you after you had mocked and mistreated them? Christ did that for us despite the fact that mankind had him crucified on the cross. He did it so that we could have eternal life. Folks, it can't get no better than that!"

"God can give you immortality – the real deal, not the sorry substitutions that man comes up with. You can't live forever through your children because at some point they're going to have to die, too. You can't live forever by having your name on a building because eventually that building will be torn down. You can't live forever by fame because in less than a generation, you'll be forgotten and your place and name removed from the history and record books, deemed irrelevant or discredited. The only way to receive eternal life is through Christ and Christ alone. Put your trust in Him. Don't believe me – believe God. Go get your Word, open it and read it. Just trust Him and see. He will never leave you and He will never fail you."

The Pastor's words were tempting. Who wouldn't want to believe in someone who had the answers to all of life's problems? Who wouldn't want to be able to depend upon someone for all of their needs? But how would she know that this God was the answer? There was a part of Allyson that wanted to believe, but she didn't want to get her hopes up. There were lots of things that seemed real to her in the past, but turned out to be fake. She didn't want to be disappointed again. The Pastor seemed genuine in his convictions, lots of well meaning people were, but that didn't mean that he couldn't be wrong.

Soon after he began the altar call for the communion. Row by row the churchgoers lined up at the altar to partake of the bread and the wine. As the people went up, the choir sang songs about the blood of Jesus. Allyson had no intention of participating. She just waited for this portion of the service to conclude. She watched as her brother went up to the altar to kneel before the serving tray with several others before saying a brief prayer and taking a chunk of bread and drinking the wine from one of the little cups. He did seem content with his life now in a way that he hadn't before. "What if his faith was genuine?" she asked herself. Allyson knew her brother had never been the church type and yet here he was, a part of this holiness church of all places. Could it have been this place that changed him? Did he really believe what that Bynum guy said? But then again, Tim could be a very convincing actor, since she herself had been fooled for so long.

Once the communion was over, Pastor Bynum offered the benediction and dismissed the parishioners. Allyson was about to try to find Mrs. Sharpe, when she saw her approaching the pew where she sat. No matter how many times she'd seen Allen's mom, she was astounded by how well she looked for her age. Sure her own mother looked young, but Allyson knew that was because of her yearly regimen of botox, spa treatments, yoga, fade and wrinkle creams, fad diets, and new age health fads. Allen's mom on the other hand, had none of that, and yet she had a flawless and wrinkle free golden-brown complexion, and though she was a little plump, her physique was noticeably toned and firm. The only things that signified her age were her outdated 80's teased out hairdo and her outfit: a simple navy seasonless wool suit that had a collarless, peplum jacket, a simple pill-box hat, and black pumps. The warmth of her smile was almost enough to melt Allyson's cold cynicism.

"Allyson! Praise the Lord and welcome back, chile!" said the older woman taking her into her arms for a hug.

"Thank you, Mrs. Sharpe," said Allyson feeling a little uncomfortable. Mrs. Sharpe almost knocked her over with the force of her affection. She was not used to all the touchy-feely-hugginess that characterized the Sharpe household. "Nice to see you again."

"How you doin', baby? Everything good at school?"

"Yes. Everything's fine there. Tim tells me you need some help today."

"Don't you know it? We're serving dinner today at the hall across the street, but most of the ladies that was supposed to be helping me got sick. I guess the flu season done started already."

"Sorry to hear that."

"You don't know how glad I was when Tim told me you'd help. Thank you so much sweetheart. I hope this isn't puttin' you out none."

"You're very welcome, Mrs. Sharpe. It isn't a problem at all."

"You don't have to call me Mrs. Sharpe. Call me Mama Lena, like everybody else."

"Okay...Mama Lena."

"There you go."

Then Mother Rose suddenly appeared dressed in a white gown that looked like an old woman's wedding dress. It had a lace bodice and silk organza skirt. Behind her were Tamiko in a stylishly retro royal blue stand collar dress with three-quarter sleeves, and Allen's cousin in a gray pantsuit with a short-sleeved jacket.

"Lena, dear, I wondered where you went. The girls and I were just about to head over to the hall."

"Allyson's going to help us, too, so I came over to get her," replied Lena.

"Is that so?" said Mother Rose who was looking Allyson over as if she were covered in feces. She reminded Allyson of Trish, but thirty years older.

"Yes," said Allyson beaming her best fake smile "Tim told me about your situation, and asked if I'd volunteer."

"I see. But if you don't feel comfortable because of your – beliefs, then know you are not obliged to participate."

"As long as I don't have to hand out tracts, I don't think there'll be a problem."

"Don't worry, dear, I wouldn't dream of it. That task is usually reserved for those more capable."

"Hi, Allyson. Nice to see you again," offered Tamiko.

"Hello, Tamika," said Allyson.

"It's Tamiko," said Riley giving her a cold look.

"Oh, yes. Sorry. And your name, again?"

"Riley."

"I'm confused. Is that your first name or last name?"

Riley narrowed her eyes, and her mouth became a thin line.

"That's her first name," said Lena, who noticed the tension stewing, "She's a Sharpe just like Allen."

"Let's head over to the hall before we're late. We don't want to keep people waiting," said Mother Rose.

Something told Allyson, this was going to be a long afternoon.

*****

"What would you like?" said Allyson for what had to be the thousandth time today. It had to be 1,000 degrees in back of the steam table she was serving from. Beads of sweat were starting to escape from under her hairnet. She would have tried to wipe them away with the back of her hand, but the plastic gloves she was wearing were covered in grease and sauce from the food she was serving. Her feet had gone numb from standing in four inch stilettos for the past two hours, and now this old woman was standing before her ogling each entrée as if she'd never seen food before and couldn't make up her mind. Not that the entrees were very appetizing to Allyson. There was whiting that looked like it'd been fried to death, pulled pork sandwiches that were oozing grease, what she could only guess were seasoned French fries, alien looking macaroni and cheese, potato salad, and biscuits. "If they're going to feed people, they could have at least offered healthier options," thought Allyson.

"Let me get one of the little whitings and some of them chips. And I'll take some of that 'tata salad and a biscuit, too, if you don't mind," said the toothless woman after what felt like ten minutes of looking. Allyson had to dig under the large pieces of fish to find her a small one and then fixed the rest of her plate. She put each entrée in a different compartment of the Styrofoam tray and handed the woman her order, just like Mrs. Sharpe had taught her. Then the next customer came up. It was a very heavy-set woman clad in spandex, who had three, disheveled looking kids with her. Allyson looked down the line, which seemed like it was never going to end. She wished she were Tamiko who was minding the dessert counter or Riley, who was on drinks. Their lines weren't that long.

"Gimme three orders of fish and chips and then I want a pork sandwich with macaroni and potato salad," said the woman.

Allyson started fixing the fish orders first and handed them to the woman who opened one to inspect it.

"How come ain't no ketchup on these fries?" she asked.

"You didn't ask," said Allyson as she finished fixing the last order and put it on the counter.

"You could've offered. After all, you the one servin'. How am I supost to know if y'all got ketchup or not?" she replied.

"And how am I supposed to know what you want? I'm not a mind reader you know."

"You ain't gotta get an attitude, snotty little half-breed."

"You're the one with the attitude, crack ho."

"Come out from behind that counter and say that, so I can kick yo' ***"

"You better hope I don't. I'll beat you over the head with one of your little rug rats."

"Yo! I'ma 'bout to jump over this counter and punch you in yo' face!"

"What's going on over here?" asked Lena who had raced over upon hearing the commotion.

"I just asked this chick for some ketchup and she callin' me a crack ho, and with my kids standing here to listen to that mess!"

"She insulted me first! She called me a half-breed."

"That's a lie! See! That's why I don't like comin' out to these things! I'm tryin' the best I can to take care of my kids, and then you got these people like Miss thing over there judging and lookin' down on you."

"Miss, I'm not judging you," said Lena putting a hand on the woman's shoulder. "And look at these three beautiful babies you got here. What's say we get them something to eat?"

"I don't want to deal with her."

"Then you deal with me and tell me what you want."

Mrs. Sharpe not only fixed the dinners for this family, but she also gave the children coloring books and crayons that she got from who knows where. It made Allyson upset. It seemed as if she were taking that woman's side over hers. When she was done with those guests, Mrs. Sharpe came back behind the steam table to refresh the dwindling macaroni tray. Allyson wanted to set things straight.

"I didn't start anything with that woman. She insulted me first. You do believe me, don't you?" said

Allyson stepping back, as Mrs. Sharpe put in a new tray of macaroni in the table.

"Of course I do, sweetheart. She's been here before and done the same thing to myself and to Mother Rose. I guess she's having a hard time in life and sometimes she takes it out on other people."

Soon another woman came up to take over the serving as Mrs. Sharpe pulled Allyson aside to talk to her.

"So why do you keep allowing her in? Why not just put her picture up and make her persona non-grata?"

"Because Jesus says to have mercy."

"You mean 'turn the other cheek'?" said Allyson trying to keep the cynicism out of her voice.

"That's right. You have to learn to let little things like that slide."

"Little things? She called me a half-breed, and she threatened me!"

"She's called me a black so-in-so. That's just words, Allyson. When you know what and whose you are, you don't let those things bother you. I know you'll disagree, but I believe we have to treat others according to what God says and not by how they treat us."

"Soooo, you're okay with people treating you like dirt and getting away with it, or are you into rewarding people for treating you like dirt?"

"I don't have to make anyone pay for what they do to me. When you're a child of God, He has your back. No one ever gets away with doing wrong to someone else."

"I prefer to mete out my own brand of justice."

"You'd feel better if you let things go. You hold onto all that stuff and all it does is eat you up inside and make you miserable. I let God fight my battles. You may not think so, but I know God can do more with your enemies than you can."

"How much longer does this dinner go on for?"

"We close at 6:00, but our shift will be over by 4:15 or so. When the second shift comes in then we can leave."

"You've given away a ton of food already. How often do you do this?"

"We do it on the first Sunday of the month, holidays, and when we have outreach events. With all the need that's out there, I wish we could do it everyday. We're trying to raise money so we can start a food pantry for the children and seniors."

"You'd need a lot to feed all these people. Would you mind if I ask where the money comes from?"

"Sure don't. Comes from tithes. Pastor Bynum is a very trustworthy shepherd. The majority of tithe offering that goes into the collection plate goes to serve the poor in the church community and the larger community. We used to spread ourselves thin and try to do some of everything, but it wasn't having as much of an impact as we would like. So Pastor decided that we needed to focus on a few things and do those well. Now we're just focusing on feeding the hungry and educating the youth and we've got a few programs to help the community in those areas."

"You seem to know a lot. How long have you been a member?"

"I been with this church ever since I was a young girl, before Pastor Bynum came."

"You mean Reverend Bynum wasn't always the Pastor?"

"No we had another pastor, but he died and the person who was supposed to succeed him didn't want to take his place, and the next in line was so radical that the board voted him out. Pastor Bynum was an associate Pastor who used to come and preach sometimes, so we asked him if he would stay with us and thankfully he did. The church has been growing ever since."

"Really?" said Allyson. Now she felt like she was getting somewhere. She wished she'd had her digital recorder with her.

"Yes, indeed. Before we were just one church, but now there are three churches. One here, one in North Carolina, and one in Virginia."

"Do those churches have a lot of members?"

"The one in North Carolina is kinda small, but growing. The one in Virginia would be the same size as the one here."

"Does the Pastor receive any money from these churches?"

"Only if he goes down there to preach. Then they'll take up a speakers offering for him, but aside from that the Pastor doesn't get anything. The churches will sometimes raise money for one another. Like when there was a storm that hit Virginia last summer, we raised money to send to the people in the church down there who were working on rebuilding their homes."

"I see. But the Pastor has control of those churches doesn't he?"

"Not really. He started those churches, but there are other pastors that direct them. He does visit them occasionally though. Sometimes we all get together for a convention with the other churches."

"Did he at least get to choose who those pastors were?"

"No, it doesn't work like that. He can recommend someone, but ultimately, the board of the church prays about it before they make their decision."

"Are you on the church board?"

"No. I'm not a church board member. But I am on the mother's board."

"Does that mean you get special privileges or stock in the church?"

"I don't know anything about all that," laughed Lena "but overall I don't come to church to get anything, I come to give: I give glory to God, and pray he uses me to give to others and lead them to Him."

"There's got to be something you're getting out of all this. Otherwise, why come?"

"Well I do want to get into the kingdom. That's the only thing I'm really looking forward to."

"You mean Heaven, right? Like after you're dead."

Now the interview was going off the course that Allyson had planned and she was losing interest. She didn't want to get into another conversation on Christian dogma.

“Unh-uh, baby. I’m going to be alive. Believe it or not, I’m going to be living for eternity in the presence of the living God.”

“But that’s the thing... how do you know that what you believe is real? It’s not like people can come back from the dead to tell you what’s out there.”

“Jesus did. He came back and confirmed everything the Bible said before he went back up into the heaven.”

“With all due respect, no one in this day and age has seen Him.”

“I have. When my parents came to this city they didn’t have two thin dimes to rub together, but I was blessed to be able to go to college and grad school. When I was 13, I had to have an operation and have most of my womb taken out. I was devastated. I had dreams of having a husband and children and after that I didn’t think any man would want to marry me. But don’t you know that in February of 1980, one of the rankest sinner’s I’d ever known came down to the altar call and got saved, and not three years later, I married him. That’s right – and he’s been a faithful husband to me for 28 years. Hallelujah! Glory to God! Then almost four years after that, I was blessed with a beautiful baby boy. I had a child, and I didn’t even have half a womb! Praise you Lord Jesus!”

To Allyson, it looked like Mrs. Sharpe was getting a little emotional. Her voice got louder, her eyes were tearing up and she was even starting to dance like she was in church. People were starting to look over and stare at them.

“Are you okay, Mrs. Shar- uh, I mean, Mama Lena? Would you like some water or something?”

"I don't need no water, I got livin' water.[7] I'm sorry, baby. I don't mean to upset you and I don't mean to make a scene, but when I think about how the Lord has been good to me...Hallelujah! There's so much more that I could tell you, but it would take all year. I just want to let you know, God is real and he's faithful, and he works! Glory! You may not think so, but I know he's workin' in your life, too."

"I'm sure," was all Allyson could say. She was in awe of the woman's candor. This woman was obviously not pretending with her. Her actions and her words were in agreement. She had never seen anything like it – ever. It made her feel afraid and yet comforted all at the same time.

"Preach, Mother!" said a short, stout dark complexioned woman in a white cotton shift that looked like a housecoat.

"Praise the Lord, Mother Hardy! I'm not preachin' I'm testifying. You know I always have a testimony, praise God!"

"Amen. So should we all. I know you have to get home and have your dinner now, so I'll take this over if you're ready to go."

The woman's words were music to Allyson's ears. She was free! Now she could go home and wash off all the grease she'd attracted from this place.

"Where's Sister Dorcas and the others?" asked Lena.

"They've been in back getting' ready for the past ten minutes or so. They should be on their way up. You can send the girls back," said Mother Hardy.

"Alright. Shifts over, you can go on back, Allyson. I'm going to get the other girls."

Allyson couldn't get out of her serving gear fast enough. First the gloves came off and went into the garbage. Then she darted for the little lounge in the back where she took off her hair net and shook out her curly mane that had been sticking to her scalp. Next, she took off her apron and flung it onto the little couch and wet a paper towel at the sink to blot her forehead. Finally, she grabbed her purse, checked the contents, touched up her make up, grabbed her coat and headed toward the door. The people were still coming in to get food so it was hard to navigate around the tables and the people who were waiting on line. She was in such a hurry to get out of the place that she didn't even notice when she bumped into someone coming in.

"Excuse me," said Allyson.

"Oh, there you are," said Tim.

"What are you doing here?"

"Bible Study just let out and I thought I'd come to see how you were doing."

"Too late. Shifts over and I'm on my way home."

"I thought you'd want to have dinner with us at Pastor Bynum's."

Allyson was about to keep walking, but she stopped when she heard the Pastor's name.

"Isn't dinner usually at Allen's?"

"We alternate."

She couldn't pass up this opportunity to see the how the Pastor lived. She could probably wrangle a whole wardrobe's worth of clothes out of her mother for this information, but at the same time she was tired.

"I feel like I've been here all day!"

"If you don't want to come..."

"No, I'll go" she said. Her curiosity and greed had won out. "I'll follow you in your car."

"Fine. This way then."

Now the moment of truth was at hand. So what if Mrs. Sharpe was one of Bynum's devoted acolytes? Many of these religious leaders had people following their doctrines while the pastors themselves were doing quite the opposite. She knew what Mrs. Sharpe thought of Pastor Bynum, but it was time to see if her account was accurate or if she was merely deceived. Allyson was trusting that it would be the latter.

THIRTY-ONE

Jim was sitting on the couch reading his Bible, and trying to stave off any morose matter that tried to find its way into his thoughts. He had decided to skip Sunday dinner. He wasn't in the mood for conversation or for any of the advice he knew the adults would be trying to give him. It was enough just trying to hear what the Lord was saying. Right now he wasn't getting anything, and found himself reading the same passages over and over as his mind kept wandering back to the landmine laying dormant within him. There was no use fighting it. He couldn't live under the same roof with Allen and continue the charade. But how would he deliver what he knew would be a heavy blow to his best friend?

In the midst of Jim's morose musings, he heard a knock at the door. He checked his watch to see that it was only a quarter to six. It couldn't have been Mama Lena or Pop Vernon because dinner had just started, and he knew Allen had skipped Bible Study and the dinner to go to a study group for law school.

"Who is it?" he said as he struggled over to the door.

"It's Callie."

Jim thought she would've been at the dinner with everyone else, but soon realized that she probably only came for Allen's sake. If he wasn't there then she wouldn't be, either. In any event, Callie was not someone he wanted to be bothered with. He'd said all he wanted to say to her at the hospital and wasn't interested in hearing anything *she* had to say.

"What do you want?" he asked through the closed door.

"Jim, don't be like this. We're supposed to be friends."

"Supposed to be is right."

"We need to talk...I only want to help you."

He had to laugh to himself about her last remark. Jim opened the door halfway, leaving the safety on.

"And how would you do that?"

"If you let me in, I'd explain."

Although he felt as if he were going against his better judgment, he let her in. He was now curious as to what she had to say. When she came in she saw him struggling and took hold of his other side to try to help.

"I'll help you."

"I can do it myself," he said pushing her away, as he labored to get back to the couch where he was sitting.

"Have you found a job, yet?" she asked, sitting down opposite him.

"Why would you care?"

"I do still care about you, Jim."

"Is that why you're cutting me out of my child's life?"

"I'm not going to go there with you, Jim. We've discussed that issue and we both understand that this is what's best for everyone involved. Yes, mistakes were made, but now we need to think about how we're all going to move forward. You need to work on yourself and how you're going to get your life together."

"Don't you think I know that already?"

"You don't seem to be acting like it. For the past week, all you've been doing is sitting around moping."

"Well it's hard to interview when you've got casts on."

"Have you been thinking about what your options are? What kind of jobs you're going to apply for when the casts eventually do come off?"

"I'm taking things day by day. I'm waiting for God to tell me what to do."

"Do you mind if I make a suggestion?"

"That's why you're here, right?"

"Listen, Jim. Everybody knows that there aren't a lot of opportunities here in New York. You might have to broaden your horizons a little."

"How's that?"

"I'm thinking that you may want to move out of the city. Go some place where you have a clean slate and can start over fresh."

"Like where?"

"How about North Carolina. You could go with your cousin Riley when she decides to return. I'm sure the Sharpes down there wouldn't mind you staying with them, and they might be able to help you get a job down there."

"I could get a job, have some money in my pocket. Later on, I could go to law school..."

"Exactly. I've heard there are some great law schools down there."

"Then you wouldn't have to worry about me ruining things for you, Allen, or Darius. Is that right?"

"This isn't about me."

"I'm not stupid, Callie. This is all about you trying to protect yourself. You'll have to excuse me if I'm not interested."

"You're wrong, Jim. This is about you protecting yourself. You should want to put space between you and your past. The further away you are the less likely it is to catch up with you."

"What are you talking about?"

"I'm talking about how you ended up at that warehouse."

"That part of my life is over and done with. I'm not into drugs anymore."

"Doing or dealing?"

"What?"

"Don't try to be cute. I know all about the operation you were in with Smoke and Bricks and them, and how you treated Way-lo, excuse me, I mean Chris."

Jim tried to conceal his shock. "How did she manage to find out about them?" he wondered.

"You've been talkin' to Chris?"

"You wish. So you could go back and try to intimidate him into silence? No, I have another more reliable source than him."

"So now what? You want me to make myself scarce before you tell the others. I could tell them all about that myself."

"You could. But once things become common knowledge, it won't be long before the police start watching you. That warehouse shooting is still an open case, and they're going to want to take somebody in for it."

"They can't if they don't have any proof."

"My friend may have all the proof they need."

"Your friend would be a liar because I didn't do anything to anybody that night."

"Maybe. But why bother to go through all of that trouble up here when you can take it easy down south with your family."

"There doesn't have to be any trouble, unless you're threatening to stir something up."

"It works both ways, Jim. I don't like to start stuff, but if you plan to stay up here and fan my stink, you can be damn sure I'll fan yours right back."

At first, Jim could hardly believe what he was hearing come out of Callie's mouth, but then he remembered this was the same woman who had tricked his best friend into a relationship, and lied to him about the paternity of her child. He had a hard time reconciling that this was the same person he'd been friends with in high school and who seemed so kind and self-less. But now it seemed that was a façade. The real Callie had finally shown up.

"So this was your real reason for coming over, right? To try to coerce me into leaving town?"

"I came to try to show you a way out of the mess you're in, but instead of taking advantage of an opportunity for yourself, it seems you'd rather cause trouble for me. I'm just letting you know in advance that I'm willing to play nice, but if you try to take me down, you will be going along for the ride."

"I think it's time for you to leave."

"Okay, if you want to be like that. I've said what I have to say. I suggest you take some time to really think about it – for your own good."

Callie got up and walked out of the door. After she had gone, Jim erected himself on his crutch and hobbled to the door to lock it. Then he leaned his back against the door. Now his burden felt like a boulder that was sitting on top of his chest, squeezing all of the air out of his lungs. Now on top of all his other problems, there was the possibility of Callie trying to get him locked up on a murder charge if he told Allen the truth. Jim didn't know how she got the information she did. The only person he knew of who could provide such information was Chris, and the fact that Callie said it wasn't him made Jim just that more concerned. What else could she know? "Could she know about what happened to Rollo and Zee?" he puzzled frantically to himself. Jim thought that after surviving the shooting, his life could only get better, but instead it just seemed to get worse. Jim wished he could just disappear.

"Going down South may be the best thing, after all," he began to consider. He couldn't think of living with Allen and seeing him every day and keeping this secret on his heart. If he went down South, there would be no secret to keep, he wouldn't have to worry about going to jail or the person who was leaking information to Callie. Most importantly, he wouldn't have to worry about hurting anybody and he could just pretend nothing ever happened. His problems would be out of sight and out of mind. Jim planned on talking to Riley about it the next time he saw her. Despite Callie's intentions her visit turned out to be helpful after all.

THIRTY-TWO

Allen had just finished vacuuming the hallway of the eighth floor and was taking the vacuum cleaner back in the little office where they ate lunch. He was only halfway through his shift but he was so exhausted it was taking all his strength to drag the machine onto the elevator. Once inside, he sat on the floor and rested his head against his knees during the brief ride to the floor below where the office was. When he got there he saw Davis putting on his coat to go outside for lunch.

"You going out man?" asked Allen.

"Yeah. I'm going to the deli down the block. You want anything?" Davis replied.

"You can get me my regular: turkey and cheese, with lettuce and tomato, and an iced tea," he said as he took a ten dollar bill from his wallet and handed it to Davis.

"You got it," said Davis. Then he noticed how drowsy Allen was. "You aiight, man? You look like you about to drop"

"I'm okay."

"You sure? I can get you a coffee if you need it."

"Nah. Just my usual. I'm good."

"Aiight," said Davis before heading out of the office.

When Davis left, Allen checked his cell phone for messages. There was one from Callie who wanted to know if he could watch Darius for her on Saturday. He decided to return her call to get the details.

"Al?" she answered after the second ring.

"Yep. You on break?"

"Yes, but it's one of my short ones."

"I'll keep it brief. What's going on Saturday?"

"Al, I know you have a lot to do and I wouldn't trouble you unless it were important. The thing is I have to go get groceries, but I can't manage everything with Darius in tow. I shouldn't be more than an hour."

"Alright. When do you want me to come over?"

"How about 10:00?"

"See you then."

"Love you."

"I love you, too."

Allen put his cell phone on the table and took a seat in one of the metal folding chairs in front of it. His limbs felt like lead weights and so did his eyelids, which kept closing against his will. Sitting may not have been the best idea. Allen got up and went over to the water closet across from the office and turned on one of the faucets. He cupped his hands under the running water and scooped enough to splash his face. Then he went back to the office and grabbed some paper towels from a shelf and wiped his face dry. The cold water gave him a quick jolt, but its affect didn't last longer than a few seconds. Allen went over to his backpack and took out a little tiny bottle that read, "Energy Boost", opened it and drank all of the contents. One of his study group colleagues, a guy named Mark, recommended this little tonic. He said it was as potent as three energy drinks, and he was right, because it didn't take more than a moment or two before Allen started to feel much more alert. He threw the little bottle in the garbage and then sat down at the table and bowed his head to pray.

"Lord, please work this out for me. It seems like no matter what I do, things aren't working together. I need you to help me balance law school, my job, my relationship, my family and my time with you. Please...I'm burning out and I don't know how much longer I can go like this without losing it. In Jesus name I pray, Amen."

Allen had finished his prayer just as Davis returned to the office.

"One turkey and cheese with lettuce and tomato and an iced tea. And here's your change," said Davis handing Allen his food and the extra money.

"Thanks, man," said Allen as they both sat down and began to eat. Davis had a bacon, egg, and cheese sandwich with a cola.

"We missed you at the Bible Study last night. You always ask the questions everyone else is too scared to."

"Yeah. I missed it, too. But unfortunately, it looks like I'm going to have to miss many more Bible Study sessions because of the law school study group I'm in."

"Isn't there one you can go to on Saturdays?"

"Yeah, but I try to reserve that day for spending time with Callie and Darius."

"Are they more important than spending time with the Lord?"

"Aw, C'mon, Dave. It's not like I've stopped going to church. It's just Bible Study. Besides, it's not Callie or Darius that's eating up so much of my time. If anything's to blame for me having to compromise time with the Lord, it's law school, which, ironically, is what I thought He wanted me to do."

"Have you prayed to Him about it?"

"I have, but I haven't heard anything yet."

"Just don't let yourself get too busy. You don't want to miss what He has to say."

"That's nearly impossible given my schedule. But I believe if I'm on the wrong track, I'm trusting that He'll lead me the right way."

"You gotta find some way to slow down, Al. You look like you been through war."

"You haven't looked so great yourself recently. It's like you caught Jim's depression bug."

"I'm not depressed about nothing.'"

"Ever since you told Miko you wanted space, you have. Is she still showering you with unwanted attention?"

"Not really."

"Then would I be correct to assume that you miss her attentions, now?"

"No. I'm glad to have the breathing room. Now that I've had time to think about it, I don't think we'd be good for each other."

"The reason being?"

"I don't think I'm her type."

"If you're a Christian, you're Tamiko's type."

"That's what she thinks, but there's a lot more you gotta think about than that."

"I have to agree with you there. Have you told her yet?"

"No, but I plan to, soon. I'm just tryin' to think about how to break it to her without breaking her."

"I hear you, but no matter how you spin it, Miko's not going to be happy. Anyway, it's your choice man. Besides, there are plenty of other women out there to choose from."

"I'm not sure if I'd be good with anybody. I think I should stay by myself. You know, like the Lord said: there are some men that are born eunuchs, and some eunuchs that are made by men, and some that have made themselves eunuchs for the kingdom of God's sake."[1]

"Wait a minute...you can't be...Davis, are you saying that you want to remain celibate?"

"That's like when you don't get married or date or nothin' right?"

"Correct."

"Then...yeah."

"You're talking about forever?!"

"Yeah. Like forever."

"ARE YOU SERIOUS?!!"

"Yeah, chief! Why not? In First Corinthians it talks about how it's better for a person to stay single, so that they have more time to focus on the Lord."[2]

"True, that calling is for some people, but how do you know it's for you? Did God speak to you and tell you that you need to remain single?!"

"No, but, its not like I'm making a decision that He wouldn't be pleased with."

"Unless it's not in his plan for you! Davis, just because you're single doesn't mean you'll be closer to the Lord than someone who's not. A good number of the prophets were married, you know. Peter was the chief Apostle and he was married."

"Still, I feel this is the best way for me."

"But why would you – hold up – you're not feeling...confused, are you?"

"Confused about what?"

"You know...confused – questioning."

"What?! Nah, man! This ain't about nothin' like that!"

"So what is this about?! Is it about the commitment, the type of women you've dated, or intimacy issues? C'mon, man. You can't just lay this type of information on a brother and not help me understand it."

"I don't know if I can. This is really personal for me."

"Davis," said Allen after taking a breath "I don't mean to brow beat you on this, and I don't want you to get the idea that I'm against this path that you've chosen. After all, it is an honorable and righteous path. But...it's one thing to live a celibate life because that's the way God has called you to live, and another if you're choosing that particular path to avoid dealing with something else."

"I'm not avoiding nothin.'"

"I hope not. I'll pray God strengthen you in this journey you're about to under take. You're gonna need it."

"Thanks."

All of a sudden, Allen felt a sharp pain in his stomach that made him wince.

"You okay?" said Davis.

"Just got a cramp, that's all. Hopefully it will go away," said Allen rubbing his stomach, but it seemed to be getting worse.

"I hope it's not that sandwich you had."

"No. I don't think so" Allen's stomach was churning like a like an ice cream maker. "I think I need to take a walk."

"You sure?"

"Yeah. I'll be right back."

Allen took the stairs to the employee bathroom on the floor below them. He hurried to one of the empty stalls where he wound up spending the rest of his break. Even after evacuating his bowels, he still felt lousy. He didn't know how he was going to manage the rest of the day and then go to school afterward, but he had no choice. When he was done, he flushed, then went to the sink and washed his hands. This just wasn't turning out to be a good day.

As he was coming out of the restroom, he ran into Davis who had come looking for him.

"Al, there you are. I been lookin' for you. For a minute, I thought you went outside."

"What's up?"

"Mr. Hardy needs you to help with some paperwork. You been in there all this time?"

"Yeah, but I'm alright."

It seemed that Allen had spoken too soon, as he was suddenly overcome by another abdominal cramp.

"Or maybe not."

"You want me to tell Mr. Hardy you need to go home? 'Cause that's what it looks like to me."

"Tell him to give me ten minutes," said Allen, as he turned to go back into the bathroom.

"You sure?"

"Yeah. Look, I gotta go," he said before letting the door slam behind him.

He couldn't hear what Davis yelled after him because he was in too much of a hurry to get back to the stall that he had recently vacated, barely making it in time to avoid making a complete mess of himself. If it wasn't enough that his life was out of whack, now his body was as well. This was not a good sign.

THIRTY-THREE

There was lots of open space affording a magnificent view of the bucolic landscape. Small houses, tall trees and lush dew washed fields spread out for miles on end. Every once in a while, one would see patches of colorful vegetation from the farms: rows of tall stalks of corn, and oranges at different stages hanging in the groves like ornaments on a Christmas tree. In his mind, Jim had transported himself into the scenes of the lovely pictures he was looking at on the internet. It made him think about all the trips he'd taken in the past to Uncle Henry Lee's farm out in Lewiston. He remembered how he, Allen and Tamiko would play in the outdoors where the air smelled like wet grass and honeysuckle plants and the sun gave everything an ethereal glow. Even the food tasted better down south. It was almost Eden like – a perfect place for him to seek refuge from the mine-strewn battlefield his life had become.

The spell the pictures had cast was broken by the smell of butter-toasted bread, bacon, and French fries. When he looked up he saw Riley had fixed a snack for them: grilled cheese sandwiches with bacon and tomato, french fries, and iced tea.

"I knew this would get your attention," said Riley as she put the tray down on the coffee table.

"You know it. I love me some grilled cheese with bacon," he said taking a plate and then taking a bite.

"What'cha looking at there?"

"Just some pictures of the south that's all."

"You thinking of repaying my visit sometime soon?"

"Actually, I was thinking of coming to stay."

"To stay?"

"Yeah. You think Uncle Henry and Aunt Shirley would mind if I came to stay with y'all for a while?"

"You know they wouldn't mind, but why do you want to go?"

"There's nothing for me up here."

"You callin' Uncle Vern, Aunt Lena, Allen, Tamiko, Pastor and your screw ball friends, nothing?"

"I'm not talkin' about them. I mean it's so hard for a black man to get a job here. Everybody and they momma comes to the city to look for work, and black men are the last ones anyone hires around here."

"And you think the south is gonna be better?"

"Wilson finally got him a good gig."

"After being unemployed for nearly two years and having to do freelance work for the businesses in the 'hood. You know that, Jim. And I was trying not to tell anyone about this, but I even lost my job recently."

"What?"

"Yeah. The owner of the salon had money troubles, so we had to close up."

"At least you didn't get fired. How you been making it since then?"

"I do heads in the neighborhood. Mostly little kids and old ladies, though."

"Hey, that's better than nothing."

"True."

"I still think I could do better down there. There's too much trouble a brother could get into up here. Unemployed brothers and police are not a good mix."

"Have you watched the news lately? Unemployed brothers and police aren't a good mix anywhere."

"Why are you being so discouraging? If you don't want me to come just say so."

"That's not it at all, Jim. Come if you want, but don't come thinking the south is some kind of paradise and get mad at us when it turns out it ain't. Just as many disadvantages to the south as advantages."

"I understand that. Remember, this isn't Allen you're talking to."

"Since you've mentioned Al, have you shared your plan with him?"

"I wanted to get everything settled first. I'll let him know soon enough."

"He's not going to be happy."

"He might not be happy, but it's for the best. He has a lot going on and I don't want him to have the extra burden of having to worry about me."

"Just because you're not here doesn't mean he won't worry. Anyway, when was you thinking of coming down?"

"I thought I'd tag along with you next week-end when you ship out."

"What?! That's a little short notice, don'tcha think? What's your hurry?"

"Who's hurrying? It's not like I said I wanted to go tonight. I'll have my casts off by then and it should be enough time for you to talk to your dad and everything..."

"Jimmy, I hope you're not running from something up here."

"I'm not! Why do you always have to try to make something out of nothing?!"

"I don't have to try. Your attitude says it all. I thought you said there was nothing else you were holding back."

"Look, the cops are still investigating what happened in the warehouse, and I don't want to get locked up over somethin' I didn't do."

"They have to have evidence to lock you up, Jimmy. So far, so good, no one's come knockin' 'round here lookin' for you. And even if they wanted to take you, running down south wouldn't do any good, they could send the hunters to take you back north."

"Thanks, Rye. That really makes me feel good right now."

"Listen, Jim. You don't have to tell me what's going on, but it's going to be found out. Going down south isn't going to make whatever it is go away. Like I said, if you want to come, you're welcome, but I'm tellin' you, you better deal with your business now before it gets too big to handle."

Jim wanted to tell Riley that it already was.

THIRTY-FOUR

Allyson was standing in front of the walk-in closet in her room, trying to decide on what she was going to wear to her surprise birthday dinner with Jason. She had already bought what she thought would be an extraordinary dress to wear for the occasion; one that would make Jason pant with desire. But after receiving the dress in the mail and trying it on, she realized that it did not live up to her expectations and she planned on returning it. Allyson could not fathom going anywhere unless she looked absolutely perfect. She had a lot of body flaws like the hips that protruded in an unsightly manner from the back and what she considered to be her thick thighs. In fact, she never really liked how she looked, considering herself very plain and boring. As such, it was important that everything she wore masked her flaws and accentuated her positive features. Allyson tried to create outfits that would transform her from her plain self into the goddess she wanted to be. She would fantasize about the reactions she would evoke when people saw her: desire, jealousy, respect, fear. Having the right clothes meant people would see her and know that she mattered. That's what her mother always said. But as Allyson perused through the rows of dresses, they all seemed to be inadequate, even the ones with the price tags still on them.

She needed something that would make her look spectacular; something that would make Jason appreciate what he had. Allyson had to hurry because she didn't have much time left. After a tortured deliberation, she finally decided on the sleeveless magenta drop front dress, a gold belt, gold stilettos, a gold necklace with amethyst pendant, matching bangles, and her gold metallic patent leather clutch. She meticulously gathered each piece of the outfit and laid it out. The last thing she needed but couldn't find, were the bangles.

Allyson raced around her room trying to find her gold bangles. The last time she wore them was three days ago and she had put them back in her costume jewelry case that was sitting on the bureau. She hoped Courtney hadn't snuck in while she was at class and borrowed them, as was her habit with regard to Allyson's costume pieces. Allyson needed them because they were necessary to make her outfit pop. She wanted her outfit to be like the night she'd planned: perfect. After all it was a special day for her, even if no one else seemed to know or care.

The day was more than half-over and she hadn't received a genuine birthday wish from anyone, not even her mother. She tried not to dwell on this fact as she continued to search for the bangles. "So no one cares. That's nothing new, Ally. Get over it," she said to herself, "Just stay focused on your goal for tonight: securing Jason's interest." She finally found what she was looking for in the nightstand drawer. Now she was certain Courtney had borrowed them because when ever she returned things she almost never put them back where they belonged. After putting them on, Allyson got out her clutch and began to fill it with the contents of her day purse. She was about to put her phone inside when it rang suddenly.

"Hello, mother."

"Hello, darling. Happy Birthday."

"Thank you, mom."

"Don't thank me yet. I just ordered two exclusives for you from the house of Sealden. They should reach you by tomorrow morning. I apologize for the belated gift, but they were inflexible about the release date of the new arrivals."

"No worries. If it's from Sealden it's worth it."

"Do you have any plans for tonight?"

"I'm almost on my way out the door to meet Jason for dinner. He thinks he's surprising me."

"Sounds wonderful, but before you go, I'd like a status update on your mission."

"Oh."

"Tell me what you have managed to glean from your last contact?"

"I volunteered at some kind of community dinner drive, and I got a chance to eat dinner at the Pastor's house this time."

"Excellent! What did you learn?"

"I'm sorry to disappoint, you mother, but this is not one of those scam churches like you see on cable TV. It's just your standard church. Nothing shady about it."

"I find that very hard to believe."

"His sermons don't have an angle as far as I can see. I didn't hear anything about money or prosperity, no pop psychology stuff, no weird rituals. It was just your standard communion service with a message about trusting God."

"But what did you observe about the larger operation, and the guru."

"The church hasn't even been around that long. I mean they have a couple of ramshackle sister churches, but it's nothing like a mega church. They don't own a lot of property, just one catering hall across the street that they use for events, which was where I was serving the dinners. They also have two church vans that they use for transporting senior citizens to and from the church. Then Mrs. Sharpe told me they have programs like any other church for helping lazy poor people who don't want to work. One of their missions is feeding the hungry, so they host community dinners and are trying to raise money to maintain a food pantry."

"But what about the guru?"

"He's not your typical guru at all. He's as poor as some of his members."

"You must be joking."

"No, I'm not. There's no entourage, no mansion, no Rolls Royce. He lives in a raggedy brownstone not far from Allen, drives a Honda, and buys clothes from places like JC Penny. He only has the one daughter and she went to the local public school with Allen. Hardly the portrait of luxury and extravagance."

"He may not have a lot of money now, but I bet he's planning on coming into a fortune by using Tim."

"I haven't seen any indication of that. Like I said, I've never heard him make an appeal for money."

"Not publicly. Believe me, my dear, these people have all sorts of tactics to get money. And what about the girl?"

"They're just friends as far as I can see."

"I just don't understand why he would want to be around those people, then."

"Could it be because they're actually nice people? I mean they seem to like having him around."

"Oh, please – everyone wants something. I don't know Allyson. I still think we're just skimming the surface of this thing. You're going to have to do more than go to church and to dinners. You need to infiltrate Tim's inner circle of friends. Go out with them when the Pastor's not around and see what happens."

"Tim's never invited me to their get-togethers."

"Find a way to get invited, Allyson. This is important!"

"Look, mom, it's getting late and I have to go."

"Fine, but I want you to forget about the church for a moment and try to get closer to Tim. I think that's where we're going to find a lot of answers."

"Will do," sighed Allyson.

"Call me when you have, and we'll do lunch. Bye darling."

"Bye, mother."

"Who cares about Tim," thought Allyson as she finished fixing her purse and headed for the door. "Today is my day and the only thing I'm going to worry about is making my life what I want it to be. Starting with Jason."

Allyson walked out to the living room and saw Monica, and Courtney sitting in front of the TV watching some reality show. They looked up when they saw Allyson approach them.

"Faaan-cy," said Courtney "Jason's going to be drooling like a saint bernard when he sees you in that."

"Agreed. You look really hot. Are you guys doing a public event?" said Monica.

"No, it's my birthday. Jason's surprising me," said Allyson.

"Oh! Happy Birthday, Ally," said Monica.

"Yes, Happy Birthday," said Courtney.

"Thank you," said Allyson.

"You're the big 2-0, now right?" asked Monica.

"Yes, and I'm planning on starting the best decade of life with renewed passion," said Allyson.

"Look out Jason. Do you know where he's taking you?" asked Monica.

"We're going to Menagerie, but I don't think that's the real surprise," said Allyson.

"Ooooh. You expecting heavy metal?" said Monica continuing her interrogation. Allyson knew it was because she was extremely nosy and a big gossip.

"I don't know what to expect, and though I would love to sit and speculate with you, I have to be going. I don't want to be late," said Allyson grabbing her coat from the closet.

Just then Trish walked in dressed in workout clothes and carrying a duffle bag over her shoulder.

"Hey, Trish. Guess what? It's Ally's birthday," said Monica.

"Oh, really? How nice," said Trish as she dropped her bag on the floor next to the couch and headed toward the kitchen. "Are you going out with your family to celebrate?"

"No, I'm going out with Jason," said Allyson.

"Really?" asked Trish.

"Duh! She told us that yesterday, weren't you listening?" said Monica.

"But I thought I just saw...never mind" said Trish, her mouth curling into a sinister smile as she gave Allyson a knowing look. "Have a good time."

"I will," said Allyson returning the look. There was no way she was going to allow Trish to play head games with her. Allyson was certain that she only wanted to instigate a break up so she could swoop in and get Jason for herself. Whatever Jason's surprise was tonight, Allyson was going to be sure to rub it in Trish's face in the morning.

*****

Allyson shifted restlessly in her seat and crossed her legs, her top leg shaking back and forth. She took a sip of the complimentary water that was on the table and looked impatiently towards the entrance of the restaurant before checking her phone. She had sent a text a couple of minutes ago and looked to see if she'd gotten a response, but there was still none. It was now 7:30 and Jason was a half-hour late to her birthday dinner. Allyson knew he was busy and that sometimes he got caught up with his work for the magazine or school, but she couldn't help but wonder how he could leave her waiting on today of all days? She decided to call him to see what was going on.

Allyson took out her phone and dialed his number, but the call went to his voicemail so she left a message:

"Jason, it's Allyson. I thought we were meeting for dinner tonight at Menagerie, but obviously you're not here. Care to let me know what's up? Bye."

When she hung up, she put her phone back in her purse and ran her hands through her hair before using them to cover her face. "Some birthday dinner this has turned out to be," she thought. She was about to get ready to leave when she heard the phone in her purse ringing.

Allyson rushed to answer it.

"Where the hell are you? It's 7:40."

"Calm down, Ally. We had an emergency meeting at the magazine. I wanted to call you, but I couldn't get out."

"So what am I supposed to do now?"

"How about I make it up to you next week. I'll come over Tuesday."

"Next week?! Why can't we see each other tonight? It's not like it's that late."

"I'm all the way downtown and there's a lot of traffic out here. By the time I get over there it'll be well past 8:00. Besides, it's the middle of the week. I have to get up early tomorrow."

"You mean you're telling me you can't even spare five minutes to see me on today of all days?"

"What's so special about today?"

“I can’t believe you’re asking me that.”

“What the hell does that supposed to mean? I don’t have time for the games, Allyson.”

“Of course. You don’t have much time for anything or anyone, so I won’t keep you. But before I go, I just want to thank you for making this the best birthday I’ve ever had.”

“Your birthday? Allyson, I’m ...”

Allyson hung up and put her phone back in her purse, put on her coat and bolted toward the doors of the restaurant. After leaving, she headed for the elevator bank and frantically pushed the buttons on the wall. Allyson just wanted to get away. She didn’t know where she would go, but it had to be somewhere far away: away from what she was feeling right now.

She paced up and down as she waited for the elevator. Her face felt hot and she could feel the pressure from the tear ducts in her eyes. “Don’t you dare. Don’t you dare cry,” she chastised herself as she struggled to maintain her composure. “This is no time for cracking up. Jason’s played his hand and you have to think about what your next move is going to be.” However, Allyson was getting tired of the chess game this relationship had become and she considered whether or not it was worth saving. After reflecting on Trish’s cryptic words earlier, it didn’t seem so. But if she gave him up, what would she have? The last thing Allyson wanted to do was to hand victory over to Trish. Allyson was getting tired of it all: of feeling as if she was constantly at war with everyone in her life, and having to constantly try to figure out ways to outwit them and defend herself. She only wanted to be loved and cared for, the way she had been so many years ago, but the notion seemed so foolishly idealistic.

Soon the elevator came and Allyson rushed inside along with some others that had joined her in her wait. She had pressed the button for the lobby but someone else had pressed the button for the 7th floor. She knew Tim lived on the 7th floor. All of a sudden, she began to wonder what he was doing now: if he was having dinner or entertaining Allen or one the others he had as friends. At least he seemed to have real friends. She had to admit the Sharpes and the Bynums weren't like the people she was used to. So what was Tim doing with them? Could she have been wrong about him all these years? He was the only other person on this earth beside, her Poppa that had ever shown her any kind of love. Happy memories from their past flooded her remembrance, which led her to wonder if it were possible to reclaim that joy.

When the elevator door opened on the 7th floor, Allyson found herself getting off. She walked down the hallway and stood in front of his door. She didn't hear anyone stirring inside. "He may not be home, anyway," she thought. She wanted to knock, but she wasn't sure what she would say if he answered. How could she explain what she wanted, when she wasn't sure of it herself? How would he react given the way she'd treated him for the past twelve years? "Allyson, what are you doing? This is stupid. You're just setting yourself up for another disappointment. It's not like he remembered, either. He could have left a message on your cell even if you didn't answer it." In the past, he used to send her cards on her birthday, even though they weren't speaking. This year, she hadn't gotten anything. Allyson turned away and walked back to the elevator.

This time when it arrived, she pushed the button for the lobby, and thought about where she could go. It was only 8:00 and she didn't want to go back to her apartment, because she knew that if she came back this early, everyone would know what a disaster her date was. She could go to another restaurant and have dinner, but she didn't feel like eating. The bar was an option, but there were too many people that she knew who hung out there, and she didn't want to risk running into any of them in the mood she was in. Not to mention she would have to drive herself home, afterward. Allyson's train of thought was broken by the chiming of the elevator as the doors opened on the ground floor. She left the building and hurried over to the parking lot to pick up her car, though she still didn't know where she was headed.

As she pulled out of the parking lot, Allyson noticed a very novel looking blouse in the window of a boutique at the end of the block that seemed as if it might be still open. She stopped her car outside and walked up to the door. According to their sign, she was just in time for a last minute shopping spree before the 9:00 closing time.

"Good evening," said the proprietor as she walked in. "If you'd like any help, let me know."

"Actually, I'd like to inquire about that blouse in the window. Do you have any more?"

"Yes. What size would you need? It comes in XS to XL."

"A small if you have it."

"I'll find it for you," she said heading over to a rack of blouses in a corner.

"Do you mind if I look around in the meantime?"

"Not at all. Go ahead."

Allyson rarely shopped boutiques because the stuff found there would often be cheaply made, but if she saw something that was really unique or one of a kind, she'd take a look. That blouse was absolutely gorgeous and it would be a great match with a lot of the other items in her wardrobe. As she glanced over the racks, there were more finds: a cute pink houndstooth pleated mini skirt, a cool brown plaid wool blazer, and a royal blue knit mini dress with a peter pan collar.

"Here you are, miss," said the woman returning with the blouse, "I see you've found some other items you like. Do you need to try them on?"

"Not necessary. I have a pretty good eye to tell if they'll fit. You can ring me up."

"Of course," said the woman smiling widely as she took the clothes from Allyson and went to the checkout desk. While there, Allyson saw some jewelry that she liked and added those to the pile of things she had. Allyson paid with the new credit card her mother had gotten for her and the woman packed the merchandise in wrapping paper before putting it in a beautifully designed bag and handing it to Allyson. By the time she opened the door to leave, the euphoria from the shopping had already worn off, and Allyson felt as miserable as when she walked in.

Allyson got back in her car and drove around aimlessly for several hours having to stop at a gas station to fill her car at one point. She didn't want to go home until she was sure everyone was asleep. As she drove, she was filled with a mix of restlessness and frustration. This had to be one of the worst birthday's she'd ever had, and she'd had a lot of crappy birthdays. She just wanted to scream. Then she could hear her brother saying, “Can you say you’re satisfied with your life right now?” like he did weeks ago. Truthfully, she wasn’t. She had thought that if she could just fight hard enough, she could make her life what she wanted through the sheer force of her will. Allyson learned that from her mother. ‘Mrs. Sharpe was right; fighting just leaves you feeling miserable,’ thought Allyson, however, it was all she knew how to do.

It was well past midnight when Allyson decided to drive back to her apartment. When she got home, she was careful not to make too much noise so no one would notice her coming in. When she opened the door, it was totally dark, so she knew the other girls had retired to their rooms. Allyson took off her shoes and put them in the bag she had gotten from the boutique. Then she hurried over to her own room. On her way, she nearly tripped over a box that was in front of her door. At first, she thought it might have been put there as some kind of a joke, but then she noticed the UPS labels on the box and realized it was a delivery. She pushed it in with her foot, turned on the light in her room and closed the door behind her as quietly as she could.

Once inside, Allyson threw the bag of clothes in the closet and went back to inspect the package, thinking the clothes her mother ordered for her had arrived early. Upon opening it there was a layer of packing peanuts and she realized that this was not from the house of Sealden. She dug through the packing to find a doll. Allyson recognized her immediately: she was olive-skinned with curly, sandy-blonde hair and was wearing a light blue dress with a jelly stained white apron, white knee-high socks and blue shoes. It was Lanie – her Lanie – the one Tim had bought for her 6th birthday. This was the doll that she took with her everywhere until the day Tim came home from California. That day Allyson was so angry, she took Lanie and all the other things Tim had given her, put them in a box and set it on the curb for the garbage collectors. But in her haste to hurt Tim, she had deeply wounded herself for she had come to love Lanie, who was almost like a friend to her. The next day, regretting her decision, she tried to rescue her, but it was too late. She would never see Lanie again until now. Allyson was awestruck. But how? And who could have sent her?

Allyson looked back at the box to see a pink envelope sticking up out of the peanuts. She kept Lanie in one hand as she grabbed the card with the other. Attached to the card was a bakery box. First she separated the envelope from the box and opened it to find a cupcake from her favorite bakery wrapped in cellophane. It was vanilla with strawberry icing. Then she opened the envelope. It was a birthday card from Tim. Inside was a picture from her 6th birthday when he had originally given her Lanie. Under the printed poem he had written in his nearly illegible handwriting:

"Happy Birthday, Cupcake!

As you can see there's an old friend who wanted to see you. She wants to know if you wanted to patch things up.

Love you always,

Your brother, Tim

Allyson eyes filled with tears that began to fall down her cheeks. She held up Lanie again and inspected her, this time noticing a note attached to her shirt. It read: 'I call dibs on half the cupcake'. Allyson chuckled, in spite of herself as the tears continued to flow. “I guess my birthday didn’t turn out so badly after all,” she thought.

THIRTY-FIVE

Tamiko sang praises to God as she picked the bones out of the can of salmon that she'd dumped into her mixing bowl. It was her night to cook, and she was in the midst of preparing salmon cakes. It was her habit to fill her mind with the wonderful ways she knew the Lord had blessed her during the day, and sing a song to express her feelings. She was in the midst of the final chorus of Lisa Page Brook's, "Thank You" as she finished mincing the meat with a fork and began to add the onions, egg, and flour. Tamiko always had a reason to praise, but this day more than others because of a special blessing she had received. When she had finished that song, she started in on another as she began to form the mixture into patties that she was going to fry in the oil that had been heating in a pan on the stove. This time it was an old time song, "Lord I Just Want to Thank You." As she was working, Riley sauntered in, and hearing Tamiko's singing, started to join in and help her finish her tune.

"Amen," said Riley once they'd finished the song, "You know I believe that one. You want any help?"

"You could check on the sweet potatoes that I'm baking over there."

"Sure" said Riley. She got a fork from the silverware drawer and walked to the oven.

"These are done," she said after poking them with the fork. "I'll turn down the oven so they'll stay warm while the cakes are cookin.'"

"Thanks."

"You ain't singin' any sad songs today. Something good happen at school?"

"Better than good. Do you remember the spreadsheet that Tim helped me to make for my assessment meeting?"

"Yeah."

"Well, everyone loved it. In fact, they want all the teachers in the school to use it."

"Aww, you go!"

"And not only that, but they want to see if they can find a way to adapt it to track our student's progress in math."

"Ye-ah! Now you gon' go git that raise, right?"

"Riley, I'm in a union under contract. I can't get a raise unless it's scheduled, and that's not for another two years."

"Well what about a promotion?"

"I don't think it's going to happen any time soon. My boss doesn't like me very much."

"Aww, man. You mean you hook them up and you don't get nothing outta that!"

"I may get a better rating and get to keep my job."

"Whoo-hoo. Teaching stinks," said Riley slumping down in a chair to watch Tamiko finish cooking.

"I'll admit that there are parts of the job I like less than others, but I wouldn't choose anything else. But you have to get through the paperwork if you want to get to the fun parts."

"Now do you realize that I was right to call Snowy?"

"Riley, do I have to keep reminding you…"

"What? I didn't call him Mr. Snow Job. I changed it to Snowy. It's a cute name now. Whaddya want me to call him? Hot chocolate? He might be a little hot, but he's definitely not chocolate."

"Will you stop. And no, I don't think you were right to do what you did. The end does not justify the means. However, I won't say I wasn't glad things turned out the way they did."

"Just say thank you, Miko. It's only two words."

"Thank you, Riley."

"Your welcome. But if you'd really like to show your appreciation, you could make me an extra cake, and make it a big one, too."

"I was thinking of something a little more special – and I want to do something for Tim, too. But he's got a lot of nice things already. I have no idea what to get him. What do you think?" said Tamiko as she pressed out some of her mix into a large patty and put it into the pan.

"You could get him a tanning bed, but that'd be a little pricey."

"Be serious."

"How would I know? He's your friend. I don't know what he'd like. Well I can think of one thing, but we won't go there."

Tamiko went to the sink to wash the excess cake mixture off of her hands. She knew what Riley was insinuating, but she let it slide. As the water ran over her hands, she continued to consider her options. Before she knew it she had what she thought was a great idea.

"I got it! I'll take him out to dinner," said Tamiko as she spun around.

"Sorry, try again," said Riley shaking her head.

"What's wrong with that?"

"It's too romantic – He's gonna get the wrong idea about your intentions. He's nuts for you as it is."

"No, he's not. He just respects me, that's all. Besides, we've been out to eat by ourselves before and he's never gotten any ideas."

"No, no, no. You gotta get him a grandpa gift."

"A grandpa gift?"

"Yeah, somethin' you'd get your grandpa - like socks with ducks on them, or an ugly light-up tie, or handkerchiefs – something that says 'you're okay, but stay away.'"

"I've actually made him some ties before for his birthday."

"You made him ties?"

"Yeah. He liked them. He even told me he got compliments on them at work."

"Tamiko, no! Unless they're ugly and poorly made, you're taking it into the romance zone again. Don't make him any more ties."

"Only because I want to do something different. I could also give him this book that I've been reading that's very good. It's called Roadblocks on the Road to Grace by Bishop Walter Simmons."

"Perfect! Once he reads it your message will be clear: you need the Lord, not me."

"I was planning to give it to him at dinner."

"Not this again. Guys like Tim look out for any kind of sign, not matter how small, that you like them as more than a friend. If you have dinner with him and give him a present he's going to think you like him as more than a friend. Is that what you want?"

"But he helped me a lot and I want to do something nice. Just giving him a book seems...like something his mom would do."

"That's the whole point! It'll shut down his fantasy!"

"Or hurt his feelings."

"You wouldn't be hurting them, just re-directing them – unless..."

"Unless what?"

"Unless you like all the attention he's been giving you."

Tamiko felt the hair on the back of her neck stand up. After flipping a over a salmon cake, she glanced over her shoulder at Riley who seemed to be looking at her suspiciously.

"What attention? I don't know what you're talking about."

"I'm talking about ever since Davis asked for space, it seems like you lettin' Tim move into his place. Please tell me you're not trying to make Davis jealous."

"Riley, you know me better than that. I would never do that to Tim or Davis. Besides, Davis doesn't mind me spending time with Tim because he knows we're just friends."

"With the way you and Tim were carrying on the other day and the way you're as happy as a clam right now, I might think somethin' else. Seems like your broken heart got mended real quick."

"I can't do anything to please you. If I'm moping, you tell me to get over him and when I'm happy, you make me feel as if I'm being cold."

"Then explain how not three days ago, you were acting like Davis was better than buttermilk biscuits, and now you got it like Tim's better than both of them. No wonder Davis wanted space. You just a hot mess."

"Now you're saying it's my fault that Davis is pushing me away?"

"You don't even know who you want!"

"Riley Sharpe, I am not some fourteen year old girl going through puberty. I am a grown woman and I know how I feel."

"So explain it to me."

"Davis is a wonderful man. He has all the qualities I've ever wanted in a husband. He's a Christian and he lives his life by his faith just like I do."

"How nice. You've said that a hundred times. What else you got in common?"

"That's the most important thing."

"If that's true, then why not hit up Elder Murty."

"He's a fifty year old man!"

"So? He's single, he loves the Lord and Pastor is always talkin' about what a great help he is to the church and how he's a light to the other men in the community."

"C'mon, Riley let's not be silly."

"Exactly! You can't go around and pick a boyfriend or a husband for that matter, based on a concept. Building relationships is not like building a car or a computer."

"Look, I don't want to be one of those women who lets her feelings cause her to walk into a relationship that's doomed to fail. I witnessed a lot of the casualties from those kind of relationships in high school and in college: so many bright girls with great futures ahead of them who threw everything away over guys who were nothing but game. Guys who made promises to them and then broke those promises over and over, while they waited for them to change, but change never came."

"Stop with the drama. No one's asking you to date a crack head, just be honest about your feelings."

"I have been."

"Ya sure?"

"Yes!"

"Positive?"

"Why can't you just believe me?"

"Okay. Sooo, you won't wind if I make my move on Snowy?"

"You said you he wouldn't be right for me and now you're saying you want to go out with him! Where's this coming from?"

"You're always telling me to give people a chance, so I'll take a chance with Snowy. I'll come with you to your friendly dinner and you can hook us up. Good idea, right?"

"Wrong! You don't even like him!"

"He's growing on me. He did me a solid for fifty bucks - can't be that bad a guy."

"I thought you didn't like preppy guys."

"I thought I didn't like Asian pork buns either until I had a couple. Snowy's pretty good looking, especially without the glasses, he's got a nice build, and he's rich. You know the more I think about him the more I like him."

"What if he doesn't like you?"

"I think he will when he sees me all fancy in my silk army pants."

"Riley..."

"Miko...boyfriends are not like donut holes. You can't have more than one at a time. If you want strawberry, it's only fair that I get to have vanilla. So, if you wanna wait for Davis, then that means I get Snowy. Oh, and I'm calling no backsies."

"Alright. If that's the way you wanna be, fine. I'll call Tim and ask him."

"You do just that."

Tamiko was sure that Riley was bluffing, but since she wanted to make a big deal of things, she was going to call her on it. After all, she was sure there was no way that Riley and Tim would ever hit it off. Yet for all of her certainty, she could not get over the uneasy feeling that suddenly gripped her heart.

*****

The basement was the most peaceful space of the Bynum residence. Because of her mother's fastidiousness and her penchant for throwing every unnecessary thing away, there was nothing in the space except for the washer, dryer, a freezer, and four large plastic containers that took up space on the periphery of the room. In the middle of the room were a folding table and a rocking chair. Many times Tamiko would resort here to pray or just to have some privacy which was her reason for coming now. She was nervous enough about the call she was going to make and she didn't want to have to worry about eavesdropping ears.

"Hey, Miko. What's going on?" said Tim.

"Not much. Just hanging around my parent's basement. And you?" said Tamiko.

"I'm was just cleaning out my closet and looking through some old stuff."

"If you're busy, I can call back."

"I wouldn't call this busy. I can talk for a minute. What's on your mind?"

"I wanted to let you know that the spreadsheet you made was a hit at school today. In fact they want all the teachers to use the format as the template for the sight word assessment in all of the classrooms."

"That's awesome news. Let's hope this puts you in a more favorable light when it comes time for observations."

"One can only hope. But I just want to thank you again for everything."

"You're very welcome, and remember, if you need anything else, just let me know."

"But I want you to know I really appreciate you giving up your time to help me and I was thinking that maybe I could return the favor," said Tamiko, her voice speeding up because of her nerves, although she had no idea why she was nervous all of a sudden.

"Miko, it's not necessary."

"For me, it is. I was wondering if you would like to have dinner with me...and Riley on Saturday night?"

"You and Riley?"

"Yes. She had a big part in my success, too, so I thought I'd invite both of you."

"Okay, sure. Where are we going?" he said in a matter of fact way. This made Tamiko feel relieved since it seemed he wasn't uncomfortable about the invite.

"There's this new place over on Audubon that I want to try. It's called the Gospel Grill. They have live Gospel music from up and coming artists."

"Sounds nice. How'd you hear about it?"

"I was reading the paper the other day and I saw a feature on it in the city living section."

"Cool. What time do you want me to meet you there?"

“Is 6:00 good?”

“Not a problem.”

“Great. So...” said Tamiko not, knowing what else to say, since she had accomplished the purpose of her call.

“So is that all that happened today? Did Jamire try to eat another glue stick?”

“Thankfully, no.”

“Makes you wonder what goes on in a child’s mind.”

“I know, and sometimes I feel like I should know. After all, it wasn’t that long ago since I was a kid and I know I’ve done some silly things myself.”

“Really? Like what?”

“Like putting liquid glue all over my hands, then letting it dry and peeling it off.”

“No way! I used to do that, too!”

“But I think the craziest thing I ever did was when I was 11 and I dyed Allen’s hair red with kool-aid.”

“He actually let you do that?”

“He didn’t think the color would take.”

“What made you think of that?”

“I don’t know, really. I guess I was just curious.”

“What did your parents say when they saw what you did?”

“My dad thought it was the funniest thing ever, and so did Mama Lena. But my mom and Pop Vernon were not happy at all...”

The conversation continued on in this way for some time as they both shared childhood stories and talked about their experiences, their hopes, their dreams, and their fears. By the time the call ended Tamiko realized that what she had intended to be a two-minute call ended up lasting two hours. There was a time when neither of them would even want to say two words to each other. Their relationship had definitely matured over the years, as they had themselves. Tamiko had to admit that Tim was indeed much different from what he used to be. He was certainly not as arrogant, cynical or irreverent as he had been and he was beginning to learn about what caring, compassion, and character meant. Their relationship was still developing and growing, and despite her reservations, Tamiko was curious and hopeful about how it would all turn out.

THIRTY-SIX

After his conversation with Tamiko and their discussion of childhood silliness, Tim couldn't help thinking about his sister and it made him a little restless. He thought about the package he'd sent her for her birthday, the first he'd sent since she was sixteen when she'd mercilessly revealed how she trashed or torched previous presents he'd given her. After that he'd only send her cards, which he was pretty sure she was trashing as well. Tim knew she had received the package because he'd tracked it online. The question was how would she react to it. Her birthday was yesterday and so far he hadn't heard anything from her. Tim was hoping that she would have sent him a text at least. He would've tried calling her, but she never answered his calls or texts. He didn't know what else to do. So went back to rummaging through his childhood treasure box, which was what he'd been doing before Tamiko called.

The box had been at the back of his closet for ages and he never thought to go through it until that Sunday after he'd returned home from dinner at Tamiko's house. He had been reading his Bible when he got the inclination to return to it, and then to send his sister her longtime companion and friend that she'd thrown away. He thought that after he'd done this that would be the end of it's usefulness, but something was leading him back to it again.

Tim's treasure box was filled with odd little keepsakes he had collected that reminded him of better days – like the time when Poppa was alive. Everyone in the family called his grandfather, the Honorable Judge Timothy Warren Russell, "Poppa." He was the distinguished patriarch, the one everyone went to when there was a crisis or a scandal and the Russell household was full of them. Poppa was the bastion of stability in Tim's life. His mother came and went, so did the nannies, and so did his aunts and Mr. Hurst, but Poppa was always there.

Tim inspected the aging artifacts, unsure of what he was looking for. There was his grandfather's old wallet, which still contained pictures of Tim's mother, Eleanor, when she was a young girl as well as pictures of Tim and Allyson. There was also and old photo album full of pictures he'd taken on their adventures together. One was taken during the summer that Poppa had taken him and Allyson camping in the woods. In the picture, they were all posing in front of the deer he'd helped Poppa to catch. There was another picture of them in a boat watching the dolphins in Australia during winter break, as well as photos from their adventures in Japan and England. There was a picture of Tim sitting on the couch in their condo holding Allyson when she was just a baby. There was even a hand drawn picture that Allyson had made for him when she was seven. In addition to the photo album were old trinkets like the plastic craft bracelets and friendship bracelets he made for her, a few awards, some old baby clothes of his, Mr. Brown, his old teddy bear, and some of the things he'd given Allyson that he managed to rescue from the garbage when she'd thrown them away.

Looking through these mementos made Tim a little misty-eyed as he remembered their happy trio: Poppa, Allyson, and himself. In a world of messy arrangements, secrets, affairs, and scandal, they clung together through it all, with Poppa as their rock and center. He was their teacher as well as their confidant. But all that changed when he died of cancer.

For months afterward, the Russell household was in chaos as all of them grieved over the loss of their beloved Poppa. Eleanor had totally abandoned them, deciding after the funeral that she needed to take a vacation to Italy to keep from losing her sanity. Hurst preferred to send his condolences in the form of a floral spread for Poppa's casket, rather than appear in person to comfort his mourning children. This left Tim and Allyson in the custody of their Aunt Morgan, who in turn, left them in the hands of their nannies and checked on them once a week, until their mother's return. In the meantime, Tim's hair grew into a curly shag that reached his shoulders, while he wore the same clothes for days on end, and went to school when he felt like it. Allyson, spent most of the time crying, and trying to follow Tim everywhere he went. She even threw tantrums when one of the nannies tried to take her to school. On the rare times she did make it there, the school would send her back home because of her hysterical behavior. Both of them spent most of their time at home, with Tim inviting his girlfriend, Nicole, on occasion to spend time with them. Then after what seemed to be an interminable three months, their mother re-appeared tanned, glowing, and with a new perspective of how they should carry on in light of Poppa's death, one that would have many implications for Tim.

Tim remembered it distinctly. After her return, Eleanor was constantly badgering him about his responsibilities toward the family. Almost everyday he was subject to a lecture of some sort, which would then turn into an argument. Eleanor had a lot of plans that she wanted him to get in line with. First, she wanted him to take entrance exams for a new school. Not long after this, he came home one day to find she had trashed all of his favorite old clothes, and replaced them with a lot of corny looking preppy ones. Then she told him about her friend who had an internship with Tim's name on it. His mother had gone from her usual laissez-faire parenting to becoming a helicopter mom almost overnight and it left Tim feeling as if he was being suffocated. At first, he had no idea what was going on or why it was happening, until she called him in for another of their little 'talks.' She had him sit in the chair in front of her desk that she used for clients while she sat on the opposite side.

"Timothy, sit up! What we are going to talk about is of the utmost importance for your future as well as the future of this family."

Tim eased himself a little higher, but had a hard time staying straight, as he stared blankly at the onyx pendant his mother was wearing. He had just gone through a joint a while ago and he was still feeling a little disoriented.

"Tim, I think I should make you aware that Poppa left a good portion of his estate to you, however, it is in trust until you turn 25. That coupled with the fact that you are the last male in this family with the

Russell name means that it is your duty to continue your grandfather's legacy."

His mother paused for a moment, as if she expected him to respond, but Tim didn't say anything. In his mind, there was nothing to say. None of what she was talking about had any meaning for him. All he wanted was for someone to explain to him why life was so unfair, that someone he loved and who had loved him so much had to be taken away.

"As your grandfather's heir, you will be the head of this family," Eleanor droned on, "There are many things you must learn in order to assume this role; there's a disposition you must develop and you are at an age where you must begin to prepare for your future. Do you understand?"

Tim continued to remain silent. He didn't care about roles, or dispositions, or the future. Right now there was a pain inside him that he didn't think would ever go away. What did he care about the future if his Poppa couldn't be a part of it?

"The staff have apprised me of your recent behavior: missing school, drugs, that girl you're fooling around with! Look at yourself -you look and smell like a hobo! Timothy this is unacceptable! You will not continue on like this! The time has come for you to grow up and fulfill your obligation to this family. From this moment forward, you will bathe and groom yourself, you will go to school, you will excel in your studies, and anything else you are told to. You owe it to me, to your sister, to your Aunt Morgan and most importantly you owe it to Poppa who did everything in his power to give you every advantage that you have now. Is that understood?! Answer me!"

Tim bolted out of his chair, dashed out of the office and into his room and slammed the door and locked it. It wasn't long before he could hear Eleanor banging on the door and screaming at him, so he got his mp3 player out, put on his headphones and zoned out to his favorite rock band. It was all getting too much for him. If it wasn't enough that Allyson was leaning on him so hard, now his mother was saying he'd eventually have to assume responsibility for the whole family. Tim knew exactly what she was doing. She was trying to groom him to become her personal ATM machine, just like Hurst, and there was no way Tim was going to stand for that. The one person who he could've leaned on during a time like this was gone. The pressure he was feeling had him dizzy. There was only one solution that he could think of. He had to get out of this house.

It took Tim a couple of days to plan his escape to California. He didn't plan to stay there, but he needed some time to think about things without having to listen to his mother harangue him about legacies and responsibility, as if he were a character in a fantasy epic. The only person he felt sorry about leaving was Allyson. He knew why she'd been so clingy lately, and he tried to be there for her, but he felt powerless to help her in the way she needed. On the day of his departure, he told his girlfriend who then insisted on coming with him. So off they went on an adventure to California.

Looking back from the present, he realized how silly his plan was and why Hurst and his mother were able to catch up with them so quickly. When he came back, he holed himself in his room for about a week before speaking to anyone, and afterward he began to notice Allyson's change in demeanor. Was this what Allyson was angry about? He didn't understand why? He'd gone mopey and silent on them all before and Allyson never took it so hard.

There was one last thing in the box: Allyson's keepsake box. He'd seen it before, but this time something was leading him to open it and go through it. Sifting through the box he found toy jewelry, a couple of beanie babies, some gum wrappers, and a diary. He never knew she had ever kept a diary. Tim decided to read it. The dates were around the time that their Poppa died. Tim surmised she had been writing about what was going on as a way to deal with everything. Some of the things he read made him feel so bad for her, like when she wrote how confused she was after Poppa died and how terrified she was when Tim went missing. It made Tim feel like a stooge for not caring for her more. Then he came to the entry of June 30, 1998:

Dear Fairy Godmother,

They found Tim. I should be happy about it but I'm not. You know why? Because he's a rat-faced bugger-head. He lied to me. He said he would take care of me, but he ran away with his girlfriend and they were going to live together like happily ever after forever in California and I had to stay here with my evil wicked witch mother who doesn't even love me. Safi told me everything then my evil witch mom fired her because she thinks Tim running away was her fault because she didn't stop him. He didn't even say goodbye to me or give me a note. He doesn't love me either, just like everybody else. I don't know if he used to love me then he didn't any more because I was bothering him too much or if he never loved me from the beginning. It doesn't matter anyway because I hate him now, too, and I'm never going to talk to him again. I hate all of them. The only one I love is Poppa, but he's gone. I hate this place. I hope I die, too. Then I could be a ghost and I could find

Poppa's ghost and we could be together forever. I know ghosts aren't real, by the way, but I wish they were.

Miserably Yours,

Allyson

After reading this portion of the diary, Tim finally understood. He was no longer stuck reasoning about the event from his 14 year old self, but with the clarity and experience that time had given him in his 26 years on the planet. He could have kicked himself for his stupidity and callousness that had brought his baby sister so much pain during an already difficult time. Tim went to his desk and grabbed a mini manila envelope from one of the cubbies and put the diary inside. Then he went to pray.

"Thank you Father for having mercy on me once again, and for blessing me beyond what I deserve. Thank you for helping me to find that diary, and for helping me to understand the pain that I've caused my sister. Lord, you know I didn't mean to hurt her. Please show me what to do now. What do I say – what can I do to let her know how much I love her and how sorry I am for what's happened. I don't want her to have to go on the way she is now. I just want to see her whole again – like when we were younger. Please, not for my sake Lord, but for hers. In Jesus name, Amen."

THIRTY-SEVEN

Jim could hear the jingle of keys and then the click of the cylinder turning in the lock as he lay on the couch in the dark. "He's back," thought Jim. Not long after, He could see the light coming from the open door and hear the sound of Allen's heavy footsteps and his wheeled backpack rolling across the linoleum floor. Jim had been waiting for this moment and at the same time he was dreading it. He lay silently on the couch, feigning sleep, still struggling within himself. 'Maybe I should wait until the morning," he thought, however he knew that Allen left for work so early that he stood the chance of missing his opportunity and he didn't have much time left, since Sunday was only three days away. He had to prepare Allen for his news, and it had to be tonight. When he heard Allen rummaging around in the kitchen getting his dinner, Jim decided it was now or never. So he peeled the covers off of him, found his crutch, pulled himself up off the couch and hobbled toward the kitchen.

"I thought I heard you come in," said Jim as he entered the kitchen and took a seat opposite Allen.

"You waiting up for me?" said Allen who was already sitting in front of his dinner of lemon chicken, baked potato, and broccoli. Allen looked tired as usual, but Jim also noticed he was sweating as if he'd ran all the way home from school.

"Kind of. You been running or something?"

"Oh, no," said Allen wiping the perspiration that had beaded up on his forehead. Just a little hot, that's all."

"You alright?" asked Jim again. It certainly wasn't hot inside the house, and it was 45 degrees outside.

"Yeah," said Allen, sitting up in his chair. "You wanted to talk about something?"

"I know you don't have a lot of time, but I thought I'd catch you before you went upstairs."

"What's up?" he said pushing the plate away after barely tasting the broccoli.

"I have some news that I was going to tell the family on Sunday, but I wanted to give you the opportunity to hear it from me first."

"Okaaay. I hope it's good news."

"To me it is."

"Alright then, let's hear it."

"It's just - since I got out of the hospital, I've been thinking about what I want to do with my life and – look, I feel like I need a change of direction, a change of scene, everything. The only way to do that is to put this city behind me."

"Jim, are you talking about leaving town?" asked Allen.

"Yeah. I'm planning on heading out to North Carolina to stay with Riley and Uncle Henry and them. I've talked to Riley about it, and she already asked Uncle Henry, and he's thinks it's a good idea, too."

Jim could hear Allen inhaling deeply and he looked perturbed. He could tell Allen wasn't pleased with his news, but that had been expected.

"Where's this coming from?"

"This city doesn't have anything to offer to an unemployed black man except trouble and I don't have the patience to deal with the games these people play with a brother trying to find work."

"We could ask around and help you find something."

"I don't want to find something up here. I'm sick of this place."

"Did you at least pray about this?"

"I know this is the right thing to do."

"But..."

"I'm not changing my mind, Al."

"When are you leaving?"

"Next week, when Riley ships out."

"What?! But I thought – you just got out of the hospital!"

"The sooner I make this break, the easier it'll be for everybody."

"This is just so...abrupt. Jim, does this have something to do with what happened to you?"

"Of course he just had to ask that question," thought Jim.

"No it doesn't."

"Then you shouldn't have any problem delaying your trip for a while."

"Allen..."

"C'mon, man. I thought you said things were going to be different this time. We just got you back and now you're going on the run again?! How do you think our parents and our friends are going to feel? How do you think I feel?"

"We're still going to be family. The only thing that's going to change between us is distance. I'll call and text and hit you on facebook every now and again. Maybe I'll come up for a visit every once in a while. It might be hard at first, but...I don't know how to explain it to you...I just need to do this."

"I understand that. If you need to start over in NC, fine, but can't you wait just a few months? I was looking forward to having you as my best man."

"Your best man?" asked Jim. He hoped he had misheard Allen.

"Aw, crap. Look, don't mention it to anyone yet, okay. I promised Callie I'd wouldn't say anything about the wedding until Thanksgiving."

"Wait - you're planning on getting married?"

"Yes. I popped the question to Callie last weekend. We were planning on getting married in June, when my first year..."

"Al, have you lost your mind!"

Jim couldn't believe what he was hearing. Callie hadn't told him any of this that night when she came to threaten him, and he thought he knew why. It was probably her idea to keep things secret in the first place. "That chick gives new meaning to the word deceptive," he thought as he began to fume with shock and anger.

"Shhh. You'll wake mom and dad."

"You are way too young and you've got too much going on to be thinking about marriage or fatherhood. Don't you think you should concentrate on finishing school and getting yourself settled in a career, first?"

"Jim, I know what I'm doing"

"No, you don't! Marriage is a huge deal. It's not something you just rush into," he said annoyed with his friend's insouciant attitude. "Have you really thought about what spending the rest of your life with Callie is going to be like?! You asked me if I prayed; did you pray about this?!"

"Are you serious? This has been the answer to my prayers. You know Callie has been my dream girl since high school."

"That's the problem, Al. You're still dreaming, but this is the real world. It's just like when you were looking for work – you looking at what you want things to be rather than what it really is."

"I can't believe this. You're talking to me like I'm some teenager who just told you he's going to elope with his girlfriend. Give me some credit. I'm a grown man who's old enough to know what's best for me. I respected your decision, why can't you respect mine?"

Jim could see that Allen was starting to get frustrated with him, and the last thing he wanted was a full on argument. He didn't want to alienate

Allen again, but at the same time, Jim desperately wanted to be able to keep Allen from making what could be the biggest mistake of his life. He wished he knew what to say to change Allen's mind and protect him from what would likely be a disaster.

"I want to, but...Al, you asked me to give my decision some time, and I'm going to suggest the same thing to you. I think you need to wait and get to know Callie better before you jump into this marriage thing"

"I've known her for years. What else do I need to know?"

"For real, Allen. I'm begging you, just wait"

"Sorry, but I'd rather not. If Callie and I are living together then I won't have to worry about putting in so much time commuting, plus I'll live closer to campus. It'll make things a lot easier than they are now."

"I can't believe what you just said. Convenience is not a reason for marriage."

"C'mon Jim, don't play. You know that is not the main reason why I want to marry Callie, and I'm not going back and forth with you on this anymore. My decision is final."

"I can't let you do this, Al."

"What you mean, let me? You ain't my daddy. There will most definitely be a wedding, but if you feel that strongly against it, you don't have to be there."

"Callie isn't who you think she is."

"Now you want to start trashing, Callie? I'm not listening to this," he said getting up from the table.

"Did she tell you who Darius's father was?"

“What does that have to do with anything?”

“I bet she’s never even given you a name.”

“What does it matter, Jim! The man’s dead!”

“He’s not dead. He’s right here. I’m Darius’s father.”

Jim felt he had to do it. There was no way that he could allow Allen to be swallowed up in Callie’s scheme. Jim knew that he stood to lose a lot, but he would protect his friend, no matter what the personal cost. The only thing he regretted was that he had to hurt Allen in the process. Allen stood staring at him, puzzled. It was as if he couldn’t process what Jim had said.

“Are you drunk? Have you been drinking again? Are you on something?”

“I’m not drunk and I’m not high. It’s the truth. We got together around the time our clique broke up…”

“Why are you doing this?” he said quietly, looking directly into his eyes. “How can you look me in the eye and say something like that to me?”

“I’m sorry, Al.”

“No, I’m sorry – sorry I trusted you, you lying…”

“You don’t know how much I wish that was the case, but I’m not lying.”

Allen began to pace up and down for a moment, running his hands over his head. He was shaking with a rage that he was trying to control.

“I never wanted to hurt you, Al.”

“Please. Just…don’t,” he said stopping by the sink and leaning against it.

“If I could go back in time…”

"Just shut up! I don't want to hear any more of your crap, alright!"

Jim noticed Allen's breathing was rapid.

"You don't look good, man. I think you should sit back down," said Jim.

"I can't wait...'til next week. I want you...out of this house...now," said Allen through short gasps.

Jim just sat there immobilized by his friends anguish. He wanted to leave, but he couldn't.

"I said...GET OUT!"

"Allen, what's all this yelling about at this time of night?" asked Vernon coming down stairs with Lena behind him.

"Allen, are you alright?" said Lena looking at her son with concern.

Without warning, Allen collapsed onto the kitchen floor.

"Allen! Allen!" yelled Lena as she shook him vigorously, hoping for some response.

"Let me look at him," said Vernon as Lena moved aside so he could kneel down next to him. Vernon, put his ear to Allen's mouth. "He's not breathing. Call 911"

"Lord Jesus, help us please!" prayed Lena scrambling to the phone as Vernon started chest compressions on Allen.

Jim sat frozen in bewilderment as he watched events unfold. The landmine had finally exploded and claimed it's first casualty.

THIRTY-EIGHT

Callie rushed through the emergency room of Harlem Hospital in pajamas covered by her jacket with a cranky Darius in her arms. She knew he was fussing because his sleep had been interrupted, and she was trying to calm him as she approached the registration desk. After inquiring about Allen's whereabouts there, she was off to the elevator bank to go to the fourth floor where he was being treated.

"Please be okay," said Callie over and over again in her head. When Mrs. Sharpe called her with the news about what happened to Allen, she thought her heart would stop. Mrs. Sharpe's voice was frantic and she could tell that she was crying. She didn't give Callie much information; just that Allen had collapsed and was being taken to the hospital. At first, she assumed that Allen got over stressed and passed out. But after thinking about things on the way over, Callie began to worry that Allen's condition might be more serious.

When she got off at the fourth floor, the nursing assistant directed her to the waiting room, where she found all of their friends and family had gathered – everyone, except Jim, and Riley. They were standing in a circle, holding hands with Pastor Bynum in the midst, leading them all in prayer. "As if that's going to help," she thought derisively. But she knew if they were praying, Allen had to be in bad shape. Callie decided to stand aside until they were finished. "I hope this isn't going to be long," she thought. Callie was anxious to know what happened to Allen.

"...Lord, we ask that you extend your mercy and grace toward him tonight and deliver him from this infirmity. Let your healing power touch his body and restore the function of his heart...."

"His heart!" thought Callie, "Could Allen have had a heart attack? But he's way too young for something like that." Then she remembered that he had an arrhythmia that had developed when he was an infant. She knew that his condition could be aggravated by physical exertion, but he collapsed at home, and not at work.

"...We're not trusting in doctors, and we're not trusting in medicine, but we are trusting in your infinite power, grace and mercy, O God, because you are the only One that can help. It is by your stripes that we have healing. When you suffered on the cross you took away not just our sins, but also our infirmities. Have mercy on this child of yours, and raise him up from this bed of affliction..."

As they continued to pray, Callie started getting restless. Even Darius was trying to wriggle out of her arms. "Enough already," she thought anxiously. But it would be another 15 minutes before she heard the 'Amen.' When they were done, Callie rushed over to Lena.

"How's Allen? Is he going to be okay?" asked Callie, as she tried to calm Darius who was beginning to whine.

"The doctors are still working on him, but even they're not completely sure he'll pull through," said Lena. Callie could tell she was trying to hold it together. Her eyes were red from crying and she was leaning against her husband who had a supportive arm around her.

"What happened to him?"

"They said he had a caffeine overdose, and that combined with his arrhythmia and all the stress he was going through..."

"Oh, no. No, noooo," moaned Callie. Suddenly, Darius let out a loud wail. Callie struggled to comfort him in the midst of her own grief.

"I'll take him for you," offered Mother Rose, as she took the crying child from her arms. Callie gave him over without hesitating. She couldn't deal with her son right now, as she was trying to absorb all of this information. Allen was probably suffering from atrial fibrillation caused by the caffeine overdose. Her professional expertise told her that if they weren't able to stabilize his heartbeat, Allen would surely die. The possibility of Allen's death was too much for her. Callie didn't want to think about raising Darius without Allen around to help. She didn't want to imagine any part of her future without him. Then she would be back where she started: alone. Callie couldn't do anything but weep. Her legs began to buckle under her and she felt someone grab her and lead her to a chair, where she slumped over and leaned her elbows on her knees.

Everyone gathered around Callie and offered their sympathies, but Callie remained silent. She didn't need or want their comfort. She knew they didn't like her and had probably been constantly nagging at him to end the relationship. She was certain that their harassment, combined with all the stress Allen was going through at school and on his job, was probably what brought on his present condition. If Allen died, Callie was convinced that they were the main cause. Such thoughts began to transform Callie's grief into an anger that she struggled to stifle. She wanted to tell all of them off, but she constrained herself for Allen's sake. If there were any chance for his recovery, she didn't want to ruin it. In the meantime, Callie covered her face with her hands, and did her best to tune them out.

"Excuse me, Mr. and Mrs. Sharpe?" said a voice.

"We're right here," said Vernon.

Callie looked up to see a tall dark-skinned man wearing scrubs and the Sharpes rushing toward him while the others formed a circle around him. Callie sprung out of her seat and broke through the crowd to hear what the doctor had to say.

"We finally got his heart beating regularly, and he is conscious..."

"Thank the Lord!" said Lena. Callie joined everyone else around her in a collective sigh of relief.

"...But we're going to keep him here for a day or two for observation. After that, he's a going to need a couple of days rest and cut back on the caffeine."

"I'll make sure of that. Can we see him?" asked Vernon.

"I'll have to say parents only for tonight. The rest of you will have to come back tomorrow afternoon between 1:00pm and 9pm."

"Can't you please just let one more person in to see him? I'm his girlfriend."

"If it's alright with you," said the doctor to Allen's parents.

"I guess it's alright," said Vernon.

"Not more than a few minutes. He needs his rest."

Callie followed Vernon, Lena, and the doctor back to the room where Allen was. They had arrived just as a nurse had disconnected Allen from the ventilator. Callie could barely see him behind the wall of bodies standing around the bed. Allen had several electrodes on his chest and he was hooked up to an EKG machine that beeped in the background. He looked weak, and while he was conscious, Callie could see that he was a bit disoriented. Lena, edged to the front and took Allen's hand.

"Everything's alright, baby."

"M-mama," said Allen weakly.

"Shhh," said Lena, "Don't try to talk. You need to rest. Mama and Daddy are here. Callie's here, too."

Callie could see a change in his expression when Lena mentioned her name. She could see his eyes roaming the room looking for her, so she broke through the wall of bodies positioning herself so he could see her. When his eyes finally lighted upon her she saw in them something disconcerting. His gaze was steady and piercing.

"Hey, Allen," she said softly, rubbing his forearm. "You had us worried there for a minute. She smiled at him hoping that he would smile back, but he didn't. He just stared at her as if he were in a trance. The beeps from the EKG machine started to speed up their pace if just a bit.

"Everyone's here. But they only let your mama and me see you, and even then they're only giving us a few minutes, so we can't stay long," said Vernon. "But we'll be back tomorrow, first thing. I'll bring you your things and we'll git you somethin' to eat. Right now, you gon' rest. You got that?"

Allen nodded his head, but he kept looking at Callie.

"I – I want – to know..."

"Whatever it is, we'll talk about it later. You need to save your strength. There'll be plenty of time to talk. You betta believe that," said Vernon.

Finally, his eyes shifted over toward his father, and the kindness that she had always recognized in them returned.

"You know I love you, right?" said Vernon, rubbing his son's head.

"I love you, too, Allen," said his mother, before placing a kiss on his forehead.

"I love – you – both, too" said Allen smiling at them.

"Love you, Al. I'll see you tomorrow, Okay?"

His smile faded and the intense stare returned. Allen was silent. As Callie looked at him, her stomach tightened into a knot. Something was definitely wrong. Even Lena noticed it and looked back and forth between them with a look of concern. It seemed as if he was upset with her for some reason. She studied his face for a minute hoping to be able to figure it out, but she couldn't.

"I hate to interrupt, but I have to remind you he needs to rest. His body has been through a lot," said the doctor.

They all bid Allen farewell and left. When they were back in the waiting room, everyone crowded around them.

"Is he really going to be okay?" asked Tim.

"I think so. He was trying to talk, but I told him, to rest," said Lena.

"That's a relief," said Tamiko.

"I'll be sure to let Mr. Hardy know what's going down," said Davis.

"I appreciate that, son. Thank you," said Vernon

"Now, I think we all should get some rest. It's pretty late," said Mother Rose.

"Wait a minute. Where's Jim?" asked Callie.

"He's back at the house with Riley," said Lena, "I hope she was able to talk some sense into him. When we left he was blaming himself for what happened."

"Why would he do that?" asked Callie.

"I guess because he and Al got into an argument before Allen got sick. I told him that didn't have anything to do with what happened," Lena replied.

"I think I know what had to do with it. I told Allen to leave off them funny drinks. That boy is just so hard-headed," said Vernon.

Callie's heart leapt up into her throat.

"What were they arguing about?" she said.

"I wish I knew. All I know was Vernon and I were asleep, then all of sudden I heard Allen yelling. When Vern and I went down to see what was going on, Allen just fell out," said Lena.

"Well, we'll sort all of that out later when Allen gets home. Right now let's get to bed," said Vernon.

Callie headed with everyone toward the elevator banks. As she waited for the elevator, she couldn't help being swallowed up by her own thoughts. She had a suspicion that Allen's response toward her had something to do with his argument with Jim. They could have fought about any number of things, but she hoped it wasn't one thing in particular. "There's no way Jim would've told him about us," mused Callie, "he's got too much to lose."

The elevator came and they all piled inside. While the others talked amongst each other, Callie was still mulling over Lena's words and Allen's cold response to her. While she was relieved that Allen was going to be okay, she was now worried about the state of their relationship. There were indications that she would have to repair any damage done by Jim's reckless words and actions. She definitely had to have some private time with Allen and make sure they were on track. Then once she had secured her relationship, she would decide whether or not it was worth it to teach Jim to keep his mouth shut.

When the elevator door opened, everyone headed toward the exit. Callie was in a hurry, because she knew she had to be to work in the next seven hours. She dragged behind the others pondering what she would say to Allen when she saw him again.

"Excuse me, young lady, but aren't you forgetting someone?" she heard Mother Rose call out to her. She looked over at her to see her carrying a sleeping Darius.

"I'm sorry, Darius," she said to her son as she took him from Mother Rose's arms, "How could I forget about you?"

"I guess we've all been through a lot this evening," said Mother Bynum eyeing her strangely.

"Yes. Thank you," she said before walking off.

Callie was startled at the fact that she almost left without her son. Darius was one of the most important people in her life beside Allen. Together they were a family and Callie was determined to make sure they stayed that way.

THIRTY-NINE

Lena and Vernon were bustling about the hospital room trying to make it more comfortable for their son. Lena was putting the flowers she had just bought into a vase she brought from home and set them on the table near Allen's bed, and then commenced to fluffing Allen's pillows. Vernon was going through a bag of things they had brought from home to cheer Allen up. In the midst of their activity, Allen felt as if he was going in slow motion. Although he was better physically, his mind was scattered and his heart felt as if someone had torn it to shreds before setting it on fire. He saw his life as a castle built on the edge of the seashore, with the waves crashing against it. Allen had tried with all his might to protect the castle, but his efforts were fruitless. Each wave took a bigger and bigger piece, bulwarks included, until it all had become dispersed in the ocean. Allen was not in a good mood, and the last thing he wanted to do was entertain his parents who were looking for reassuring signs that he was on the mend. But after all they'd done for him he'd try to do his best acting.

"How you feelin' now, son? Better?" asked Vernon.

"A lot better than last night," said Allen.

"You don't know how glad we are for that," said Vernon. Then he slapped Allen in the back of the head.

"Vernon!" said Lena.

"What was that for?!" said a shocked Allen, as he tried to rub away the sting his father's slap left.

"That's for drinking them energy drinks when I told you not to. You betta hope I don't take my belt off right now."

"Vernon, must you? He's still recovering. You'll bother his heart."

"The doctors done fixed his heart. I'm tryin' to fix that head, so he won't end up here again."

"Look, dad, I've learned my lesson. You don't have to worry about me even drinking coffee anymore."

"You know you betta not. I don't even want to see you drinkin' soda anymore."

"The doctor said that for the next couple of days, you're going to have to take some time off. No school, no work, no nothin'."

"I can't not do my school work. I'll fall behind again..."

"Fallin' behind? You always told me and yo' mama everything was okay. How you done got behind?" said Vernon.

"Okay, I got into a little trouble in the beginning, because I wasn't prepared for how different law school is from undergrad. But now that I've been attending the study groups, I was catching up. I don't want to lose that."

"But you have to look after your health, Allen," said Lena.

"You should have thought about that before you started drinkin' that mess. And anyway you need to cut down on all this stuff you tryin' to do. You ain't no superman."

"I already gave up the Bible study."

"The Bible study isn't what you should be giving up. You need to cut back on all them hours you workin'. You can't go to school and work no full time job and not have something suffer. I done talked to Mr. Hardy and Davis, and they said that they were willin' but you the one don't want to cooperate."

"At the time I was thinking I needed the money."

"Money ain't worth yo' life! And I think there are other things you need to cut back on, too. I know you might not want to hear it, but I think you need to cut back on seein' that girlfriend of yours."

"You might be right about that."

Both Lena and Vernon looked at each other in astonishment.

"Now, Allen, I hope you not gon' sit here and agree with me, then go out and do the opposite like you did last time."

"No, sir."

"You betta not if you know what's good for you," warned Vernon.

"Allen, what were you and Jimmy fighting about last night?" asked Lena.

"Nothin'"

"Couldn'tve been nothin' if you was hot enough to wanna throw him out."

"I'd rather not get into it right, now."

Allen didn't want to tell his parents what Jim had told him because he was still struggling with himself over whether he should believe it or not. Jim, like everyone else, strongly disapproved of his relationship with Callie. Allen suspected it was because he was jealous. Jim's reaction to the news of the engagement made it highly likely. Allen considered the possibility that Jim concocted that lie to break them up. Then again, Jim had never lied to him –ever, not even when they were at odds with each other. Allen thought back to the time when he saw Jim at the hospital and showed him Darius's picture. He recalled Jim's strange reaction. "But it couldn't be true," thought Allen. If it were true then that meant the woman he loved and his best friend had betrayed him in the worst possible way.

"Why? You still angry?"

"I don't know how I feel right now"

"You betta find out, 'cause when you get home we gon' settle this. Ain't no reason why you and Jimmy can't put whatever this is behind you and move on. Y'all been friends too long to let some foolishness come between you. You hear me?"

"I hear you"

"It's probably better that you have time to yourself to think about things for a while. While you're thinking, I hope you read your Bible. It's in that bag there. Sometimes we need to take a step back and consider what God has to say about things"

"I will"

"We'll be back tomorrow to take you home. If you need anything in the meantime, call us. Okay?"

"Definitely"

After some final hugs and kisses, Allen's parents left him alone with his thoughts. He kept thinking about what Jim had said the other night. He had to know whether or not it was true. There was only one person that could help him find out, and with the way things were right now, he didn't know if he could trust her. The more Allen went over things in his mind, the more depressed he became. There were so many questions that he had and he didn't know if any of them would or could be answered in a way that would satisfy him. In the midst of his meditation, he heard a knock at his room door. Not long after that, Callie eased the door open, and peeked in smiling at him uneasily.

"Hey, Al" said Callie.

"Hey"

She rushed over to hug him, but Allen wouldn't return the embrace. Callie pulled away and they looked at each other for a moment. Allen could sense that she had been unnerved by the change in his demeanor. Her eyes seemed to be pleading with him in a way that made her appear guilty.

"I brought you flowers," she said handing them to him.

"I see. I didn't expect to see you until later," said Allen, tossing the flowers on the bed tray.

"There was no way I could go to work, without checking in to make sure you're okay," she said taking his hand and sitting beside him. She squeezed his hand, but Allen wouldn't squeeze back. "When I heard you'd collapsed, I thought they'd have to take me in next."

"Hmmm."

"You are okay, right?"

"Yeah. Don't I look okay?"

"You seem like you have something troubling on your mind."

"Lately my mind has been full of problems."

"Your mom told me you were arguing with Jim before you collapsed. Is that what's bothering you?"

"He laid something on me that I've been having a hard time dealing with."

"What was that?"

"First, he said he wanted to move away to North Carolina. Next week in fact."

"Really? Knowing how close you two are, I guess you weren't too thrilled to hear that."

"I wasn't really upset, just shocked. It was kind of weird that he wanted to leave so soon after getting back, but I was okay with it. The thing was, I told him that I was hoping he would stick around for our wedding."

"You told him about our plans?"

"I wasn't meaning to. It came up in conversation. Anyway, he wasn't happy with the idea of me getting married, especially to you."

"Why's that?"

"He said I shouldn't trust you."

“What on earth?! I can’t believe Jim would say something like that!”

“Neither could I.”

“You know he’s just hating on our relationship because he’s jealous. He sees you making progress in your life, while his is falling apart, so he wants to sabotage you. He’s trying to cause problems in our relationship so you’ll be as miserable as he is. I told you this would happen.”

“That’s what I was thinking, but...Callie, I’m going to ask you something and I want you to look at me when you answer.”

“Go ahead.”

“Is Jim Darius’s father?”

Callie’s eyes grew wide with apprehension, and the hand that had been holding his started to tremble.

“Did he tell you that?” she said looking away.

“Look at me, Callie. I want a straight answer.”

She looked back at him again.

“Allen, you know me better than anyone. What do you think?” she said, tears dropping from her eyes like the start of a spring shower. Her evasiveness had already given Allen his answer, but he would make her say it.

“Answer the question, Callie.”

“You’re the only father Darius will ever have.”

“It’s either yes or no. Is Jim Darius’s father?!”

“No!” she said, “Jim is not his father!”

“I guess it’s settled then.”

"Of course it is. How can you even consider taking the word of some fake, hating, jealous, brother over that of the woman who actually loves you?"

"Because he's right."

"Allen!" she said looking startled, "I can't believe...how could you think I'm lying to you?!"

"I saw the look on your face when I first asked you the question."

"I was shocked that you could even ask me something like that! To imply that I would sleep with your best friend?"

"Please, don't even try to cover yourself because you can't. I've been thinking about it for a while and it's all starting to make sense now: the way you tried to convince me not to reconcile with Jim, your plan for me to talk to him about moving down south and then when I wouldn't do it, you snuck behind my back and talked to him yourself."

"What?! How could I have talked to him about something that I didn't even know he was going to do?! That's ridiculous!"

"No it's not, really. Where else would Jim have gotten the idea? You were the only one kicking it around, and not a week later, he's saying the exact same thing."

"He could have gotten the idea from Riley for all we know! They have been spending a lot of time together, and she does live in the south."

"Aiight, then," said Allen slipping into Ebonics, as he usually did when he was angry, "if it's like you say, then how 'bout we take Darius for a paternity test?"

"What?!! I'm not going to put my son through something so intrusive, just because your boy is a liar!"

"Had a feeling you would say that."

"So I'm just supposed to be cool with having my son's personal information being made public?"

Allen wasn't in the mood to rebut such a ridiculous argument that had been brought up for no other reason than to take the conversation off topic because she had no reasonable excuse for not wanting a paternity test given the circumstances.

"Callie, give it up, already. You've been found out. It's over. We're over – the engagement, the relationship, the friendship, everything."

"Allen how can you just throw away everything we have together?! How can you do this to me after everything you promised me?!"

"Are you serious?! What about what you've done to *me*! How could you sleep with my best friend behind my back? How could you bear his child and then lie to me about it, and string me along for nearly two years?"

"Al, please..."

"No, I loved you, Callie! I loved you with everything I had and I trusted you with my heart, and this is how you do me?! "

"I'm sorry," said Callie sobbing.

"Not as sorry as I am."

"I made a mistake...and I know I hurt you – but there has to be a way for us to get past this and start over."

"If you had been honest with me up front when I first asked you, I might have considered it, but – that's what I can't get over – you lied to me."

"I'm being honest with you now!"

"Only after I called you out. I just don't understand why you felt you had to lie in the first place. Why didn't you tell me that night that I called you? I would have listened to you, Callie. I would've tried to understand."

"I didn't want you to walk out on me the way you did before."

"I didn't walk out on our friendship; you threw me out. I guess you were too busy with Jim."

"It wasn't like that. We weren't in a relationship, it was just..."

"I don't care what it was. It doesn't matter at this point."

"What about Darius? You're the only father he's ever known. Think about what this is going to do to him."

"Don't you dare bring Darius into this. You know I'll always love him, but how I feel for him has nothing to do with what's going on between us. Don't use him like that."

"I'm sorry, Allen...please...I love you."

"There's no way I can believe that after what you've done. Now, I'll have to ask you to leave. Make sure you leave the ring on the table before you go."

"Allen...please."

Allen looked away from her out the window. He wouldn't look back until after he heard the sound of the ring hitting the table and the door of the room closing. It was over. This time it was really over. Callie was gone along with the remnant of the hopes and dreams from his teenage years. As he studied the ring lying on the table, his heart flooded with waves of pain. After all the disappointments that he had to endure for the past several years, he was certain that God would bless this relationship. It was the one ray of light in the midst of what was becoming a very gloomy life. He had prayed, and prayed and prayed, and just when it looked like his blessing was coming into fruition, it turned out to be a curse. "God, I just don't understand," prayed Allen as the tears started to fall. "What is this all about? What are you doing to me?"

FORTY

"The doctors are here to administer emergency aid to a patient in distress in room 411!"

Allen looked up to see Richard, Tim and Davis bringing in burgers, fries, soda, and fried apple pies, paper plates, napkins and cups. His friends were a welcomed sight given everything that he'd gone through in the past 24 hours and the food was as well, since the dinner they served at the hospital didn't even put a dent in his appetite.

"What is all this?" said Allen.

"Its called dinner, my friend," said Tim.

"Yeah. Since we all know how nasty hospital food is, we thought we'd stop by and bring you some real eats," said Davis.

"That's right, so just sit tight while we will fix you a plate. Dr. Russell, prep this brotha for a cheeseburger transfusion. Dr. Martinez, start a line of cherry cola, 20 CC's, stat"

"Will do, Dr.," said Tim.

Richard, and Tim set up the food and beverages on the available tables, while Davis went to wrangle a few more chairs from the waiting room outside. Soon the room was filled with the scent of freshly grilled burgers, as well as the camaraderie of close friends.

"Thanks guys. You all know how to have a brother's back, for real"

"That's what we're here for, dude."

"Oh, and before I forget, Mr. Hardy wanted me to give you this," said Davis. He took an envelope out of the inside pocket of his coat that he had on the back of his chair and handed it to Allen.

"It's a get well card," said Allen after opening it. Then he began to read it. "He's giving me the next two days off!"

"Cold snap! You lucky you got a real chill boss, Al."

"Word. Just make sure you use those days to rest."

"I intend to. Tomorrow, God willing, I'll be sleeping in until noon."

"Don't forget to pray. This whole thing might be God's way of getting your attention."

"That thought has crossed my mind more than a couple of times. If that was His plan, then I'd say it was effective and the message has been well received. Getting sick has helped me to realize that my most important relationship is with Jesus. That's where my strength was coming from. Leaving Him for caffeine supplements and other nonsense was not a good idea."

"I'm glad you seein' that, now. So you think you gonna start dialin' down your workload?"

"Yes, Davis. You don't have to worry. I'll be talking to Mr. Hardy about cutting my hours to part-time."

"That's going to give you a lot more time to study. Trust me," said Davis.

"And that's just what I need. I'll probably be cutting out other things, as well. Nothing wrong with having less things to do."

"Exactly. It's one thing to have a work ethic and another thing to become so busy with work that you have no time for God. Everyone needs balance," said Tim.

"Right, and I intend to make that my priority."

"I see you got a lot of other cards and flowers stacked up there. Has everyone else been by already?" asked Tim.

"Pretty much. My parents were here bright and early of course. Callie stopped after that and then Riley and Tamiko stopped by with the Pastor and Mother Rose. You guys were last, but I like your visit best."

"Because we brought food?" said Davis.

"And good food, too. Where did you guys get these burgers? These are the joint,"

"From the new chain across the street from here," said Tim.

"You know I'm going to have to start finding excuses to come by this way."

"Hey, wait a minute. What about Jim? He ain't stop by this way to see you?" asked Richard.

Everyone stopped eating and the conversation came to an abrupt halt. The light in Allen's eyes faded and his lively expression was replaced with a more sober one. Tim and Davis looked at Allen then gave each other wary glances. Richard kept his gaze on Allen as he waited for his answer, totally oblivious to the change of mood in the room.

"No, he hasn't" answered Allen.

"Is everything okay between you two?" said Tim, "I heard you guys had a bit of a disagreement before you fell ill."

"I didn't really want to have to get into this now, but I might as well. You're going to find out everything soon enough, anyway. Jim and I are going our separate ways."

"Again?! Why?" asked Richard.

"I just can't take any more from him. He's proven to me that he doesn't want to be my friend anymore." Allen put his hand over his mouth. All of the emotions that he thought he had been able to temper, started to rise to the surface. There was no way to put into words the depth of the betrayal he felt. "I think I should just accept that before either one of us can cause the other any more pain."

"What'd he do, chief?" asked Davis.

"I can't even talk about it right now. All I will say is that I trusted him, and he proved that he wasn't worthy of it. In my mind, he's dead to me."

"Al, I understand that you're probably still feeling a little raw right now because you're just starting to deal with everything, but I think you should give yourself time to think about things before you write him off completely. From what I've heard, he's been feeling a lot of remorse about what happened," said Tim.

"I don't care how he feels. He obviously didn't care about how I felt when he was stabbing me in the back."

"But you two have been friends for so long, and you've been able to get past your differences before," said Tim.

"That was before, this time he really spit on our friendship."

"You gotta forgive him, Al. You know what the Word says. If you want God to forgive you, you've gotta forgive others," said Davis.

"I'll forgive him, but that doesn't mean I have to forget."

"Then that's not real forgiveness," said Davis.

"Sorry, but it's all I have right now."

"But how's that going to work wit' you two livin' in the same crib for who knows how long?" asked Richard.

"It won't be that long. Jim is supposed to be moving to North Carolina with Riley next week."

"What?!" the other men exclaimed in shock.

"Was this decided before the argument or after?" asked Tim.

"Before. Jim was the one who decided it was time to move on, most likely because he felt guilty about what he'd done. But I thank God the truth came out before he left."

"Wow. This is blowing me away," said Tim.

"Word. This clique is going through too many changes," said Richard.

"But even though he's leaving soon, I still can't see myself living at home in the meantime. Tim, would you mind if I bunk with you for a while?"

"Of course not. Why do you think I keep the spare room?"

"Thanks, man. I promise I'll try not to get in your way."

"Trust me, there's not much to get in the way of nowadays."

"You sayin' you don't have no more female company?" asked Richard.

"Not since my last dating disaster."

"Tim, just because you made one mistake doesn't mean you shouldn't date anymore," said Allen.

"I'm well aware of that, but I'd rather wait and let God lead me to that someone, if there even is someone out there for me."

"I guess I can understand that. You don't want to rush into something and end up in a bad situation you can't get out of."

"So what you gon' do in the mean time, yo? You just gon' be by yourself?!" said Richard.

"As a Christian, I don't think there's any other choice, Rich," said Tim.

"You gon' be livin' like one of them monks!" said Richard.

"Nothin' wrong with going solo. I been solo for a while myself," said Davis.

"Hold up, I thought sho' you and Miko was gonna git together. You not gonna try to git that?" said Richard.

"Richard!" said Allen.

"Chillax, Al. I'm not talkin' about hittin' it, just datin.'"

"Like I was tellin' Al, the other day. I don't think Miko and I would be a good fit in a relationship," said Davis.

"Fa real?"

"Yeah. As a matter of fact, I think it's best for me to stay the way I am."

"Wait, wait, wait. You sayin' you wouldn't mind being single for right now, or for the rest of your life?" asked Richard.

"For the rest of my life."

"Hold up – I know you don't mean to tell me you don't ever want to be with another woman again?" asked Richard incredulously.

"Yeah. I mean, I don't mind having female friends, but I can do without all the romance stuff."

"Say What?! Brotha you need an intervention!"

"Rich, I understand your shock. I felt the same way when he told me, but now I don't think Dave's idea is so far fetched. Sometimes when you're in a relationship you can get caught up and end up serving that other person more than the Lord," said Allen.

"Where did that come from?" asked Tim.

"Like I've said. I've had a number of personal revelations in the past 24 hours."

"I don't know if I'm gon' be able to hang wit' you guys for much longer. All this talk about no women and what not – I don't know. Next thing you know, y'all all holed up in Tim's crib, wearing those brown robes and them funny sandals, burnin' incense, shaving the top part of your head bald," said Richard.

"First of all, we're not Catholic, and nowadays modern monks do not shave their heads," said Tim.

"Still, y'all sound a little extreme," said Richard.

"When you live for God sometimes you gotta make a sacrifice," said Davis.

"That's a pretty big sacrifice. Too big if you ask me," said Richard.

"When I think about everything He's done for us, I don't think any sacrifice can be too big," said Davis.

"Hmph. That's what y'all sayin' now 'cause ain't none of y'all found that tenderoni yet. I have a feelin' before the next summer is over somebody here gonna be puttin' a ring on somebody," said Richard.

They all laughed.

"Sounds like wishful thinking, Rich," said Tim.

"You'll see brother. You'll see."

FORTY-ONE

"Evening, Brad," said Tim as he walked into the New Towers. It had been an incredibly long day and with all the running around he'd been doing, he really hadn't had a chance to rest. Tim was looking forward to going through with his evening devotion and then going to bed. He'd wait until morning to fix up his spare bedroom. He hoped in the meantime, the Lord would show him something he could do to help Allen and Jim reconcile.

"Good evening, Mr. Russell," said Bradley, "Late night at the office, sir?"

"Nope. Just visiting a friend in the hospital," said Tim leaning against the station desk.

"I'm sorry to hear that."

"It's okay, Brad. He's fine, now. In fact, he'll be out tomorrow and he's going to be staying with us for awhile."

"I look forward to it, sir. I take it Mr. Sharpe will be our guest."

"Yes. How'd you know?"

"Just a guess. He visits often, and you seem like close friends."

"Indeed we are."

"You're very lucky. Not many people are so blessed."

"Thanks, Brad. Any news?"

"You have a delivery..." began Brad handing Tim a small box.

"My books! Awesome!"

"...and you have a visitor," he said as his face became grave and nodded his head to the waiting area.

Tim turned in that direction to see Allyson, casually dressed in a blue and white striped, cotton breton, dark rinsed skinny jeans and red platform sneakers, sitting with a red coat over her lap, listening to music on her cell phone, or at least that's what he assumed she was doing since she was wearing her ear buds that were plugged into it. She was so absorbed in what she was doing that she didn't even notice him. "Broke again," Tim surmised to himself, "What in the world is she doing with all of her money?"

"How long has she been waiting?" said Tim.

"Not more than five or ten minutes."

"Thanks, Brad. Here's something for looking out," he said handing him a twenty-dollar bill.

"Thank you, sir. It's always a pleasure."

As Tim got closer to where she was sitting, he realized he might have been wrong. Instead of music, he heard the voice of someone talking. When he was right behind her he could see, a video was displayed on the screen of her phone. It looked like a classroom lecture. Tim was practically standing right over her and yet she still was unaware of his presence. He crouched down where she was sitting, and removed one of her ear buds.

"That looks interesting," said Tim in Allyson's ear.

Allyson shot up and let out a short high-pitched shriek, while her coat fell to the floor, and her phone swayed near her legs from the cord of the earplugs.

"I wish you wouldn't always do that!" she said struggling to collect her belongings. She tried to reel in her phone, but it became disconnected from the ear buds and dropped to the floor next to her coat.

"Sorry, but I was trying to get your attention. You seemed so focused," said Tim, as he helped her gather her things.

"It's just a seminar."

"The professors at Columbia allow you to record them, now?"

"Some. The ones who aren't popular or knowledgeable enough to demand speaking fees."

"Speaking of fees, I thought that with all the extra money mom's giving you to spy on me, you wouldn't need another subsidy for quite some time."

"I'm not here for money."

Tim couldn't help gaping at her in disbelief. He wanted to believe that this was a positive development, but judging by the sour expression on his sister's face, he wasn't sure he should get his hopes up.

"Sooo why are you here?"

"If you don't mind, I'd prefer to discuss it in private," she said as she looked over his shoulder at Bradley.

Tim followed her gaze and noticed that Bradley was indeed staring at them. He would be annoyed with Bradley, but he knew nosiness and eavesdropping were the unspecified duties of a building doorman.

"Fine. After you," he said before they started toward the elevator banks.

Tim swallowed hard as he walked along with his sister. Ever since their falling out, any kind of conversation that did not involve pecuniary matters would end up in a shouting match with Allyson occasionally getting physical. He didn't know if he had the strength for whatever his sister had in store for him.

*****

"Would you like something to drink?" said Tim after he and his sister entered the apartment and he had locked the door. He hung their coats on the rack near the door and then laid his package on the coffee table.

"Depends. What do you have?" she said looking around as if she'd never been there before.

"There's sparkling water, regular water, orange juice, and berry smoothies."

"Just water."

"Coming up."

Tim went into the kitchen and grabbed a bottle of water from his fridge and brought it back to Allyson, who spent a good several minutes just staring at the bottle.

"Allyson, is everything okay?"

"I'm fine," she said before taking a sip and then a long drag and then putting the bottle on the table. He noticed that she seemed a little fidgety, and avoided looking directly at him. All of a sudden, her expression went from her usual sour, 'I'm annoyed with the world,' look to a more somber one. It made Tim less wary and more concerned.

"You sure? You look..."

"I told you I'm fine," she said, as her sour look returned, "I didn't come here because I had a problem. I wanted to let you know I got that little package you sent."

"Did you like it?"

"Where did you find her? I threw that doll in the garbage years ago."

"Yes, I remember going out to ride my skateboard, when I saw her lying outside in a box of trash, and I rescued her before the garbage collectors got to her."

"Why?"

"She was special to me. She reminded me of the good times between us."

"So why not keep her? Why send her to me now all of a sudden?"

"You read the card didn't you?"

"Yes."

"Then you know my reason."

"If this is some sentimental ploy that you're using to try to broker a reconciliation, then consider it a fail."

"Ally, I don't do ploys, or games. I am not trying to trick you into reconciling with me. I'm well aware that you're angry with me and probably will be until the day you die, but in spite of all that, I still love you. I always will. That's all that present was about."

"How magnanimous of you, Tim, but I'm not the one that needs mercy. As always, you forget there's a reason why we don't get along and I have every right to feel the way I do."

"Look, Ally, I know that I hurt you...obviously very deeply. But you have to know that I never meant to. I'm sorry, Ally."

"You can't be sorry if you don't even know what you're sorry for."

"I'm sorry for breaking my promise to you...to be there for you when Poppa died. I'm sorry I abandoned you and left for California, and then for boarding school. I'm sorry for not being there for you when you needed me the most. I'm sorry for being so caught up with myself that I didn't consider your feelings. I know things probably won't ever be the same between us and I'm not asking for them to be if that's not what you want. I just want you to forgive me."

"So you finally figured it out. What happened? Did you have some kind of epiphany or did your God tell you all this?"

"He led me to find this."

"This is my old diary," she said looking it over, and noticing that the lock was broken, "You read it?"

"Yes."

"It figures. You just don't get it, do you?"

"Are you saying you didn't want me to read it? You threw it away!"

"Duh! That in and of its self should have told you I didn't want anyone reading it. Those are my personal feelings! You had no right to read any of it without my permission!"

"I'm sorry, Allyson, I didn't realize you'd feel this way. But how else was I supposed to know why you were angry with me? After all, you flat out refused to tell me whenever I asked and I'm not a mind reader."

"You didn't need to be. It should have been obvious."

"Sometimes it's not. Two people can have different views of the same events you know."

"That's because the selfish can never properly empathize with anyone or understand the effect their actions have on other people. They only see things from their own narrow point of view."

"Okay, so I'm a jerk. Fine. If you can't forgive me for my sake, then do it for your own. If you haven't noticed, all that misery and anger you're holding inside of you is only going to attract more of the same. If you want to have some peace in your life, I suggest you let it go."

"Please. I have lots of money, I'm on the path to a promising career in journalism, I have lots of connections and I'm dating the heir of a multimillion-dollar publishing and entertainment mogul. I would hardly call that miserable."

"Sounds very brave, but you can't fool me. If all that stuff could satisfy you, then you wouldn't be as upset as you are now."

"I'm not upset!"

"If you're not upset, then why are you yelling?"

"I'm not! - Why did I even bother coming here?"

"That's a good question. Why did you come here tonight, Ally? I know you couldn't have possibly come out all this way in the middle of the night, and even be willing to wait around for a bit, all so you could tell me you got your birthday present, especially when there are easier and faster ways to do it and you wouldn't have had to put up with my irritating presence."

"You are so right. Thanks for the insight. In fact, I think I'll do myself a favor and leave."

"Allyson, wait!"

She stopped in her tracks but she didn't turn around to face him.

"I'm tired of things always ending up this way between us."

"I'm tired, too, Tim. I'm tired of mother, I'm tired of playing detective, I'm tired of church, and I'm tired of you."

Allyson left leaving Tim standing in a puddle of disillusionment. He thought sure that after discussing the real problem, things would change between them, but Allyson was just as bitter as she was before.

"Lord, I tried. I've done everything I know how to do and I've done everything you've told me or at least what I thought you told me. But now it's in your hands. If Allyson and I weren't meant to reconcile then I accept that. I pray you give me the strength and courage to move on."

FORTY-TWO

Jim tried to stand up. He eased himself up on the crutch until he was standing. Then he tried to shift his weight onto his formerly encased leg. At least he could stand on it. Yesterday, he couldn't do much of anything with it. Next, he tried to walk across the floor. He managed to take a few steps, but his knee seemed to be locked up and he had a hard time flexing it. Jim was getting frustrated with his lack of mobility. He'd had his casts off for two days, but with the way his body was responding, they might as well still have been on. Jim wasn't expecting to have his full range of motion, but thought he should be able to walk about without the use of his crutch by now. He was hoping to be able to have enough mobility to be able to get himself back to his old apartment. There was no way that he could stay with the Sharpes any longer.

It wasn't that the Sharpes had been angry with him. If they were, he would have felt better about staying under their roof. After confessing everything he'd told Allen to Mama Lena, Pop Vernon and Riley they all agreed that they'd been disappointed, but were willing to look past his indiscretions. Everyone was willing to move on as if nothing had happened and nothing had changed. But Jim knew better than that.

Allen was now at Tim's place, and had no plans to return anytime soon. Mama Lena and Pop Vernon had told him that maybe it was a good idea for him to go away for a little while with Riley so he could clear his head. Even Riley didn't hang around as much any more. When she was, she didn't have much to say. The Sharpes were too polite to say it, but he knew they were tired of dealing with him and the problems he was constantly raining on them. Jim wasn't going to continue to put a strain on this family. So he decided he was going to do them a favor.

Jim looked at the clock. It was almost 4:00 and he knew Mama Lena would be back from work soon, so he tried to move as fast as he could. It took him a good five minutes to get to the door, but Jim was determined to continue on. Once he was out the door, it was another ten minutes to the end of the block. By then he started to feel a pain in his foot that shot up into his leg, and his left armpit was sore from the crutch digging into it. Ordinarily, he could just walk home, but in his condition it would probably take him all night to trek the few blocks, so he decided to hail a gypsy cab instead.

Several passed him by before a brown 1996 Cadillac slowed down a little past the curb where he stood. Jim hobbled up to the door and eased himself in.

"I need to get to 123rd and St. Nicholas."

"St. Nicholas?"

"Yeah."

"I take you."

The ride lasted not more than a few minutes before he was outside the front of his building. Jim paid the fare, and struggled out of the cab, like a hermit crab shedding it's shell. Once he was out, he stood in front of the building for a moment gazing up at it. He had only been away for a little more than a month but for some reason the place seemed strange and forbidding. It seemed less like a home and more like a towering prison fortress. The last time he'd been here was the morning before the ambush. His most recent memories of the place were marked by loneliness and despair and now he'd returned plagued by the same feelings. He didn't want to be here, but he felt he deserved to be – in exile, where he could do no more harm.

Jim trudged slowly through the gates until he reached the entrance where he stopped to rest for several minutes. Sweat was dripping down his back from the workout. Then from the entrance he headed toward the elevator in the lobby, where he rested again as he waited for the elevator. A half hour had passed by the time Jim finally reached the door of his apartment. He tried his old key, which still worked and went in.

It wasn't like he remembered at all. He distinctly recalled leaving his apartment in a state of disarray. After Angela died, he didn't care about anything and let the place go to pieces. Since then someone had been by and had cleaned up. All of a sudden, fear took hold of Jim's heart. He closed the door behind him and struggled to the bathroom. He was tired and his left leg was throbbing when he got there, but that didn't stop him from his purpose. Jim sat himself on the toilet and inspected his old spot, but when he tried to remove the toilet paper dispenser, he couldn't. Someone had fixed the hole and sealed it up. The stash that had been there was obviously gone.

Jim gave himself a few minutes to rest as he tried to remember his other hiding places. Then he eased himself up off the toilet and hobbled to his bedroom, stopping at his desk. He looked through all the cubbyholes. He found the old mirror he used, and a random rusted razor blade, but there was no stash here either.

In his frustration, Jim knocked some books that were on the desk onto the floor. Jim didn't just come here to help the Sharpes, but he came here to help himself, too. He was tired of living with the pain, the shame, and the guilt of his actions. He was tired of feeling depressed all the time. Jim wanted just a little bit of happiness, even if it was just for a moment. Prayer hadn't made him feel better, and reading the Bible hadn't made him feel better, either. He even thought that once his secrets were revealed, the pressure would unload, but it didn't. He had asked God for help, but it seemed He was nowhere in sight. He didn't care about his future anymore. As far as he was concerned, he didn't have one. He was content to spend the rest of his life in a haze, sheltered from his feelings and the world around him. Jim had piled his hopes onto the little vials he had hidden away, but now they were gone.

"I still have $20.00 on me. There's got to be something I can get," Jim thought. There was only one thing he could get that cheaply. Under any other circumstances Jim would have hesitated to engage in such a risky experiment, but he was desperate. He knew about a dude named Mickey that had spots in Harlem, one not far from here. Jim had to get there.

Jim was back up on the crutches, taking one step at a time, ignoring the burning muscles in his leg, the soreness under his arm, and the cramps in his left hand. There was something much more urgent driving him. Before he knew it he was back outside on the street thinking of how to get to Mickey. If he took another cab, he wouldn't have any money for his hit, so he decided to inch along to the nearest train station that would take him over to the east side.

"Jim!" he heard a voice call suddenly. Jim looked around, but he didn't see anyone he recognized.

"Jim! Hey, Jim, wait!" he heard again. This time he looked behind him. He was carrying two grocery bags. Jim couldn't believe his good fortune. If anyone would be able to help him, he could.

"Chris! What you doin' around here?"

"I moved, remember? Now I live across the street. I was just comin' back from the store," he said showing Jim his grocery bags. "I see you got your casts off, now. You makin' out alright out here by yourself?"

"I'm good. The doctor says I have to exercise, you know."

"True, but you don't want to overwork it though. You looked liked you was havin' a little trouble."

"No, no. I'm managing."

"You walked all the way out here from Al's?"

"No, I took a cab here. Came to check on my old apartment. I used to live in that building over there."

"Word?"

"Yeah. While I'm here I thought I'd get reacquainted with the old hood and check out some of my old haunts. I was about to try to find Mickey, unless you know somebody that's closer," said Jim trying to bring up the topic of his interest in a casual way.

"You lookin' to score?" said Chris whose countenance fell with disappointment.

"Don't look at me like that. You of all people should know how hard it is."

"I do."

"Not everybody can go straight all at once. I'm not trying to do this on the regular, I only need a little somethin' to get me through today. You understand what I'm sayin'?"

"Yeah. I understand. I been there."

"That's just what I thought, man. So you willin' to do a brotha a favor?"

"Yeah. Just follow me."

*****

Chris had both of his grocery bags in one hand and tried to hold Jim up with the other as he led him to the door of his apartment. When they entered, Jim was amazed by how clean and orderly the place was. It was a studio apartment, and Chris had a number of screens up to divide the living space. He was also astonished by how much open space there was. Chris led him to the section that he had made into a living room that was furnished with a futon and matching bean bag chairs. Jim rested himself on the foldaway futon while Chris put away his groceries.

"This place looks nice."

"Thanks. Al and the others helped me put everything together."

"You still doin' that welfare job?"

"Yeah, but I been puttin' out applications to other places and I'm hopin' to find a real job. The section 8 I got ain't gon last no more than a couple of years."

"I hope you find somethin' soon."

"Thanks."

"So you got somethin' 'round here to float on?"

"I got some Advil to help your leg, but I ain't got nothin' for floatin."

"Then what you brung me by here for? I thought you was fixin' to hook me up."

"Jim, you don't need that mess."

"Now you gon' tell me I need the Lord, right? I tried that, man. He don't have no more grace for me. I done messed up too much."

"That ain't true. Ain't nobody out there messed up too much for God's mercy. If He's helpin' me, He'll help you. You couldn't have done nothin' worse than I done, and believe me, I done a whole lotta wrong."

"If that's the case then, why do I feel the way I do? Everybody talkin' bout the joy of the Lord. When do I get to that joy? Hunh? Right now all I got is a lot of pain and problems that I can't see my way out of. Y'all like to say He's a burden bearer. When's he going to bear mine?"

"When you trust him enough to give 'em to Him."

"What you mean, 'when I give them to Him? I done prayed my heart out to Him."

"Prayin' is one thing and trusting him is another. Lot's of people pray, but they don't have the faith to believe that He's working on their situation."

"I listened for Him. I did what I thought He told me to do, but now I feel like I'm in a worse situation than before with even more problems. It's like he's punishing me, and I know I deserve it, but – I can't take this anymore."

"I can't say what God's doing to you. Only He can tell you that. But I do think it's safe to say he don't wanna destroy you. Remember, you coulda died in that warehouse."

"With everything that's going on now, I wish I did."

"Don't say things like that, Jim. We talked about this before. Just because the situation isn't how you want it to be doesn't mean that God's not workin'. Look at the things He *is* doing: you're alive, and you have a family to support you"

"I don't know about that last part."

"What you mean? What's goin'on?"

"When I was out there in the streets, I did a lot of stupid things I shouldn't have including stabbing my best friend in the back. Now that they all know what went down, I don't know if any of them is going to want me around. Can't blame them, either."

"Did you apologize to everyone?"

"Al doesn't even want to hear what I have to say. The others say they understand, but they don't act like it."

"Anyone say they wanted you to leave?"

"I was thinking about going down south for a while, and they think it's a good idea."

"That don't sound like they want you out. Might mean they want you to take some time away so Al can cool off. You got to be careful, sometimes your guilt can make you see things that ain't there."

"They're all acting different around me now."

"You can't take that to heart. Everybody got to have time to process things. Think about if you were in their position, or Al's position."

"I'd want me out."

"I don't know Jim. From what I'm understandin', your peeps care about you too much to just throw you out like that. But let's play devil's advocate and say it's true. You're still alive, you still got God on your side. He's forgiven you even if the others don't. Now you gotta forgive yourself and move on, and if no one else will be your friend, then I will – that is, if you want me to be."

"Why would you want to be there for me after everything I did to you?"

"Jim, that was the past. I done forgive you for all that a long time ago."

"Thanks man. It's just that this is so hard."

"I know it's hard. Sometimes it's down right painful. It's human nature to want to avoid it all – to do a few lines, take a hit or a drink or whatever you like to do to get away from it all, but you can't grow like that. Times like this you gotta grit your teeth, trust God and go through it."

"I thought being with Him was supposed to make it all easier."

"He does make it easier, but only when you trust Him. Let go and trust Him. Don't think about what might happen in the next hour, or the next day, or the next week. Trust what he's doing now."

Right now Jim was sitting with a good friend, rather than being holed up in a drug spot getting wasted. Right now, Jim was starting to feel a little better about his situation, instead of being anxious to get high. Maybe he had not been forgotten after all.

"I guess if He wasn't lookin' out for me, I could've been down at Mickey's by now."

"That's the last place either of us needs to be."

"Level with me Chris. You been clean this whole time?"

"Yeah. But that don't mean I never been tempted. But in the times when I have, I know I have to hold onto His hand just that much tighter."

"Where you learnin' all this stuff from?"

"Just goin' to church, Bible Study, counselin, and spending time with the Lord. I'm going to counselin' service tonight. You can come with me if you want."

"I don't know. I don't want a lot of strange people in my business."

"The people down there ain't like them folks at the rehab that gets paid to deal with people. These Christian people that want to help."

"Yeah, but that Davis dude is gonna be there and I don't know about him."

"Trust me, he's a good brother. He's helped me better than family. But there's plenty of other people workin' down there besides him if that's your worry."

"Still..."

"Just come one time, and if you don't think it's worth it, I won't bother you 'bout it no more."

"Aiight."

"I was going to fix myself something to eat before I left. If you want you can stay for dinner and then we'll take a cab down to the church. I got lots of soups: vegetable, chicken noodle, tomato, cup o' noodles, ramen. Which one you want?"

"Vegetable sounds good. I guess you're a soup fan."

"Not really. It's one of the few things I can eat - that and things like bread, and pasta, and fresh vegetables. That junk I was takin' did a number on my stomach. Can't really even look at dairy or fast food anymore."

"Word?"

"Yeah. It's messed up because I been trying to gain some weight like the doctor say, but it's hard when there isn't much that'll stay down."

"Looks like you're gaining weight to me."

"That's 'cause last time you saw me I was skin and bones. But the doctor say that a guy with my height and frame should weigh at least 190 pounds. So far I only got up to 175 and can't seem to get no higher."

"What about grits? You can eat that can't you? That'll put some weight on you."

"What's grits?"

"A brotha like you never eaten grits? How come? Your mama didn't know how to cook?"

"My mother was Puerto Rican. My father was black, but he was married, so he didn't come around. After him, she was married to a black guy for a while, but he always spent what little money we had on forties, cigarettes, and fast food."

"Well, one day when I return the favor, I'll make you some."

"You cook?"

"Some. I can make grits and eggs, toast, and cake. That's about as far as my expertise goes."

"I used to go to one of them trade high schools where they taught you how to cook. I used to know how to make some things, but it's been a long time since I used those skills."

"Once you learn something, you never really lose it. Maybe you should try to do something with that again. I wouldn't mind being a guinea pig. Me and food are no strangers."

"I'll think about it."

"Chris."

"Yeah."

"You're a good guy. I'm glad I know you."

"Back at you, man."

FORTY-THREE

Tim was sitting on his couch in sweatpants and a t-shirt, the only thing he'd ever wear for pajamas aside from the sleeveless t-shirt and boxer shorts he'd don in the summer months. He was getting his briefcase ready for the next day, arranging all of his files and notes in order of priority. Tim was the master of organization when it came to his work, and wished that he had the power to work the same kind of magic on his social life. He hadn't heard from his sister in days and true to her promise, she hadn't shown to church last Sunday. His best friend had been camped out at his place for nearly a week and he still didn't know what happened between Allen and Jim. He had called Jim once to make sure he was okay, but he seemed like he wasn't in the mood to talk, and Tim wasn't going to try to press him for information. Once again, their set was falling apart, however, he realized that no matter what, he had to accede authority to the master of it all who could do more than he could.

After fastening the locks on the briefcase, he checked the clock on his living room table and realized that Al would be home soon, so he went into the kitchen and got the other half of the pizza he had ordered for dinner and put it in the oven. After that, he grabbed a Bavarian pretzel from a jar on the counter as a snack. His timing was perfect for just as the aroma from the pizza began to waft through the apartment, he could hear Al unlocking the living room door.

"How was class?" asked Tim shouting from the kitchen.

"Good. Now that I have time to study and get some rest, some of the information from my readings is sticking. I felt like I knew what I was talking about in class today."

"Glad to know things are working out for you. I've got some pizza heating in the oven if you want. It should be hot by now."

"Thanks. I'm so hungry, I could eat my own foot," said Allen stopping at the sink to wash his hands before grabbing an oven mitt to retrieve his pizza.

"Lucky for you there's pepperoni and sausage instead."

Allen took a seat at the kitchen table with his meal, while Tim sat across from him, bringing another pretzel with him.

"How was work?" asked Allen as he wiped pizza sauce from his mouth with a napkin.

"Fine. Things are starting to slow down there as of late. I'm not taking home much work anymore. Sometimes I just stay an extra hour or so and just get things done rather than bring work home with me."

"Smart. Still nothing from your sister?"

"Nope."

"Don't worry. Things tend to get worse before they get better."

"One can only hope. Oh, by the way, Callie left a message for you on my voicemail for some reason. She asked me to tell you that she wants to talk to you."

"That's interesting."

"I'll say. I was wondering why she didn't just leave the message on your phone."

Allen just kept eating his pizza without responding.

"I mean she is your girlfriend, after all. Although...I have noticed that you haven't mentioned her the whole time you've been here, and she hasn't stopped by to see you, either."

"If you get anymore messages like that, just erase them. Callie and I broke up."

"I kind of suspected that. When did this happen?"

"Just before you guys came to see me at the hospital."

"So that's why you seemed so bummed when we came in. This wouldn't happen to have something to do with the fall out between you and Jim, would it?"

Allen was silent again.

"C'mon, Al. I gave you some space earlier because I knew that you were still trying to figure things out, but it's been nearly a week now. What's going on?"

"I don't even know where to start. The only person who I feel sorry for in all this is Darius and what he's going to have to go through. I'd like to be there for him, but I don't know if that's going to be possible."

"Darius? How does he figure in all this?"

"You'll never guess who Callie hooked up with before Darius was born. No, actually, you will."

"Jim?"

"Told you."

"Dude! Are you implying that Jim is Darius's..."

"I'm not implying anything. He told me himself."

"Whoah, dude! Are you serious?! Hold on, I think I might need a minute. This information's blowing me away."

"Now think about how I must've felt."

"I'm not going to even pretend to know. Sorry, Al. I can't imagine what could've happened to..."

"Neither can I."

"Are you sure Jim even knew how much you liked her?"

"Trust me, he knew."

"We all know he was under a lot of emotional stress at that time, and was definitely drinking if he wasn't using yet. You think maybe he was under the influence when this happened? I'm not saying that excuses his behavior, but it might explain it."

"I don't know. Maybe. Only God knows. Not that it matters anyway."

"Are they going to be a couple now?"

"No. Whatever they had together was just physical."

"Figures."

"Now, I'm just trying to move on, and forget about them."

"Al, I can understand your being upset and all, but I think you should try to work things out with Jim."

"Believe me, for the past couple of days I've thought about that, but Jim's got a lot of issues that he needs to work out. I used to think that God could use me to help him, but I think I'd just be setting myself up for more pain."

"Not necessarily. He's given his life to God and I know he wants to do the right thing. He could have gone down south and kept everything a secret, but he told you the truth."

"That might have been more like an accident."

"No, he made a decision, even if it was in the heat of the moment. Besides, this thing happened years ago when you knew neither of you were on good terms. It's not like he did this yesterday and if what your mom says is true, he is sorry about it."

"Or sorry his secret's out."

"Despite what everything looks like, I can't believe Jim could be that malicious. He was still grieving over his mom. Sometimes people get so wrapped up in their own pain that they're not thinking about the real impact of their actions."

"It's called selfishness. I'm not sure if it would be good to have a friend like that."

"All right, I'll grant you that. But we've all been there. I know I have. I've done a lot of stupid, selfish, irresponsible things to you in the past, like the time I left you stranded in the middle of Allentown, Pennsylvania."

"Yes, I remember, but that wasn't as bad..."

"It was bad enough. You could have been killed or abducted or something. Yet, the next week back on campus, you forgave me, despite my very lame excuse. As a matter of fact, there were a number of other times you could have written our relationship off, but you didn't. Why?"

"Because I knew that the real Tim, the good guy that was hiding, would show up eventually."

"Well, I think the real Jim is about to make a comeback, too. You've known him since you were little kids. Friendships like that are rare and definitely worth the effort to save."

"I always thought if our frienship was so special, stuff like this couldn't happen."

"In an ideal world it wouldn't. But we're living in a fallen world with imperfect people, and that includes Christian people. You have to forgive Jim. That's not what I'm saying, that's what the Bible says."

"Funny. You're the last person I would've expected to hear this from given that you and Jim were never that close."

"I've always respected him even when we didn't agree, and I think I can understand what he's been through. When my grandfather died, I was in an emotional funk for a while, too, and ended up hurting Allyson in the same way he hurt you."

"I'm not sure that's possible. Anyway, I thought you didn't know why she was mad at you."

"I didn't – until I came across her old diary about a week or so ago."

"So..."

"So, you remember when I told you I ran away to California when I was 14?"

"Yeah."

"She felt that I had abandoned her. Come to think of it, I did abandon her."

"That's why she's so nasty? All because you ran away from home?"

"It's not that simple, Al. She was a kid. I was the only real family that she had left after Poppa died. Instead of being there for her, I ditched her. I get why she's so bitter."

"I don't. It's not like you didn't come back."

"But I didn't stay very long before I was off to Boston for boarding school."

"Have you talked to her about this recently?"

"Yes, and she's still angry. I thought that once everything was out in the open things would change, but, no deal. Al, you don't know what I'd give to have my baby sister back."

"Sorry, man. I wish there was something I could do."

"There's not much that any person can do. We have to wait and see what God will do."

"Makes sense. I think I'll do the same."

"Allen..."

"On another note, I heard from Miko that you two are supposed to be having dinner together this weekend. Is that right?"

"Yes, that's right. We were supposed to go last week, but then a certain person got sick and we had to change our plans."

"Maybe I should get sick again."

"Relax, Al. It's not what you think. She just wants to thank me and Riley for helping her with her work from school."

"Good. I thought I'd have to remind you of the conversation we had when you were staying at my place."

"You mean when you threatened me to leave Miko alone for yet the second time."

"I was not threatening, just trying to persuade you to see things logically and to consider all of the possible consequences that could follow if you chose to continue your pursuit."

"In which you concluded, and let me know if I'm paraphrasing you correctly, that I am an emotional retard who would only mess things up with Tamiko, destroy our friendship, and create rancor and division among our friends."

"I know it hurts, but I had to keep it real. Your track record in relationships is like the NY Knicks basketball stats. Am I wrong?"

"Okay, I will admit that in the past I was very immature and self-serving. But I've outgrown that stuff. I really do want a genuine relationship now."

"I've heard that one before."

"You're not going to bring up the whole thing with Mya are you?"

"Well..."

"C'mon! You're like the fifth person this month that's brought that up. Is anyone going to let me forget about that? Is there anyone who thinks I can be different?"

"Tim, I know you're trying, but you need to reflect and think about where you went wrong with that, bro, or you'll keep making the same mistake."

"I have. It's like Daniel said, I should have set some boundaries and expectations. Better still, I should have followed the leading of the Lord and never taken her out in the first place."

"Yeah, she wasn't right for you, bro."

"Tell me about it. Not that I was really that into her anyway."

"You always say that. C'mon, man. Haven't you ever met a woman that you felt like she might be the one."

"Truth be told? Yes, but you just said she's off limits."

"Tamiko?!"

"Who else?"

"All this time, and you still haven't gotten her out of your system?"

"I've been trying, Al."

"So try harder, 'cause I'm not sure if you two are meant to be. You know she still likes Davis?"

"He doesn't like her. You heard what he said."

"Davis is just having some cold feet because of something that happened in a past relationship. Once he gets over it, I think he'll change his mind."

"You think it's fair that she wait around until he does?"

"Tim, I'm telling you. If you go after her now, she'll probably go out with you because she feels bad about losing Davis. Then when Davis comes out of his funk and opens his heart to her, she'll go running back to him."

"And he and Tamiko will get married and live happily ever after."

"And you, the rebound guy, will be all alone. Don't waste your time chasing something that wasn't meant to be. All you're going to get is a lot of heartache. If you need proof, you can consider me exhibit A."

"Tamiko's not like Callie."

"That's not the issue. You need to think about finding someone that's into you. There are lots of other women out there, some that may be even better than Tamiko."

"Hmmm. Doubtful."

"C'mon, man. Don't put that face on. You saying she has you that deep?"

"That's what it feels like sometimes."

"You know Dan said: if that's how you feel then you should be ready to pop the question. You think you're ready for that?"

"Did you want to marry Callie?"

"Between you and me – we were engaged. I was going to let everyone know on Thanksgiving."

"No way!"

"No, I was serious. I thought she was the one and I was willing to back it up with a ring. Blood aside, Miko's my sister, and I think any brother who wants to step to her, better be prepared to do the same. She deserves no less than that. Wouldn't you agree?"

"Absolutely."

FORTY-FOUR

It had been a while since Davis had called on Tamiko privately, and he wished he had a more positive reason for coming, especially with the way things had been going between them as of late. But there was no use in delaying things. He'd had his space and he'd made his decision and it wouldn't be fair to keep Tamiko in the dark any longer.

After knocking on the door, he stood and waited, his heart racing as he tried to prepare himself. It never really worked. Just like when he met with his old girlfriend, Janice, the other day and she slapped him with a litany of insults before letting him know she never wanted to see him again. At least Stephanie was kind and forgiving. The rejection never ceased to hurt, but he knew that he deserved it, and had to endure it. There was probably going to be some rejection in store for him here, but he had to man-up and go through.

"Who is it?!" asked a very stern voice that was definitely not Tamiko's.

"It's Davis Martinez, ma'am. I was wondering if I could talk to Tamiko for a few minutes."

"What is it that you want?"

"It's something personal, ma'am."

"Personal! Did you hear that Pastor Bynum? Too personal for us to know about in our own house?!"

"Mother, why don't you just open the door instead of making the boy stand out there all night," said Pastor Bynum from within.

"I'm not opening my door at night for these strange men I don't know who have personal issues. Tamiko's got this place like 42nd Street in the 80's. This is going to have to stop!"

All of a sudden, the door opened and Davis was greeted by the warm smile of Pastor Bynum.

"Hello, Davis. How are you tonight?"

"I'm fine, sir. I hope I'm not causing you any trouble or nothin' like that. I know it's a little late."

"Not at all. It's only 6:30. Come in and have a seat."

"Actually, I'm not planning to stay long. I was wondering if I could talk to Tamiko for a minute in private."

"What for?"

"Rose, please" he said to his wife before turning back to Davis. "Is everything okay, son?"

"Yeah - I mean - yes. It's just that we had talked about something a little while ago and I just wanted to..."

"Davis? I thought I heard your voice. What are you doing here?" asked Tamiko as she glided down the stairs. She was wearing a pink cotton dobby peter pan collared short-sleeved shirt and a grey pencil skirt. Even with her hair in a messy ponytail, she still looked pretty. It made his task even harder.

"I just wanted to talk to you about something. It's kinda personal."

"Alright. Let me get my coat. We'll go outside."

"If she's not back in five minutes. I'm calling the police."

"Nah, fa real, Mrs. Bynum, Pastor, I don't want to do nothin' to her. I can talk to her right here, but...maybe I should just go home and call you."

"No, that won't be necessary, son. Mother Bynum and I will go upstairs. You two can talk down here"

"Pastor!"

"Let's go, Rose," said the Pastor as he escorted her away leaving Davis and Tamiko by themselves.

"That's all they better be doing is talking," said Mother Rose as she made her way up the stairs.

Tamiko rolled her eyes and sighed before she addressed Davis.

"So...can I take your coat?"

"I'm not staying long."

"Oh. Can't we at least sit down?"

"Aiight."

They both took seats on the couch and faced each other.

"What's on your mind?"

"I know that a little while ago, I said that we needed to put some space between us so we could think about things."

"Yes, I remember."

"First off, I really appreciate you hearing me, and giving me time so I could figure things out."

"Of course."

"During that time, I had to come to terms with a lot of things - a lot of stuff from past relationships that I had to deal with - and a lot of stuff about myself, too."

"Okay."

"Lemme get to the point. You're a really good friend, Miko. In all the time I've known you, you've really put yourself out there for me and that means a lot. I don't want to lose that. I think us being in a relationship might mess all that up."

"Sooo, you can't date me because I'm such a great friend, is that right?"

"Friendships can last a lifetime. Can't say the same for relationships or marriages for that matter."

"Where'd you get that? An episode of Dawson's Creek?"

"Look, Miko, I know you're upset and I can understand why, but you should know me well enough by now to know I'm not some player running game."

"Then be honest with me instead of pitching some lame, patronizing, excuse! Tell me the real reason, you don't think we should be a couple, like maybe I'm not your type, or there's something about my personality that bothers you, or maybe there's someone else you're interested in."

"This isn't about none of that. I'm just trying to protect you."

"Or maybe you're trying to protect you, because you don't have the guts to actually put yourself out there and risk being hurt."

"I'm not afraid of being hurt, okay. I don't want to end up hurting you."

"It's a little late for that," said Tamiko, who was beginning to choke up.

"Okay, you're right. This is my fault. I should've never even given you the idea that there could have been anything between us, I just thought that..."

This was a lot harder than Davis anticipated. He couldn't leave her there like this. He had to tell her everything. It was the only way she would be able to understand.

"Listen, I'm not like Allen, and Daniel, and Tim, okay...I have problems..."

"Don't tell me you're going into the 'it's not you it's me' speech again."

"That's right, because it is me. It's not a line it's the truth...I've hurt people..."

"Sometimes that happens in relationships..."

"Tamiko, please! I'm not talking about them silly little games people play! I'm talking about stuff I should've been put in jail for..."

She was now stunned into silence. Davis didn't know if he could go on, but he had to. It was as much an admission to himself as it was to her. Over the past couple of weeks when he apologized to his former girlfriends, he had never come out and said it – what he'd done. Often he'd refer to it indirectly, talk around it, but that wasn't enough. He needed to hear it come out of his own mouth as much as she did.

"I – I was in a relationship with this girl named Evie a while back, and one time – one time, we was at the crib and she got a phone call from her sister, but her sister was using her male friend's phone and when I saw his number come up, I thought he was calling her. I got angry because I thought she was playing me...so I snatched the phone from her and I grabbed her by the hair, punched her in the face, and threw her into the table..."

"What?"

"One time, I even held a girl over the edge of the roof and threatened to drop her because she wanted to leave me. That the kind of dude you lookin' to hook up with? A beater?"

"Was this when you were...I mean before you got saved?"

"Most were before. But even after I got saved, I still had problems. I've prayed about it. I'm still praying about it."

"He can help you overcome this."

"I know, but, sometimes – it's like the Word says – if your hand offend thee, cut it off.[1] I think I gotta cut this relationship stuff off. Sometimes I feel like there's a spot on my soul that just won't come off. But that's my problem. I'm not gonna force nobody else to deal with my madness. I promised myself and I promised God, that I'm not going to hurt anyone anymore."

"Davis – I – I'm sorry I – I didn't know."

"Bet you're glad we didn't get together, now. Maybe you're even rethinking our friendship, too."

"That's not what I'm thinking."

"It's what you should be. I wouldn't hold it against you. No woman in her right mind should want to be with someone like me."

"That may be who you used to be but that's not the you I know now."

"You don't know me like you think you do. I can't even say I know me like I should."

"A lesser man wouldn't be doing what you are right now."

"I don't deserve credit for telling you the truth, especially when I should have done it sooner."

"Davis..."

"Believe me, Miko, we're both better off this way. Anyway, I've said what I came to say. I'll see you around."

"Davis, wait!"

Davis rushed out of the house and down the street, not bothering to look back. It was over now. All of the skeletons were out of his closet. He thought he should have felt relieved, but there was a shadow of uncertainty that followed behind him. He wondered what Tamiko thought of him, and if she would be afraid of him now. He knew she probably was, despite her brave front. He had to admit that he even scared himself sometimes. That's why he had to give up this part of his life. There was no way that he could risk that darkness taking control again.

FORTY-FIVE

Allyson was sitting at her desk in the offices of the Columbia Spectator, putting the finishing touches on a story she had been working on that was due within the hour. The controversial Professor Wayland Gibbons had been invited by one of the African-American student organization groups to speak at a fundraiser event, to the chagrin of other students on campus. Gibbons was widely known for his outspoken, liberal views on police reform, and had also been associated with what was being called reverse racism due to some off-color comments he'd made about the police that caught a sound bite. Allyson had been assigned to cover the event, which turned out to be a lot of drama: exactly the way she liked it. From the start, the event was plagued by protests from other student groups that had surrounded the venue. At the end of the day ten people were arrested and Gibbons had to be escorted out by police. It was the biggest story Allyson had ever done for the paper so far, and she wanted to make sure it was perfect. She knew that if she did well on this kind of a story, she'd get more of the same, rather than be limited to reporting on changes in the menu at JJ's place.

Reporting was the only other thing in the world that Allyson liked aside from shopping. She was particularly good at it because her early family life had trained her for investigative reporting. Tim had trained Allyson in how to snoop around and find information on all the things the grown-ups tried to hide from them. He'd taught her how to ask questions that on the surface seemed innocuous, but in a series of other leading questions would eventually get the interviewed person to give up the information they needed and then some. So that's what Allyson did when she was at the conference: ask an open-ended question that people would not be afraid to answer and then allow them to implicate or exonerate themselves.

Allyson had just saved and sent her file to her editor, when the phone near her desk rang.

"Spectator. Allyson Russell, speaking."

"Before you hang up, please hear me out," said Jason.

It was the tenth time he called since that Wednesday Allyson wanted to forget. He knew she wasn't answering her cell or email, so of course he'd try the paper.

"What would I hear that I haven't heard before?"

"I really miss you, Ally."

"You're not acting like it. You have to put some work into this you know."

"I know that. Didn't you get the roses and the necklace I sent?"

Allyson got them indeed. At first, she was more than ecstatic. The necklace was platinum with four carats of diamonds and emeralds each. Couldn't have been worth less than $11,000.00. She made sure to rub Trish's nose in it. But the glory was short lived. Allyson remembered that Hurst used to treat her mother the same way.

"I got them."

"I want to make things up to you. Let's go out tonight."

"Where would we be going?"

"Anywhere you want."

"Hmmm. Then I think I'll cash my rain check for Menagerie. I love their eggplant cutlets."

"I don't know about that, they're pretty out of my way. I was hoping you'd pick that Bar and grill you love so much that's close to the magazine."

"Why tell me anywhere if you don't mean it?"

"I'll rephrase it: Anywhere within driving distance of the Expose offices."

"Fine. We'll do Shenandoah. When do you want me to meet you?"

"Does 6:30 sound good? We'll meet at the bar."

"Sure. I'll see you then."

*****

"I'm only waiting another five minutes and then I'm outta here," thought Allyson as she sat at the bar of the Shenandoah grill. He was already ten minutes late and she wasn't about to be made a fool of again. However, not long after she made her declaration, she spotted him heading toward their table with more flowers in hand.

"Hey, there" he said.

"Hey yourself. Are those for me?"

"Of course."

"Thank you. They're beautiful."

"Not half as beautiful as you."

"I've heard that one already, but I'll take it."

"What would you like to drink?"

"Drink? I thought we were having dinner?"

"I thought we'd have a drink or two before heading back to my place."

"This is what you call making things up to me? A booty call?"

"So I rearrange my schedule at the last minute so that we can spend some quality time together and this is what I get? Attitude?"

"How would you feel if every time someone wanted to spend time with you it was always with your clothes off?"

"I'm doing the best I can here. You of all people should know how busy my schedule is..."

"Do you treat your other woman like this?"

"What are you talking about? There is no other woman."

"I'm not stupid, Jason. The least you can do is be honest with me."

"Let's talk outside in the car," said Jason, scanning the room at the same time.

Allyson followed him outside to his sport scar and sat in the passenger's seat, while Jason sat on the other side.

"I'd rather you hear this from me than find out from someone or someplace else. I have to go to LA next week to do a promotional junket in order to get some publicity for the company. It also means I'm going to have to entertain the daughter of a really big media mogul."

"You're probably already entertaining her."

"This is business, Allyson. My dad is thinking of selling the mag to her father. In order to do that, we have to get them to buy in. That's all this is about."

"Oh, I'm sure."

"I'm not enjoying this, Allyson. But sacrifices have to be made. At the end of the day, I'm thinking about us."

"How's that?"

"The more money I make, the more you'll benefit. That necklace I gave you was just a sample of what you could have."

"You mean like a condo over looking central park, a nice ride, tickets to fashion week."

"And who knows? If all goes well, I might be able to connect you with some people that could help you find a sweet position at a news station."

Allyson had heard this all before, but from a different perspective. It made what could have been a tantalizing offer seem cheap and hollow.

"I don't know, Jayce."

"You don't know? What does that mean?"

"I mean...I want to know if you're serious about us."

"Allyson, I totally intend to keep my promise to you..."

"I don't want to be a kept woman, or a sidepiece, Jayce. I want to know if there's a possibility that we could have a real relationship."

"Allyson, why can't we enjoy each other and let things ride? I'm not into labeling things. What this is and what it turns into, only time can tell. But if you want me to commit to you, you're going to have to show me that you can stand by me no matter what's going down. As someone who works with the public, you're going to have to accept that certain things come with the lifestyle I have to live."

"You're right."

Allyson opened the passenger side door and got out.

"Wait a minute – where are you going?"

"Home. I need some time to think about things – like whether or not your lifestyle is for me."

"Are you serious?! Do you realize just how much I have had to sacrifice to make time for us? I'm putting off my school work, and I blew off a meeting with a big sponsor, just to spend time with you and you just want to walk away?"

"You know what? I'm getting sick of you guilting me all the time about how much time you're sacrificing, especially when you've never had more than two hours to spare at a time – and that's just to screw me."

"I'm starting to get sick of your ungrateful attitude. I just made you an offer some women would die for, and you wanna act like it's nothing!"

"That's because it is!"

"Oh, so you're too good, right? Well let me tell you something Allyson, you're not the prize you think you are. A lot of guys on my level wouldn't even want to be seen with you."

"Oh, please. Stop it with the sour grapes. I saw what you were dating before I came along."

"Get over yourself, Allyson. Daria may not have been as fair as you are, but she comes from way better people and has a lot more class. Everybody who counts knows your mom's a crazy whore who tricked her way to the top and from what I can see you're cut from the same mold."

"Go to hell, Jason!"

"Gladly, to get away from a psycho whore like you! And don't try to come crying back, either!"

Allyson got into her car and sped off. It was over. She couldn't fool herself anymore. While she knew that Jason didn't love her, she thought that he at least respected her. Then he confirmed what she had already suspected. The words hit her like boulders, shattering the flimsy veneer she'd erected of herself. She felt as if she had been thrown into the street naked.

Tears spilled down uncontrollably, blurring her vision. She couldn't hold it back anymore. She was alone in a world where everyone was against her. Where could she go? What could she do? As she was driving aimlessly about she found herself on a stretch of roadway not far from the George Washington

Bridge. The ramp was a low one and over it she could see the streetlights reflecting off the river. All she had to do was speed up and turn, and all of her suffering would be over.

As Allyson was about to shift her car into top gear, she could've sworn she heard someone talking to her. "Go see momma." At first she was puzzled, but then it became clear to her. She knew where she needed to go. She pulled onto the bridge and headed uptown. After about twenty minutes she found herself in front of the Sharpe residence. The lights were still on.

Allyson walked up to the door and rang the bell.

"Who is it?" she heard Lena's musical voice ask.

"Allyson – Allyson Russell. Tim's sister."

"Hey, girl. You know, I was just thinking about you," said Lena as she opened the door. Then she paused as she got a good look at Allyson's face. "Chile, are you alright?"

"I'm fine," she said wiping at her eyes. She had forgot she'd been crying, and it dawned on her that her make-up must have looked a mess.

"You look like you've been crying."

"No, its just allergies."

"Now Ally, I done been around too long not to know better than that. What's wrong, baby?"

Allyson looked into Lena's eyes and saw her concern. It touched her.

"I...I just came from a bad date."

"Oh my goodness! He didn't hurt you did he?"

"Not physically."

"Well, come on in and have some tea and we'll talk about it."

Allyson came in and followed Lena into the kitchen. Allen's house wasn't very fancy, but it was cozy. There were lots of pictures of Allen, the midget girl, the crippled guy and even a few of her brother in some group photos. The furniture was old, but you could tell it was clean and in good shape most likely thanks to Lena's housekeeping. The whole place smelled like cookies baking in the oven. It wasn't just a house. It was a real home.

"I know it's late, I won't stay long. It's just that I was driving around and I was getting tired."

"Don't worry 'bout that none sweetheart. It's not even 8:00" said Lena as she started the tea using the little machine Allen had given her for her birthday. "Did you and your boyfriend have an argument?"

"We broke up."

"Aww. I'm sorry."

"Don't be. I'm not."

"Then how come you look so down?"

Against her will, the tears started to come again. Lena came over to put her arms around her. Allyson welcomed it in spite of herself. She had always wanted a mom to hug her and to listen to her.

"He never cared about me. Nobody cares about me," she sobbed.

"Oh, Allyson, that's not true. There's plenty of people that care about you. I care about you, and I know your family must care about you."

"My mother's not like you. We barely even talk unless she wants something – and I don't even want to talk about my father."

"Well I know for a fact that Tim cares about you. He's never said a bad word about you that I've heard."

"I bet he's never said anything good about me, either."

"No, chile. He loves you. He always asks the elders to pray for you. I don't think he'd do that if he didn't."

"You don't know him like I do."

"I suppose you're right about that, but tell me dear, what could he have possibly done to make you think he doesn't love you?"

"He abandoned me. He didn't even say goodbye."

"When was this? When he went to college?"

"No. It was when we were younger. I was about eight and he was fourteen. It was just after our grandfather passed away. He promised he'd be there for me and then the next thing I knew, he was gone."

"Gone?"

"He ran away from home."

"Kids will do that. Allen tried it when he was 12. Ended up down the street at our friend Merta's house. Vernon tore his behind up when we got him back. Where'd your mama find Tim?"

"California."

"California?! How in the world was he able to get all the way over there by himself at 14?"

"My mom gave us a lot of freedom – at least with some things."

"Too much, I'd say. You're lucky nothing happened to him."

"Maybe something should've."

"Ally! Don't say things like that."

"But he didn't even think about how I'd feel."

"He probably couldn't, Ally. I don't know too many 14 year olds that would. Given what he did, he likely wasn't thinking at all."

"He thought enough to take his girlfriend."

"But you're judging him as if he was a grown man. Remember he was young, too. Think about it from his perspective. He's 14 going through all the crazy hormone changes of puberty, and trying to figure out his place in the world, and on top of all that, he loses his grandfather. He probably wanted and needed someone to take care of him, too."

"I would've taken care of him. We could've taken care of each other."

"You couldn't raise your brother any more than he could raise you. That's what parents are for. Now that's not to say you can't give each other support when you need it, but you can't expect Tim to be like your daddy. It wouldn't be fair to him. It wouldn't be fair to you either. Trust me I been there."

"What do you mean?"

"You see I have a sister who is nine years older than me. When we were younger she was always protecting me and looking out for me, which was nice sometimes, but by the time I got to be a teenager, you couldn't tell her she wasn't the boss of me. She wanted to tell me where to go to school, who to date, how to dress, and how I should act. She was worse than our mama and daddy combined."

"Did you ever tell her how you felt?"

"Yes I did. Just before I went away to college, I told her that she needed to live her life and let me live mine. Then she got as upset as you are right now, moved away to D.C. and didn't speak to me for a whole year. But she was still my sister, so I wrote to her and sent her birthday and Christmas gifts even though she never sent any back. After a while, I started to get a little angry at her about how she was treating me. Then one day, I got an invitation to her engagement party, and I wasn't going to go just to hurt her as much as she hurt me."

"So you weren't always so forgiving?"

"Of course not. No one's born perfect. I like to think God had to do a lot of work on me to get me where I am today, and I still got a long ways to go."

"What happened when you ditched your sister's engagement party?"

"Oh, I went to the party, alright. My daddy convinced me to go. When I got there she apologized for everything. She told me that she realized that I was right. That she had been so caught up in my life that she wasn't even thinking about what God's plan was for her own life."

"I know we're supposed to have our own lives. But I thought...he wasn't supposed to..."

"Hurt you? Ally, understand that sometimes, whether it's by accident or on purpose, you gonna get hurt, even by the people you love the most. Especially by the people you love the most. In fact, the more you love someone, the more it's gonna hurt. But you can't hold onto that and let it shut you up. You gotta let it go. Otherwise you gonna block out all the love that's gonna help you to heal."

"I suppose you're right. But I've held on for so long, I feel like I don't know how to let go."

"Now, I know you'll think I'm crazy, but I know there's Someone out there that can help you with that. He loves you, even more than anyone on this earth ever could."

"You say that, but I've never felt it. I've always felt alone."

"Believe me, Ally, you are never alone. Don't always trust feelings. They can fool you. I'm certain that if you took the time to really think about your life, you would see He's been there all along."

"Lena! Where are you?" said a voice interrupting Allyson's thoughts. It was coming from outside the kitchen.

"In the kitchen," she replied.

Just then the kitchen door opened and Vernon came in carrying some catalogues and a few pieces of snail mail. He stopped when he saw Allyson, who just kept staring down at her mug of tea.

"What's going on in here? And where'd you come from?" asked Vernon.

"Allyson just stopped by to chat," said Lena.

"Uh-oh, another long face. What done happened to you?"

"Nothing really. I just broke up with my boyfriend, that's all," answered Allyson.

"Another one. Girl, how long was you seein' this boy?" said Vernon.

"A couple of weeks I guess," said Allyson.

"A couple of weeks! You ain't got no business making that pretty face all long for some knucklehead you knew for a few weeks. You young folks today don't know nothin' bout no courtin'. Y'all get involved too deep too fast. You got to take your time with this kinda thing – go slow," said Vernon.

"And he should know. It took him almost 2 years to pop the question to me," said Lena.

"That's right. I had to make sure you loved me as much as I loved you," said Vernon.

"You don't have to worry about that," said Lena.

"I know," he said kissing her on the cheek.

Allyson couldn't help but smile at their display of affection.

"Is that a smile I see?" remarked Vernon.

"Maybe," said Allyson.

"You gotta pretty smile, girl. You could probably get any of these boys you want. I'd ask Allen to take you out, but he's too busy actin' like a fool right now. Holed up at yo' brother's place over some girl. You talked to him today, Lena?"

"Yes."

"What he say?"

"He's determined to stay there until Jimmy leaves. He even asked me to come get his laundry."

"That boy got some nerve. Don't you go nowhere. This foolishness has gone far enough. I'm letting him know that I expect him to bring his behind home by the end of the week and if he don't, I'll come over there and make him wish he had. Now if you'll excuse me. Evenin' ladies."

The ladies wished him goodnight before he turned and stormed up the stairs.

"It's getting late and I better be getting back," said Allyson.

"You sure?" asked Lena.

"Yes. I have things I have to do tomorrow."

"Alright then, but remember what I said."

"I will. Goodnight – Mama Lena."

"Goodnight, Ally."

"Mama Lena?"

"Yes, dear?"

"Just so you know. I don't think you're crazy."

FORTY-SIX

Tamiko was sitting at her vanity trying to make up her mind about how she wanted to style her hair, but as she deliberated stray thoughts kept weaving their way into her head. She tried to comb them away along with the few loose strands of damaged hair, but it was no use. She was not thinking about Davis. Tamiko was actually surprised with how quickly she was able to come to terms with the fact that she and Davis were not going to be a couple. Although she was feeling some disappointment that evening after he had left, it was far from the total devastation she expected. She ended up going back upstairs to her room to pray and read her Bible, turning to the book of Matthew to read about the last supper.[1] It was this particular portion of the Bible that she was meditating on at the moment.

She had read the part where Jesus prophesied about Peter's denial. Peter was sure that he would never deny Jesus. He professed his loyalty and his love. However, the word of the Lord could not be denied and he did in fact deny his Lord. Yet, Jesus would make Peter the chief Apostle on which the church was built. It gave Tamiko pause for a moment. She thought about what she knew about Peter from the scriptures. Peter often spoke before he thought[2], acted hastily[3], and denied his Savior[4]. Given his pattern of behavior, it didn't seem like he was worthy of being a chief Apostle. If Tamiko had had a say back then she probably would've suggested Peter be kicked out of the twelve entirely, but Christ overlooked his shortcomings. He would even die to atone for them. It was like what Riley had told her earlier: God sees what we can't. Christ's decision to choose Peter was not based on who he was in that moment or who he used to be, but was based on what He already knew He would make Peter into. This revelation caused Tamiko to reflect on how she had been judging people lately. The awakening that followed humbled her and caused her to re-think her understanding of relationships.

"You don't choose to love someone because they're perfect, rather, in spite of their imperfections you've chosen to love them. I guess I would want someone to feel the same way about me. After all, I'm not perfect either," thought Tamiko to herself. Then she made a decision.

"You do realize you've been combing your hair for the past 20 minutes. I think you're good, Miko," said Riley breaking into Tamiko's train of thought as she squeezed next to her on the vanity seat.

As Tamiko looked at her cousin's reflection in the vanity, she was floored. Riley had straightened her hair, which was now hanging loose and flowing over her shoulders. She was also wearing a navy blue, silk, sleeveless v-neck dress with a flared skirt that gently caressed her hourglass figure, paired with some two-inch leopard print heels. Riley was absolutely stunning. Tamiko always knew that Riley had the ability to shape shift from tomboy to princess but she didn't expect her to do it for this occasion.

"You're certainly showing out tonight. What happened to the silk army pants I thought you were going to wear?"

"I changed my mind," she said as she began to finish styling her hair. As Tamiko looked at their reflections in the mirror, her heart sank. All of a sudden her blue and white bib-front, tie neck blouse and navy skirt made her feel like an old lady.

"Is this your attempt to impress Tim?"

"Girl, I don't have to attempt anything. He will be impressed. You can bet your last dollar on that."

Riley was right. The way she looked now, she was exactly the kind of girl Tim would drool over. It made Tamiko feel faint.

"You're actually going through with this? You're going to try to hit on Tim?"

"I'm no slut. I'm not gonna hit on him. It's called getting to know him and seeing if he would like to court me, as daddy would say."

"I can't believe you would play with Tim's feelings like this."

"Who said I'm playin'? You're not the only one that can like somebody."

"Oh, don't even go there. You know you're only doing this to prove a point."

"And what would I be trying to prove?"

Tamiko didn't want to go there. Despite her recent realizations, a part of her was still afraid to face her true feelings.

“Never mind.”

“No, not never mind. Why is this such a big deal for you?”

“Tim is my friend, and I don’t want to see him get hurt.”

“Really? You sure this doesn’t have anything to do with the fact that Davis gave you a pink slip the other night?”

“What?!”

“I was sitting in the kitchen listening to his confession, in case you didn’t know.”

“You were eavesdropping?!”

“Don’t act surprised. You know that’s what I do. So now that Davis is not available, you want me to back off of Tim so he can be your backup? Is that it?”

“No, absolutely not! I would never do that!”

“Then you’re going to use Tim to make Davis jealous so he’ll come running back?”

“No!”

“So what is it then? Last week, I asked you who you wanted and you said that was Davis, but now that he’s not interested it seems like you’re changing your mind.”

“I do like Davis. Despite what he told me, I still think he’s a good guy. If he wasn’t he wouldn’t have been as honest with me as he was. But...that night, our conversation led me to think about things.”

Tamiko put her comb down on the table and looked down.

“Like what?”

"Like the reasons why I liked him. I liked Davis because I thought he was a safe choice for a perfect marriage. But I've learned there's no such thing as a safe choice, even if you share the same faith. Everyone has something that they struggle with, whether they've been with the Lord five days or fifty years. No one is perfect."

"There's no such thing as a perfect marriage either."

"You're right, and Davis deserves someone who sees him as more than just a safe choice. Everyone should have someone who appreciates and loves them for who they are. You know, take their good with their bad, the highs with the lows."

"For richer or poorer, better or worse..."

"Exactly. You trust God first and each other second. It's funny because I accused Davis of being afraid of getting hurt, when I was the biggest chicken in the henhouse. But now I understand that I can't let my fear get in the way of what I know in my heart."

"Which is?"

"I don't know when it happened or how, but...Tim reaches a part of me that no other guy can come close to. For a while I've tried to deny it, and unfortunately my attention to Davis was a part of that. But I can't do that anymore."

"Snowy's player past doesn't bother you?"

"That's who he used to be. Nowadays when we're together I don't really see that guy anymore. I see the man I believe God is making him into."

"I guess you are calling backsies, then."

"Sorry, cuz."

"You should be – you should've been honest from the beginning instead of leading Davis on, and making Snowy feel like the third wheel."

"I know, I know."

"Are you going to tell Snowy how you feel?"

"I don't know. Just because I feel that deeply for him, doesn't mean he feels the same way about me. Besides, the last time I did that, the guy ran."

"The last time you were lying."

"I wasn't lying. I told you – I did like Davis, but not in the way that I should have."

"You better tell Snowy before some other chick, who is not your cousin decides to try to get his interest."

"When I'm sure he feels the same way, I will. Otherwise it will just make things weird between us. The last thing I need to hear is Tim asking for space."

"I think he'd ask for less space, not more."

"A girl can only hope."

*****

As Tamiko and Riley approached the entrance of the Gospel Grill, the former's heart was melting like the wax on a lit candle. When they went inside it was a little crowded, and she had a hard time spotting Tim right away.

"There he is! At the table at the end near the stage" said Riley.

Tamiko scanned the area until she saw him. He was sitting at the table watching the performers who were on stage. They waded through the patrons and other tables until they got to the spot where he was sitting. Tim was so taken by the performance going on he didn't see them even though they were right up on him. Tamiko was afraid of what might happen next. In the past, Tim would look right past her, arch one eyebrow and flash a crooked grin right at whatever beautiful woman came into his view. She decided to wait until the performers had finished their set and the applause from the patrons died down, before attempting to get his attention.

"Tim?"

He started for a moment and turned to see who was calling him. Their eyes met and he stood up to greet her. At first he seemed a little awestruck. His expression softened, and there was a look in his eyes she had seen before. Then he smiled, and his whole countenance lit up.

"Hey. You kinda snuck up on me there," he said.

"Sorry. I didn't mean to," said Tamiko.

"I know – it's okay. You look...amazing," he said as he continued to study her.

"Thank you. So do you," she said.

He was dressed in a moss green tweed blazer and a light brown shirt with brown moleskin pants and Chelsea boots. He made a very handsome picture indeed. But then again, Tamiko believed Tim could wear a paper bag and rock it.

"I like your hair. Did you stop by the beauty parlor?" said Tim.

Tamiko had the front of her hair in an upswept ponytail and the back was out and down on her shoulders.

"Thank you, but no, I did it myself kind of last minute."

"It's still beautiful. But where are my manners? Let's sit down," he said leading her to the table, when suddenly he stopped. "Oh, wait. Where's Riley? I thought you said she'd be coming with us."

"I'm over here," said Riley.

As Tim looked up, Riley waved at him to help him find her. For a moment Tamiko felt as if she couldn't breathe.

"Riley?" he said looking at her quizzically.

"That's right," she said.

"You look different. I didn't even recognize you. Sorry about that. Anyway, come on over and have a seat," said Tim.

Tim seated the two ladies and then took the seat next to Tamiko. Tamiko relaxed a bit. Despite Riley's efforts, Tim certainly wasn't giving her, 'the look.'

"So what do you think?" asked Riley.

"You look nice – a little more feminine at any rate. Did Miko talk you into letting her give you makeover or something?" said Tim.

"No. I don't need Miko to make me look beautiful. I mean, I am a beautician," said Riley rolling her eyes.

"Sorry. I forgot about that. Well, so far this is a nice little spot. Good music, nice atmosphere, and the menu looks appetizing from what I've seen. Now if the food is any good, we can bring the others here," said Tim.

"Speaking of food, I think we should order. And I want you guys to get anything you want. Don't think I can't afford it," suggested Tamiko.

"Yeah, but I don't want to take advantage of you, Miko," said Tim.

"It's alright Tim, I've saved my money, and I want to be able to do nice things for you, just like you've always done for me," said Tamiko.

Tim signaled for a waiter who took their orders. Then some new performers came out to start a new set. They listened to the music and drank the complimentary water provided while they were waiting for their food. Tamiko's mood began to brighten and she was able to enjoy herself and the entertainment. Every once in a while Tim would put his arm around her chair. Sometimes he would lean over and comment to her about which songs and artists he liked. Sometimes when she looked over she would catch him observing her. Then after the set was finished the waiter came with their food, and it wasn't long before the conversation started again.

"You know you guys never told me how you liked that play," said Tim.

"It was aiight. A little slow, though," said Riley.

"You slept through most of it," said Tamiko.

"So what'd you think of it, Miko?" asked Tim.

"I thought it was awesome," said Tamiko who was in a good mood and ready to gush "I don't want to tell you too much about what happens because I think you should see it for yourself. There's this twist at the end that you won't see coming at all. It will definitely make you think about what our walk with God is really about."

"In that case, you've helped me make up my mind. Since you've seen it already, I'll probably get one of the guys to go with me. And speaking of things to make you think, I started reading this book the other day, called Roadblocks on the Road to Grace, by this guy, Bishop Simmons..." said Tim.

"Get out! I can't believe this. I got you that book!" said Tamiko.

"No way!" said Tim.

"Yeah. I was going to give it to you as a gift tonight, but I guess now I don't have to."

"I guess it's true what they say. Great minds think alike."

"I guess so. I've read it myself at least three times. What do you think of it?"

"I've only gotten about three-quarters of the way through, but from what I have read I'd say it's really good. Like chapter three when he talks about the roadblock of compromise. It helped me to see how something that I think is innocent, can lead to other things that can separate you from God. The whole time I was reading it, I started to realize that I do some of those things. It made me start taking a closer look at my behavior and holding myself more accountable."

"Chapter two really spoke to me where he talks about the roadblock of pride. For a long time I thought pride was just about being arrogant, but he taught me how a lot of times fear and anxiety can be linked to pride, too."

"Like the connection that he makes with King Saul."

"Exactly. And did you notice with every point he makes, he takes time to elucidate the scripture that it's coming from. So it's not like he's just giving you his opinion on something."

"I don't know about you guys, but I'm starting to experience the roadblock of boredom," said Riley trying to enter the conversation. “I thought this was supposed to be a dinner, not Sunday school.”

“Sorry. It’s just it really is a good book,” said Tim. “Maybe Miko can give you the extra copy.”

“Miko already sent me a copy for my birthday. Not my thing. I prefer fiction,” said Riley.

“Oh” said Tim.

“How does everyone like their meal?” asked Tamiko.

“Girl, you know I love me some catfish, I don’t care how they do it. What ‘bout you? You ever had catfish?” said Riley.

“Yes, but I didn’t like it very much,” said Tim.

“I noticed that when ever we go out the only seafood you ever order are lobster, shrimp, salmon and scallops,” said Tamiko.

“They’re the only sea food I’ll eat. I’m not a fish fan. I can’t believe you noticed that,” he said.

“We’ve been friends for a long time. How could I not? Anyway how’s your salmon?”

“Pretty good. How’s your pasta?”

“Could be better. This Soul food gnocchi is not what I expected. Usually when I order gnocchi its white. This one’s orange and it has that white pasta sauce that I hate.”

“Let’s see,” said Tim spearing one from her plate and tasting it. “It’s got ricotta and sweet potatoes in it. And it’s got like a butter sauce on it, not that Alfredo sauce you hate. Just try it. You might like it”

“I guess I could give it a try. Riley would you like to try it, too?”

"Sorry sister, you on yo' own," said Riley.

Tamiko put one in her mouth. It wasn't long before she grabbed her napkin and spat the half-chewed food into it.

"I don't think that's for me," said Tamiko.

"Just goes to show you: the only thing sweet potatoes belong in is pie," said Riley.

"I didn't think it was so bad. I've had something like this before at a soul food restaurant in Baltimore. It's gourmet cuisine. But not everyone has a palate for it," said Tim.

"I certainly don't," said Tamiko.

"So I'll get you something else if you want," said Tim.

"No, Tim. I'll be alright. I'm supposed to be treating you tonight, remember?"

"Miko, seriously, I don't mind."

"Well I would. I don't want you to have to pay for my mistake. Maybe Riley and I..."

"Don't look at me, you're not getting any of mine," said Riley.

"Then how'd you like to switch with me? I haven't eaten much of my salmon. You could have the rest of it, and I'll eat your gnocchi," said Tim.

"I don't know. I don't want to ruin your dinner by making you eat something you don't want."

"I couldn't enjoy my dinner watching you starve. Anyway, it's not that big a deal to me. The gnocchi is just as good as the salmon."

"Are you absolutely sure?"

"Yeah, go ahead."

"Aww, Tim, you're so sweet."

"Sweet my foot! That's nasty. You gon' eat off his plate after he put all his germs in it with his fork and breathed over it? Yuck," said Riley.

"It's okay Riley, I don't have cooties. I got my shots yesterday. Promise," said Tim.

"Actually, I have heard that people who interact with a lot of different people and have a wider circle of friends, get sick a lot less often than people that don't. It's actually the exposure to all the germs that helps people build their immunity," said Tamiko.

"Nice to know I'm helping you build your immunity," said Tim.

"I can't believe he said that. He's like a talking Ken doll," muttered Riley under her breath.

"What was that?" asked Tamiko who gave her cousin a very annoyed look. She had heard what Riley had said.

"Nothing important," Riley replied.

The trio finished their dinners and stayed to listen to the music as several more artists performed. Tim had put his arm around her chair again and Tamiko found herself resting her head on his shoulder. After the final performance they all decided it was time to end their evening out and head for home. They paid the bill and headed out to the street where they parked their cars.

"Thank you for inviting me out. I certainly had a wonderful time," said Tim.

"Your welcome. I must say I enjoyed our evening as well," said Tamiko.

"The food was good, but the portions were too skimpy. I'm still hungry," said Riley.

"You're always hungry," said Tamiko.

"I guess I'll bid you ladies good evening here. I parked in the garage down the block from here," said Tim.

"Bye, Sno – I mean, Tim."

"See ya around, Riley."

"Tim, before you go. I wanted to ask you something?"

"What is it?" he asked.

Tamiko turned to Riley and gave her, the "we need privacy look."

"Aiight, I got the hint. I'll go wait in the car," said Riley.

Tamiko waited until she was out of sight before she addressed Tim.

"You remember that fundraiser I told you we were having?" she said walking up to him so that the thinning crowd of patrons still milling about wouldn't be able to hear their conversation.

"You mean the Christian Singles thing?"

"Right. You see I still haven't found anyone to help me host it, and I was wondering if you'd like to help me. After all, we do make a great team, don't you think?" she said taking his hands.

"I do think we make a great team and I would love to help you. If it were any other kind of project, I would, but this – I don't think it would be a good idea."

"Why not?"

"Because – it might – complicate things between us."

"How?" she asked.

He stepped closer to her. Now their faces were barely inches apart.

"I don't know how to explain this, but – every time we're together – It's like – I like spending time with you Tamiko – sometimes maybe – a little too much."

"I like spending time with you, too, Tim. I always have."

"But there's someone else who you'd probably like a little better than me. Right?"

"Not that I can think of. To tell you the truth, there's no one else I'd rather be with."

Then came what neither of them expected as they were each drawn into the other's magnetic pull. Their lips met, followed by an embrace, igniting the embers of emotions they both had long been trying to quench. Tamiko's heart was beating wildly and she could feel herself getting lost in the moment, and then...Tim pulled away.

"We can't," he said. She could see the anguish on his face. "I can't do this."

"Why not?" she asked as her heart began to sink within her.

"It's not that I don't care for you, Miko. I do – more than you can imagine, but...I won't be the understudy for Davis," he said before walking away.

"Tim, wait!"

This time he didn't stop. He didn't turn back.

“You were always my first choice,” she said weakly into the night as tears spilled down her cheeks.

FORTY-SEVEN

Callie lay in bed where she had been for the past two days. In the aftermath of her break-up with Allen, she tried to struggle on and trudge through her daily routines, but the more she tried to move on the harder it was to do so. She had made so many plans, and invested so much into her future with Allen, that losing him made her feel that she had lost everything.

"What am I going to do now?" she asked herself as she lay beneath her quilt, shivering from fear rather than lack of heat. "Get a hold of yourself," A voice told her, "You still have a job, and you still have a place to stay. You can move past this" The voice was right, but still it all seemed empty. Nothing mattered if Allen wasn't there. She didn't care about the job or the apartment. She just wanted Allen, back.

She got up and grabbed her cell phone from her purse that was hanging from the foot of her bed. "It's been almost two weeks. Allen's a very reasonable guy. He always gets over things. He should be ready to talk to me by now. He has to be," she considered hopefully. Her hands were shaking as she scrolled through her contacts to find his number. She dialed and waited anxiously for him to pick up. When she heard the pre-recorded message from his voice-mail, she threw the phone across the room. It crashed into some bottles on her vanity sending some of them to the floor. Then she heard the sound of wailing.

"Damn it!" she said. The last thing she wanted was to deal with Darius. "Why couldn't I have had a good baby," thought Callie. She thought Darius's crying spells would have stopped once he passed the six-month mark. But here he was over a year old and he still spent a good portion of the day and night crying – for no good reason. She could do everything she knew how to do for him, and he'd still cry. Her frustration with him was starting to get to her. At first, she thought about getting her earplugs and just ignoring him, but she knew he would just get louder and she didn't want the neighbors knocking on her door. Callie got up and went to the bathroom cupboard and got out the cold medicine she had given him a while back. Then she went to the nursery and picked up Darius from his crib. His face was contorted in an ugly grimace. Callie was sure there was nothing wrong with him. She took him to the rocking chair and sat him in her lap. She pinned him against her with one arm as he squirmed and tried to measure the medicine in the dropper with the other.

"Cut it out!" she said as she jerked Darius by the arm and forced him back onto her lap upright after he had almost wiggled out of position and landed on the floor. She almost spilled what was left of the medicine as well.

When she was sure she had the right amount, she squeezed the medicine into his mouth. He must have liked the taste of it, because he lapped it down and was whimpering as if he wanted more. Then she put him back down into the crib and waited for the medicine to make him drowsy as it always did. Within ten minutes he had quieted down, and not long after that he was asleep again.

As she watched him sleep, Callie was reminded of how much Darius resembled Jim in terms of his personality, and she became annoyed if not angry. All Jim did was whine, and his son was the same way. Jim was the one who had caused all her problems in the first place. He was the one who had got her drunk and seduced her into having an affair, and left her pregnant. Jim was the one who had turned Allen against her, and had ruined her life. Soon he would be headed down to North Carolina to start a new life for himself without a care in the world. “It’s not fair!” thought Callie, “Once again he gets to turn my life upside down and then run off to do whatever he wants.”

“You can’t let him get away with that,” another voice told her. “Jim needs to pay for what he’s done to you. It’s time you let him feel what its like to be in your shoes.”

Callie felt the voice was right. There was no way she could let Jim run off to live happily ever after given what he’d done to her. He had to pay. The only thing left to figure out was how she’d enact her revenge. It would have to be something that would make Jim deeply regret he’d ever made an enemy out of her.

FORTY-EIGHT

"I am not my past, I am what God is calling me to be. My life is in Him. I let go of all my burdens and desires that I might surrender to His will and trust that He knows what's best for me. He is with me no matter what I feel like. He is gives me the strength to go through. As long as I remain in Him I have already overcome."

With this declaration, the men in the counseling group ended their session for the evening. This was the third session that Jim had attended, and at this point all his earlier fears and apprehensions about counseling had dissipated like fog in sunlight. Here he found a lot of solidarity amongst people who he felt understood what he was going through. As the meeting began to disband, Daniel came over to where Jim and Chris were standing.

"Jim, before you go. I just want to let you know about this job-counseling program in NC that I found online. It may help you get a lead. Here's the flyer."

"Thanks, man. I appreciate that."

"They're right by Allen's folks. When you get down there check it out. And remember, if you need something just call me. I got people down by there, too, and I can even jet down there if necessary."

"It's okay Dan. Don't think you have to come all the way down. A call will do."

"Just make sure you do."

"I will – and Dan?"

"What?"

"Thanks for having my back these past couple of days. I want you to know I appreciate you"

"That's what brothers are for, man."

Daniel and Jim gave each other the pound before going their separate ways.

"Hey, Jim. Davis said he was gonna meet up with me to hit the donut shop for some coffee. You want to stick around and join us," said Chris.

"I don't know, man. He may not be down."

In the fallout of his disagreement with Allen, Jim was sure that most of their set had been taking sides. Since he hadn't seen much of any of them lately, he could guess whose side they'd taken. As such, he didn't think that Davis would welcome his company.

"C'mon, Jim. He's chill. Here he comes now. I'll ask him," said Chris.

"Chris, you ready?" said Davis.

"Yeah. But I asked Jim to come along. You don't mind, right?" said Chris.

"Nah. We cool. How you doin' man? You gettin' around any better?" said Davis.

Jim was surprised by his casual attitude. He was certain Allen had been badmouthing him to everyone they knew. However, Davis didn't seem to be influenced by it.

"Every day is better than the day before. I'm getting used to the fact that it's going to take time, ya know?" said Jim.

"I feel you. But you don't have to worry about gettin' a work out, we only going 'round the corner," said Davis.

The three men left and headed out down the street and around the corner to a popular donut chain. Jim ordered coffee, Chris had tea, and Davis ordered a whole-wheat donut to go with his java. At first, Chris and Davis did most of the talking, with Jim staring sullenly at his coffee, getting lost in his own thoughts. There were going to be a lot of changes in store for him in the coming weeks. He was moving down south for an indefinite stay. He and Riley were supposed to have been headed out to North Carolina by now, but Pop Vernon and Momma Lena insisted that he extend his time until after Thanksgiving. They were stalling for time, waiting for Allen to come back home to patch things up. However, Jim had given up that hope and made peace with the fact that maybe he had lost his best friend and brother forever. Jim didn't deal well with change, but he had no choice but to relegate his fate to the will of the Father. This wasn't what he wanted, but if it had to be, then so be it.

"You got any plans for North Carolina?" asked Davis. It was almost as if he had been reading Jim's mind.

"Not really. Just going to take it day by day."

"You been down there before, right?" asked Chris.

"When I was a kid, I'd visit there sometimes. Haven't been there in about eight years."

"That's a long time. But why you stayin' with Allen's people? Don't you have any family down there?" said Chris.

"No. My grandparents died when I was a baby. My mother was an only child, and my Dad had one brother who was killed when he was young. Technically that makes me an orphan."

"Sorry to hear that, man," said Chris.

"It's all right. I'm not alone," said Jim.

"That's right, you got the Sharpes," said Chris.

"Even better, you always got God," said Davis.

"Amen," said Chris.

"I take it Allen is still angry?" asked Jim.

"I don't think I'd put it like that, chief," said Davis.

"Haven't heard anything from him. But then again, I can't blame him. It's like you said before, I gotta man up and accept my punishment," said Jim.

"Look, Al's still sorting things. Just give him some time," said Davis.

"Didn't want to leave with all the loose ends hanging around," said Jim.

"Sometimes you can't help it. We're not in control, God is," said Chris.

"True, but that doesn't mean we don't have choices to make. Jim, if Al, won't talk to you, maybe you should try to get in touch with him," said Davis.

"Now you sound like Riley. I don't want to go over there if he doesn't want to see me," said Jim.

"It may not be what he wants, but it's what he needs – what you both need," said Davis.

"What if we end up getting into an argument and things get worse?" said Jim.

"And if you don't it could get worse. It's like the Bible says: Agree with thine adversary quickly whiles thou art in the way with him; lest at any time the adversary deliver thee to the judge, and the judge deliver thee to the officer, and thou be cast into prison. Verily I say unto thee, Thou shalt by no means come out thence 'til thou hast paid the uttermost farthing.[1] Sometimes resentment builds over time and makes things worse than when it started. The longer you wait, the harder it's gonna be. And you don't want this thing to block your relationship with God. It's best to deal with things now," said Davis.

Jim looked away and played with his coffee cup.

"Look, I'm not telling you to do nothin' I've never done myself. There's risk involved, yes, but you have to trust that God will have your back. He knows your heart, he knows you're tryin' to do what's right. Promise me you'll pray about it – see what the Lord says," Davis continued.

"That's about all I can promise," said Jim.

Davis's words made sense, but Jim knew he couldn't do it. However, he knew who could.

FORTY-NINE

Allen was startled out of his sleep when he heard the buzz of the intercom. He was hoping Tim would answer it since his room was closer, and Allen didn't want to have to get up out of bed, especially since he had just gotten into it after a monster study session for his contracts class. To his disappointment the only thing he heard was Tim's loud garbage-disposal-like snoring and the intercom buzzing again. "Can't believe he's out that deep. It's not like he came back home late last night," thought Allen as he got out of bed, put on his robe and walked to the living room, where he saw the clock. It was 7:30am. Allen had no idea who would be calling on them at this time in the morning. Then he had a second thought. "Maybe it's mom coming for my laundry."

"What's up, Brad?"

"Mr. Sharpe to see you Mr. Sharpe."

"My dad? Why would my dad come all the way here this early? I hope something hasn't happened," mused Allen. "Okay" he said to Bradley.

Allen went to the door and unlocked it. As he waited for his father, he tried to anticipate what he'd come for. His dad was not the type of person to make a long trip to talk to him, when the phone was readily available. Allen was so busy thinking he didn't hear his father approaching and was startled when the doorbell rang.

"Dad, what are you doing here so early? Is mama alright?"

"Yo' mama's fine. I came to talk to you."

"At 7:30 in the morning?"

"What you talkin' bout 7:30. I been up since 5:00. You young folks just too lazy for any good."

"It's Saturday – and I was up studying 'till late last night."

"I don't want to get into nothin' bout no studyin'. I want to know..." began Vernon before he paused and looked around. "What is makin' that noise like that?"

"That's just Tim's snoring."

"Boy needs to get his adenoids checked – anyway, I want to know when you gon' cut this foolishness and bring yo' behind back home. This baby-boy temper – tantrum you havin' done gone on long enough."

"Temper tantrum! How can you say that after what Jim did to me? How would you feel if you found out the Pastor was having an affair with Ma!"

"That ain't nothin' like what we talkin' 'bout. And even if it did, you think I'm gon' run to Smitty's house and never go to church again."

"Dad, Jim is not the same person he was when we were growing up. His actions have made that clear. Now, I'm over what's happened and I'm not angry anymore, but I can't help but think that all of this came out when it did for a reason. Maybe this is the way God wants it to be. I'm just trying to go along with the inevitable progression of things."

"Or maybe it's the way the Devil wants it to be. Allen, you and Jimmy been friends for too long to let some shady gal come between you two."

"Jim's just as shady as she is. She had a partner, after all."

"Jimmy told you the truth and apologized. Did she do that? Cause those actions tell me a lot more than what came before."

"Still..."

"Don't you 'still' me when I'm talkin' to you – Listen, that boy been wearing out the prayer rug at the church over this thing."

"If he'd done that before, this would've never happened."

"Allen, I know you ain't gon' allow yourself to be so hardened against Jimmy. Especially after everything you been through."

"What are you talking about?"

"I'm talking 'bout when you prayed that Davis would forgive you for runnin' your mouth in his business, and if that's not enough, what about when you prayed to God to have mercy on you and speak to you after you'd turned your back on Him lookin' for that corner office job. Even now, when you shruggin' off Bible study, and cuttin' out of church, He's still being merciful. And look at how you repayin' that."

There was nothing that Allen could say.

"The Bible say, "seventy times seven". Remember that man Jesus talked about that threw his friend in prison over 100 dollars after his boss forgave him for 10,000.00.[1] Don't ask God for mercy no mo' if you ain't willing to give it."

Just then Tim stumbled out of his room, half asleep.

"What's going on, out here?" he said through a yawn as he stretched himself. Then he rubbed his eyes. "Mr. Sharpe?"

"Boy, how you coming out half-naked like that in this cold!" scolded Mr. Sharpe.

Tim looked down at his grey t-shirt and black sweatpants, puzzled. Then he sent another puzzled look towards Allen's way. Allen merely shrugged.

"Go git yo' robe and put it on! You makin' me cold just looking at you! No slippers or nothing.'"

"But I'm not..." began Tim, before Allen shot him a look of warning. "I'll – just – be – right back."

"Allen, you're not the first person that was wronged in this world, and you haven't been wronged in the worst way. Jesus died for sinners - all sinners - and that means you don't have the right to hold nothing against nobody. Now you chew on that for a while."

"Dad..."

"I've said my piece – I'm going. But also know that I expect you back in our house for Sunday dinner. Is that clear?"

"Yes, sir."

"Cause even if you gon' be a grudge, you can at least be civil and say goodbye."

As Vernon headed for the door, Tim reappeared wearing a dark green full-length terry-cloth robe.

“I’m properly robed now, sir.”

“Good. And get your adenoids checked ‘cause your snoring sounds like construction” returned Vernon before leaving.

“I will, sir.”

Allen closed the door, leaned against it and let out a sigh.

“What was that about?”

“Just my dad being a papa bear, that’s all. If he nags you that means he sees you as his kid.”

“That I know. What did he want to see you about?”

“I think you probably already know that, too?”

“So are you going home, or are you going to have your mail re-routed?”

“Maybe.”

FIFTY

The sun was out this November morning, enlivening the grounds around the Wakefield cemetery. The cold winds and bare trees the only reminders of the present season. Allyson would only come to the cemetery during daylight hours because she was afraid to come at night. Not that she was afraid of ghosts (or so she tried to convince herself), but it was a matter of general safety. She came devotedly, every year since Poppa died. Today was the anniversary of his death. Though he had left her, she had purposed that she would never leave him, but would honor his memory until her own eventual demise.

She walked slowly among the graves until she came to her family plot. Every Russell who'd ever lived had been buried here going back to the late nineteenth century. Poppa's was the one with the large rectangular headstone with his visage engraved in the center. When she came to it, Allyson kneeled down - her knee socks and boots doing nothing to protect her from the shock of the cold from the hard ground below. Slowly, she ran her fingers over the words etched into the frosty marble:

In loving memory of our Poppa: Honorable Judge Timothy Warren Russell, 1943 – 1998. “When evidence fails, trust your gut.”

Allyson had always been in awe of her grandfather and his uncommon perspicacity. The Sharpes reminded her of him. She knew that if he were alive today, he would probably like them. Allyson had always tried to live by Poppa’s advice: trusting her gut, or at least she tried to. Many times fear got in the way, like what was happening to her right now.

She took something out of her pocket. It was a handmade key chain that she had made herself. Carefully she dug a little cavern with a stick she’d found around the grounds, placed the keychain inside, and covered it with the dirt. Allyson would never put flowers on her grandfather’s grave because he always hated them. Instead, she would bring a memento that she would make for him. Wherever he was, she wanted him to know that she still loved him, even if he couldn’t love her back anymore. It was times like these, when visiting her grandfather’s grave that she felt the most alone. But today, she couldn’t help thinking about what Momma Lena had said to her.

Her reflection on that conversation was disturbed by the sound of dry autumn leaves being crushed under foot. She didn’t have to turn to know who it was.

“Is it okay, if I take a spot over here?”

“Whatever.”

Tim sat next to her cross-legged. The two were silent for a while, listening to the wind blow the leaves around.

"You think he can see us?" said Allyson.

"I'm not sure. Maybe. In a way, I hope he can't."

"Why's that?"

"I don't think he'd be okay with what's happened with our family over the past 12 years. He was adamant about what he'd call 'family cohesion.'"

"I remember. He'd always say, 'family is family no matter what.'"

"You know, before you were born I wasn't quite thrilled about mother having another baby, and I think Poppa must've known somehow. One day he took me aside in his office and he said to me in his deep officious tone, 'Now, Tim you must know that since you're mother's going to have another baby, we're going to have to take on more responsibility. I don't think she looks after you the way she should and you've heard some of the silly ideas she's got for this little one – nonsense about painting rabbits on the walls and lace curtains. This little baby's going to be ruined unless you and I take decisive, immediate action.'"

"Sounds like Poppa alright."

"He made it seem like we were this team on a mission to protect you. He'd tell me that when he wasn't around it would be my job to look after you and make sure my mom didn't turn you into a spoiled brat. We even went to the mall sometimes and he'd let me pick out toys and outfits for you – things we liked that he knew mother would hate."

"Is that why I was wearing that awful looking baseball onesie when I came home from the hospital?"

"Poppa liked it. He felt it would be better if you had a bit of tomboy in you rather than be the girly-girl mom was planning to turn you into. He wanted you to have some spunk, and to not always think you'd have to conform to the common mold."

"I know. So...Poppa was able to trick you into wanting a sibling."

"Maybe at first. But then after a while, I started to like the idea. I even started to think that you were going to be my baby, too. When mom brought you home, the first thing I said was, "Is that my baby?"

"So I've heard. That was a long time ago. So much has changed since then."

"Some things haven't. I remember that when I first saw you, I thought that there could never be anything I wouldn't do to protect you. I still feel that way. Believe it or not, I really do love you, Allyson."

"Tim..."

"Listen, Ally, I know that saying you're sorry doesn't magically fix things. I can't change what has happened in the past, but I want you to know that no matter what happens down the road, I'll always love you."

"I love you, too."

"What?"

"You heard me. I want my big brother back," she said looking directly into his eyes.

Tim reached over and took her into his arms. Allyson held on tight.

"Tim...I'm – I'm sorry," she sobbed.

"It's okay cupcake. It's okay."

FIFTY-ONE

Allen stood in front of the mirror in his room trying to knot his tie and ignore the one in his stomach. The church was normally his refuge and his sanctuary, but for the past couple of weeks, going had been torture. He'd been on the evasive trying to avoid Jim, even skipping Sunday dinners with the excuse that he had to study for class. Today he'd be ushering so there would be no awkwardness from having to sit in close proximity to his old acquaintance. After thinking about what his dad said, Allen knew that he'd have to actually settle things with Jim. However, he didn't know if he wanted to do it today. "I've got too much going on right now to have to deal with that," Allen reasoned to himself. Finals were going to be right after the holiday break and Allen wanted to be prepared. A knock on the door interrupted Allen's thoughts.

"Come in."

"Ready?" asked Tim, who poked his head around the door for a brief moment before disappearing.

"Just about," said Allen as he finished his tie. He grabbed his jacket and bag before heading out. When he came into the living room, he saw Tim securing his guitar in its case and whistling a gospel hymn.

"I see someone's in a good mood."

"How can I not? It's Sunday. Sundays always remind me of all the things I have to be grateful for."

"And this doesn't have anything to do with a certain relative of yours."

"It might have something to do with a relative of mine, if I must say."

"Is she going to be with us today?"

"No, but she might come back to have dinner with us in the near future. We're taking baby steps, Allen."

"I hear you. I'm also happy for you."

"Thanks, dude – and I have to thank the Lord while I'm at it. Nothing ever happens without Him."

"Amen. At least someone's able to get a prayer through."

"Not just my prayer a lot of people's prayers. Don't worry Al, your change is coming, too. Just stay focused on what God wants you to do."

"I'm trying. It's just that – sometimes I think about my life and it's nothing like I imagined it would be. I mean, I always thought that by the time I was 24 I would be in an entry level finance job, I'd have my own apartment and the girl of my dreams. Instead I'm a broke janitor, living with my parents, going to law school, of all places, the girl of my dreams has just broken my heart, and my best friend... well no need to go over that – It's just like there's one disappointment after another. I just wish He would let me know what's going on. Is this a punishment? A joke? A trial? I need a word – something to hold onto."

"You have that already. You know what He's promised us in His Word. Now you just have to trust in spite of everything you feel. In fact, you just have to let go of all those feelings – the disappointment, the hurt, resentments – they'll just choke your faith."

"It's hard."

"So was getting a Harvard Degree, but you persevered to get it. This is worth a lot more."

Their conversation was interrupted by the sound of the intercom.

"Who in the world could that be?"

"Let's find out," said Tim walking to the intercom, "Roger, Brad."

"It's a Mr. Reid, sir."

Tim sent a look to Allen. A lump formed in Allen's throat. After a moment of deliberation, Allen nodded.

"Send him up."

"It's best to get this over with," thought Allen. He didn't know what he would say or how he would feel coming face to face with Jim after so long. For the past couple of weeks, his job and his law school responsibilities kept him preoccupied so that he didn't have to think too much about everything that had happened. Some things he had resolved, but others he had stuffed down deep and he could feel the emotions stirring as his meeting with Jim drew nearer. "Lord, please watch over my mouth and my actions," prayed Allen inside himself.

“How ‘bout I take our stuff downstairs and wait in the car?” said Tim.

“Sure you don’t want to stick around and clean up the blood?”

“Knowing the two of you as long as I have, I’m sure that won’t be necessary.”

Tim left and not long after there was a knock at the door. Allen walked over and opened it. At last they were both face to face after so long. Allen thought he would be angry. He had felt the bile and heat radiating through his body just a few moments ago. But when he looked in Jim’s eyes he did not see what he expected.

“May I come in?”

Allen backed up to allow Jim to enter into the apartment.

“I had to come. Even though I know I’m the last person you want to see. I had to see you – to set things straight.”

He paused as if he was waiting for Allen to say something, but Allen couldn’t say anything.

“Ever since things fell apart, I never really came to you to apologize. I’m sorry, Allen. Sorry for cutting you off- and for all the trouble I’ve caused you. I’m not going to try to give you reasons or excuses because there really aren’t any. As Pop Vernon would say, I let the devil fool me”

“There’s one thing I agree with,” thought Allen.

“I can’t blame you if you don’t want anything to do with me anymore,” Jim continued, “I know the past couple of years I’ve put you through a lot. Trust me, Al, I don’t want to hurt you anymore. You might not believe it, but it’s killing me to know how much pain I've caused you. You're like my little brother. I've always tried to protect you – wanted the best for you..."

Jim started to choke up. His words reminded Allen of everything they had been through together when they were young – like all those times Jim stepped in to protect him from bullies and thugs. One time, when Jim was 12 and Allen was 10 they both got jumped by two older boys from the rough junior high school from around the corner. Allen was useless, but Jim fought like a junkyard dog to keep him from being hurt. Then he thought about all the times that Jim would loan Allen his last five dollars if he needed it and never even ask for it back. When Allen got into Harvard, Jim seemed to be happier than he was about it. Allen was starting to realize that Jim was indeed looking out for him. His dad was right. Jim could've gone down south and kept everything a secret and allowed Allen to make a mess of his life, but he didn't. But even if Jim hadn't done any of these things, Allen still couldn't justify his grudge.

Jim's manner had no anger, malice, bitterness, or shame – just a quiet humility, sincerity and the love that Allen knew had been buried deep inside him. It made Allen feel somewhat ashamed of his behavior and actions of the past few weeks. As a Christian he was supposed to be a reflection of God's love. It made Allen feel like he should be the one seeking forgiveness.

"Don't let what I've done mess you up, man. I want you to have a good life. You deserve that. And even though things are the way they are, I'm still going to miss you. Good-bye, Al."

"Are you leaving today?"

“No. I just wanted a chance to speak to you before I did, that’s all.”

“Oh.”

Jim turned away, to leave, but Allen knew he had to stop him.

“Don’t I get a chance to say something?”

Jim turned to face him again and nodded.

“I don’t want you to go, Jim. You’re my brother. You always will be. I love you, man.”

“I love you, too.”

The two men embraced briefly in a man-hug, each trying not to let the other see the tears that were trying to escape from the corners of their eyes.

“How’d you get all the way here, anyway? I know you’re leg’s still jacked up.”

“I got up early and took the bus.”

“The bus?”

“Yeah. I’ve had the casts off for a little while now and Riley’s been helping me with the rehab exercises. It’s gettin’ easier to get around – not as stiff anymore.”

“Still, I’m betting you could use a ride to the church, right?”

“You sure?”

“Positive.”

They walked out into yet another chapter in their friendship. The last blocks of the invisible wall that had stood between them, finally broken.

FIFTY-TWO

Spade was heading toward the projects on 153rd street, when Callie spotted her. Now was the time to put her plan into action and get her revenge. She had previously been to the police, but they were skeptical of her allegations. They weren't interested in the warehouse shooting because they felt the case was closed. According to the detective, there was no evidence that tied Jim to any wrongdoing except maybe an attempt to buy illegal narcotics, but no drugs had been found at the scene. Then Callie tried to tag Jim as a local dealer, but they didn't seem to give much regard to this accusation, either. She knew they would take her seriously if she could produce a witness. Callie only hoped the story she concocted would be enough to get Spade to cooperate.

Spade was walking so fast that Callie had to run to catch up with her. She tried to catch her breath before talking to her to make it seem like a chance encounter.

"Hey, Spade! How you doin'?"

"Hey, Cal! I'm fine. How you? I'm seeing you a lot here lately. You on your way to pick up your baby?"

"As always. But I also wanted to give you a shout from Chris."

"Really?"

"Yeah, he says hi. He would come by, but he's afraid to come by this way."

"Why?"

"You know that guy you said got shot up in the warehouse – I think you said his name was Jay?"

"Yeah."

"It turns out he's not dead. He's alive and he's been threatening Chris."

"Word?"

"Word."

"Cold snap," said Spade quietly, "But why would Jay be botherin' him now? Last time I spoke to Chris, he said him and Jay had made peace."

"I think he's trying to get Chris to buy from him again. But I was thinking we have to protect Chris and get this guy off the street."

"How we gon' do that?"

"I was wondering if you would go with me to the police about him. You've seen him before and you know what he does..."

"Nah, nah, Cal. I can't do that. I don't have a lot of positive 'sperience with the police. I got warrants, myself."

Callie's heart was gripped with fear. She had her plan all worked out, and now it was all coming apart.

"But what if this guy ends up hurting Chris or worse?"

"I know Chris. He's a real smart n**ga. He know how to keep himself."

"Think of it this way, if you turn states evidence against Jay, you might be able to make a deal on some of those warrants. That way you'll be helping yourself and Chris. I'll even help you pay for a lawyer if you need it."

"Sorry, Cal. Once you get processed in, it's hard to get out. But like I said, I don't think nothin' gon' happen to Chris," said Spade as she began to back away and head across the lawn to continue to the projects.

"But..."

"Fa real – don't worry about it. I'ma always have Chris's back as long as I'm livin'. There's other ways to take care of Jay, if he's back in business like you say."

"Like how?"

"You go on and pick up your baby, and let Chris know I got him," she said before walking away and out of sight.

Callie began to shake with frustration and anger. After everything she had lost, there was no way she was going to let Jim walk off free. She had to find a way to make Jim pay before he left for North Carolina. Then the idea came to her. "After I'm through with him, there's no way he'll be going anywhere anytime soon."

****

"You're late," said Bobby as he counted a wad of twenties.

"Sorry, but that guy you sent me to over on 143rd and Willis didn't know when it was time to go."

"Don't worry about it. I'll just add it to his bill next time. Time is money."

"Speakin' of money..."

"Don't worry, I got you. Here," he said as he handed her a five twenty-dollar bills and three tiny bags of brown powder.

"Thanks. You know Bobby, you always look out for me, and now I'm gon' do you a solid."

"How's that?"

"I got some information."

"Like what?"

"I heard that Jay ain't dead. He back on the streets and he's tryin' to get an operation started."

"Where you heard that from?"

"A friend of mine from back in the day. She knows Way-lo. She said Jay was leaning on him to buy and she wanted me to go to the cops and snitch to help Way-lo out, but I said I wouldn't do it. There's other ways to take care of Jay, right?"

"Forget about Jay for a minute. How do you know you can trust *her*?"

"We've always been cool."

"Since when?"

"I shout at her every now and again. She a nurse that works at the hospital."

"She straight?"

"Yeah, but..."

"Please tell me you didn't run your mouth to her."

"All I said was that I'd look out for Way-lo. I didn't say nothin' bout you."

"Good. 'Cause I think she's lying."

"Her boyfriend is friends with Way-lo. They go to church together."

"It don't sound right, Spade. How the hell Jay gon' threaten anybody as busted up as he has to be? I saw them take 'im out in the ambulance. He probably just got out the hospital recently, if at all. If he leaned on Way-lo, that n**ga could just bust him in his head or go to the cops for himself. Jay all by himself and he ain't got no juice no more."

"But why would Way-lo..."

"Think, Spade!" said Bobby, who seemed to be growing frustrated with his employee, "When was the last time you actually saw Way-lo? Hunh?"

Spade just put her hands in the pockets of her cut off shorts.

"That's right, you don't know what Way-lo said. All you know is what she tellin' you Way-lo said. And that's another thing, if Jay is going back in business, why would he lean on somebody that done gone straight like Way-lo? That n**ga could barely pay his bills when he was usin! Why not hit up Dray or Passion who still usin' and good for the money? What this chick is sayin' don't make no sense. Nothin' she sayin' is addin' up."

"So why she comin' to me with all these stories all of a sudden?"

"Now that's the million dollar question right there. It sounds to me like she's dropping names and making up stories because she's fishing for somethin.' She knows about Jay and Way-lo, but she don't *know* them. Probably using third hand information to set up a sting. She could be a cop, or she could be down with those dudes over in Washington Heights."

"You think so?"

"I know so. Don't forget, there's a reason why I run this and not you. You see that chick again, let me know. Stay close to her. I'ma whisper in yo' ear and you gon' whisper in hers and see what she say. And I'ma give you a little extra for lookin' out like you did," he said handing her two more little bags of brown powder.

"'Preciate you, man. You know I got you, Bobby."

"Your little friend gon' learn you need to be careful when you go fishin'. You might just catch a shark."

FIFTY-THREE

"Lord, I'm coming to you this morning once again to thank you for what you have been doing for me and my friends. You blessed us with another day and another chance to worship you. You've given us our health, and strength and a mind to serve you, and I'm really grateful for that. You've stood by us through our problems and changes, and I'm just askin' that you continue to be with us. Be with my friends Allen and Jim, and keep the devil's nonsense from separating them from each other and from you. I ask that you look out for Miko, and help her to find a good brother who's worthy of her. I pray for Tim and his family and that you bless them to reconcile their differences and use Tim to bring the rest of them to you. Please look on Chris, too and keep him on the straight path that leads to you..."

Davis had come to the sanctuary early and was in one of the prayer stalls of the upper room, tarrying in prayer. He came because he felt burdened. Even though, he had dealt with everything that he had been avoiding, there was still something that bothered him. It was that stain, that darkness that he knew existed somewhere inside him.

"...Lord, please deliver me from this anger and evil that's inside me. I've been dealing with this for so long and I don't know what to do anymore. I've confessed it, I've been to counseling and I've tried to make things right with those that I've hurt, but...I feel like – it just won't leave me. Please, Jesus, I'm willing to do anything. I'm not even going to do the dating thing anymore. Just take this thing out of me and make me more like You..."

He continued in prayer for some time and when he was done he sat in the stall for a few minutes just to listen for the voice of the Lord. He knew he needed strength for the path he was undertaking. He just wanted to lose himself in the Lord – for Jesus to dwell in him, take over and do the work that he couldn't. In the midst of his meditation, he felt as if he should go downstairs to the sanctuary. He didn't know why, he just felt that he should go.

Davis got up and headed downstairs. As he reached the pulpit, he looked over all the pews and the church seemed empty, as it usually was at this time of morning before the service. The only other people that would be here at this time were the elders and Pastor Bynum, all of whom spent their time in the church offices across from the prayer room. The choir wouldn't have rehearsals for another half-hour or so. So Davis sat in one of the pews and folded his hands. "So much for that," he thought to himself. "Maybe it was just me being restless."

"Is everything okay?" he heard someone ask. He didn't have to look to know who it was. There was no mistaking the deep baritone voice.

"Everything's fine. I'm good."

"You sure? You kinda look like you lost your best friend. Seems like that's something that's catching around here," said the Pastor taking a seat next to him.

"Nah, I'm not really sad or nothin.' I guess it's just the way I look."

"It's a new look. You're usually more placid and composed. For the past few weeks I've noticed you look like something's been bothering you. Kinda like the time when you came by to talk to Tamiko."

"Okay, maybe I have been struggling with some things, but it's got nothing to do with Miko. She's a really nice person, and I don't want my problems to affect her. That's all we was talkin' about that night. I'm not tryin' to get with her or anything like that."

"You don't have to explain anything about that to me, Davis. I trust you. And even if you did have feelings for Tamiko, I don't think I'd mind if you wanted to court her. You're a nice young man, after all."

"I don't think I am."

"Why would you say that?"

"I – It's just – the Bible says when you get saved old things are passed away, and all things become new, but – sometimes I feel like the old me – the guy I used to be, keeps hanging around.[1] I been prayin' about it, but just when I think I don't have a problem with it any more, it comes back."

"That's just the flesh, Davis. As long as we're in these bodies, we're always going to be subject to the different temptations of the flesh. It's how we handle these temptations that matters. If you're going to the Lord, you can always be sure you're going in the right direction."

“Sometimes it seems like going to Him isn’t enough.”

“You’re right. You have to believe in Him - that He can and will change you.”

“I know that He’s God and He can do anything, but when I think about my past and all the things that I’ve done, I can’t help but think, why would He want me. Maybe this thing is His way of rejecting me.”

“Davis, no. That’s not true. Everyone that comes to Him, He has called to Himself.[2] Every single one of His children is precious to Him – even you. Forget about your past, that doesn’t matter any more.”

“But I feel like, if I don’t hold myself to account, I might go back there.”

“Holding yourself accountable is one thing, but tearing yourself down is another. No one should do that. As children of God we are supposed to see ourselves the way He sees us.”

“You might not be saying that if you knew me back then.”

“It doesn’t matter what you were like back then, it who you choose to be now that matters. Everyone has a dark side, and there isn’t anyone on this planet that’s not capable of doing what you’ve done or worse. Think of how the Lord changed the life of Paul the Apostle. The difference is in the choices that we make every day. You’ve chosen Christ, so now just keep on choosing him. Like Paul said, with every temptation, he makes a way of escape.[3] When you choose Christ, He will show you that open door, so you don’t have to fall to the devil.”

"But there are times when I feel like I can't trust myself. I'm afraid I'll lose it."

"You're not supposed to trust yourself. It's when you try to handle things yourself that you really do lose it. Trust Jesus. He knows where your will and your heart are. He won't fail you. He loves you too much for that."

"He loves us, but that doesn't mean we can get away with the things we've done. The Bible says you gotta reap what you sow. David was a man that God really loved a lot, and he had to get punished for what he did.[4] Look what happened with Absalom and everything."[5]

"True. But even though David had to go through all those things, God remained with him and vindicated him from his enemies. Though David suffered some hardships God did not allow him to be overcome by them. God had mercy and that's what the grace we stand in today is all about. Then think of what you are sowing in the now, that you will also reap. Right now, I see you sowing good things, Davis – spiritual things that have an everlasting reward.[6] Remember Davis, your past sins aren't any worse than anyone else's sins. All sin is sin and Jesus died for all sin. Of course we don't deserve it, but still it is the gift that he has given us – a very precious gift that came at a great cost. Don't throw that gift away trying to punish yourself for things He's already forgiven you for. Even if others don't forgive you, it's still okay to forgive yourself."

"I don't think I'd even know where to start with that."

"Forgiving yourself is hard, but its even harder if you allow yourself to get too caught up in you. Forget about you and what you've done, and think about what you can do for others. That always helps me."

"You're right. I Guess oughta stop feeling sorry for myself like I'm the only guy going through this."

In the midst of their discussion, Sister Gaines, the choir director came down the aisle in her usual quick-paced trot.

"Davis, I've been looking for you. I thought you were in the upper room. Rehearsal is in five minutes. Chop – chop."

"I'll be right there Sister Gaines. If you'll excuse me Pastor."

"Go ahead. I know how sister Gaines is. Wouldn't want you to get kicked out of the choir. I just hope you think about what I said."

"I will."

He had already begun to think about what the pastor said and with each step he made toward the choir room, he could feel the burden he'd been carrying getting lighter and lighter.

FIFTY-FOUR

"I tell you mother, I think we're going to have to get a bigger dining room table for our Sunday dinners," said Pastor Bynum.

"Yes, Pastor. I've noticed that our Sunday dinners are becoming very popular all of a sudden, especially with the young men of the church. It seems like every week there's a new fellow stopping by, like this young man here," said Mother Rose, gesturing with her fork in his direction.

"His name is Chris, mother Rose. I invited him because I didn't think anyone would mind," said Jim.

"Of course we don't. However I do find it interesting that he should suddenly show up when our friend Tom is curiously absent. Strange indeed, since that young man has never missed a dinner since Allen first brought him here," said Mother Rose.

"He was planning on coming, Mother Rose, but his sister called and she wanted to talk to him about something," said Allen.

"Really?" said Tamiko, "He and Allyson are talking again?"

"That's what he told me."

"Well praise God! I was praying for them," said Lena.

"So you don't have to worry, Tim will be back and he said his sister may stop by now and again, too. At any rate, the next time I see him, I will tell him how much you missed him Mother Rose," said Allen.

"She's not the only one that misses him," said Riley.

Tamiko kicked Riley's leg under the table.

"Ow!" she said wincing in pain.

"Once we start these kids on the ladies cookin' you know they gon' be back. Ain't that right, Davis?" said Vernon.

"I have to admit, I'm hooked on Mama Lena's meatloaf," said Davis.

"I hope they find more friends and family to invite. I love watching our family grow. We started out with just three between us and now I think we got more than twice that. Makes me feel like a mother hen," said Lena.

"Well that's all well and good when everyone's getting along, but when the conflicts starts that's something different," said Vernon.

"Everyone here is getting along fine," said Jim.

"Is that right?" said Vernon looking toward Allen.

"Yes. Just so you know, I should have all my stuff back in the house by the end of the week," said Allen.

"I'm glad to hear you done came to your senses," said Vernon.

"Praise the Lord! Another prayer answered! Hallelujah!" said Lena.

"Does this mean I'm going back to NC solo?" said Riley.

"I don't know. I might tag along for a short vacation, but I definitely wouldn't be staying as long as I originally intended," said Jim.

"Since Jim's not in such a rush anymore, maybe you could extend your visit here a little longer," said Tamiko.

"Though I know you would love to have her here indefinitely, we have to think about what's best for Riley and her family. I'm certain her father is beside himself with worry by now and is anxious to have her back for the holidays," said Mother Rose.

"With all due respect, Mother Rose, I just spoke to my daddy yesterday on skype, and he said that as long as I'm close to Uncle Vern and the Pastor, he's not worried a bit. Now that's not to say he doesn't miss me," Riley replied.

"Of course he misses you. You're his only daughter. I'm sure you're probably missing them as well," said Mother Rose.

"Kind of. But It's not like I've been here that long."

"Whatever you decide, just know that we don't mind having you here. So if you want to stay through the holidays, you're more than welcome," said Pastor Bynum.

"Thank you, Pastor. I'll think about it," said Riley.

As everyone continued to alternate between dining and conversing, the doorbell rang.

"Don't worry, I'll get it" said Allen rising from his chair. He walked out to the living room and stopped in front of the door.

"Who is it?" he asked. He listened for a response, but there was none. Then he looked out the peephole to see if there was someone outside. He didn't see anyone. Then he heard something. It sounded like the muffled moans of a baby.

Cautiously, Allen opened the door. Someone had left a child alone in a stroller. Allen recognized the stroller and turned it to look inside. Just as he'd suspected, it was Darius. He looked weak and glassy-eyed. He was moaning and moving his head from side to side. Allen brought the stroller inside and picked up Darius. As Allen held him close, his suspicions were confirmed. The child had a fever.

"Mom! Mother Rose!" said Allen, "I need your help out here."

The two women came rushing out of the dining room followed by the others who were curious to see what was going on.

"Allen, dear, what on earth?"

"What's Darius doing here? I thought you and Callie broke up."

"We did. She just rang the bell and left him here. I think he's really sick though. His color's off and he's really warm."

"Let me have a look at him," said Mother Rose taking the child from Allen. "You're right, I'm afraid. This baby is very ill. We're going to have to take him to the emergency room right away."

"Will they let us? When I went for my violence and abuse training for school, I was told you had to be at least the legal guardian of a child to get them care at a hospital or register them for school. If not, they could remand Darius to foster care," said Tamiko.

"What?! No!"

"Tamiko's right, son. We've got to think about this for a second," said Vernon.

"Darius may not have a second."

"Do you think they'd let me…" began Jim.

"Only if Callie named you on the birth certificate," said Tamiko.

"You know she wouldn't have done that," said Jim.

"What about you, Allen?" asked Tamiko.

"Callie left it blank," said Allen.

"Did she at least leave his health insurance cards or something?" asked Lena.

"There's a diaper bag on the back. We could look through that," he said handing it to her.

Lena looked through it with Tamiko peering over her shoulder. She took out several diapers, bottles, toys, and a stuffed animal before he got to an envelope. She opened it and started to read the contents.

"Oh, my stars," said Lena.

"What?" asked Allen.

"I found his medical papers, but I also found this note for Jim. I think you need to read this."

Jim took the note and read it out loud with Allen looking over his shoulder.

"'Now it's my turn to run. Welcome to single-parenthood.'"

"How could she – this is her baby!" said Tamiko.

"I can't believe this," said Allen.

"I can," said Jim, "Forget about her, Darius needs us right now."

"And if we try to get him help, they may take him away from us," said Allen.

"Even so it'll only be temporary. Me, Lena and the boys will take the baby to the hospital and I'll call Ballard and ask him if he can meet us there. Maybe he can help us get temporary custody until things get worked out in court. Anybody know any good family court lawyers?" said Vernon.

"Let's try to get in touch with Tim and see if he knows anyone," said Allen.

"We'll do that," said Davis.

"In the meantime, pray for us," said Vernon.

"We will," said Tamiko.

*****

"Lord, please watch over Darius. He's just an innocent baby. He didn't do anything to deserve what he's going through right now. Please protect him, and heal him of any disease or illness. Cover him with the blood that you shed for our sins and deliver him. Please, Lord God. Please," prayed Allen as he sat in the waiting room of the pediatric wing of the hospital. His parents were in consultation with officer Ballard and the hospital social worker, while he and Jim were waiting for the results of Darius's blood tests. His heart hurt for little Darius who he had always considered as his son. Then he looked over at his friend Jim, who he could tell was just as tortured as he was.

"You okay, man?" asked Allen.

"I was just thinking – I never even got the chance to get to know him," said Jim.

"He's going to be okay. We have to have faith."

"I know."

Just then a young woman wearing scrubs and carrying a clipboard approached them.

"Is either of you Detective Ballard?" she asked.

"No, He's upstairs with the social worker. I'm Allen Sharpe. My family and I were the ones who brought Darius here. Is he okay?"

"Unfortunately, I can't give you any other information except to say that we have the child stabilized."

"What?! Are you serious? We're the only family that child has right now!"

"I'm sorry, but I've no choice in the matter. This is the law. Now if you'll excuse me, I have to find the detective."

"Can't we at least see him?"

"Under the circumstances, you're not allowed. I'm sorry," she said leaving them and looking warily at Allen.

"This is insane!"

"Al, calm down. Us getting upset like this isn't going to change the situation. Besides we can find out about Darius from Ballard when he gets the information."

"If this is Callie's way of getting back at us, then she deserves to..."

"Don't go there, man. Don't even entertain that thought. We gotta forgive her, too. We also gotta stay focused on that little boy and what's going to happen to him now."

"You're right. But the idea of him being handed over to some strangers in foster care – I just can't – Jim, you have to petition for custody, ASAP."

"I can, but do you think they'd let me have him? I have no job, and I'm practically homeless. What kind of father could I be?"

"The kind of dad that God wants you to be. Don't worry so much about the circumstances. The Lord has a way of working things out."

"I know, but it's enough to have to worry about my future, and now I have to think about Darius, too."

"You're not going to be alone. Mom, Dad, me, our friends – we're all going to be there to help you."

"He doesn't even know who I am. He'll probably want you more than he wants me."

"Maybe at first. But you'll have time to get to know him and he'll get to know you. That's how it works, man. That's what being a dad is all about."

"Al, I know how you feel about Darius. I want you to know, that no matter what happens, you're always going to be a part of his life."

"Thanks, man. I'd be honored."

"I know this will work out for all our good."

"It has to."

Just then, the Detective had reappeared along with his parents. None of them looked very happy.

“So?” said Allen who had raced over to meet them.

“Darius is suffering from acetaminophen poisoning,” said Detective Ballard.

“You mean like the stuff in the cold medicines,” said Jim.

“Right. It seems Callie must've been giving it to him over several days and wasn't careful about the dosage,” Ballard explained.

“But she's a nurse. How could she not know?” said Allen.

“Unless she was using it to knock him out,” said Jim.

“They're going to keep Darius at the hospital for a while to conduct more tests, but right it now it's looking like he might have liver damage. He may even need a transplant,” said Lena.

The words hit Allen in the stomach like a sucker punch from a world-class boxer.

“He's barely more than a year old yet and he may have to have surgery and they won't even let us see him,” said Allen.

“It's okay, good news is, I'm working with social services to have Darius placed with your mom and dad. We were just starting the preliminary paper work. In the meantime, we're also going to have to get Jim's petition in for paternity and the blood test done in order to get legal custody of Darius. You'll need to go down to the court tomorrow morning and file papers,” said Ballard.

"Thankfully, Tim got a lawyer already working on the motion," said Vernon.

"I pray God keeps things working in our favor," said Lena.

"I know He will," said Allen.

FIFTY-FIVE

"Hello, mother dear," said Allyson beaming brightly as she sat down to join her for lunch at an upscale midtown eatery.

"So you avoid my calls until I threaten you, and you have the nerve to saunter in so casually."

Eleanor wouldn't look at her, but kept staring at her menu, her face like stone. Allyson could tell a storm was brewing in her mother's heart, but she wasn't the least bit worried.

"I was busy working, trying to get you as much information as I could. That is what you wanted, isn't it?"

"With the way you've left me hanging, this better be more than the school girl gossip you've been bringing me. We need to get Tim back with us ASAP," she said tossing the menu down on the table.

"Thankfully, she has delivered," said Tim walked up to their table.

"Tim! How – What are you – I mean, this is such a nice surprise. I wasn't expecting you to join us."

"Allyson invited me," he said taking a seat.

"What?" asked Eleanor.

"I was thinking, 'why hear things second hand from me when you can get all your information from the source," said Allyson.

Eleanor looked at them both curiously as if she was wondering if they were playing some kind of a joke on her.

"Allyson said you've been missing me. Is that right?" said Tim.

"Yes – uh, since we came back from Baltimore – you seemed so upset about what happened. Allyson and I were under the impression that you were avoiding us."

"You mean you were under the impression that he was avoiding us," said Allyson.

"What would give you that idea?" asked Tim.

"Maybe the way you banished us from your bedside at the hospital, and the way you sent away the private nurse I hired for you..."

"No one banished you anywhere. All I did was ask for my phone back and request that you wait outside while my friends were visiting with me – and I told you from the beginning I didn't need a nurse. No where in any of that did I ever say I never wanted to see you anymore."

"Though he would have been justified," said Allyson under her breath.

"Still, you rarely call anymore," whined Eleanor.

"I left a message on your service three months ago that you still haven't returned," said Tim.

"Okay, so maybe there were some issues of miscommunication on both our parts, but regardless, we have to remember what's most important. You remember what Poppa used to say: Family must stick together."

"I agree."

"So does this mean you will be spending more time with us?"

"I'm always open to spending time with you."

"Excellent!" said Eleanor beaming, "In fact, I was hoping that you would be able to attend a luncheon this Sunday coming. I wanted to introduce you to the congressman and there's a young lady I've been dying for you to meet..."

"Wait a minute, hold the phone. Look, when I said I was open to spending time with you, I meant one on one family time. I'm not doing any business related stuff – and you know Sundays are off the table because I go to church."

"You're still going to that, that..."

"It's a church, mom - a plain homely little church. It's really not a big deal. Lot's of people go to church," said Allyson.

"Don't tell me they've got to you, too."

"Please. I'm not even a member there. I hardly think I've been gotten to."

"Then how can you condone your brother's involvement with that place and with those people?"

"Honestly, they're not bad people. Why don't you go down there sometime and meet them? I'm sure they'd love to meet you," said Allyson with a smirk.

"Or my pocketbook," she snarled to her daughter before returning her attention to her son. "Timothy, that is not the kind of place where you belong. You need to be around people of means and position. People that can help launch your career, not a bunch of cotton-headed dreamers looking for mansions up yonder."

"That's where you're wrong. There's only One with the power to launch anything, and that's God. Wherever He is, is where I belong."

"You sound like a child."

"Despite what you think I sound like, at the end of the day I'm a grown man. That means I am entitled to live my life as I see fit. Now I am willing to share that life with you, but the key word is share. You can have some of me, but you can't have all of me, and I'm sorry, but I can't allow you to run my life. That's my final offer. Take it or leave it."

"Timothy, I'm just trying to look out for your interests. That's what a mother does. The last thing I want is to be forced to have a front row seat to watch you self-destruct."

"I said take it or leave it. What's it going to be?"

"Remember, this is going to be your decision, mom. Tim is holding out the white flag," said Allyson.

"Alright, have it your way, Tim. I just hope that when you finally wake up from the dream world you're living in, it won't be too late to fix things."

"Thank you for respecting my decision, even if it is grudgingly."

"I just don't know what has happened to you, Tim. You've changed so much in the past couple of years, I hardly recognize you."

"I agree, mother. But I think that actually might be a good thing," said Allyson taking her brother's hand.

FIFTY-SIX

It was a lovely late fall day. The sun shone brightly and the winds gently blew the bare branches making the trees look as if they were waving to a beat. Davis found himself whistling as he approached the Bynum homestead dragging his tools in the rollaway bag behind him. He rapped gently on the door to alert the residents to his arrival. He had no apprehensions because he knew that Mother Bynum was at the church hosting a prayer meeting that had started well over an hour ago. After a moment, the door opened.

“Hey,” said Riley. She always looked at him as if she was sizing him up.

“Hey,” he said, feeling a little unsettled.

“Miko’s not here. She went food shopping.”

“S’aiight. I’m not here for a visit. The Pastor asked me if I could take a look at the garbage disposal.”

“Oh,” she said still looking a little uncertain.

She backed up so that he could enter and led him to the kitchen. Davis parked his tool bag near the table, and then got to work on the disposal. He had already inspected it before dinner the last Sunday and knew that it only needed a new gasket. He decided to get started right away. As he began to work, he noticed that Riley had planted herself in a chair and was watching him silently like a cat in a shop corner and he wondered if it was out of mistrust or simple curiosity. But considering what he believed was her moody disposition, he was wary of trying to start a conversation with her.

"So what is it with you?" She asked him out of nowhere. "You don't talk much, or you just don't like talking to me?"

"Depends. I don't mind talking to people that can be chill, but if you're gonna bite my head off for no reason, then I think its best if we…just kept things civil," said Davis.

"I know I can be a bit direct sometimes, but I don't usually bite unless there's a reason,"

"If you say so," sighed Davis who was trying to keep his mind on what he was doing. He would keep it brief. The last thing he wanted was to get into an argument with her. But then somehow he sensed there was something different in her manner with him.

"So I guess we're not going to be friends then."

"Not sayin' that," he said as he stopped his work to look at her. She seemed to be a little nervous. "Do you want us to be friends?"

"If you don't want to be…"

"I never said I didn't. Okay, I know we didn't get a chance to start things off right. How 'bout we start over, right here, right now?"

"Are you for real?"

"Yeah, why not?"

"How does that work?"

"Like this. Hi," he said as he wiped his hand before extending it to her, "Name's Davis Martinez, and you?"

"Riley Sharpe," she said taking his hand.

"Nice to meet you, Riley."

"Nice to meet you, too, bra."

"Now was that so bad?"

"I guess not," she said.

Then she smiled in spite of herself and Davis couldn't help but notice the way it made her whole face light up. Her radiance was absolutely stunning. So much so that Davis almost forgot about the work he had to do.

"Sorry about what happened earlier. Miko and Al always say that I'm abrasive or whatever. Not tryin' to be though."

"S'aiight. But just so you know, the Word says the best way to make friends is to be friendly."[1]

"I try," she said shrugging her shoulders.

"You don't mind if I work while we talk?"

"Not at all."

"How you likin' it up here?"

"Not bad. Nice to have the stores in walking distance when you want something. I'm from Lewiston, and that's like in the middle of nowhere."

"When you get back I'll bet you'll 'preciate the quiet, though."

"You city people call it quiet. I call it boring."

"I wouldn't mind trading places with you for a while. Sometimes I think the city can be a little too exciting."

"If you're talking about all the so called dangers here, I think that stuff can happen anywhere."

"I guess you're right about that. So what do you do for a living?"

"Hair, mostly – sometimes make up."

"You like it?"

"Yeah. I like working with my hands. There's no way I could sit at a desk all day."

"Me either. You get a lot of customers?"

"I got some regulars in the neighborhood where I'm from. Don't get hit with any complaints or lawsuits, so I guess I do a pretty decent job."

"My sister's kinda like you. She don't do hair, but she does makeup, facials, manicures, and stuff like that. She works at a spa in Queens."

"I studied that, too, but I just prefer working with hair. More interesting to me – ya know?"

"So how come you don't like – make your own hair fancy?"

"Excuse, you?"

"No, I mean, like you always got your hair – uh – uh."

"It's called an afro – or a natural, not nappy or a bad hair day. And let me tell you something, you have a lot of nerve to assume that just because I wear an afro, that I'm not doing anything with my hair."

"Chill, girl. I wasn't tryin' to say you don't do nothin' to it, I only meant like you don't change it up that much..."

"Don't try to clean it up, I get what you were trying to say. For your information, it takes as much time, if not more, to care for an afro than a straight style – that's right, straight hair is just a style, it is not the default for perfection as you wanna make it out to be. And for your information, sometimes I do straighten my hair if and when I feel like it, not because people like you think I should."

"Okay, fine. I stand corrected. That's how you roll, it's fine with me."

"I don't really care if its fine with you or not. It's my hair and I think natural hair is just as beautiful, as straightened hair. After all, it is the hair God gave me."

"How about we talk about something else?"

"No, I got one better; how about we not talk anymore at all," she said before she sprung up from her chair and stormed out of the room. "I can't believe I was actually starting to think you were chill."

She left just as Pastor Bynum walked in.

"Hey, Riley. How's..." said the Pastor, who was unable to finish his address before she left. Then he sent a very confused look toward Davis. "What's with her?"

"She was watching me fix the disposal and then we started talking about her hair..."

The Pastor began to chuckle. "Son, Allen or Tamiko should've told you – you don't ever talk to Riley about her hair."

"Lesson learned."

Riley was definitely not like Tamiko at all. Whereas Tamiko was like a tomato, Riley was more like an artichoke. He found himself hoping that Riley would extend her stay with the Sharpes for a while. He was curious to discover what lay beneath all the layers of her prickly personality.

FIFTY-SEVEN

"Dinner's Ready!" called Lena from the dining room. Vernon, Allen, Jim, and Chris were watching a football game in the living room, while Mother Rose, and Tamiko were setting the food on the sideboard and tables, and the Pastor was beginning to carve the turkey.

"You don't have to tell me twice," said Allen who got up from his seat on the couch and headed to the dining room.

"That is a huge turkey," said Chris.

"I thought we'd have more people over, but Tim and Allyson are with their mom, and Davis is with his family," said Lena.

"Don't you worry, there's still a lot of people here. I don't think we'll have much left over after tonight," said Jim.

"I am actually glad to have a smaller party this year. Reminds me of when all the children were younger before all the interlopers arrived," said Mother Rose as she brought in a casserole of sliced rutabagas. "No offense, Christopher, dear."

“None taken – and you can call me Chris, ma’am.”

“Of course, dear.”

“Are you alright, Miko?” asked Allen, “You haven’t seemed like yourself in the past couple of weeks.”

“I’m fine. I guess I’ve been a little preoccupied with what’s been going on with Darius and everything.”

“Sure you haven’t been moping about a certain young fella?” asked Pastor Bynum.

“Daddy, can we not discuss this right now?”

“Davis? Again?!”

“Allen, please. I’m over him already – and I’m not moping about anybody!”

“No, not Davis,” said Pastor Bynum chuckling.

“Then who?” asked Allen.

“No one!” insisted Tamiko.

“You know who,” said Jim.

“Oh, no!” exclaimed Allen, “Tamiko, we’re going to have a brother-sister talk after dinner.”

“No, we’re not. There’s nothing to discuss, nothing’s going on.”

“Yes, I think you do need to talk with Allen and I hope he can talk some sense into you. Heaven knows I’ve tried,” said Mother Rose.

“Can we please change the subject?” said Tamiko.

Fortunately for Tamiko two more came to join the celebration.

“Guess who’s up and ready for dinner,” said Riley who was bringing in a bubbly Darius. She sat him in the high chair that was between Allen and Jim.

"Hey, Darius! You ready to get your grub on, little man?" said Allen.

Darius smiled and babbled excitedly.

"Me, too," said Allen.

"Aww. He looks so cute in that little outfit, Miko got for him," said Lena.

"Hi, sweetheart," cooed Tamiko at the little boy. "Jim, he looks so much better, now."

"Yeah, the medicine they gave him is helping, but he's still going to need the surgery," said Jim as he put a bib on Darius.

"When's he going in?" asked Mother Rose.

"Monday. I'm trusting that God will bring us through," said Jim.

"That's the way to believe. He's brought us this far and I don't think He's gonna leave us now," said Vernon.

"It was fortunate that Jim turned out to be a match for Darius. A lot of times, the parents aren't," said Tamiko.

"God knows how to work," said Vernon.

"Still nothin' on where his mama went?" asked Riley.

"No, but wherever she is, may God bless her," said Jim.

"For Darius's sake I pray God changes her," said Allen.

"I pray, she doesn't try to cause any trouble for Jimmy," said Lena.

"I wouldn't worry about it, that's old stuff. But you gon' have to be careful from here on out, Jim. Once you're known for being in the game, the cops are gonna be watchin' you."

"I know, but it's like mom says: as long as the Lord is watching over you, you'll be alright."

"How's your job search going, Jim?" asked Pastor Bynum.

"I was hoping you'd ask me that. I was keeping it under wraps until today, but I got a job at the seminary school Dan goes to. He put in a word for me there a couple of weeks ago and I got the call yesterday."

"Now if that's not something to thank the Lord for, I don't know what is," said Vernon.

"That's great, man! So you're going to be working at New York Seminary?" asked Allen.

"Yeah," said Jim.

"Congratulations, Jim. What kind of position is it?" said Tamiko.

"It's in the admissions office."

"When do you start?" asked Lena.

"Two weeks."

"Please tell me the pay is decent," asked Riley.

"Not as much as transit, but enough to cover the bills."

"I told you Jim, this is just the beginning. Your change is just around the corner," said Pastor Bynum.

"I agree, sir," said Jim.

Everyone sat down at the table and they joined hands as Pastor Bynum led them in the grace.

"Lord, we thank you for showering us with your blessings once again in that you have allowed us to be able to come together for another Thanksgiving – giving us yet another opportunity to come together as a family and give you thanks for all that we are and all that we have. So much has transpired from the time that we last gathered around this table until now – so many trials and tribulations we have experienced, but you have brought us through them all and so we each give our thanks this day. Lord, I thank you for expanding our family and blessing the lives of those who are here as well as those who are not here. I thank you for mending the broken hearted and turning them to the light of your eternal glory. May as many come to thy light as you see fit."

"Lord thank you for restoring this family and settlin' the strife the devil tried to sow," said Vernon.

"Lord God, I thank you for all of the love that you have shown us and blessed us to be able to give to each other. I thank you for making me the mother of many children," said Lena.

"Thank you Lord for giving us wisdom and insight to know right from wrong and good from evil. I pray you give us the strength to continue to walk in it," said Mother Rose.

"Dear Lord, I thank you for the faith to trust you, when there's nothing else that we can do," said Chris.

"Lord I thank you for your mercy and for the second chances that you give us everyday, because you don't pay us for our sins nearly as much as we deserve, but as far as the east is from the west, so far have you placed our sins from us," said Jim.[1]

"God I thank you for looking out for us and providing for our needs, despite the fact that we tend to pray a lot about what we want," said Riley, "because you always know what's best.

"Father God, I thank you for all the things you are going to do for our future, because I trust that you will always be there for us, even when we make mistakes," said Tamiko.

Then Allen said:

"Father God, I thank you for the gift of grace that you purchased on the cross. It is the gift that gives life - for by this grace not only are our sins are forgiven but you have shown us how to forgive others, and even ourselves."

And all the others said "Amen."

Notes

Five

1. Proverbs 18: 22
2. Proverbs 31:10 – 11
3. Matthew 5: 23 – 26

Seven

1. Psalms 54: 1 – 3

Seventeen

1. 1 Samuel 16: 1 – 4
2. 1 Samuel 16: 11 – 12

Eighteen

1. Psalm 61: 1 – 2

Twenty

1. Matthew 10: 35 – 36
2. Matthew 5: 23 – 24
3. Proverbs, Leviticus 11: 1 – 47
4. 1 Corinthians 6: 15 – 20
5. Leviticus 11: 44
6. Romans 12: 1
7. 1 Corinthians 6:13
8. 1 Corinthians 6:20
9. Deuteronomy 22: 28 – 29
10. (See #8)
11. Romans 6: 16
12. Romans 8: 28

Twenty-One

1. Deuteronomy 22: 5
2. Psalm 100: 1
3. Luke 23: 34
4. Romans 1: 19 – 25
5. Ephesians 6: 12
6. Numbers 25: 6 – 11
7. Genesis 28: 6 – 9

Twenty-Six

1. Matthew 10: 26

Twenty-Seven

1. Proverbs 31:10

Twenty-Nine

1. Matthew 10:26
2. Job 13:15
3. Matthew 26: 41 – 42

Thirty

1. Psalm 39: 5
2. Psalm 49: 20
3. Numbers 23:19
4. Romans 3:4
5. Romans 5:6
6. Romans 4:8
7. John 4: 10 – 14

Thirty-One

1. Matthew 19:12

2. 1 Corinthians 7: 32 – 33

Forty-Four

1. Matthew 5: 29 – 30

Forty-Six

1. Matthew 26: 1 – 36
2. Matthew 17: 4
3. Matthew 26: 51
4. Matthew 26: 58 – 75

Forty-Eight

1. Matthew 5: 25 – 26

Forty-Nine

1. Matthew 18: 22 – 35

Fifty-Two

1. 2 Corinthians 5: 17
2. John 6: 37
3. 1 Corinthians 10: 13
4. 2 Samuel 11
5. 2 Samuel 15
6. Galatians 6: 7 – 9

Fifty-Six

1. Proverbs 18: 24

Fifty-Seven

1. Psalms 103: 12

ALSO AVAILABLE FROM LAWRENCE CHERRY

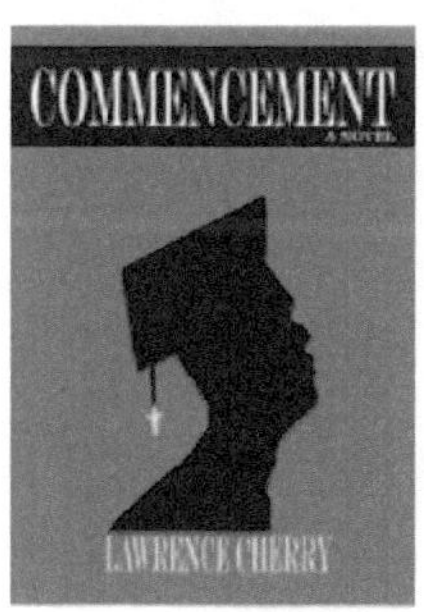

Commencement

ISBN: 978-0-615-48546-1

Allen Sharpe thought he had it all. As a graduate of one of the nation's most prestigious Ivy League Universities, Allen believed he was poised for a six-figure position as a financial consultant and "the good life". In Allen's world, nothing else could be more important. However, after experiencing a major detour on his road to success, Allen learns there is more to life than what the University has prepared him for.

As Allen tries to pick up the pieces of his broken dreams, he is forced to re-evaluate his aspirations and priorities. As a result, he embarks on a spiritual journey to develop a deeper relationship with God. On this journey, Allen and his friends learn many invaluable lessons they could never get from a textbook.

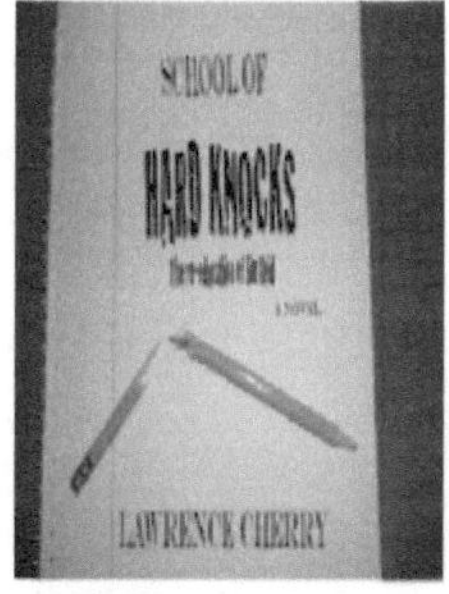

School of Hard Knocks The Re-education of Jim Reid

ISBN: 978-0-615-845586

Nearly a year after his arrest and subsequent conviction for drug possession, Jim Reid is struggling to rebuild his life. All he wants is a second chance, but it seems society will not allow him to forget the mistakes of his past. Battling unemployment, financial ruin, and his own personal demons, Jim realizes that he needs help. Instead of turning to the only one who can help, Jim begins to rely on his new friend, Smoke, a small time drug dealer who dreams of making it big.

Smoke promises Jim that he will find the solution to all of his problems in "the thug life" and teaches him how to navigate the underbelly of the inner-city. "The thug life" turns out to be much more than Jim bargained for. Ultimately, Jim finds himself trapped in Smoke's perilous world with no way out, except one. But will Jim take it before it's too late?

www.ingramcontent.com/pod-product-compliance
Lightning Source LLC
Chambersburg PA
CBHW020623020726
47494CB00001B/23

* 9 7 8 0 6 9 2 4 6 2 1 6 4 *